THE
CEMETERY KEEPER'S WIFE

BY

MARYANN MCFADDEN

Three Women Press
www.threewomenpress.com

For information, or special discounts for bulk purchases, please contact: Three Women Press, P.O. Box 208, Allamuchy, NJ, 07820 or publicity@threewomenpress.com.

Interior layout: Booknook.biz   Cover Design: Alan Donaghey

Also available as an Ebook: ISBN 978-0-692-99899-1

Publisher's Cataloguing-in-publication data

Names: McFadden, Maryann, author.

Title: The cemetery keeper's wife / by Maryann McFadden.

Description: Allamuchy, NJ : Three Women Press, [2018]

Identifiers: ISBN: 9780692974773 (print) | 9780692998991 (ebook)

Subjects: LCSH: Smith, Matilda, -1886—Fiction. | Murder—New Jersey—Hackettstown—Fiction. | Union Cemetery (Hackettstown, N.J.)—Fiction. | Date rape—Fiction. | Women—Fiction. | Spouses— Fiction. | Family secrets—Fiction. | Cemetery managers—New Jersey—Fiction. | GSAFD: Historical fiction. | Mystery fiction. | LCGFT: Domestic fiction. | Historical fiction.

Classification: LCC: PS3613.C4375 C46 2018 | DDC: 813.6—dc23

Also by Maryann McFadden

The Richest Season

So Happy Together

The Book Lover

For My Son and Daughter,

Patrick and Marisa

PROLOGUE

November 1883

T ILLIE STUMBLED OUT OF THE CABIN, the stench of sickness nearly making her vomit. She stood in the cold a bit, bent over, gulping in fresh air. They were all with the fever, but Catherine was coughing so fiercely, she brought up blood. If her mother were still with them, she'd know what to do, but her mother had been gone for too many years already, her presence like a shadow Tillie couldn't seem to grasp. The doctor was what they needed, but the doctor and his medicine cost money. And there was none. It was Nora who said to maybe go over to Waterloo and see if the uncle might lend them some.

Tillie went over to the well, careful not to slip on icy patches of mud, thanking God she wasn't sick, or who would have helped them? She stood there a moment, a bucket in her hand, shivering and trying not to cry. The last she'd seen any of the uncle's family had been in town that summer, her cousins in their fancy store-bought dresses and bonnets with feathers and ribbons, like something out of a newspaper advertisement. They'd looked right at her and at Nora, too, and then stuck their noses up in the air as if she and her sister smelled of manure. She'd be damned if she'd go begging to the likes of them.

Catherine's fever was burning up for the third day, and her pa was delirious when he wasn't passed out from the whiskey he insisted would make him better. Nora tried not to make it harder on Tillie, but she had it in the bowels and couldn't make it to the outhouse. Yesterday one of her pa's customers came to pick up an ax handle but wouldn't come near the cabin when he heard of the sickness. Tillie wanted to curse him because the coins for the handle would have at least paid for some medicine.

1

She brought the bucket to the door, set it down, then gathered wood, carrying it into the house in batches, sweat running down her camisole by the time she was done.

"Tillie?" Catherine's voice was barely a whisper. "You must rest up, Tillie. If you were to get sick, what would happen to the lot of us?"

She went over to Catherine, older by seven years, lying in bed, her face flushed with fever, her eyes like glass marbles. "Hush up. I'm just fine."

Catherine took her hand, and Tillie's stomach seized with fear. Her hand was like ice. "I wish Mama was here," Catherine whispered.

Tillie had to turn away a moment and bite her lip to keep the tears from coming. Then she stood up and in her high-falutin' play voice said, "Well, Duchess, I'm going to do one better. I'm going to fetch the doctor to come look at you all."

"But Tillie, you know we ain't got that kind of money."

"I do. I've saved a bit and hid some," she lied. "So you take a good rest, and I'm going to walk up to Waterloo and see if I can fetch the doctor now. It may take me some hours, so just be patient."

She left her sisters each a cup of tea laced with whiskey, thankful her father had been too sick to drink it all. She hoped that would keep them all asleep for the hours she'd need to be away and get the doctor. But first to get the money.

Despite the cold, she stripped down at the well and washed herself with the icy water as well as she could, then went back in the house, brushed her hair, and put a few drops of her ma's cooking vanilla behind her ears. She put on Nora's Sunday dress, which was tight on her, though maybe that wasn't such a bad thing. Then she looked at herself in the piece of mirror hanging on the kitchen wall beside the stove, wishing she looked a bit older than sixteen.

Star Port at Saxton Falls was a three-mile walk each way. She would be gone most of the day and prayed they'd be no worse when she got back. She wondered if she would burn in hell for what she was about to do. But God, she told herself, had to understand there was no choice for her, was there?

Tillie kept her mind busy during the long, bitter walk, praying the wind would ease up. She thought over what she knew about the relations between men and women. It wasn't a secret what happened and what the result could be. Anyone who lived on a farm knew such things. Catherine had warned her to be careful there when she'd first explained about monthlies and all that. Not that she'd had much opportunity as of yet. Still, sometimes she felt her heart might burst out of her chest from wanting. To be held. To be kissed. That handsome fella who came sometimes and talked to her sisters, picking up his pa's handles, made her cheeks flush when he looked at her. And she dreamed at night about what it might be like to kiss him. He hadn't come there in a long time now.

Just ahead she saw a clearing for the turn into Saxton Falls and knew that Star Port was just up the road a piece. Her feet seemed to slow of their own will. She knew of the house there, where the canal and mine workers went for sport. A rough lot they were. Crossing the little bridge, she looked down at the river, the water so clean and clear as it rushed over the rocks. She thought over what she was about to do, her heart beating so fast, it was like a baby bird was caught inside her chest trying to fight its way out.

She took a long breath, forcing her feet to keep moving.

She'd get through it, she told herself. Because then her sisters could get better. And though she knew she could manage now without her ma and would without her pa, she also knew that without her sisters, she wouldn't want to.

Walking up the porch steps, she heard a man's laughter inside the house. Her stomach lurched with fear when she imagined those hands on her, and worse. Before she went inside, she made herself a promise. Somehow she'd make a better life for herself and her sisters. Or she'd die trying.

There is no such thing as chance; and what seems to us mere accident springs from the deepest source of destiny.

Friedrich Schiller

CHAPTER 1

March 2014

THE MORNING I MARRIED ADAM MILLER, I'd said a prayer for the first time in more than fifteen years. I'd asked God's forgiveness for what I was about to do.

As I was cutting the tags off a knee-length lace dress in my furnished studio apartment, my worldly goods packed into just a dozen boxes and bins, I reasoned that if you looked at the past, rarely did marrying have to do with love. It had to do with convenience, fortunes, need, etc. So what did it matter if my intentions weren't completely honorable? I was quite certain I was falling in love with this man. Though what did I actually know of love?

I was thirty-five years old and, for all intents and purposes, a virgin. I wasn't normal; I knew that. I'd been a loner since college, the weird girl who didn't get invited to parties. The cat lady without the cats. I'd been broken.

Now, five hours later, I turned to look at Adam driving us home, still not quite believing what I'd done. *Husband.* That improbable word kept turning over in my mind. He glanced at me with a smile of anticipation, resting his hand on the gearshift, a habit I'd already learned about him, though we hadn't known each other very long. His plain gold band caught the sun, flashing for a moment, as if telling me something. A warning, perhaps. *Don't hurt him.*

Three months ago, he'd walked into my life as I stood in the flooded cellar of his great aunt Eleanor's house. It was the middle of the night, and I was bailing water in nothing but my underwear and rubber boots after my clothes had gotten drenched. I'd been trying to salvage antiques I would be selling for the estate when the power went out, and then the sump pump stopped working.

"Can I help?"

I turned with a scream, not knowing anyone else was in the house. And then I realized I was mostly naked and reached for my dripping sweater. But Adam had already taken off his flannel shirt, handing it to me.

"Well, I guess I've made worse impressions than this," I joked awkwardly as I slipped it on, the scent of him filling my nose.

"I'd say you're making a pretty good impression. I don't know too many people this committed to a job."

"And you are?"

"I'm Adam Miller, executor of the estate."

He stepped into the candlelight, extending a hand. We shook, and it was in that moment I saw the birthmark and froze. A port wine stain across his throat. I'd seen it before, just once.

"Getting excited?" Adam asked now, bringing me back to the present.

"Yes," I said, barely a whisper.

A bride *should* be excited. And nervous. But I knew the growing panic squeezing at my insides wasn't what most brides felt. Then again, I wasn't most brides. People didn't do what we'd just done that morning—get married by a justice of the peace after knowing each other just twelve weeks—except in novels. Or maybe some did. Those who'd given up hope long ago. Or perhaps those like me, desperate for a normal life, saw a chance, and grabbed it.

I glanced over at Adam. To me he seemed none of those things. In fact, he seemed like the perfect guy. But I knew no one was perfect. We all have our dark sides. We just hadn't seen each other's yet.

My new husband wasn't handsome but was good-looking in a rugged way, his dark hair just reaching the collar of his flannel shirt. There was also something boyish in his grey eyes, the way they lit up at times, though he was a few years older than me.

How was he not taken long ago?

We began descending the mountain, thick woods on both

sides of the road. The highway and Budd Lake, its edges still laced with ice, were now behind us. I reached over impulsively and slid my hand inside the collar of his shirt, my fingers grazing his birthmark. His skin was smooth and warm. I could feel the rising of his breath, the quickening of his pulse. Touching, an act so foreign to me, and so thrilling. He turned again, smiling, and the longing in his eyes told me what was waiting for me at the end of this drive. My stomach squeezed harder.

Had I just made the biggest mistake of my life? I'd made so many already. My life was like a minefield, littered with bad decisions. *Rachel, you are your own worst enemy*, my mother used to warn me.

"There it is," Adam said, breaking into my thoughts again.

I looked out my window, and through a gap in the bare trees, I saw Hackettstown below, stretching across the valley. It was like a Norman Rockwell painting, tree-lined streets and houses with porches, complete with a white church steeple. In the middle of town, rising above it all, a gold dome shimmered in the late afternoon sun.

Suddenly the curves sharpened, and we picked up speed, winding down the mountain as my ears popped. Then the woods opened up, the road flattened, and we were in the eastern edge of the valley, driving past a strip mall and car dealer. Tucked between them was a lovely farm with a stone house and horses grazing in a small pasture. Then we were driving over a small bridge.

"The Musconetcong River divides the counties. Now we're officially in Hackettstown."

"It's charming," I said, "though I don't remember much, really."

"Well, you were a little girl. And you were here for only a few months."

"Right."

"Now, let's go home."

Home. Another word that was foreign to me. It had been years since anyplace had felt like home.

* * *

FROM THE MOMENT WE DROVE through the grey stone arch into Union Cemetery, its huge wrought iron gates wide open, it felt as though we were entering another world. Two fields, already turning a rich green although it was early April, stretched on either side of the narrow blacktop road. A moment later we were rumbling across a small wooden bridge, the weathered boards clattering beneath the truck tires, the river glistening like liquid crystal just below. The scent of the Musconetcong hit me suddenly, dank, earthy, a pungent odor of fish.

"I love that smell, Adam."

"So do I."

As we came into the cemetery, a small hill rose before us, the road splitting in either direction. A tiny white building sat on the edge of the river to my right at the foot of the hill.

"That's the office," Adam said, stopping the truck.

"It looks like the seven dwarfs' cottage."

Adam laughed. "Well, we don't need much."

Adam turned right, going past the office toward the southern tree line, the narrow gravel lane, rutted in spots, veering left, then around the knoll. The cemetery rose before us, small hills and rolling fields studded with headstones stretching into the distance, bisected by these winding little lanes. I glanced at the small mountains ringing Hackettstown, like protective arms surrounding this small valley.

"What do you think?" Adam asked.

"It's so beautiful, Adam. If not for the gravestones, it would be an enchanted park."

"We work hard to keep it that way."

He stopped the truck and turned to me. I could see the worry in his eyes.

"I told you, I'm not afraid," I assured him. "I work with dead people, too, and as we both know, they can be a lot nicer than the living. Besides, at least I don't have to worry about the neighbors liking me."

"You're too much," he said, laughing again, then leaning over and kissing me. "Hey, you're trembling."

"No, I'm just excited." I turned away, gazing out the window again. "I can see why you love living here."

"Well, hopefully it stays this way."

I looked at him. "What do you mean?"

Adam shook his head. "Nothing. Not to worry."

But I could see something there in his eyes.

We turned left up a hill, and as I looked toward the highest point of the cemetery, a tall white monument caught my eye. "Who's buried up there, the marble monument with the angel carved on it?"

"Oh, that's Tillie Smith. She's something of a local legend."

"She must have been quite prominent." And there was something...familiar about the stone.

But Adam took my hand then, and I turned to look ahead. On the far side of the fields of graves, obelisks, and tiny mausoleums, I saw the white house, three stories with a wide front porch and gabled roof, the long windows bathed in the afternoon sun. Behind it I could see an old wooden garage that must have been a barn at one time.

A few moments later, Adam pulled in front of the house and parked. I got out of the truck, looking up. The house rose imposingly before me, a gothic look to it, like something from a Bronte novel. Old flower beds surrounded the front porch, a scattering of daffodils and tulips popping up haphazardly, hinting at neglect. This would be a good project for me, though I'd never really gardened before. Still, I could learn.

We walked up the porch steps and I stopped, turning for a moment. I could see the river, a silver slash of water bordering the western edge of the cemetery, but nothing else beyond. I felt as though I'd stepped into a fairy tale, with the seven dwarfs' cottage, the big old house, the enchanted fields and trees surrounding us. And Adam, the cemetery keeper...would we really live happily ever after?

"Tomorrow we'll go for a walk, and I'll show you everything," he said, "but now..." Adam paused, suddenly lifting me.

"Oh, Adam, don't. You're going to need a chiropractor—"

But his lips silenced me. I could feel him trembling. Then he pushed the door open with his boot, carrying me across the threshold. I felt the heat of his body through his clothes, his citrus cologne and a hint of sweat, an odor so masculine it filled me with longing. He set me down in the front hallway.

"Welcome home, Mrs. Miller."

I stood in the silence of the foyer while Adam went to get my things. For me, walking into a house for the first time was like opening the cover of a book. I'd learned throughout my years handling estates and auctions that every house has a history— lives unfolding through knick-knacks, memorabilia, furnishings, and pictures. But what I also knew was that almost every house held secrets, ferreted away years ago under floorboards, inside coat pockets, tucked inside a book, and often long forgotten.

In Adam's aunt Eleanor's house, a sense of grieving hit me on the first day, and it was confirmed when I found the letters from World War II hidden in an eave of the attic, from the soldier she'd never stopped loving. No one in the family knew anything about it, Adam had told me, impressed.

Now my eyes traveled up the staircase to the portraits lining the wall, the generations of cemetery keepers going back nearly a century and a half. Adam was the seventh. I waited for a feeling, for something...but the moment was broken as my husband came bounding up the porch steps again. He looked at me, shaking his head.

"There are no mysteries here, Rachel." Then he pointed through the open front door. "But there are plenty out there."

I gazed out at the sea of graves surrounding us, the white marble monument at the top of the hill, the gravity of it all flooding me. What was it going to be like living amidst the dead day after day? Knowing that beneath the rolling fields of sweet green grass and the towering arms of the old trees lay hundreds of lives that had come and gone? Would I sense the yearnings, the heartache of spirits unable to rest, as I did in the houses I auctioned? Would I become consumed, as I often was, with the need to somehow soothe them? In that moment, it was as if each headstone, each obelisk and tiny mausoleum, radiated some kind of energy, like a grey mist floating above each grave

until it flooded the entire cemetery. Suddenly I could feel the burden of all those souls pressing on my chest. All those people and
their stories. How many had taken secrets with them? Left
unmet dreams behind? How many lives had been cut short?

I inhaled suddenly, not realizing I'd been holding my breath,
and the mist disappeared, the afternoon sun once again casting
its cheerful glow. Then I closed the door.

THE HOUSE WAS AS I'D EXPECTED for its age: high ceilings, creaky
wood floors, old furniture that hadn't been changed in decades. It
was a bit cluttered but clean, and I wondered if it always was or
if Adam had worked hard for me. I was pleased to see one wall of
the living room lined with bookshelves. There was just one TV,
also in the living room.

The dining room was quite large, with a big bay window and
heavy mahogany furniture, including an oval claw-foot table
that would easily seat twelve. It was furniture of another era,
another way of life.

In the back of the house, I found the kitchen and saw some
attempt had been made to update it over the years. It had light
oak cabinets, white Formica counters, and a porcelain sink. I
imagined myself washing dishes, staring out over the fields of
granite and marble, wondering about the lives lived and now
gone. A square table sat in front of a triple window. I sat a
moment looking at the view. A curve of silver water was visible
where the river curled around the low side of the cemetery. Just
above it I noticed a row of small markers, perhaps the oldest
graves.

Finally, I went upstairs, passing each of those portraits, noticing in several the resemblance to Adam, the strong jaw and
wide shoulders. When I reached the upper hallway, I found four
doors. Two were bedrooms with old floral wallpaper and twin
beds; another was for a big bathroom with pink and black tile
harkening back to the fifties and its last renovation. I realized it
was probably once a bedroom, back when there was an outhouse. I was happy to see a claw-foot tub.

I opened the last door and looked at the master, the bedroom I would share with Adam as his wife. A double bed with a brass headboard sat between two long windows. Several mahogany dressers lined the walls, and a long mirror sat in the corner. What drew me, though, was the window seat covered in a cabbage rose floral. I sat there and parted the sheer curtains, looking at the cemetery below, surrounding the house. What kind of life would I have here? Would I even still be here tomorrow?

And then I heard Adam coming up the stairs. He put my two suitcases down and looked at me, his face flush with exertion. And anticipation. Slowly he came to me, taking my hands and gently pulling me up. He cupped my face and kissed me over and over until I felt as if I were turning to liquid. It had been twelve weeks since we met, four since he asked me to marry him. There was no way of putting this off any longer.

CHAPTER 2

I HEARD A NOISE JUST AS ADAM BEGAN removing my sweater. Someone was pounding on the front door.

"I'll be right back," he said.

I sat on the window seat, waiting, trembling as I watched the sun setting just above the mountain across town, wondering at the men's voices downstairs. When he came back, I could see Adam was upset.

"What is it?"

"I'm sorry, something's...happened. It's work, and I need to take care of it."

"Now?"

He smiled ruefully, then nodded. "We need every hand. Besides, it's not like they knew I just got married this morning."

"You...you didn't tell them?"

He shook his head.

"Why?"

He hesitated. "I was afraid you might change your mind. About living here."

"Oh." But I wondered if it was more than that.

"Hey," he said, taking my hands and pulling me close. "It'll be like this sometimes, I should warn you. Unpredictable. Intense."

"It's your job. I understand. Mine can be like that, too."

"I think I saw that for myself at my aunt Eleanor's. Why don't you get settled? You must be exhausted. I'll be back as soon as I can."

"I'll be here."

I sat back on the window seat and waited for the trembling to stop, hating myself for the relief coursing through my veins. It wasn't as though I didn't trust Adam, or I wouldn't have been sit-ting there in his bedroom.

I watched the truck drive across the cemetery. I couldn't help thinking about that first morning, after we'd worked all night in his aunt's old cellar, clearing it of antiques and bailing water. Having no idea how my life was finally about to change. How the miracle I'd prayed for had finally walked in. When I woke on the couch that next morning still wearing his flannel shirt, sunlight was streaming through the front windows. I looked over and there was Adam, asleep in the dining room, his head on the table, snoring softly.

I walked over to him as though transfixed. Adam Miller. I couldn't quite believe he was there. His lashes were impossibly long against his cheek. His dark hair was still curling from the dampness we'd worked in all night. A woman, I thought, would kill for those lips, full and sensual. I already knew he had a good heart before he lifted a finger to help me. I knew that as soon as I glimpsed his birthmark.

My hand reached out, longing to touch him. Aside from the hug of a client or a handshake, I hadn't touched another person in eight years. Instead I pulled the sleeve of his shirt that I was still wearing to my face, breathing in the scent of him.

I watched him quietly for a long time before he finally woke up. He insisted on taking me for breakfast at a diner nearby. As we talked, I felt the door to my heart, bolted tight so long ago, open a crack. He had a deep voice and spoke slowly, and I found the sound of it calming. I explained that my father had left when I was young, and my mother had been killed in a car accident when I was a freshman in college. I'd gone home, barely able to function. I had no other family, and I couldn't bring myself to go back to school. I stopped there, though, knowing I would never share the rest.

I did tell him that I'd eventually lost the house. When I had to sell off most of the contents, I met a kind auctioneer who showed me a way to make a living. And escape my past.

We talked for three hours. I liked him a lot, and rusty as I was, I could see that he liked me, too. A lot. He talked about his own loneliness living in the cemetery, a place that didn't appeal to most women. I laughed. We had things in common; that was pretty obvious. We were both a bit removed from what might be considered a "normal" life. Ours revolved around dead people.

Afterward, when we were sitting in his truck, he leaned over, and while looking into my eyes, he lifted my long braid, slipping off the elastic band. Then his fingers slowly separated the braid until my long hair fell around my face like a halo.

"I've been wanting to do that," he whispered.

I sat there frozen. And he suddenly looked embarrassed.

When he kept coming back to his aunt's, I asked him if business was slow, and he laughed. It took him weeks to work up the nerve to kiss me.

Now, sitting on the window seat, I wondered if he'd put his job in jeopardy spending so much time with me over the past three months. Or was it something else? Because I sensed something was off here.

I got up from the window seat to unpack, then glanced out again and changed my mind. I went downstairs and put my jacket back on. It was still light enough for a walk. And the cemetery was drawing me.

I headed out the front door and down the porch steps, the smell of spring grass filling my senses. Fields of green stretched into the distance, sloping down to the river. I turned and rounded the house, a sea of gravestones as far as I could see, up and down grassy knolls, bordered by paths and dirt lanes. Huge old trees were scattered here and there, lending a pastoral look to what I hoped wouldn't unnerve me once darkness settled.

I walked toward the lane by the river, the one we'd driven in from. Every so often, as I passed a particularly old-looking headstone, I'd stop and read. Most of this section was dated in the later 1800s. As I neared the bridge, the path branched. I turned left where it began to rise, and I stopped suddenly at a row of four small arched stones. The carved words were worn and barely visible, and I struggled to decipher them. I got down on my knees and wiped away years of dirt with my sweatshirt sleeve, excited to discover they were dated late 1700s. Then I saw that one of them held the names of four children, all dead by the age of two. I knelt there a long moment, imagining the unbearable grief that mother had endured losing one baby after another and living long afterward.

This mother and her children had been gone more than two centuries, yet in that moment my heart ached for her. The human body, I thought, had such a capacity for loss. You could lose everything and still your heart would go on beating. Your lungs would draw breath. It was the mind, I knew only too well, that took longer to heal.

Looking at the headstone, I wondered what became of this woman, how her life had turned out after losing all those children. Turning, I surveyed the hundreds and hundreds of graves. Like the houses I'd been mining for more than fifteen years now, each represented a life lived. A story with twists and turns, loves and disappointments. Secrets. And things sometimes beyond imagining.

I thought of Aunt Eleanor's secret love letters and her never marrying. The rolls of old hundred-dollar bills stuffed in a rifle barrel in an old man's house before that. Photographs taped to the underside of a doctor's desk drawers. And of course there was my own mother's diary, wedged inside a covered casserole dish in the china closet. They were like clues to a mystery. Who was each person, really? What drove them through life? What dreams remained unmet?

Some might call my love for my job a passion. Adam did the day he came back to his great aunt's and found me kneeling on the living room floor, where I'd fallen asleep the night before. I was surrounded by her jewelry boxes, imagining how each piece came into her hands, when and where she wore them. It was one of the things I loved about my job, touching the things they treasured most. Unearthing their secrets. And in my mind, bringing that person back to life for a brief time.

And what I realized was this: we never really know another person. Not really.

I turned in a circle, imagining the stories buried in each grave. Unlike my houses, there were no beloved things here, no artifacts or clues. There were simply words: names and dates. Husband. Wife. Mother. Father. A line of scripture or poetry, an ornament or flower. Adam was right; this place was full of mysteries.

I walked on, climbing the path, continuing past a break in the graves, my eyes now fixed on the tall white monument at the very top I'd noticed on our drive in earlier. I stopped, and my mouth opened with a tiny gasp, knowing now I'd seen it before. It was stunning, a work of art unlike anything else I'd passed. It rose at least ten feet high with the sculpture of a young woman stretching from bottom to top, wearing a tunic with one shoulder bare. She was reaching to the heavens, placing a laurel wreath above the inscription:

SHE DIED IN
DEFENCE
OF
HER HONOR
Apr. 8th 1886
Aged 19 years

I stared at what was written just below the epitaph: *Erected by An Appreciative Public*. Across the pedestal at the very bottom, in rough lettering that was incongruous with the rest of the elegant monument, as if carved into the stone by a child, was her name: *Tillie Smith*.

I closed my eyes, and a memory came flooding back: *Mommy, is that an angel?* It was the only time we'd ventured into the cemetery.

Yes, baby, that's an angel. She's in heaven now.

But Mommy, how does an angel die? Can someone hurt an angel?

And then my mother knelt on the grass, her hands digging into my shoulders. *That's why you must always listen to Mommy. Someone bad hurt her. That's why Mommy makes sure you're careful.*

But of course I hadn't always listened.

I shook my head, opening my eyes, noticing what should have caught my attention from the first. On the pedestal beneath Tillie Smith's name sat a row of old votive candles. A small bouquet of silk flowers, wind battered and dirty, clung haphazardly from fishing line that someone had tied around the monument.

I looked back up at the epitaph and the maiden reaching toward heaven. Tillie Smith was obviously a heroine. I wondered who was still alive to put candles and flowers on a grave so old. Then I remembered Adam saying she'd become something of a local legend.

Looking at the rectangle of grass on which I stood, I wondered who she was and what had happened. I tried to imagine the girl who had once lived and breathed, who had laughed and dreamed. My heart quickened at the idea of trying to fill in the pieces of this girl's life. Then I looked up at the inscription once more: *SHE DIED IN DEFENCE OF HER HONOR.*

Stepping closer, I reached for the bouquet, tucking it in securely. Suddenly I gasped as a searing pain shot up my hand. I yanked it back and saw a bead of blood oozing from my thumb where the wire had sliced into my skin. I stared, transfixed, a slow crimson line trickling across my hand. It felt as though the ground was tilting, and I leaned against the white marble. I couldn't breathe as an image flashed in my mind. I was alone on a bed. Unable to move. My thumb oozing blood where a belt buckle had pierced it. I turned from the monument and began to run.

In the far corner of the cemetery, I saw Adam and another worker erecting three tents. I forced myself to slow down and walk, my breath coming in little gasps. I started counting like I used to, distracting my mind and shutting down racing thoughts. Darkness was falling quickly, and bats began to swoop low for insects. I was halfway across the cemetery when I couldn't see Adam or the workers anymore, and they couldn't see me. It took 384 seconds until I climbed the porch steps.

The house was dark. I turned on every light. I checked to make sure every window and door was locked. Then I poured myself a big glass of wine. Before I even stopped shaking, I opened all the cabinets and began to rearrange everything.

CHAPTER 3

I WOKE TO SUNLIGHT STREAMING through the sheer curtains. I turned with a start to the other side of the bed. Adam hadn't come home. I got up and threw on my robe, and the room spun suddenly. Sitting on the window seat, I began to remember. Walking back to the house from Tillie Smith's monument in the falling dusk. Downing a glass of wine and bandaging my thumb. Turning on every light in the house as the cemetery grew black outside. Finally noticing the note from Adam on the kitchen table: *I'll probably be gone all night. I'm sorry. I'll explain when I get back. Love, Adam.*

I heard a car door then and looked down to see Adam getting out of the truck. I went downstairs and met him in the hall.

"Hey, I'm so sorry, babe," he said. "We just had one problem after another."

I could see he was still upset. And exhausted.

"It's okay, Adam." I slipped into his arms and hugged him.

"This isn't how I pictured things our first day back. Or night."

I looked up at him. "What happened?"

He sighed. "There was an accident. Three...teenagers."

"Oh my God."

"And there was some confusion over plots. But it's complicated, and it's all fixed now."

"You must be starving. I'll make some breakfast."

"Do you mind if I just sleep for a while?"

"Of course not."

He caressed my face. "I wanted our first night to be perfect," he said softly.

How could that even be possible? I wondered.

21

While he showered, I dressed and started coffee. I went back up to kiss him good night, but he was already asleep. I stood there staring at him, flooded with guilt. I did not deserve this man.

* * *

AFTER BREAKFAST, I CARRIED TWO BOXES into the kitchen from the pile Adam had set in the living room. The first box was small. I ripped off the tape and carefully pulled out several soft towels before lifting the brass urn that held my mother's remains. I put my lips to the smooth, cool metal, then held it to my chest and closed my eyes, trying so hard to feel my mother's spirit.

I'd taken her urn with me from one rental to another, always struggling with where to place it. On a shelf surrounded by candles? In a sunny window? It always seemed that when she was sitting in the yard with her face to the sun, she was some-how at peace. I went to the big window over the sink and looked out at the cemetery. Maybe it was time for something more per-manent. A place she could finally belong. I could adorn her grave like so many others I'd passed on my walk, honoring her memory with flowers, solar lights, or an eternal flame candle.

Late last night when I couldn't sleep, when I'd finished organizing the kitchen, I turned out that light and looked out this same window over the darkened fields, the soaring trees like shadow soldiers guarding over the dead, the golden glow of the eternal flames like fireflies hovering over the graves. It would be a beautiful place to spend eternity.

I looked at the urn, carved in filigree. "Are you here, Mom?"

What happened to a soul, a spirit, after that final breath was taken? My eyes scoured the cemetery, imagining again all of those souls. Did something invisible rise up and leave the still warm flesh after the heart stopped beating? Go to another dimen-sion? Was there really a heaven of sorts? Because I certainly didn't believe the fairy tale of angels and white clouds and pearly gates. But I did believe in souls, an essence, an energy, some-thing that went on. I prayed that my mother's was at rest, as it had never been in life

I couldn't help but look up at the little hill, the white marble monument visible even from this distance. Was it possible Tillie Smith's spirit was not at rest?

The phone rang suddenly, and I jumped, turning at the shrill sound to see an old-fashioned yellow wall phone with an actual cord. I hesitated, unsure whether to answer it. Did people call the house for cemetery business? I wondered. It kept ringing loudly, and I didn't want it to wake Adam.

"Hello?"

"Oh," a woman said, clearly surprised. "Would this be Rachel?"

I was stunned. Who could be calling for me?

"Yes, this is Rachel."

"Well, I've been trying to call Adam on his cell, but he's not answering."

"Oh, I'm sorry. He's asleep. He had to work all—"

"It doesn't matter. I was actually trying to reach you."

"Who is this?"

"I'm his aunt Helen. I have a job for you."

* * *

AN HOUR LATER, I WAS DRIVING through the cemetery on the winding gravel lane. It seemed winter had returned, and though it was sunny and the cobalt sky cloudless, the air was frigid. Spring in New Jersey was unpredictable, and a snow in April was not uncommon.

In one of the fields, I spotted a worker cleaning up old flowers from graves and straightening the small American flags that marked the service people who'd died. I turned toward the river then, and a moment later Adam's pickup rumbled over the boards of the old bridge. I wondered just how old the bridge actually was because it didn't seem safe.

Coming out from under the huge stone arch, I turned right, pausing a block up as I approached Water Street, then continued on. I wasn't ready to see the little green house we'd lived in all those years ago. I drove up Mountain Avenue toward Main Street, glancing at the handwritten directions once more.

In the center of town, I turned and pulled in front of the

house on Sharp Street. I'd been in many of these before, a typical Civil War–era Colonial, a two-story box with a gable roof, front porch, long windows, and shutters. The rest of the block was lined with similar homes, and the street was quiet on this early spring morning.

From the moment I stepped into the front hall, I knew that something was off. Walking into the living room, I could tell someone old had lived there, though that was nothing new. Handling estate sales and house auctions usually involved old sick people or those who had just passed. There was a sense of sadness, though that wasn't uncommon given the circumstances. No, this was something else, something I felt but couldn't name yet.

Looking out the side window, I saw the driveway lined with forsythias in full yellow bloom. Yet a pile of Christmas presents sat on the coffee table, as if wrapped that morning awaiting the big day. Library books were stacked on the hall radiator cover, a reminder, no doubt, to return them.

The dark furniture and the big floral wallpaper were all a throwback to the fifties, or perhaps even a decade or two earlier. The old metal kitchen table, so retro it was back in vogue and would fetch a nice price, was cluttered with the beginnings of someone's breakfast. But the thing that made me pause was the open pill bottle. Beside it, a single pill sat waiting to be swallowed. I stared at that tiny yellow pill, round and familiar, but my mind was suddenly seeing a little mound of yellow pills, a handful you could swallow all at once.

"Hello?"

I jumped, banging into the edge of the table. Footsteps were coming closer. I turned, expecting Adam's aunt, but the short-haired brunette looked about my age.

"I'm Gail, Mr. Trimmer's secretary. He's the attorney handling the house sale." As she spoke, her eyes roamed over everything. Then she looked at me.

"It's nice to meet you," I said, extending a hand, relieved it wasn't a nosy neighbor looking to grab something for a steal, which wasn't unusual. "I'm Rachel Dem...I mean Miller."

"Oh, right. Helen told us Adam got married. Congratulations. I'm on my way back to the office from an errand and thought I'd stop in. It's amazing, isn't it?"

She began walking through, picking up knick-knacks and even sitting on a cane-seated chair. "I can't imagine who buys this stuff, but I guess what they say is true: one man's junk is another's treasure."

Her sing-song tone and casual attitude with the house's items were annoying, but she worked for the attorney, so I put on my best professional voice. "You'd be surprised what's valuable, sometimes things that most of us wouldn't give a second glance. Old tools, for instance, can bring incredible prices."

Gail got up and headed into the dining room. "I love antique jewelry, so I'd be curious to see what's going to be auctioned off."

"Well, I'm about to do a preliminary inventory, so I can give you an idea."

She stopped then in front of a wall of family photos I hadn't noticed yet. "I doubt she'll want these." She turned to me. "You know, I had Mrs. Freeman for kindergarten. She was such a great lady."

"Did she die suddenly?"

"Oh no, she had a stroke and went into a nursing home. All those years, though, I had no idea who she was, that she was related to *him*," she said, nodding to the picture.

In the center of the pictures hung a family portrait that must have been taken back in the forties, judging from their clothes and the car parked out front as they gathered on the porch.

"That's him," Gail said, her finger landing on the old man in the rocker.

"I don't understand. Who do you mean?"

"The murderer. James Titus. He lived here all those years."

"A murderer lived in this house?"

"Oh, I just realized you're not from around here. But it was like the O. J. Simpson case back in the late 1800s."

"Who did he murder?"

"Tillie Smith, a poor young kitchen maid from the college."

I opened my mouth, but my words stalled, picturing the

white marble monument to Tillie Smith where I'd stood last night. How was it possible I was now in the house of her murderer? A prickle of nerves crawled up my back as I stared at him. He must have been in his nineties when the picture was taken. He looked so old and sweet. I fingered the bandage on my thumb. I knew how a person looked meant nothing.

"Are you okay?" Gail asked.

"Oh...yes. I was just startled by what you said."

"It is kind of shocking, especially in a little town like this. Those poor women. Can you imagine?"

My eyes then went to the women in the photo. One was in her sixties or seventies; his daughter, I imagined, her face unsmiling. And a younger woman about my age stood on the end, the granddaughter who'd live here until a few months ago, unsmiling as well.

"What about Tillie?"

Gail shrugged. "She was a kitchen maid. That's all I ever heard."

"Oh, I thought she was someone prominent. The monument—"

The front door opened then, and we both looked over.

"Oh, hi, Helen," Gail said, then turned to me. "I'd better be heading back. Nice meeting you. Good luck with all this."

And then I was face to face with Adam's aunt, and she wasn't anything like I expected.

"So, you're the one who stole my nephew's heart," Aunt Helen said, walking toward me and extending a hand. But her tone and her taut smile belied the friendly expression. It was neither joking nor teasing. My own smile froze.

She was probably in her late fifties, dressed to kill in heels and a red silk jacket. Her platinum pageboy must have been sprayed stiff because her hair didn't move as she assessed me with obvious surprise. Short, plain, a few pounds overweight. No doubt wondering how I'd ever stolen her nephew's heart. Should I tell her how he loved my long hair?

I reached over and shook her hand. No warm hug from Aunt Helen.

"Well, your nephew stole my heart as well," I said nicely.

"Obviously. But he didn't tell us much about you, dear, though we know you're supposed to be an amazing auctioneer. And you did do a fine job at Aunt Eleanor's, thank you. So where are you from originally?"

"I was born in Pennsylvania, but we moved a lot with my father's jobs. I've lived in New Jersey, mostly, and when we met, I was living near Kearney."

"And your family? Where are they?"

"I...I don't really have any family. My father left when I was young, and my mother...she died when I was in college."

"No siblings?"

I shook my head, trying to take long breaths to control a building irritation. I felt like I was on trial. "Nope. My mother lived in foster care after her parents died, and my father was an only child. Not everyone is as lucky as Adam, I guess." That last part had come out a bit snarky.

"I wouldn't exactly call Adam lucky, dear."

"Why is that?"

She gave me a little smile. "Let's just say there are better options for him than staying in that cemetery."

I was stunned. "But he seems to love living there."

"And what about you? Think you can handle it?"

"I'm used to dead people. It's the living I sometimes have a problem with."

Now her smile froze.

"I'm sorry, I..." I didn't even know what to say.

Helen put her briefcase down. "Look, I'm sorry if I seem harsh. But you have to imagine how shocked we all were to learn forty-eight hours ago that Adam was planning to elope with a woman we'd never met. Why, you two hardly know each other."

"I don't know. The time we spent at your aunt Eleanor's was pretty intense. Getting through a crisis situation with someone... well, I think you can learn a lot fast. And I know the important things: he's a good man, he loves music, he's played outfield on the same softball team in town for ten years, he loves to read and prefers biographies over novels. I know he has a tenderness and passion for his work, which is something we share. Besides, we actually met when we were kids. My family lived here for a few months when I was a little girl."

Helen actually frowned and gave a little smile at the same time, as if to say, "Come on." So I kept going.

"We lived over on Water Street near the cemetery. I'd just gotten my first two-wheeler bike, and it was too big for me. I took it out that same day by myself, though I hadn't ridden without training wheels before. Anyway, I took a nasty fall near the corner by Main Street and ran home crying with my knees all bloodied. And then I remembered my bike and really got upset because I was afraid it might be stolen. I ran to the front door, but when I opened it, there was this young boy walking the bike right up to my house. I was so relieved. I had no idea who he was. But I remembered that birthmark all these years. He rescued my bike."

And that's exactly how I felt when he walked into my life again. Here he was once more, to finally rescue me from the mess I'd made of it.

"That's a charming story. And very much Adam. He can't stand to see anyone hurting." And then she turned and looked around the room. "Well, I guess we should both get down to business. We can share more at the party."

"What party?"

"Oh, I'm having a little reception for you two this weekend. I hope you'll share that lovely story with Adam's grandmother. They adore each other."

"Yes, I know."

I stood there a moment after she went upstairs, and thought about what I told Helen I knew about Adam. And what I didn't say, that I guessed there was something in his past. It was there in brief moments in his eyes, like in my own sometimes when I saw my reflection in a window. I wondered if it might have something to do with her comment about his not being so lucky living in the cemetery.

TWENTY MINUTES LATER, when she was done measuring the

rooms for her listing, Helen came back downstairs. I was in the dining room, once again looking at the photograph of James Titus.

"Did you know the family?" I asked her.

She walked over and glanced at the pictures. "Yes, they were lovely women."

"And James Titus? He was the one who murdered Tillie Smith?"

She turned to me. "No, I didn't know him. He died in the early fifties. But do me a favor, please, especially if you want this job. Forget about Tillie Smith. Mrs. Freeman has been through enough in her life because of her grandfather. Whatever time she has left, let her have peace."

There was a long silence. "I do want the job. Advice taken."

Helen seemed to relax then and gave me a hint of a real smile. "Well, I'll see you at the party, then."

I wasn't really sure what to think about Helen. Adam had told me he and his aunt were close, as she had no children of her own. Here I was, a stranger, suddenly married to her darling Adam. Of course she would be protective. I decided the wisest thing would be to give her the benefit of the doubt. Hopefully she'd do the same for me.

* * *

DRIVING BACK INTO THE CEMETERY a few hours later, I couldn't help myself. I didn't go right home. I turned the truck up to the highest point, rolled down the window, and stared at the beautiful monument to Tillie Smith. In the distance I could see the gold dome of the college shimmering in the sun, where I now knew she had worked as a maid. And yet here she was in the most prominent place in the cemetery, with a monument that must have cost a fortune back then. Something didn't make sense. Not only that, it seemed something was at play here.

Just then bells began to ring across the valley, and I realized it was the college bells ringing the hour. "Who were you, Tillie Smith?" I whispered.

CHAPTER 4

December 1885

TILLIE WALKED UP CHURCH STREET, her eyes on the big building three blocks ahead where the dirt road ended. Losing her balance, she quickly caught herself, knowing she'd best keep her eyes on the wooden sidewalk, slippery from the night's snow. It would do her no good to arrive wet and dirty. This job was her last hope.

The December wind cut through her old wool coat, and she shivered, wishing for a better one. And perhaps some gloves. She expected that if she was lucky enough to get this job, it was possible all of that could happen. The Centenary Collegiate Institute was now the plum landmark of Hackettstown, Mrs. Conover had advised her just that morning before she left. It sat on a ten-acre tract donated to the Methodist Church in an effort to lure it to build its new seminary here rather than Princeton or Newark, where it seemed more fitting.

"The society of people you will meet at the institute can make a big difference in your future, mind you," Mrs. Conover had gone on in that whispery voice of hers, as if she were too weak to get the words out. And sometimes she was, which was why Dr. Conover had hired Tillie to help out in the house. But now a niece, who she'd overheard them saying had some troubles, was coming to take over, which meant Tillie had best find another house that needed a domestic, unless she could find employment at the institute.

Two years ago, Tillie wouldn't have dared come here for a job, though she'd worked in several households. She wouldn't have thought it possible. But now she was able to read, thanks to Dr. Conover. Going to work for him and his wife had brought her advantages. In the evenings, the doctor and his wife sat around the fire reading or even singing, and it was peaceful and comforting, so different from her own home, though those were the times she found herself yearning most for her sisters, and her ma. One night, when they asked if she'd like to borrow a book and join them, Tillie was pressed to admit she couldn't read. There was a long silence, and she saw them look at each other.

"Well, I'm sure we can arrange to fix that," Mrs. Conover said in her soft voice.

Tillie could barely take her next breath as excitement and nerves set a fire in her belly. Lots of people she knew couldn't read, but it was something she had always yearned for, ever since the time she was six and had seen her rich cousin, but a few days older than herself, open a book and read aloud to the lot of them. It was the only Christmas they'd ever been invited. There'd just not been opportunities to learn or money for books. Not in her house, especially not after her mother had left.

"You know, Tillie," Dr. Conover then said, breaking into her thoughts, "I think teaching you to read would be an advantageous thing. Perhaps then, when Mrs. Conover isn't quite up to it, you might read aloud to her?"

"I should like that very much. And I'm a fast learner. You'll see."

"My dear, we already know that," Mrs. Conover said, reaching over with one of her dry, cold hands.

And for the next months, each night Tillie sat with the doctor in front of the fire learning words, and Mrs. Conover simply watched, seeming delighted with this new arrangement.

Now, Tillie was almost to Jefferson Street and the front gates of the seminary. She looked up at the building, five stories, the highest she'd ever seen, and her blood stilled. She studied the long rows of windows, the odd clock tower, and the railing at the top of the roof. There was something a bit fearsome about it, reminding her of the mansion in that book Mrs. Conover once had her try to read aloud, *Jane Eyre*. A prickle of nerves crawled up her back and she shook herself. There was no time for such foolishness.

Tillie stepped through the front gates and stopped at the big wooden doors. Should she go around back to where the servants' entrance was, no doubt? No, she'd go through here, because if she didn't want to work in the kitchen, then why start there? She had to keep all of her wits about her right now because not only did she need this job in a fearsome way, but here was a chance for her to perhaps move up a bit in the world.

She stepped into a front parlor filled with rose-colored couches and long velvet drapes. The shining wood floors were covered in beautiful rugs, and the soft light of gas lamps was everywhere. Tillie stood there frozen, her mouth about to drop open, never having been in any place quite so grand, and warm, not even her cousins' at Waterloo. She rubbed her icy hands together, hoping to get feeling back into them, when a young girl in a maid's black uniform walked in. The girl looked Tillie up and down, not in a kindly way.

"I'm Matilda Smith. I'm here about a job," she said, perhaps a bit too loud.

The girl left, and a minute later, an older woman came in. "You are Matilda Smith?"

Tillie nodded, her heart about to pound out of her chest as she faced the matron. "Everyone calls me Tillie, though."

Now the matron studied her with a quick sweep of her eyes. Her clothes were freshly ironed but nothing to set store by, hand-me-downs from Mrs. Conover's sister, who was a bit more her size, not like the doctor's wife, who was little more than skin and bones. The laced boots were tight, pinching her toes. If she were to secure this job, the first thing she'd do was buy a proper pair of shoes and those handsome kid gloves she'd seen in the dry goods store on Main Street.

They sat on one of the settees, and Tillie told her about her previous employment.

"Well, you look strong enough," the matron said. "Are you handy with a potato peeler?"

"But...I thought there was a position for a parlor maid, ma'am. I've been working at the doctor's residence for quite a while now, and I think I'd be very good at that job. I can read and do some fancy stitching as well."

"These are professional men and women, Matilda, um, Tillie. Some soon to be ministers. Your hair is..."

"Oh, sorry, ma'am. The wind was a bit blustery out there." She tried to smooth back the stray wisps curling around her face, her hair always taking on a life of its own. More hairpins— surely that's what she'd need first thing. "I know my hair's a bit wild....I mean unruly. I'm fixing to get it cut proper once I'm settled."

"Well, I'm afraid it's potato peeler or nothing. That's all I've got for someone with your background right now."

"Would there be a chance of perhaps advancing after a while?"

Tillie waited a few heartbeats as the matron considered. She regretted her boldness. She needed this job, even if it was only to peel potatoes for the rest of her life, because her only other option was the farm way out in Great Meadows, a sad place if she'd ever seen one. Five young ones and no mother. The farmer eyeing her with a toothless grin like he was starving for something more than domestic help. She would do whatever she had to so she wouldn't have to work there. And there was Nora and Catherine to think about. With a position here, there might be enough money not just to send to her sisters but perhaps to help them get on as well.

"The job is yours if you want it. But I can't make any promises about advancing."

"I'll take it. Thank you, ma'am."

"We have strict rules here, mind you, as we're a Christian institution. You'll get two Sundays off a month. There is to be absolutely no fraternizing with students of the opposite sex. And curfew is ten o'clock each evening, with no exceptions. This position is open because I've had to let someone go for ignoring curfew more than once."

"Of course. And I truly do appreciate this, ma'am. I'm a hard worker; you'll see."

The woman's face seemed to soften. "I'm sure you are, Tillie. And call me Mrs. Ruckle."

"I'm most obliged." She hesitated, then asked, "I know this is a seminary, ma'am, but did you say there are ladies attending here as well?"

"Why, yes, Tillie. We're a seminary for men; that's true. But we are also a college for both sexes and give girls a wonderful opportunity to have not just a classical education but a spiritual one as well."

She'd had no idea.

When she stepped back outside, Tillie turned, looking up at the big building once more, not seeming so fearsome now. She was hardly able to believe this was where she was going to work. And live. She'd done it! This was truly grand.

Because this was a place that could perhaps change all of their lives.

CHAPTER 5

W HEN I LEFT THE MONUMENT, I drove home and sat in the truck, staring up at the house, still having a hard time processing everything that had changed in my life so quickly. I lived here now. I had a husband. I was loved. I should be focusing on that.

Maybe it was the weight of all the souls, all the graves surrounding me. I looked at the bandage on my thumb, thinking about the odd coincidences of the past twenty-four hours. I felt as if I had stepped into a shadow place, that I was standing on the invisible line between past and present, and it was beginning to blur. It wasn't just with Tillie Smith and James Titus. It had to do with me and my own past, a past I had fought so hard to leave behind. I didn't want this happening. I wanted to be happy, to bask in the miracle of this marriage.

But where did the past really end and the present begin? Was it in this moment right now as I sat in the truck? Or in my next breath? When did it stop mattering if someone had once suffered?

Just then the front door opened, and I watched Adam come out, one hand holding the phone to his ear, the other raking through his hair. He didn't even notice me as he paced, obviously upset.

I needed to get a grip on myself. Adam was a good man. I was going to be a part of his family. Finally, here was a place I belonged. I needed to be a good wife. Nothing else should matter.

* * *

I WENT INSIDE AND BEGAN making shepherd's pie, one of Adam's favorites. Here was that moment I used to imagine on lonely weekends. Coming home to a sunny kitchen, preparing a meal for someone. Anticipating the evening ahead. It was like a mirage I could never reach and eventually gave up on, resigned to spending the rest of my life alone, burying myself in the lives of those whose houses I auctioned. But here I was, with Adam. I couldn't let a feeling about someone who'd been gone for over a century get in the way.

"You're a million miles away."

I jumped, not hearing him come back inside. He stood in the kitchen doorway, looking exhausted.

"Oh, you're off the phone," I said, wiping my hands and walking into his arms. He pulled me so close, I could feel his heart beating through his flannel shirt. "I could stay like this forever, Adam."

"Well, I have a few other things on my mind," he whispered in my ear. "But first, let's eat. I'm famished."

"Is everything okay? You look like you've barely slept, and you seemed upset on the phone."

But he put a finger to my lips. "Everything is fine. I'm sorry. You know this isn't how I imagined things our first couple of days."

"I know, but I want to help if there's a problem."

"Rachel, there's no problem."

"Okay."

He opened a cabinet for a glass, and then I watched as he opened another and another.

"Rachel..."

I should have warned him.

"I know I'm not the neatest guy in the world, but...you seriously alphabetized the spices?"

"I'm not OCD, I promise, Adam." I could hear the tremble in my voice. I actually was a bit OCD when I was worried, nervous, when I needed order to calm me. As I did last night when I came back from Tillie Smith's grave.

"It...looks great," he said, though I could hear the hesitation in his voice.

"I couldn't sleep last night, and I wanted to see what you had already and what I'd need at the store, and then...I just started organizing a little."

"I know you do this with your job. I just didn't realize..." He shook his head and gave a little laugh.

"You don't mind?"

"I don't mind at all. Did you get unpacked and settled today?"

"Actually, no." I slid the casserole in the oven, then told him about the call from his aunt and going to the house on Sharp Street.

"I told her I was worried about your leaving an established business behind, and here she gets you a job already."

"Well, I don't have the job yet. I have to put a proposal together."

"I'm sure she's going to push for you."

I wasn't so sure about that. I wondered if it was simply her way of checking me out alone. "The house I went to once belonged to a man named James Titus. His granddaughter, Marion Free-man, just went into a nursing home."

"You're kidding."

"You know of him?"

"I had Mrs. Freeman for kindergarten. She's a wonderful lady. I didn't know she was ill. I'm sorry to hear that."

And then I couldn't help myself. "Apparently her grandfather murdered Tillie Smith?"

"That's true, yes."

"I saw her monument when I was walking last night, Adam. The attorney's secretary, Gail, popped in. She seemed to think it was a big deal."

He laughed. "I went to school with Gail. She's a drama queen if there ever was one. But in this case she's right."

"Do you know what happened?"

"Well, Mrs. Freeman is a good friend of my grandmother, so we never talked about it, really, out of respect for her."

"You must know something."

He shrugged. "I've heard lots of things over the years, though I'm not sure what's really true. Tillie's become something of a local legend. She was raped and murdered on the grounds of

Centenary. I do remember as a kid, though, asking my father about the monument, and he said I should let it go. It was all in the past. And that James Titus wasn't really to blame."

"Seriously? The man raped and murdered her, but he wasn't to blame?"

"Whoa, Rachel." He stared at me with eyebrows raised. "I'm sure that's not what he meant."

"I'm...I'm sorry. I'm sure you're right."

After a moment, Adam said, "It is kind of weird, though, your seeing the monument and then hours later walking into the murderer's house."

"I know. What an odd coincidence."

"Maybe it's God winking at you."

"What?"

"It was a book someone gave me a while back, actually, about how random coincidences are sometimes really God, the universe, whatever you want to call fate, giving you a nudge about something." And then he smiled. "Like you and I meeting that way again?"

I smiled, too. "It did seem like fate, your walking into that flooded cellar during the storm."

"Yeah, really, what were the odds?"

"So why do you think the universe might be nudging me about Tillie Smith?"

He shrugged. "Maybe you should find out."

But his aunt had specifically told me not to if I wanted the job. And I did want it, probably more than any job I'd ever had. Because I could only imagine what might be hidden in that house. Or simply forgotten over the years.

* * *

WHILE I FINISHED MAKING DINNER, Adam got wood from the porch and lit a fire in the living room. When I brought our plates of steaming shepherd's pie in, I couldn't help but smile. He'd laid a blanket on the floor in front of the roaring fire and also lit candles all around the room. Light music was playing from somewhere.

"Oh, Adam, it's lovely."

"Sit," he said, taking the plates and gesturing to a throw pillow on the blanket near him.

"This is so romantic," I said, smiling, yet a humming of nerves running through my veins.

"This was what I had planned for last night, actually. I'd like to propose a toast," he said, holding a glass of wine out to me. "Some people might think what we did was crazy."

"Actually, most people would."

He laughed, then went on. "Eloping, no honeymoon...though there will be one, I promise. But I'm going to make you happy here, Rachel. I know we haven't known each other very long, but I started falling in love with you that first night I saw you bailing water in your underwear. And then when you sat there with tears streaming down your face, reading those love letters...that kind of sealed the deal. I'm looking forward to spending my life getting to know you."

We touched glasses, and I swallowed hard. "I hope you're not disappointed."

"I highly doubt I'll be disappointed."

We ate in silence for a few moments, Adam murmuring over and over how good the meal was. I was pleased. Though I'd learned to cook as a little girl when my mother wasn't capable, I was hardly a gourmet.

"Tell me something I don't know about you," I said. We had begun playing this game a week after we'd met, learning about each other in bits and pieces over the weeks. Each time, I could see him thinking, as he was now, as if deciding which memory to share.

"When I was a kid, I always thought I was lucky living in the cemetery, you know?" he began, a faraway look in his eyes. "I had all this room to roam, and the river, which you could imagine was an amazing place to play and explore for a boy. It really was like living in a park because after a while, I didn't even see the headstones. Just the beauty. But I'd get teased by the kids in school, and my mom would tell me to say I felt sorry for them, so I did. Then one day..." He paused, looking out the window before turning to me again. "I started getting teased about some-thing else. About my dad being a drunk."

"Oh, Adam."

He gave a little shrug. "That was worse, but it was true. He did drink a lot. My mother said it was the job, that it was a heavy burden for some men. And it's a small town."

"Why are kids so damn cruel?"

"It's all right. That was long ago. I still see that kid—well, he's a man now—and I wonder if he remembers saying that to me. I punched him, and I got suspended. I was twelve. My mom made me promise I would go to college and do something else with my life. I did go to college, but...obviously, here I am."

"Wasn't there something else you wanted to do?"

He shook his head slowly. "This is my family's legacy. It has been for seven generations. I don't want it to end with me."

There was more. As there was with me. But I let it go. Because now we had each other. I made him laugh; he made me feel safe.

We finished our wine, and then he put his glass down and leaned over to kiss me. As the fire burned down, he kept kissing my throat, my neck, lifting my hair, causing goose bumps to run down my back.

"You're shivering," he said, pulling away. "I know this is your first time and you're nervous, but I'll be gentle, I promise."

I wanted him so much. And I knew this was my chance. That with Adam, this would be possible. But I also knew that this could be the moment it might all fall apart.

HOURS LATER, I WOKE IN THE DARKNESS, my heart pounding. The room was lit by the moon, soft white light coming through the sheers. Beside me, Adam snored softly, the sleep of a man whose body was exhausted. A good man. I knew that the moment I saw the birthmark that day in Kearny. My fingers touched his cheek, ran down the stubble of his chin, and lower still across his wide chest. He murmured something and I stopped, not wanting to wake him.

Slipping out of bed, I pulled his sweatshirt over my head, then tiptoed out of the room, down the stairs, past the wall of cemetery keepers, and stood in the big foyer. I looked at my boxes still piled in the living room. There weren't many. I'd lived in a series of furnished rentals over the years. Though I loved exploring the houses I worked in, I preferred to keep my own life sparse. I didn't need much. Besides, if I wanted to move, it made things easier. And I moved frequently.

I walked into the dark kitchen and looked out the window at the eternal flame candles, little pinpricks of amber scattered across the fields of graves, rising up the hill to the monument. I shut the curtains then, turning on the lights in the kitchen. Remembering the wine, I filled a water glass, then sat at the table, thinking about how I'd convinced Adam I'd not been with a man before, that I was that rare and precious woman who wanted to wait until I was married. He'd admired me for that.

But now he had to be disappointed.

As he kissed me, stroking me so gently, I closed my eyes, willing this to happen. But in the final moment, I couldn't. I pan‑icked, my body tensing as I held back little screams of pain. I looked up at him and gasped, unable to breathe.

He stopped, rolling off and holding me tenderly. "It's okay," he whispered in my ear. "We'll take our time."

I sat in the quiet now, wondering just how much time Adam would give me. And why, if I really trusted him, I couldn't just tell him the truth.

That when I looked up, it wasn't his face I saw.

CHAPTER 6

A DAM WAS ALREADY IN THE KITCHEN eating breakfast when I came down the next morning. He'd made pancakes and had some keeping warm in the oven. We made small talk about the day ahead and the party his aunt Helen was hosting for us that weekend. But to me the air seemed to vibrate with his disappointment.

It wasn't until I went into the dining room to work on my proposal for the house on Sharp Street that he finally pulled me into his arms and stared into my eyes, as if searching for the truth.

"I'm sorry," was all I could manage.

"No, I'm sorry I hurt you. Maybe you should see a doctor."

"No!" It came out way too loud. "I mean, there's nothing wrong with me. I was nervous."

"I know the first time can hurt, but..."

But. Right.

"Maybe I was in too much of a hurry," he suggested.

I knew that wasn't the case. The problem was me. It was always me.

"And things got off to a rocky start here, me disappearing on our wedding night to work. If we were on our honeymoon now..."

"Please, Adam, I don't want you blaming yourself. This is your job, and you took a lot of time off to be with me in the past three months. I'm fine waiting until after Memorial Day. It gives us time to plan."

He pulled me into him. "You're so damn sweet."

"I love when you touch me, Adam," I whispered. "I'll try to relax more." And perhaps more wine wouldn't hurt.

He kissed me, and then he left for work.

* * *

INSTEAD OF UNPACKING, I wrote up my proposal for the house on Sharp Street and decided to walk into town. As I came through the stone arch and headed toward Main, I stopped at the corner of Water Street. This time I turned, walking half a block to the small green bungalow across from the river. This was where we'd lived for those few months when I was a little girl.

I imagined myself at six years old, crying at that front door with bloody knees, my mother locked in the bathroom, unable to help me, then moments later watching a young boy wheeling my new bike back to me. Did I say thank you? Did he speak? I couldn't remember. The only thing I did remember was the birthmark across his throat, as if a fiery hand had clutched his neck, burning his skin.

Who could have imagined almost thirty years and miles later, fate would bring us together again? Had God been winking at us when Adam and I met at his aunt's house in Kearney? Was there really such a thing as fate? If so, how would that explain everything that had gone horribly wrong with my family? My life?

I swallowed hard, remembering the three of us in that little house. The longing for normal beginning right there as I watched my mother fall apart for the first time when my father was away on a business trip. Paralyzed myself with the fear of something I couldn't even name yet.

Turning away, I continued walking through town, trying to forget those sad images. I focused on the town, reading each street sign to learn my way. The sidewalks were lined with older Colonials and Victorians with porches and gingerbread. Tulips, daffodils, and pansies bloomed in flower beds and window boxes. Near the center of town, I walked up to a small white Cape with a sign out front. Gail looked up as I stepped into the office, giving me a brief smile.

"Oh, your proposal. Thank you. Mr. Trimmer is hoping to make a decision by the end of the week. We'll call you either way."

I handed Gail the manila envelope with a dozen questions about Tillie Smith on the tip of my tongue, but she was already back at her keyboard. There was none of yesterday's chattiness.

Once outside again, I headed to Main Street, glancing into store windows. There were several barbershops, a bakery, a number of restaurants, as well as antique and consignment shops. Tall lanterns lined the sidewalks with baskets of Easter flowers. The benches in front of the stores were painted with M&M characters, and I realized that was why the air was so sweet. I'd forgotten about that. It was chocolate cooking.

This was my home now, where I would shop and walk and make a life with Adam. But would I fit in? Could I really belong? I was so used to being alone. In a few days I would meet his grandmother, see his aunt again, and be introduced to countless others. This was the normal life I'd longed for. Yet a prickle of nerves crawled up my back.

Turning onto Church Street to find the library, I wondered what would have happened if Adam hadn't come into my life. Where would I be now? Lost in thought, I nearly collided with an old man who was walking from his car across the sidewalk.

"Sorry," he muttered as he brushed by. "I'm late opening."

I'd been walking with my head down and hadn't realized I was right in front of the library. It was a small brick building with mullioned windows and a little front stoop. But the man kept going, and I turned to see him hobble up the porch steps of a weathered yellow Colonial. I read the placard next to the front door: *Historical Society.*

I stood there a moment, staring. *Don't do this*, a voice inside my head warned me. But I couldn't help thinking about Adam's comment the night before. I'd never believed in synchronicity. How could I? Because if I did, it would mean that the disasters in my past, so perfectly aligned, were somehow meant to be. Still, wasn't meeting Adam again a seemingly perfect alignment of fate?

As I hesitated in front of the historical society, knowing that to step inside could possibly open a door to my past that I'd slammed shut long ago, I couldn't deny that there was something larger at play here. Was I meant to meet Adam? To come back to this town and see that grave once again? And then, against all odds, find myself in the murderer's house?

It was just too much to ignore.

IT WAS LIKE GOING TO ONE OF MY JOBS, an old house stuffed to the gills with memorabilia, only in this case, it was a museum of the history of the area. I walked through a cluttered front hall and into a back room that was no doubt once the kitchen, where the old man I'd nearly run into now sat at a desk catching his breath. There were pictures and maps all over the walls, uniforms from different wars, medals, and I already felt a sneeze coming on.

"Hello there. What can I do for you?" the man asked, suddenly noticing me.

"I'm actually new to the area and wondered if you might have anything on Tillie Smith. I saw the monument at the cemetery, and I got kind of curious."

He nodded and began to rise. "We have a folder on the murder, and we have one on the Smiths. Do you want them both?"

"Uh, sure." Why not?

He opened one of several filing cabinet drawers that lined the other side of the room and pulled out a file. Then he opened another drawer, and I watched him scan through the *S*'s.

"There's a table in the other room where you can sit and look through these. If you want copies of anything, it'll be twenty-five cents each."

"Okay, thanks." I walked into the other room, no doubt the former dining room, sat at the dark table, and opened the file in front of me. *Tillie Smith*. My heart quickened.

The article on top was from the *New York Times*, dated April 10, 1886, with the brief headline *Found Dead in a Field*, and directly beneath that a subhead, *A Domestic in Hackettstown, N.J.*,

Brutally Assaulted and Murdered. I was surprised that a national newspaper covered an event in what must have been a tiny town back then, but then I remembered Gail saying that it was the O. J. case of its time. I continued reading:

This town was thrown into great excitement this morning by the report that a young girl had been murdered sometime in the night after having been brutally assaulted. A. J. White, passing through a field just southwest of the Methodist seminary, early in the morning discovered at the corner of a fence the body of a young woman. She appeared to be sleeping, but upon closer inspection he noted finger marks on her throat and a bead of dried blood from a wound on her thumb.

I gasped, as though the breath had been sucked from my lungs. My eyes drifted to the bandage on my thumb. A scab was forming, but a little blood still oozed from underneath.

"Everything all right?"

I looked up, and the old man stood in the doorway with a frown.

"Oh, yes, I...I'm sorry. It's just so awful."

"Yes, it was a terrible thing."

"But it says she was killed on the grounds of a seminary."

"Yup. The college actually started out as a Methodist seminary."

"Oh."

He went back to work, and I turned to the article again. *There were no signs of a struggle in the vicinity, and the girl's clothing was covered with dust but was not muddy, as it would have been had she been assaulted in the spot where she was found. White gave an alarm, and the body was soon identified as that of Tillie Smith, a domestic employed at the seminary.*

The article went on to say that Tillie had gone into town to see a theatrical company. She attended the show with friends of hers and a male friend of theirs who was a drummer, or travel-ing salesman. Afterward, they walked down Main to Church Street and there parted, Tillie heading back to the seminary accompanied by the drummer.

I looked out the window a moment. This was Church Street.

I'd just turned off Main Street to get here. Had I just inadvertently followed in Tillie's footsteps on the night she died?

Tillie apparently did not make it back inside the seminary building. *Her absence caused some comment last night, but no search was made, as it was supposed that she had remained overnight with a friend.*

Instead, she was being brutally attacked.

It is believed that more than one person was concerned in the crime and that murder was not intended, but that the persons who assaulted the girl only desired to render her insensible or to choke her into compliance with their wills.

Someone had been trying to rape her, and she fought so hard that they ended up killing her on the seminary grounds. What if she hadn't fought? Would she have lived out her life? The one she should have had?

The drummer who'd left town that morning was under suspicion. But yesterday I was in the house of the man who was eventually convicted of the crime, James Titus. I wondered why they thought it was two men at first. What happened to the other man?

I leafed through the rest of the file, and there on the very bottom was an actual sepia-toned picture of Tillie Smith. I picked it up and stared at the girl. Tillie wore a brown jacket—at least in sepia it appeared to be brownish—with a white lace collar and three-quarter sleeves, cinched in tightly at the waist. She no doubt wore a corset beneath the dress and possibly a bustle under the long skirt. On her head was a straw hat topped with flowers. Was she pretty? It was hard to tell. She seemed solidly built and had an upturned nose and round face, and her lips were set in a line, with perhaps the hint of a smile.

But it was her eyes that drew me in. At the moment the picture had been taken, there was such intensity in her gaze as she looked off into the distance, just above the camera. It was as if she were looking right at me now. What were her thoughts at the moment it had been taken? Her hopes? At just nineteen, she must have been filled with dreams. I could remember my own as if they were yesterday. I was a freshman, my whole life ahead of me, raging inside.

I grabbed a tissue from my purse and wiped the tears that threatened to spill from my eyes. Poor Tillie. I took the picture and a few of the articles to the old man to have photocopied.

"It says in one article that Tillie was buried in Potter's Field, yet I saw the beautiful monument to her at the cemetery," I said to him. "Do you know anything about that?"

"I'm not sure exactly what happened except that it was a big to-do back then."

"There wasn't much about her at all in what I saw. Just about the different suspects and the case, and then that the janitor, James Titus, became a suspect."

"Newspapers from all over the country came to cover it," the old gentleman said as he made the copies.

"But why?"

"I'm not actually sure."

"But this time they got their man convicted, right?" I said, handing over another article headlined, *TITUS FOUND GUILTY*.

"Not everybody thinks so."

"What do you mean?"

He shrugged. "I just remember years and years ago hearing that Titus was railroaded. 'Course my mother worked at the library next door with his daughter, and they were friends."

I thought about the two women I had seen in the family photo, the granddaughter still alive in a nursing home. The gossip she must have endured. And I couldn't help remembering Aunt Helen's warning to leave it alone.

"But who knows what's truth and what's fact after all these years?" he then said.

"What about Tillie, though? Everything I see here is about the crime or the trial. Do you have anything more on her? You know, where she came from, what her life was like?"

"She was nobody, really. Just became a bit famous in these parts because of the crime."

"She wasn't nobody," I said, then regretted my sharp tone

when he looked up at me with raised eyebrows. He handed me the copies.

"Well...thanks for all of this," I said, mustering a grateful smile.

"You know, every so often, someone comes in just like you wondering the same things, hoping to find out the truth of what happened."

"And?"

He shook his head. "They all give up after a while."

It seemed that no one had cared enough to find out the truth about Tillie Smith's life, or her death.

I LEFT WITH MY COPIES, STOPPING on the sidewalk out front, turning to look all the way up Church Street, where I could see the front of Centenary College. I began walking toward it. Tillie had walked these same blocks on the last night of her life. Three blocks later, I stopped in front of a wrought iron gate and looked up at the brick building, four stories tall, stretching from corner to corner, with a grand front portico.

I stood there and could almost picture Tillie in the long dress and bonnet as she walked through these very same gates, going inside and donning her apron. Was she in awe of the big build-ing? Did she have hopes for a future there?

I thought going into the historical society that I would find out enough to satisfy my curiosity and be able to let it go. But after everything I read, I only had more questions. Something wasn't right. I felt it in my gut.

I fingered the bandage on my thumb, thinking about the strange coincidences adding up now. Was Tillie Smith reaching out to me somehow?

Just then the college bells began ringing the hour. I jumped as someone tapped my shoulder. Turning, I realized it was just a tree branch. And then I shivered, despite the warmth of the sun.

"What happened to you, Tillie?" I whispered.

CHAPTER 7

O N THE WALK BACK TO THE CEMETERY, Tillie Smith dominated my thoughts. I couldn't wait to get back to read more. When I walked in the house, I saw that my things were no longer in the living room. I went upstairs to find my boxes in the guest room across the hall, where Adam had told me to set up my office for work. He must have come back for lunch and moved them. Had he waited for me, wondering where I was?

I couldn't help staring a moment at the plastic bin I hadn't opened in years, that I simply moved from one rental to another, unable to bring myself to look inside. Opening the closet, I saw that it ran deep. I pushed the bin far back, but it hit something that fell with a melodic crash. I kneeled inside and pulled out a Martin guitar. My fingers grazed the strings, and they made a deep, lovely sound. I wondered who had played, Adam's father or his mother? He'd never mentioned anything about it. I put a few boxes of off-season clothes in as well and emptied the box of books and CDs, filling up a bookshelf. All the while I worked, my mind kept drifting back to the questions swirling in my head since I'd left the historical society. Finally I sat at a small desk set in front of a double window and opened my portfolio.

I paged through it, glancing at the names of people I had, in a way, brought back to life after they were gone. There were dozens. In the back of the book, on the first line of a blank sheet, I wrote, "Tillie Smith." The empty page lay before me like a dare. No one had tugged at me like this before.

I chewed on the end of the pen for long minutes. I knew that if I pursued this, I would be risking everything I'd spent years trying to forget. As I stared out the window, though, I couldn't help thinking about how it all seemed to be set in motion. Was there really a sort of destiny at work here?

I opened the folder with the articles and began to read. After a while, I sat on the bed and propped up pillows to try to stay awake. I lay my head back, closing my eyes for a moment, the next article still in my hand.

"RACHEL?"

Opening my eyes, I saw Adam sitting on the edge of the bed.

I sat up. "I'm sorry. I should have started some dinner."

"What's wrong?" he asked. "I don't think you've slept a full night since you got here."

"I told you I'm a night owl," I said with a little laugh, trying to make light of it.

"You sure you're not spooked being here? My mother used to leave sometimes and go visit her sister when it got to be too much, after a big accident like we just had or...a child."

"I'm not spooked. Promise."

"I'll be glad when Easter is over and things slow down so you're not alone so much. Though in a few weeks, we'll be clean-ing the graves all over again and getting ready for Memorial Day. I can't wait for you to see that. It's really special. And then we'll take our honeymoon."

"You're a hard worker, Adam."

He shrugged. "It's my job."

"It's more than that; I can see that. And everything's okay? With the board?"

"Sure." Then he picked up a page from the bed. "What's all this?"

"Oh, I kind of stumbled across the historical society when I was walking through town. I was reading some articles I copied when I guess I fell asleep."

"'Titus Found Guilty,'" he read out loud and looked up.

"I thought I'd see if I could find a little information on Tillie."

"And?"

"Well, as you just read, Titus was found guilty and sentenced to hang. But there he was in the picture in that house. He was really old, and he obviously didn't hang."

"I wonder what happened?"

"I don't know. There were lots of suspects in the beginning, and he was never even mentioned."

"Wow," Adam said, continuing to read. "They brought in the Pinkerton Detective Agency. It's kind of like a whodunit."

"It's not a whodunit. This girl died a gruesome death fighting off some bastard trying to rape her."

Adam stared at me. "I'm sorry, Rachel. But...it was a long time ago."

"Oh, shit, Adam, I'm sorry. I just... it's just so horribly sad."

He took both of my hands. "Listen, let's leave all this. Let's get back to you and me. I've been neglecting you, but I have plans for us tonight. I'm going to run you a nice warm bath. I want you to take your time. And when you come out, I have a surprise for you."

He gathered all of the pages into a pile and handed them to me.

* * *

ADAM RAN ME A BUBBLE BATH. There was a full goblet of wine beside the claw-foot tub. My robe hung on the hook behind the door. I sank into the tub, making it hotter. I finished the entire glass of cabernet, trying to calm my nerves. Thirty minutes later when I stepped into the hall, Adam was waiting for me, his shirt off, wearing nothing but blue jeans. I was warm and more than a little buzzed. I felt giddy with possibility. God, how I loved his wide shoulders, the muscles on his arms, the place I could be cocooned and feel safe.

He kissed me, then took my hand and led me into our bedroom. It was filled with candles. Rose petals covered the bed, and the last rays of sun bathed everything in a golden light.

"This is what a wedding night should look like," he whispered in my ear, the hum of his voice sending goose bumps up and down my body.

"It's just beautiful."

He took off his pants, then sat on the edge of the bed, looking up at me, the wanting so evident in his eyes. He untied my robe. I stood there, my breath coming in spurts, as he took the strap from one shoulder and pulled until it slid down my arm, baring my left breast. He did the same with the other strap, and my robe slid to the floor.

He pulled me onto the bed with him, devoured me with kisses, and I gave myself over to his tenderness, kissing his shoulders, the birthmark across his throat. Suddenly he was above me, looking into my eyes.

"I love you, Adam."

He smiled. I meant it. I really was falling in love with him, despite any uncertain moments I may have had. He was a good and loving man, and I would give myself to him as he was to me. But in the next moment, as he tried to enter me, my body tensed and closed up. I whimpered in pain.

"It might hurt a little," he whispered as he continued to push, "but once we—"

"Stop!" I shoved his chest until he rolled off of me.

He lay looking up at the ceiling, and I could hear the frustration in his breathing. I ran to the bathroom and pulled on my clothes. It was over. I knew there was no hope for us after this.

Then I ran out the front door and into the cemetery, wondering what the hell I would do now.

* * *

I RAN UNTIL A CRAMP IN MY SIDE doubled me over, forcing me to stop and catch my breath. My heart was pounding so hard, I thought it might burst through my ribs. I hated myself. How could I ever face Adam again? Why hadn't I been honest with him from the beginning?

I kept walking toward the river in the falling light, through fields of headstones, the still before nighttime with just the rush of the river and the calling of birds for a last feeding. My tumbling heart began to slow down. Dusk thickened. The beauty of this place in early evening surrounded me, and I realized I was no longer afraid here. But I felt a weight on my heart as I walked beside all of those lives passed, wondering about the mystery of it all. What happened when everyone who remembered you was gone? Weren't you forgotten then? My God, for your life to not just be over, but to be erased from memory. As if it had never happened.

Who would remember me when I was gone? I wondered, my eyes filling with tears. Probably no one.

I climbed the hill to the highest point and stopped, looking up at the white marble monument. *Tillie Smith*. Who, really, remembered *her*? Not the crime or James Titus. Not the ghost I'd just read about that was said to prowl the college. But the real girl.

If she hadn't fought off her attacker, what would her life have been like? Would she have married? Had children? Would her dreams have come true? I sat there on the ground, my fingers stroking the grass just above where I imagined she lay. The silk bouquet hung upside down now, the petals mostly gone. I felt silent tears spill down my cheeks.

"Rachel?"

I turned. Adam was standing on the gravel road. Quickly I wiped my face.

"What's going on? Tell me, please, what it is."

I shook my head and looked away, so embarrassed by what I'd done.

"I'm sorry I hurt you. I should have stopped," Adam said, kneeling beside me.

I couldn't speak.

"There's nothing you can tell me that will change how I feel about you, okay?"

I looked up at him, this man whose hands dug the dirt that became graves, who witnessed the wailing and grieving of those who couldn't bear their losses. Was that how he'd become so tender?

"I've never told anyone. Ever."

"That's okay." Adam waited.

"It was a long time ago. I..."

How did you finally speak words you'd buried for years?

Words that would make it all real again. The shame. The horror. He squeezed my hand.

"I was...raped."

His eyes widened, and for a moment he looked stunned. "Oh, Rachel."

"I should have told you before we got married. But we could probably just get it annulled because we haven't—"

"Stop!" He looked at me a long moment, and I thought he might cry. His voice when he spoke again was so gentle, it was almost more than I could bear. "Tell me what happened."

I stared at him. "Date rape, I guess they would call it, but that just makes it seem like it was something less than...what it was."

"I'm so sorry."

"I was just eighteen, and...I was a virgin."

"I hope he went to jail for a long time."

I didn't speak for a long moment. He kept squeezing my hand.

"I never pressed charges."

Adam said nothing.

"How could I? It was my word against his. I know you're probably thinking, *Are you kidding? How could you let him get away with that? Were you a fool?*"

"I'm not thinking any of those things. Just that I'd like to kill the bastard."

"I've felt that way, too." I took a long breath,

"I don't want to relive it by going over all the details. I was just...an idiot. I wasn't very experienced, and I trusted him. I thought he was such a nice guy, and how could he be interested in me, right? I didn't scream, Adam, because I...I couldn't breathe. I should have, somehow, but...he was crushing me. I felt like I was being torn in half, and I was terrified my lungs were going to collapse. I..." Even now in that moment, I could feel the terror of his weight on me, gasping for air. "I...thought I...was going... to die."

"It's okay. Try to catch your breath."

I closed my eyes then and took long slow breaths.

"Better?"

I nodded. "Maybe things would have turned out differently, but...then my mother was killed. I had no one. I went to bed each night terrified, wondering if I'd be alone the rest of my life. Looking back now, I think I was probably in some sort of post-traumatic stress. I had no idea how to move forward. Over the years I've tried to trust men, but...they always lost patience, and I guess I just couldn't let anyone in. Until you, Adam. I knew you were different."

Bats began to swoop above us, diving for insects, and it was nearly dark. Adam was silent, his face hard as stone, and suddenly I was afraid.

"I should have been honest from the beginning, but I just always felt so ashamed. You waited until we were married because I told you I was a virgin. Obviously I wasn't, and I don't blame you if—"

"Oh, Rachel." He cut me off, shaking his head. "I was more than willing to wait. I wanted tenderness with you. Everyone thinks guys just want sex anytime they can get it, but to me it's a commitment. I've seen it wreck lives when people aren't careful."

"Yours?"

"Just...friends when I was younger. I decided that was never going to be me." He took my hand again. "I really felt like we had something special right from the beginning. And I wanted to do it right."

"But I've ruined it."

"Don't ever say you're sorry about this. You did nothing wrong. But you should have trusted me."

There was a long silence, and I knew I should tell him the rest now. The door was wide open, and I might regret it one day if I didn't. But coward that I was, I just couldn't.

"I'll help you in any way I can," Adam said then. "There's no rush. We've got all the time in the world."

"Thank you, Adam. At least I still have my life. And I don't want to waste it anymore on the past. That bastard took years from me. Years I wasted. The only thing I want now is to be a good wife and to make you happy."

"He could still be punished, you know."

"I'm sure it's too late. Besides, it would be hard to prove anyway. It would have been even then."

"There are other ways."

"What...? No, Adam. I just want to put it behind me, okay? Maybe now I finally can."

He nodded to the monument. "Is this why you're so caught up in what happened to Tillie?"

"We were the same age. And I can't help but think that these coincidences do mean something."

"God's nudging you?"

"I almost feel as if Tillie is reaching out to me. I can't change my own past, or Tillie's, but she wasn't a 'nobody,' as I've heard her called. She was the victim, just like I was. And in so many ways, the victim becomes invisible, forgotten. Except now it's like she's occupying a corner of my mind, and I can almost imagine what she felt, what she dreamed. She was nineteen years old, her whole life ahead of her. Maybe if I can find out the truth about her and her life, it could be some kind of...atonement."

"If it helps you to heal, then do it. But Rachel, you do not need atonement. You should not feel guilty or ashamed."

I opened my mouth, but again the words didn't come.

Adam stood and held out his hand. We walked back to the house through the dark graves. I was relieved that I had finally told him about the rape. He held me all night, with no expectations. But talking about that horrible day, the day that ruined my whole life, it became real again. I could see the red hair, smell that awful cologne. And I could hear my mother's voice on my answering machine, pleading with me to pick up.

As Adam began to snore softly, I wondered if it would ever really be possible to put it completely behind me. A few minutes later, I got out of bed and went to the desk in the bedroom across the hall, trying not to think of it all. I pulled out the copy of the picture of Tillie Smith, staring into her eyes for a long time. Then I opened my portfolio and picked up my pen.

And so it continued, a passion to learn about this girl's life. And to once again forget about my own.

CHAPTER 8

THE MORNING OF THE BRUNCH, Adam had to take care of some equipment problems. He spent the previous day at the shed on the other side of the cemetery tinkering with a riding lawn tractor he'd been unable to fix.

"It's seen better days," he said after downing a quick cup of coffee.

I glanced at the old tractor on the back of his truck, rusted with peeling paint. "Maybe it's time to trade it in."

"Not while it's still got some life left in it," he said, then smiled. "I'll be back by eleven to change for brunch. My aunt's a stickler for promptness."

Why was I not surprised? "I'll be ready," I said, a little drumbeat beginning in my gut.

"Don't be nervous."

"They don't think what we did was kind of weird?"

"I've never let what other people think influence my decisions, Rachel. Besides, they'll love you. You're family now."

He kissed me then, searching my eyes. Something had changed between us since I'd told Adam about the rape. There was a protectiveness there that melted my heart. He'd done nothing but kiss or hold me at night. But he made me promise I'd call and get checked by a doctor. I promised I would on Monday.

I went upstairs and took out the dress I wore for our wedding, beige lace with an empire waist. It was knee length and simple, but it reminded me of a dress I'd had for one of my dolls when I was a little girl and imagined what my own wedding would be like one day. It was the first dress I had bought in years. I'd gone to Lord & Taylor, and when I tried it on in front of the big mirror, I couldn't help wondering what my mother would have thought. It wasn't what she'd have expected, any of it: eloping, no bridesmaid, no fanfare. She would have controlled it all. But after everything I'd been through, I didn't need any of that. Adam agreed and seemed relieved. He didn't want a big fuss.

The dress had gotten wrinkled in the move, so I got the ironing board out of the bathroom closet and plugged in the iron. A minute later, the lights went off, and so did the iron. Old houses and electricity. I was used to this. I had tripped a breaker.

Adam had already warned me that the basement was a disaster, but I had no choice. Besides, I was certain it was far better than some I'd encountered. Still, when I opened the door off the kitchen and saw the steep wooden steps, narrow and pitched to the right, I paused. Then I noticed a flashlight on a shelf above the railing. I flipped the light switch up for later, hopefully, then held on tight to the railing with one hand as I carefully made my way down, smelling the dampness already. The cellar had thick stone walls and a dirt floor, and as I scanned the flashlight for a breaker box, I shuddered at the cobwebs hanging from the low beams of the ceiling.

He was right; it was a disaster. And I imagined it hadn't been touched in years. Paint cans, rusting tools, pieces of wood, and more were piled on makeshift shelves that lined one wall. An old coal bin under the front porch was filled with furniture, no doubt ruined by years of moisture. Newspapers and magazines from decades ago were stacked on a metal shelf on the opposite wall. Then the light caught a flash of color, and I walked over to a tiny window. Old bottles lined the sill. My foot hit something, and I saw boxes of them on the floor below. Someone, I realized, had been a collector.

I turned, searching again, and found the breaker box. I flipped the switch, and the lights came on because I'd been smart enough to turn them on before coming down. A little trick I'd learned over the years. I went back to the window.

The bottles were thick and colorful, covered with grime and dust, but you could still see the different shades: amber, blue, gold, and of course clear glass. But it was a small emerald green one I picked up, holding it to the light. The raised letters on the front of the glass read, "Palmer," and at the bottom, "2 ½ ozs Average." It was beautiful, a tiny work of art.

Old bottles could be valuable, but usually not very. I wasn't familiar with this brand. I turned, once again studying the cellar. Someone had once spent a lot of time down here, collecting things. But nothing had been touched in years. I wondered why. "There are no mysteries here," I recalled Adam saying the first day I arrived. I wasn't so sure about that. But for Adam's sake, I wasn't going there. Besides, my mind was already occupied with Tillie Smith. Tucking the bottle into my jeans pocket, I went back upstairs to get ready for the brunch.

I wanted to make the best impression I could with Adam's grandmother.

* * *

THE DAY WAS UNSEASONABLY WARM for April, so the wedding brunch was being held in the yard of Aunt Helen's rambling blue Victorian in the historic district surrounding the college. The streets were lined with other beautiful Victorians and Federal-style homes, some with gas lanterns and even a hitching post here and there. As we got out of the car, I paused a moment. People had already arrived and were seated at white tables and chairs on the back lawn, as we were a few minutes late. Daffodils, tulips, and grape hyacinths were everywhere, and the trees were festooned with white ribbons. Aunt Helen had outdone herself, for Adam, no doubt.

I saw her coming toward us then. My knees went weak at her big smile because I could see the frosty look in her eyes as they set on me. I felt as though I were on a set in a Hallmark movie, the plucky heroine with a troubled past suddenly finding herself in a place of honesty and goodness. And here was the suspicious aunt.

I was introduced by Aunt Helen to one person after another. "And this is Adam's wife," with an inflection that told me they were all still having trouble believing that quiet, steadfast Adam had gotten hitched to a stranger he barely knew. I made small talk—yes, I had a house auction business; oh, it was full of great stories. Then I was assured that in no time everyone in town would know me and I'd be drowning in business. But for now, I was still Rachel, the stranger who happened to be married to their darling Adam.

"Your grandmother's waiting to meet the bride," Aunt Helen said then, looking at Adam. "She's getting dottier by the day, refusing to believe you're really married. This has thrown her for a loop."

But Adam just smiled. "Well, we'll have to go show her the proof right now."

We finished our rounds in the yard and walked up the back porch steps, stopping in a large kitchen as Adam was waylaid by a cousin I'd already met, who had a question about a summer job for his son. I wandered into a large dining room, impressed with the antiques and collectibles. I stepped into the big living room and immediately felt eyes on me.

There in the corner of the room I saw an elderly lady in a wheelchair looking at me quizzically. A moment later, Adam was beside me taking my hand again, and those eyes shifted, the look of joy unmistakable.

"Oh, Ronnie, where have you been? I've missed you."

Adam dropped my hand and walked ahead, then knelt at the old woman's feet. "It's me, Gran, Adam. Dad's been gone a long time, remember?"

I watched confusion, then sadness settle in Gran's eyes.

"Of course, Adam. I'm so glad to see you," she said in a voice softened by age. "It's just…you look so much like your father. And you never stop missing those you love, no matter how long they're gone."

"I miss him, too, Gran."

I wondered if that were really true after hearing how Adam had suffered because of his father's drinking. And then Gran looked at me.

"Sandra?"

Adam stood then. "Gran, this is my wife, Rachel."

Gran looked at me again, frowning, but then she smiled,

shaking her head. "I'm sorry, dear. You must forgive me. My mind seems to wander sometimes."

"I'm so happy to finally meet you, Gran. Adam has told me so much about you. Maybe sometime you can tell me about your years living in the cemetery."

"That would be great, Gran. Maybe help Rachel get over her nerves a bit."

"Why, there's nothing to be afraid of there. It's one of the most peaceful places in the world."

Adam squeezed my shoulder as if in relief.

"And what about your family?" Gran asked. "How do they feel about this wedding?"

"Oh...my mother died when I was in college. And I don't really have anyone else. A few distant cousins of theirs, but no one they really kept in touch with."

"So you're all alone, my dear?"

"Yes, I guess so."

"Not anymore. You've got a wonderful man in Adam, and of course all of us now."

I couldn't help smiling.

"Why don't you come visit me for lunch one day soon, and I'll tell you all about my adventures in the cemetery? I'd move back in a heartbeat if I could."

Adam's aunt was suddenly beside us with a plate of food for Gran.

"Come along, you two. There are lots more people here waiting to meet the mysterious bride."

I held my face in check and forced myself not to roll my eyes. Before long, Adam and I were caught up in different groups of friends and relatives. My cheeks began to hurt from smiling so much and answering the usual questions: How did I like their little town? What did I think of living in the cemetery? What did a house auctioneer actually do? How did we meet? And of course when I told the story, I left out the part about being in my underwear. I was able to keep it all light.

THROUGHOUT THE PARTY, I caught Adam's eyes on me from across the yard as we both mingled. He'd had a few beers, and his face was flushed with heat since it was an unusually warm day for April. But the message in his eyes was clear. He was happy, and he wanted me. My pulse quickened. And then it was as if everything froze in place as I watched a tall man with bright red hair coming round the driveway. I felt my mouth open, but no words came. How was this possible?

"There you are," I heard from behind, turning with a start. Aunt Helen was beside me. "Can I steal you away for a few minutes? Gran was hoping to spend a little more time with you."

I turned back toward the driveway, nearly sinking to the grass in relief. Hair that color, a bright orange-red, wasn't common. But it wasn't him.

"Rachel?"

"Of course," I said, flashing her a bright smile. "I'd love to spend more time with Gran."

I followed Helen back into the kitchen, suddenly feeling overwhelmed by the crowd of people, the sudden fright. I wasn't used to social settings like this, or the pressure to make small talk with people I hardly knew. I also felt a wave of sadness, looking at this wonderful family, all the friends. This was what I'd missed all these years.

Adam's aunt stopped to top off her wine glass and turned to pour me some.

"Oh, no thanks. I'm just having iced tea. Wine makes me sleepy during the day."

Helen stared at me a moment. "I'm sorry you didn't get the job on Sharp Street."

"Oh..." She meant the Titus house. I pictured the house—the contents, the secret nooks and crannies I wouldn't be able to explore, especially in hopes of finding anything related to Tillie—and was disappointed. "I didn't realize they'd made a decision."

"Well, I thought you knew. I'll be listing it in a few weeks, and someone in town will actually be selling the contents."

"Thanks for putting in a good word for me anyway."

Helen hesitated as if about to say something, then thought

better of it. "Well, let's go find Gran before she's ready for her nap."

Gran smiled as soon as she saw me, and my unease lightened. I sat in the chair next to her and was surprised when she reached for my hand and squeezed. I had an ally.

"My grandson looks happy," she said, smiling.

"He's a wonderful guy."

"You know, his grandfather and I eloped, too."

"Really? I was afraid that maybe the family might be disappointed."

Gran shook her head. "Oh, Helen was. You know, she loves a big to-do. But I remember well being young and in love, and after all, isn't that an intimate thing? My husband and I had just four dates before he was about to be shipped off during the war. You know, I'd never been out of New Jersey, but I took a bus to Maryland, and we were married the day before he left. I didn't care about anyone else. I understand wanting to keep it to yourselves. That's how we felt. Besides, here we are celebrating. So it all turned out fine, didn't it?"

"Thank you for saying that." I loved this woman already. I knew Adam was close to her, and I imagined he had learned a lot of his caring ways from her. Not his aunt.

"Now, I had Helen get out my old photo albums," Gran said, nodding to a small stack on the table beside her. "Would you like to see some old pictures of Adam and the family?"

"Oh, I would love that."

She opened a beige leather album.

"Is that Aunt Helen?"

"Yes. She was quite a beauty, wasn't she? Had all the boys after her."

Helen looked like Doris Day, in saddle shoes and a poodle skirt, her hair in a chin-length bob. She was a stunner, and in her youth I could see her resemblance to Adam, too.

"Was she ever married?"

"Twice, but no children. Such a shame."

"She must be a good realtor. I've seen her signs all over town."

"Money isn't everything. Family is. It just breaks my heart

she couldn't seem to make that happen." Gran shrugged. "Some people don't allow themselves to be happy. Don't you think that's true?"

I was surprised at this revelation. "My mother was like that," I said before I realized it.

"You poor dear," she said, giving my hand a squeeze once more.

On the next page were pictures of Adam, including one where he was standing beside the river with a fishing pole, tall and skinny, the birthmark looking so big across his throat.

"And there's my Ronnie." She pointed to Adam's father, beside him in another photo. "They looked so much alike, don't you think?"

"They really do." The resemblance was marked, except for the birthmark.

"Oh, but my son was very different from him. Adam didn't have it easy, you know. My Ronnie was a good man, but he had his demons. It's not an easy job sometimes. And Ronnie was hard on Adam. He'd have his dark moods from time to time and...well, Adam's mother was a good woman, but she was an enabler, as they call it. But my grandson values family. He loved his father despite it all, and when he was needed, when it was time for him to take over, he came home. It's his legacy, and he's doing a wonderful job. My husband, Sam, would be so proud of him. They were close, you know."

"Adam told me about his grandfather, teaching him how to fish and to carve things from wood. And of course his stories, the legacy of the cemetery keepers."

"'The keepers of the souls,' Sam used to say." Gran smiled, a faraway look in her eyes. "I used to love walking the lanes there, reading the headstones. Wonder at all those lives and their stories."

"Oh, Gran, I've done the same thing. In fact—"

"It's important to honor the end of a life," Gran went on, seeming to be lost in the past, "as important as marking the beginning. Why these people who throw ashes in a river or scatter them somewhere, or simply stick an urn in a closet...where's the honor in that? The proof for future generations?"

And then she turned and looked at me. "Oh dear. I'm sorry. I do seem to ramble on at times. Where were we? Oh yes." She picked up a very old album and opened it. These pictures were priceless, small black-and-whites glued with corner tabs to thick black pages.

"Oh, Gran, look at you!"

"Oh my, I haven't seen this in decades. I was the homecoming queen."

"You were hot!"

There was a picture of her a few pages later with a handsome sailor in front of an old train. She was wearing a tailored suit, with a little hat that had a netted veil, and carrying a small bouquet.

"My wedding picture. Can you imagine? The only evidence of that day."

"Oh, Gran, our wedding picture is in my phone. I still have to get it printed." Neither Adam nor I had even thought of pictures. It had all happened so fast.

"And there's my Ronnie, his christening." Gran and Sam stood with another couple, and the other woman was holding the baby, smiling.

"Gran, who is that other woman? She's familiar somehow."

"Oh, that's my friend, Marion Freeman. She was Ronnie's godmother."

"Gran..." I couldn't seem to put words together.

"Is something wrong, dear?"

I turned and looked at her. "I was just in her house, assessing it for a house auction. I saw her picture on the wall, and then the attorney's secretary came in and pointed out her grandfather in the picture, James Titus."

"Oh, we don't talk about him."

"But—"

"It's best you forget about him. What heartache that situation brought her. Can you imagine? I remember in home economics in high school we were all talking about when we would get married. You know, the color of our bridesmaids' dresses, the flowers, then where we would live, how many children we'd have. All those girlish dreams. When it was her turn, Marion refused to talk. Later she whispered to me that she wasn't sure anyone would want to marry her. But if they did, she wasn't going to have children."

"Because of him?"

"Yes. She wanted the stigma to die with her." She sat there shaking her head. "She's a good woman, and now...well, there's no one for her. She's all alone in that nursing home."

"Did you know him?"

"He was a quiet man, kept to himself. No one wanted to cause them anymore hurt."

It was horribly sad. I imagined Gran with no one. "I'm surprised the family didn't move away. Start over somewhere else."

"Oh, it's not always that simple. You have to remember the times, the Depression and then the war. Marion's father died when she was little, and her mother, well, she had a life here, friends, despite the gossip." She sighed. "Maybe it would have been different if he hadn't lived with them all those years, but that's how families were back then."

"But what did he have to do with Tillie Smith? Do you have any idea?"

"Oh, there was quite a bit of talk about Tillie Smith."

"You mean about Titus and Tillie?"

"Rachel!"

I turned to find Helen in the doorway, her face pinched in disapproval. Beside her was a girl who looked to be in college, with short spiked hair.

"Oh, Justine," Gran said. "You're here already?"

"Helen asked me to pop in and see if you wanted to rest for a bit," Justine said, with a slight lisp due to the stud pierced through her tongue. "The party will be going for a while."

Then Gran introduced me to her home health aide. "Oh, I hate to miss any fun," she said next, "but I could use a quick rest."

I gave her a quick hug, and off she went.

LATER ON, I MANAGED TO SLIP OUT to the front porch, which was empty. We'd had cake, and Helen made sure a photographer captured every moment. Then we opened gifts. Gran gave us an envelope with a nice check and a note to put it toward our honeymoon, as well as a photo album for today's pictures. I stood there leaning against the porch railing, emotionally and physically exhausted, wanting desperately to belong yet uneasy creating these memories when I wasn't sure about anything lasting. Would Adam really have the patience for me? It could all disappear. Evaporate in an instant. And I would be alone again.

I looked across the street at the college campus stretching from where the main building fronted Jefferson Street back to ball fields in the distance, pushing my thoughts elsewhere. I tried to envision it back in Tillie's era when it was a seminary with just the main building, surrounded by farms. Staring at the big brick structure, I wondered where exactly the old kitchen was.

I pictured poor Tillie, whose round face and hopeful eyes were now etched in my brain, down there early in the mornings, beginning her day of peeling potatoes. That was her job, I'd learned. Peeling potatoes day in and day out. What a hard life it must have been. And then I couldn't help picturing the green bottle I'd found in the cellar that morning. It was from Tillie's era. Salon Palmer had been a perfumer in the 1800s and one of the first in the country, I'd learned after doing some quick research. As a servant, it must have been hard living in such a beautiful place, surrounded by girls who had so much more. Did she own nice things like that, or did she simply dream of them?

My mind jumped then to the handwritten letter I'd discovered last night in the pile of pages I had photocopied at the historical society. There was something so eerie about seeing someone's actual handwriting, reading the language of the era and knowing he'd known Titus. And Tillie. That he'd also known the truth about what happened to her.

Who was this Peter Mead?

CHAPTER 9

January 1886

B ECAUSE SHE SPENT MOST OF HER TIME in the kitchen peeling potatoes and washing pots, Tillie still hadn't seen much
of the big building that was now her home. There was but a bit
of time for herself in the afternoons between meals, and she
mostly went upstairs to rest up. In some ways the work was just
as grueling as that of a domestic on a farm. But there were
differences.

Tillie wasn't used to being around so many people, which
could be unsettling at times. Hoping she was saying the right
things to the other help, or especially the matron. Wondering if
they were questioning what she, a poor girl from Lubber's Run,
might be doing in such a grand place. Her belly churned most
mornings, hoping to get her potatoes peeled quickly enough, not
to cause any fuss that might cost her job. She knew her manners
weren't the best, in spite of Mrs. Conover's constant advice. But
she was learning. In the quiet moments in her room, before
sleep would claim her, she even found herself beginning to have
dreams...dreams she dared not put into words yet.

But in her working hours, Tillie knew enough not to get
caught up in all that. Mrs. Ruckle could pop in at any time, and
she needed to be doing her best. Now with the breakfast and
lunch cleanup all finished and the others all gone for a bit, she
walked through the long, narrow hallways past the big laundry
and drying rooms in the basement. The hall was full of the
smells of damp linens drying, and Tillie thanked God at that
moment she wasn't working in the laundry, with all the boiling
water and lye soap that could peel the skin off your hands.

No one was about in the furnace room, the boilers blazing so fiercely that the heat hit her as she passed by. And the repair room, where they tended to and fixed things, was empty as well.

Ahead was the staircase to take her to the floor above the kit-chen and laundry, where the sleeping rooms of all the female help were. Tillie shared her room with Stella Sliker, a chatty thing who worked as a choir maid. Stella lived in town but stayed over during the cold months. Tillie wasn't sure she liked her yet 'cause of her gossiping. Not the innocent kind like Brid-get, but words that were not always kind and could rustle up trouble for some if she didn't like them. It was Stella, though, who'd come in gushing last night about the Salon Palmer drum-mer who was to come today to sell perfumes and toiletries to the college girls.

"Did you ever notice how lovely they all smell?" Stella went on as Tillie was trying to fall asleep. "I particularly like the ones that smell like roses, don't you, Tillie?"

"I prefer lilacs. And sleep, Stella. My bones are crying they're so tired."

"Oh, then go to sleep, why don't you?"

That was the last thing Tillie remembered Stella saying. She thought about the perfumer now and paused at her stairs. Instead, she turned and went up a short flight to the dining room, all cleaned up from breakfast and quiet now, though in a matter of an hour, preparations would begin for the evening meal. Quickly Tillie walked through, then opened the door that led into the front parlors and the adjoining rooms where musicales and programs were held. She paused a moment.

"And where do you think you're going, missy?"

With a gasp she turned to see one of the divinity students just steps behind her.

"Why, I...I heard there was a perfume drummer coming, and I thought I...might purchase something." Her voice came out little more than a squeak, she was so nervous.

"I don't think the fine ladies will be expecting the kitchen servants to attend, now, do you? Besides," he said with a tiny smile, stepping closer, "I think you smell just fine as you are."

Tillie knew who he was now, remembering the glint of light

flashing from those gold-rimmed spectacles in the workroom downstairs. He helped Janitor Titus from time to time, caning chairs and whatnot to help with his tuition. Peter Mead, she remembered hearing Titus call him.

She turned to get away from him, but he grabbed her apron string and pulled. Turning to face him, she hissed, "Don't you dare, or I'll..." but the words caught in her throat.

He stared at her, and she knew she'd best tread carefully here. A divinity student could have her job at a moment's notice, whether she'd done wrong or not. Especially one with connections to the higher-ups.

"I'm sorry, sir. I must have lost my way. I'd most appreciate it if you'd just let me by," she said then.

He backed away, holding up his hands. "Don't know what you're getting at, missy. I'm just going up to fix a bed frame that fell apart."

He turned to the stairway for the gents' rooms up on the higher floors. Tillie took a deep breath. The last thing she needed was for trouble to start brewing. She liked it here, though she was tired of peeling potatoes. But she'd gotten paid some already and was saving to bring a bit home soon. Her birthday was coming up, and she was hopin' to get the day to make a trip back to Lubber's Run and see her sisters. She missed them something fierce.

She entered the front parlors, skirting the sides of the hallway until she was at the edge of the big entryway into the grandest of the parlors, where she'd met Mrs. Ruckle that first day. The couches were full of the girls, all in their Sunday best, passing around bottles and giggling as they smelled one fragrance after another.

"You won't find a finer perfume anywhere but Paris, ladies, and I can guarantee that," the drummer said as he held up a bottle. The color caught the light. "Now, I have a limited supply with me, including a new Spring Lilac scent that is all the rage, so if you don't want to wait for delivery, you should order quickly today."

Tillie thought about how her hair smelled like boiling potatoes and onions and how she'd love to have one of those beautiful green bottles, though she was certain she wouldn't have enough for it. Just that moment, she saw one of the girls stand and come across the room. She was lovely, in a pretty blue dress that was certainly store bought and a strand of pearls around her neck. Tillie's breath stopped. The girl was coming straight at her, no doubt to chastise her for being where she shouldn't. Quickly she turned, hurrying back through the halls, glad that fellow Mead was nowhere to be seen.

She ran up the stairs to her room and sat on the bed to catch her breath. Then she opened the drawer where she kept her money safe. She sat there counting her coins as her heart stopped its galloping. She couldn't help imagining how lovely that lilac perfume must smell and how she might even be able to share it with Nora and Catherine when she got home on her birthday. She could just picture their surprised smiles. Why, they would think they'd about died and gone to heaven. And wouldn't they be so proud of her?

The bells rang the half hour. She wouldn't have much time to get back down there. And she'd have to be extra careful this time, especially with that Peter Mead lurking about. But perhaps when the girls were all gone, she might catch the drummer before he left. Hopefully he'd have some lilac perfume left for her.

CHAPTER 10

THE NIGHT WE GOT BACK FROM THE WEDDING PARTY, Adam seemed distracted by a sudden cemetery board meeting and said he'd probably be up late catching up on paperwork. Once again I asked him if everything was okay, if I could help. Instead of answering, he took my hand and led me upstairs.

"It's been a crazy week, and you look drained," he said, kissing my forehead.

I couldn't argue with that. Eloping, moving into the cemetery, meeting Adam's family and dozens of others. All of that would have been enough. But I knew it wasn't that. It was the feeling again that something was at play here.

"And about Tillie Smith," Adam said then, as if he were reading my mind. "I think you should let all that go. It didn't even occur to me it might upset my grandmother or my aunt. I wouldn't want to cause Mrs. Freeman any more anguish, especially now after her stroke."

I stared at him and finally said, "Of course."

I lay in the dark then, wondering if that was even possible, letting her go. Though I often felt close to the deceased persons whose homes and possessions I became intimately involved with, I'd never felt anything like this before. It was something I couldn't even name, really.

But I'd never had a grandmother, and I cared for Gran already. I could imagine the times we would spend together in the future. I didn't want to hurt her. As for Helen, it wasn't so simple. But perhaps one day she'd warm up to me.

Years ago, when he still lived with us, I could remember my father whispering to me that the easiest way to keep peace with my mother was to simply keep quiet. "What she doesn't need to know won't hurt her," he used to say. I had to wonder now if that wasn't my best option with Adam's family.

I understood that Mrs. Freeman was like part of the family and that she'd suffered. But how was that Tillie's fault? Gran had alluded that Tillie had had a reputation. "There was quite a bit of talk about her." I knew what that meant. It made what had happened to poor Tillie even more awful. To be raped, to have your life taken, and then, after more than 130 years, to have your name smeared. It was unfair. Unjust.

In the quiet bedroom, I could still hear the giggles, the whispers about me. Even now, years later, I could feel the burning shame crawling up my skin as I hid in my room.

I turned over, willing my thoughts to stop. I knew if she could, my mother would tell me to let Tillie Smith go, that it was only going to lead to no good. I would try. But I was on a slippery slope.

* * *

I WAS UP FIRST IN THE MORNING, not sure what time Adam had come to bed, but I knew it was late. I was surprised to hear him coming into the kitchen as I finished making tea. He grabbed a coffee cup, leaving the cabinet door open as usual. I got up to close it out of habit, but before I could, he turned quickly and shut it.

"You don't have to close doors behind me, or drawers," he said, a definite edge of annoyance in his voice.

"I'm sorry. I know it can be annoying."

We stared at each other.

"No," he said, shaking his head. "I'm an ass. I'm sorry."

"Are you okay?"

"Yes. I'm just worried about you. I want you to call a doctor."

"I'm calling a gynecologist this morning, I promise."

"Good. You need to see if there's anything wrong as a result of..."

"I know."

"Don't be nervous. I can go with you."

"No! I mean, I'll be fine going myself."

He poured his coffee, and I put more water in the teakettle.

"Did you get everything done that you needed to last night?" I asked.

He was standing at the sink, staring out the window at the cemetery. "Yes, but...I'm going to need to push the honeymoon back a bit." And then he turned to me. "If that's okay with you."

"Oh, Adam, is it because of all the time you lost these past months with me?"

"No, not at all. It's...complicated. I want to have everything in order before we leave for a few weeks. It's just going to take a little longer than I thought."

I didn't push, though I couldn't help thinking once more about Helen's words, implying this legacy was something that Adam would be better off without. She was wrong, though. I knew that for Adam, keeping his family's tradition alive, being the seventh-generation cemetery keeper, was vital. It was who he was. And to him this was sacred ground.

"It's fine," I said then, walking over to him and taking his hands. "We could even go in the fall if that would be better. I don't care if we ever go on a honeymoon. I'm just happy to be here with you."

The teakettle began to whistle, breaking the silence.

"I think I'll go shower," Adam said as I turned off the stove.

"Adam, wait. I forgot to ask you something." He turned in the doorway to look at me. "At the party, Gran asked me to remind you about playing her favorite song, 'Let Me Call You Sweetheart.' Is that your guitar upstairs?"

"I used to play."

"You never mentioned it before."

He shrugged. "No reason to. I don't play anymore."

"Your grandmother said you're really good."

He smiled, shaking his head. "Lots of people are good. I just... lost interest."

"Okay. But maybe you'll play for me sometime?"

"We'll see." He turned and went upstairs.

And I knew there was more to that as well. As I made

another cup of tea and sat to read again, I realized that the man I married was not as simple as I'd first thought. Of course, neither was I.

WHEN ADAM CAME BACK DOWN from his shower, I was making breakfast. Then I was going to start looking for business, I told him.

"Don't pressure yourself. It takes time to build a business in a new area, and you've only been here a little over a week. Sleep in. Get a massage. You can even redecorate if you want. This place hasn't been touched in years."

"Try decades," I joked, thinking of the basement.

He laughed. And I felt better.

"Come out on the porch a minute," he said then. "I want to show you something."

It wasn't quite light yet, and on the porch he led me to the end of the railing.

"Oh..." My words caught as I looked far across the darkness to a cross lit up in the sky.

"It's the Easter cross on Buck Hill. It's lit every year during Holy Week."

"It's beautiful. It looks like it's hanging in the sky."

"Wait until Christmas. There's a star, and it's lit for the entire month."

"Who does it?"

"There was a doctor years back who was kind of the town's Good Samaritan. He started the tradition when he lived there. When he moved, he apparently put it in the deed that whoever bought the place had to keep it up."

"It's just magical. He must have been a good man."

"He was."

I put my arms around him. "So are you, Adam."

He kissed the top of my head, then looked down at me. "I'm sorry you didn't get the job. I know you're really disappointed."

"It's okay. I'll find work."

"You need a car."

"No, not until I can pay for it myself."

He shook his head but smiled. "You are one stubborn woman. But I kind of like that about you."

When he went back in, I stood there for a long moment looking up at the cross shining over Hackettstown and thought about what it represented. Forgiveness. Redemption. Rebirth. Everything I needed.

* * *

LATER THAT MORNING I TOOK THE TRUCK and drove into town, dropping my business cards at the various attorneys' offices, trying to stay busy, trying not to think about the doctor's appointment I'd made. And then I couldn't help myself, I turned onto Sharp Street. A big van was parked out front: Finegan Auction House. An elderly man limped down the porch steps.

I parked and got out. "Are you Mr. Finegan?"

He turned to me and stopped. "Why, yes, I am. And who might you be?"

"I'm Rachel Miller. I'm an auctioneer also. Congratulations on getting the job."

"Oh...no hard feelings I hope?"

"Of course not."

"Well, I've been around these parts a long time."

"I understand. I just had a personal interest in this one."

"Oh? Well, why don't you come back inside, and we can talk? I was just grabbing some things I forgot in the van. The mind's not as sharp as it used to be."

It turned out Mr. Finegan was hoping to retire soon, and none of his kids were interested in the business. Too many weeks without a day off. But there was a nephew who was working with him, though he was off fishing in Canada and due to return in a few days. Hopefully he'd take over the business one day.

"It's not an easy job these days, as I guess you know full well."

I nodded and smiled. "With eBay and the internet, we're becoming like dinosaurs."

"That's not the same thing," he said wistfully. "There's nothing quite like walking into a house and...getting lost in it all, eh?"

"Absolutely. I think you and I are kindred spirits, Mr. Finegan."

"So you mentioned a personal interest in this place."

"I was wondering if you knew anything about Tillie Smith."

He was already nodding. "Yes, I know about James Titus, though not personally. You know how rumors spread in small towns. It doesn't take much to fan the flames."

"What have you heard?"

"Well, I just remember back when we were kids, my mother telling my sister she was never to go inside this house. My sister was a bit older than me, and she was friends with the granddaughter who just went into the nursing home."

"Did your mother ever say anything about Tillie Smith that you recall?"

"No. I do remember hearing somewhere that she was dirt poor, though the relations were pretty prominent. They were the Smiths who started Waterloo Village."

"What's that?"

"Well, it was once a pretty bustling place a ways out of town on the old canal. Now it's a restored historic site. All the houses and little stores are there. You should go see it. It's quite impressive."

"Is that where Lubber's Run is?"

He frowned. "Haven't heard of that place."

"It's where Tillie's family lived. I'd read that in an article."

"You might try the historical society. They probably have old maps. Or even at Waterloo Village. They have tour guides who might be able to help."

"Thanks. I'll try that."

Before I left, I took a picture of that family photo of James Titus in the rocking chair with my cell phone. Then I got in the truck, again hearing my mother's favorite refrain: "Rachel, you're your own worst enemy."

I drove across town, past the hospital, and out Waterloo Road, following directions I jotted down from Mr. Finegan. The

Musconetcong River came into view then, weaving in and out of the trees as it paralleled the road. In a few places I saw wide grassy paths I imagined were the old canal towpaths. It was seven miles to Waterloo Village. As I drove further, the woods thickened until the river and all evidence of the canal disappeared. I stopped just as the sign for Waterloo Village came into view. It was quite a distance from town without a car.

I sat there thinking of Tillie working at the seminary. I could only imagine what it must have been like for her if she were to make this long journey home.

CHAPTER 11

January 20, 1886

I T WAS TILLIE'S FIRST SUNDAY OFF since she started her position at the seminary. And though she longed so to see her sisters, she dreaded the journey home to Lubber's Run, eight miles north of Hackettstown. The bright sun wasn't much use at all as the temperature had dipped to near zero last night.

She donned her heavy drawers over her bloomers and then three petticoats. No matter what she wore, she was going to be right cold before long. If she was lucky, she might hitch a ride with a wagon heading out to Waterloo. No doubt there'd be miners traveling back or even workers who'd be heading for the canal. There was always the train since they'd just opened a station in Waterloo, just a few miles from home, but there weren't enough coins left for that anymore.

Tillie left the seminary after breakfast, tucking half a loaf of bread and a hunk of cheese into a paper sack to eat later on, as well as the cakes and breads she'd saved from the past few nights' kitchen scraps. Bridget had watched her without saying a word when she'd taken the plates before they could be scraped and picked out the best of the leftovers.

"I'm goin' home tomorrow, and I know of some who could use this."

Tillie hadn't told the other girl much about their way of life back in Lubber's Run, but Bridget had told her all about the famine back in Ireland. Bridget nodded, then squeezed her arm.

"I'll just have me a little rest," she said and set a chair in the doorway to watch for anyone coming by, especially the matron.

She walked up Church Street. The town had laid wooden sidewalks to keep the students from getting mud on their clothes, but today even the mud was frozen. When she got to Main Street, it was all but deserted. Her toes were already about numb, and the skin on her face was stinging. Still she pressed on. Today was her birthday. She imagined her sisters would make a bit of fuss, and her heart lightened at the thought.

Just past the Presbyterian cemetery, she turned left onto the road that would take her out of town and past the mines, past the canal, and through long stretches of woods. Near to an hour later, before she reached the first lock, she heard horses and a wagon rattling. She turned. The wagon stopped beside her.

"You got far to go?" the man asked. Beside him, the woman smiled.

"Out past Waterloo," she said, walking toward them, hope coming alive.

"Well, we'll be turning off at Saxton Falls. We can take you that far."

"Oh, I'm much obliged," she said and came toward the wagon. The man got down and helped her up. Tillie sat beside the woman, who lifted the blanket on her lap to share with her.

"I'm mighty grateful, ma'am," Tillie said, wrapping it tightly around her and burying her hands beneath it. "It's god-awful cold out."

"You're most welcome. I'm Mrs. Pritchard, and this is Mr. Pritchard."

That was the end of the talk, it being too cold to even think about conversation.

An hour later, Tillie climbed down and saw a canal boat docked at the lock near Saxton Falls. She thought a minute about trying to get a ride on the boat, which would no doubt stop at Waterloo, but when she saw the men coming out of the lock tender's house, she decided not to. Miners, most likely, and they were a rough lot, spending their off-hours in the local taverns like Elsie's and causing all sorts of trouble.

She kept walking, not even halfway home, and soon the canal disappeared into the thick woods. She kept to the dirt road, trying to avoid the frozen puddles and ditches. Just as she was thinking she might turn around, fearful of the journey back in the dark, another wagon stopped and offered her a ride. She hesitated a minute, looking at the two men on the buckboard. Then the one at the reins jumped down and took off his hat.

"And what's a fine lady like this doing all the way out here in the cold?"

"Well, I'm heading out to Lubber's Run to see family."

"Then this would be your lucky day, miss. We're heading right past there on our way to Stanhope." He put his hat back on and offered her an arm. "I'm Frank Weeder, and that's my friend, George Search."

"I'm Tillie Smith," she said, taking his arm and climbing on the wagon. George Search offered her a hand as Frank Weeder gave her a little push, and even through her layers of petticoats and drawers, she thought his hand might have wandered where it shouldn't have. The friend barely said a word, but Frank Weeder chattered like a bird, full of questions, impressed that she worked at the seminary.

She had them drop her off at Waterloo, deciding to walk the rest of the way to Lubber's Run, though they'd be going right by. She lollygagged a few minutes, waiting for the buckboard to disappear. It was best they not know exactly where she lived.

* * *

THE SUN WAS HIGH when Tillie turned off the road. She followed a wagon path through thick woods until she saw the clearing for the cabin. She stopped, staring, and her heart seemed to go still in her chest. It looked so...sorrowful. How had they all lived there? Is this what her ma had thought the first time she'd come back? She'd reckoned they were poor, but now, well, now she saw what poor really was.

The mud around the cabin was frozen up, and Tillie took care not to slip and fall on patches of ice and dirty snow. She glanced over at the chicken coop, but it was so bitterly cold, even the animals chose not to venture outside. To the right of the cabin was the well and behind it the outhouse, where she'd had to dump the night's slop buckets each morning. On the rare occasion of a winter bath, they had to haul and heat bucket after bucket of water, then share the tub. In warm weather, they simply washed in the creek bend nearby, something that would no doubt send Mrs. Ruckle and the rest of the staff at Centenary into conniptions.

Just then the door opened, and Nora stood there, bucket in hand, her chin about hitting the floor.

"Tillie!" she squealed, then turned and yelled inside, "It's Tillie!"

CHAPTER 12

I PARKED THE TRUCK IN A GRAVEL LOT and walked on an unpaved road through a canopy of trees. I entered a clearing and gasped. It was as though I'd stepped back in time and landed in Tillie's era. There before me was an entire little village looking like it was straight from the set of *Little House on the Prairie*. I stood there, unable to move, knowing what it would mean to continue further into this place and ask questions. I would be going against Adam's family. But perhaps worse, it might ignite further images in my brain, jarring bits of memory that could undo me, that were best left buried.

I closed my eyes and saw Tillie's face. I began walking.

The road was lined with old Colonial homes with porches, bay windows, and cupolas. Placards showed the dates they were constructed and the original owners' names. The third house, and grandest of all, was the Smith home, built in 1830. Yellow clapboard with white shutters, it was three stories, with long windows and a wide porch. Directly across the road sat the Smith General Store beside the canal. It was all real, and it amazed me. These were Tillie's relatives, and they were wealthy.

I climbed the porch and went into the Smith house first. It was filled with the finest of furnishings: velvet draperies, crystal chandeliers. Formal portraits hung everywhere in gilt frames.

"Welcome to the Smith mansion," said a woman dressed in eighteenth-century finery, a long mauve gown with bustle and lace collar. "I'm Joni, and I'd be happy to walk you through and tell you about life here in Waterloo in the 1800s."

"Actually, I was wondering if you knew much about the Smiths. I'm particularly interested in Tillie Smith and her family." I hoped this woman didn't somehow know Helen. What were the odds, really?

"Well, that's not the name of one of Captain John Smith's daughters. But there were lots of Smiths. They were a big family. We have a family archive set up in the back parlor. Let's go see what we can find."

In the parlor, Joni pulled out a big book, *The Smiths of Waterloo*. When she opened it, I saw page after page of names and dates. "Do you have any idea who her parents were?" Joni asked

"Her father's name was Nathan. That's all I know."

"Oh, well, I think he may be buried in the cemetery here. I used to do those tours back when I didn't mind the summer heat outdoors. The church land was donated by Captain John Smith, who fought in the Civil War, and in fact, he was the first one to be buried there."

"I read that Nathan's family was from Lubber's Run. Do you know of it?"

"Well, this whole area was called Waterloo back then, but it may have been a little enclave nearby." She turned some pages, going slowly, then stopped and pointed. "Here they are."

"Oh wow, it's the 1880 census. This is six years before Tillie died." It listed Nathan Smith as forty-seven at the time and a farm laborer and his wife, Sarah, fifty, as "keeping houses." "I read in one of the articles that they didn't live together. Maybe that's why she was working somewhere else."

"Yes, women often found work as domestics in other households. It looks like there were four children," she said, pointing to a list of names below. "In 1880 there were three girls at home: Catherine, twenty-one; Leonora, seventeen; and Matilda, fifteen. A brother, James, was twenty and also a farm laborer."

"Matilda—that's Tillie." It was a thrill just seeing her name there. My finger slid to a slim column to the right. "Oh my God, they were all illiterate."

"That wasn't uncommon then," Joni said, "especially for those who were poor. School was a luxury."

"But the age can't be right. Tillie was nineteen when she was murdered. This would make her twenty-one."

"Oh, census records are often inaccurate with names and dates. When people couldn't read or write, things got recorded inaccurately."

"Is there any way to figure out where they lived?"

"Well, let's pull out some of the old maps," she said, going to a filing cabinet tucked in a corner. She spread a big parchment map on the table. "Back then, most maps showed the owners' names for each plot of land because there wasn't much population. So sometimes it's not hard to find where someone resided, though some of the roads today may not have existed."

I followed her finger as it traveled from the village in ever-widening circles to the outlying areas. Besides the canal, I noted the various mines throughout the region.

"There it is," she said, pointing to a spot north of the village. "Nathan Smith."

"So is Lubber's Run a settlement?" I asked.

"It's actually a stream that runs through the area. That's what they were called back then—a run. My own grandfather had a farm in Pennsylvania on Mudd Run."

"So it's not a settlement, then? They simply lived near the stream?"

"Not quite a settlement, but you can see there were a few other houses back then."

"Would I be able to find this house, though, do you think?"

She looked at up at me with raised eyebrows. "I doubt it's even there anymore."

"No one else has ever asked about this?"

She shook her head. It wasn't hard to read her thoughts. I could just imagine the game of telephone that would ensue as she told the story of the weird woman looking for Tillie Smith's house a hundred and thirty years later. In the middle of the woods. Knowing the odds were against it even being there. And how it would eventually get back to Helen and Gran. And Adam.

"I'd like to try."

She looked back down at the map again. "Well, you might be able to find it. If you keep going up Waterloo Road," she said, her finger tracing the route, "you'll see here on the left a sign for a big parcel that was purchased by the Boy Scouts a few years ago, where they have their campouts and jamborees. That's about where Lubber's Run crosses the road. If you follow the stream, there might be enough landmarks. There's a mine not too far in, and the stream bends sharply right there. The old dirt road may be nothing but a path through woods now, or even completely overgrown."

I borrowed a piece of paper and made a hand sketch of the map before I left. Joni wished me good luck with a doubtful smile.

* * *

A FEW MILES NORTH OF WATERLOO VILLAGE, I pulled over on the side of the road just across from the sign for the Boy Scouts' property. It was already three o'clock, and I wondered if Adam was back yet. If he was wondering where I was. If Joni had started talking about me to others.

I saw the stream, not much more than a tiny brook now as we'd not had rain in a while. I crossed to the other side, where it disappeared in the thick woods. There was no visible entrance, much less an old dirt road. Walking up and down the shoulder, I looked for an old path or even an area not so thick with trees. It was like looking for a needle in the proverbial haystack.

After fifteen minutes of walking up and down the road, I considered just pushing my way in, hoping I might have better luck. I was so close. Somewhere not far from where I stood was where Tillie had lived as a little girl with her sisters and a brother, where she dreamed of what she would be when she grew up.

It was getting late, and I was growing frantic. I closed my eyes and said a prayer to Saint Anthony, the patron saint of finding things. My mother prayed to him all the time. Her ring turned up in the yard a year after she lost it. I was digging in mud and found it. She'd just made a novena to him.

Suddenly another image of my mother flashed across my brain. I could see her sitting in the kitchen with her head on the table, crying, praying to Saint Anthony to find me. I could almost hear her begging, and a sob rose up in my throat. I shook my head, turning from the tree, pushing back my tears. Then I saw it. A slight gap between two huge oaks.

I stepped into it, turning sideways to fit through, desperate to escape the scene of my mother. A few feet ahead, it widened, and I pushed ahead, trying to focus. I went as quickly as I could, following a narrow rutted path that continued deeper, probably nothing more than a deer trail. The trees had barely begun to bud here, so it wasn't that dark as I continued. I needed to be quick. I couldn't let myself get distracted again.

I thought about Adam again, waiting for me with questions.

Five minutes later, there was a small clearing and a limestone kiln. The mine should be nearby. I turned, surveying the woods around me nervously, knowing how vulnerable I was out there alone. Then I spotted the mine, nothing more than a crevice in a swell of earth surrounded by large stones. I looked at my hand-drawn map. Due east of the mine was the stream, Lubber's Run, and a little north of it the sharp bend. I headed that way on the path for what seemed like long minutes, growing more nervous, hoping I'd find my way out later. Suddenly I stopped.

"Dear God," I whispered.

It was an old log structure, nothing more than a big rectangle that could have been mistaken for a hunter's shack. The wood was blackened with age, and there were gaps between the logs. The roof was completely gone, and a tree was growing through the middle.

It was so tiny. I knew now there had been six of them living there. It couldn't be more than a room or two. How had it not been struck by lightning or burned to the ground? It looked like a tinderbox.

I walked closer, intending to just peek inside because it didn't look safe to venture in. I pushed open the front door, a crooked slab of pine hanging by one hinge. It fell with a crash, and I screamed. There were patches of light inside where sunlight came through the trees overhead. This place had been abandoned for decades or longer. *Anything of value would have been looted long ago*, I told myself. But I wasn't looking for anything of value. I was hoping to find something that would bring me closer to Tillie.

Despite every alarm bell ringing in my head, I went inside.

CHAPTER 13

January 20, 1886

NORA DROPPED THE BUCKET JUST IN FRONT of the door and ran to Tillie, hugging her so hard they near fell on the ice. "Tillie, I swear you've gained a few pounds."

"Oh, Nora, I've been pining so for home. But the food is so wonderful. I've got to watch myself or I'll never fit into anything," she laughed, then caught herself, knowing how little food they had.

Nora was two years older, but Tillie looked at her now, thinking how skinny she was, with that light hair all wild about her shoulders. In a dress patched and stained, she looked little more than a girl.

"Is our Catherine home as well?"

Nora's smile left her. "She is, Tillie. She's lying down, feeling a bit peaked."

"And Pa?"

Nora shrugged. "At Elsie's, I suppose."

Tillie had wondered as they passed the tavern. It had been crowded with horses and wagons, the windows steamed up and smoke billowing from the chimney.

"Catherine's going to be tickled," Nora said, taking her hand, pulling her into the cabin. "You might be just what the doctor ordered."

The smell hit Tillie before she was fully inside: smoke, dirt, onions, coffee, body smells and waste. Aside from the small kitchen, here in this one large room, six of them had lived while her mother and James were still there. Slowly they'd been scattering, her ma first, then Nora for a bit, but Tillie was glad she was back. She hated for Catherine to be here alone.

She found Catherine lying on the bed in the back corner, her long, pale face and dark hair peeking above a ragged quilt. Tillie imagined her soft bed at the seminary, the clean sheets and warm blankets.

"Good morning, Duchess," Tillie said in her high-falutin' voice. "How's the royal pain in the arse today?"

Catherine's eyes remained closed. "Oh, I'm just having myself some beauty sleep, so you'll just have to wait with my strawberries and clotted cream. Perhaps go and press my silk gown."

They'd been playing this game as long as Tillie could remember. Catherine, who was seven years older, was more like a mother than a big sister since their own ma had gone off when Tillie was eleven. When Tillie began asking questions about their rich uncle and her beautiful well-dressed cousins, Catherine began pretending that they were royalty, even higher class than those uppity Smiths at Waterloo.

"I've got better than strawberries or a fine gown," Tillie said, sitting on the side of the bed. "I've got sweet cakes. And stories!"

Catherine's eyes opened. Then her hand went to her belly, and she moaned a little. Her eyes filled with tears. "Oh, Tillie, is that really you?"

"Yes, dear sister. What's wrong?"

"Oh...just my monthlies."

Tillie looked at the dark rings below her eyes. "You never could bear the cramps, could you?" She opened the paper sack and pulled out the cakes, wrapped in newspaper.

Catherine and Nora each took one, biting into them hungrily, crumbs falling.

"There's more; don't worry," Tillie said, going over to the kitchen for plates. There were just three left from the last time she'd been home, and they were all cracked. The pantry shelf was nearly bare. She went to the corner behind the hearth and jiggled the log where she knew her father kept his coins in a jar, hidden away. It was empty.

She went back to Catherine, Nora sitting on the other side of the bed, and handed them the rest of the cakes as well as the bread and cheese she'd not had time to eat yet.

"Now, sit down and tell us all about what it's like in that big, fancy place," Catherine said.

They both looked at her.

"Some days I can't quite believe I'm in such a grand place. I think I've died and gone to heaven. Do you know I had a bath last night in a real bathroom? And I didn't have to haul in buckets of water. I just turn on a spigot, and hot water comes flowing out!"

"Imagine that," Nora sighed.

"Even better, every single room is nice and warm. There's central heat throughout that whole big building, and when I go to bed at night, I have my own bed with sweet-smelling sheets, and we change them every single week."

"Do you have to wash them all?"

"No, someone else does the laundry. Several of them, actually. That's all they do. I work in the kitchen, mostly peeling potatoes and washing up the pots and dishes. But yesterday, I got to wait tables." She didn't say that she only waited on the other servants in the kitchen, 'cause it wouldn't be considered proper yet for her to wait on the students in the dining room. Still, it was something.

"Are the students handsome? Have you got your eye on any of them?"

"Oh, lots of them are handsome. And rich."

"Maybe you could find yourself a husband there," Catherine said. "You're pretty enough, Tillie."

"Yes, and have a big house, and we could come and live with you, and..." Nora hesitated.

Tillie swallowed hard, then took Nora's hand. "Why not? I'm coming up in the world, don't you see?" And wasn't she their only hope, really?

They were quiet a spell until Catherine asked, "Have you been to see her yet?"

"Ma? No, not as yet. I'm planning to on my next Sunday off. I just missed you two so much." And she'd hoped for a bit of fuss over her birthday. But she wouldn't show a speck of disappointment. Even if there were a calendar, they couldn't read. She stood and straightened her skirt. "When will Pa be back?"

Catherine shrugged; then her face lit up. "Did you hear our James is at Cape May? He got a job on a ship and is off to sail the world, just like he always dreamed."

Her brother, James, who'd worked on the local farms all his life, had always talked about one day getting out of Lubber's Run. "Well, imagine that. He really did it." Would she ever see him again? she wondered.

"And you're doing it, too, Tillie," Nora said. "Making your way and changing things. Perhaps I'll be next. I have an interview for a domestic's position in Newark with a wealthy lady. It's just kitchen work, really, but I'm a bit nervous about living in a city. I've never been as brave as you, Tillie."

Tillie wanted to tell her that in truth, it wasn't being brave, because inside, wasn't she afraid a lot of the time? It was the desire for something more. A better way.

"Oh, I almost forgot. I brought you a present," she said. "But I only have the one, so you'll have to share."

Opening her purse, she pulled out the tiny green bottle. "A drummer from Salon Palmer came to the school, and all the girls were buying his perfume. When he was leaving, I stopped him and got one for you." She pulled the stopper out and sniffed it before handing it to Catherine. "Silly me, I spilled some, but there's plenty left, and doesn't it just smell wonderful?"

She hadn't spilled it, but she didn't want to spoil her surprise by telling them that she couldn't afford the regular perfumes, so she talked the drummer into selling her the sample bottle, which had been only half full.

"It smells like a bouquet of lilacs," Nora said, her nose pressed to the open bottle. Her finger traced the raised lettering in the glass. "What does it say?"

"Well, it says 'Palmer.' That's the company. They're quite grand, Salon Palmer, and all the girls at the institute have lovely colored bottles of their perfumes. They're from New York City."

"You mean there are girls attending the seminary, too?"

"Oh yes, it's not just a seminary but also a college for fellas and ladies. The gals are quite grand as well."

"You've surely found quite a place for yourself, little sister," Catherine said.

Tillie pulled her into a quick embrace. They weren't ones for shows of affection, but she had no idea when she'd see them again. Then she gave Nora a quick peck on the forehead. Nora giggled, embarrassed.

"Now, it's god-awful cold, and I've got to start back."

"But you just got here!"

"I know, Duchess, but your lowly one must walk all the way back, and dark is coming fast. The institute doors lock at ten, and I dare not be late."

"You must come back soon, Tillie. Promise?" Catherine cried.

"I promise. And tell Pa I was here and I'm doing well, all right?"

They each nodded with tears in their eyes. Nora walked her out, and when they were past being heard, Tillie asked her, "Has Catherine been to see the gypsy woman over in Stanhope?"

"No, Tillie, she hasn't left the house in weeks. Why?"

"Oh, nothing, really. Now be good and keep an eye on her."

"I will, Tillie. I...I wish I could go with you. What if I get the position in Newark? When will we ever see each other?"

How could she leave with Nora standing there in the cold, shivering, a shawl wrapped tight around her thin shoulders? And Catherine inside looking all hollowed out? "Here," Tillie said, opening her purse and taking out what coins she'd brought. "For you and Catherine, for food. And make sure Pa doesn't get hold of that."

She turned away then, the frigid air stinging her skin, but she took a deep breath, grateful for the clean, fresh smell. By the time she turned onto the road, heavy snowflakes began to fall. She walked as fast as she was able. She had a long way to go, and ten o'clock wasn't so far off.

CHAPTER 14

I SAT IN THE DOCTOR'S WAITING ROOM. It was a cheerful place, with pictures of newborns blanketing the walls and light classical music playing in the background. Still, I felt as though I'd run up ten flights, my breath shallow, my ribs closing in on my lungs. I fingered the shard of emerald green glass in my purse, the smooth edge and the jagged point, which had become like a talisman for me since I'd found it.

The door opened, and a nurse called a very pregnant woman, who chatted happily. I was next, but there was nothing pleasant about why I was here. I reached over for a magazine on the coffee table, but instead my eyes landed on a pamphlet. *A Girl's Guide to Understanding Her Body.* I stared at the words and the silhouette of a young girl. It was as if my life rewound in that moment to the year I was in fourth grade. And I could hear my mother's reaction when I brought home a similar pamphlet from school one day. "You have got to be kidding!"

I'd been embarrassed just giving it to her, knowing a bit about what was coming. All the girls had been giggling and whispering since the teacher announced the movie just for girls. The boys would be seeing another movie in another room. My face flamed as my mother stood there looking at me and shaking her head. Then I watched in horror as she picked up the phone. I begged her to wait. She called the school, lambasting them for taking it upon themselves to teach her daughter about the facts of life. "This is not your place," she'd gone on, her voice getting louder. "God knows the kinds of things you'll be putting in their heads. This is a parent's job, and ten years old is a little young to be talking to children about sex."

The day when all the other mothers went to see the movie with their daughters, she kept me home. We didn't talk about it. Two years later, when I got my first period, she still hadn't told me anything, except to be careful of boys. They were after one thing.

"Mrs. Miller?"

I looked up. "Oh, yes."

I followed the nurse to the examining room and put on the blue-flowered gown tied in front, a sheet of tissue paper across my lap, naked and trembling underneath. I sat there for long minutes until the door opened, and in walked a middle-aged woman with a laptop in hand.

"Mrs. Miller, I'm Dr. Roberti. How are you today?"

"Fine."

"Let's go over your history before the exam since this is your first time here."

Dr. Roberti opened her laptop, and I realized the forms I'd filled out in the little notebook computer must have already been transferred.

"Okay, thirty-six years old, last exam was...eighteen years ago? Is that right?" The doctor looked up in surprise.

"I just...I don't really like these exams."

Dr. Roberti smiled. "No woman does. I understand. But we're very gentle here. You should be getting a pap every two years at this age. And in a few years, you should start doing an annual mammogram." She glanced at the computer again. "No history of cancer in your family. That's good. But early detection is the key, so make sure you come back in two years for another pap, okay?"

"Of course."

"You're not on any medications at all?"

"No. I took an antidepressant for a while, but I stopped that a few months ago."

She nodded. "How long have you been married?"

"A few weeks."

"Well, congratulations. Do you want to have children?"

I didn't answer right away, and the doctor looked up again.

"I don't know." I tried to find the right words, how to put it tactfully that I wanted to be sure things were going to work out with Adam.

"You might as well enjoy your honeymoon for a while," Dr. Roberti said with a grin. "Though each year after thirty-five, it does get a bit more difficult to conceive. But I wouldn't worry about that. Now, let's have a look."

Dr. Roberti closed her laptop, then came over to the table. "Lie back and put your feet in these, then slide down to the bottom of the table, okay?"

This was the part I dreaded. How could I ever possibly have a baby? At the first touch of the doctor's fingers, I jumped.

"I'm sorry. Just relax. This will be quick. I promise." She began to probe as I winced. "Uterus, ovaries, everything feels just fine. Now I'm going to insert a speculum and do a quick pap." Despite my discomfort, she kept me distracted, asking questions about what I did, where I lived, and so on.

"All done."

I sat up and pulled my feet out of the stirrups. My legs trembled so badly that the tissue kept making crinkly sounds. "Everything looks okay?"

"Perfect."

"I'm not...too small or..."

Dr. Roberti leaned against the counter, her head tilted. "Everyone's a little bit different, but you're certainly normal." She hesitated a moment. "Are you having a problem?"

I nodded.

"With a new marriage, sometimes it takes a while."

"It's just that it...really hurts. I thought maybe there was something wrong with me." I didn't want to disappoint Adam anymore. And how much longer would his patience hold out?

"Rachel, a lot of times something like that isn't physical. It's more an emotional thing, perhaps tied to something in your past. And it can be hard to relax, you know?"

"Yes. I guess I'm a bit of an oddball. I don't really have much experience, and I know that's not the norm for someone my age."

"Did something happen to you? Did someone hurt you in the past, maybe when you were young?"

I started to shake my head, then stopped. "Yes."

"Were you sexually abused?"

She waited while I sat there chewing my lip, knowing I had to be honest if I was going to get help. "I was raped. When I was a freshman in college."

"I'm so sorry, Rachel. Have you had intercourse since then?"

"Not really. I tried a few times, but...I just couldn't."

The doctor nodded, processing this information.

"I want to now. Before, I was just trying to see...if I could. They were short relationships. Neither one was going to work out."

"Did you ever go for any kind of counseling after the rape?"

"A few times, but I just didn't want to keep talking about it."

"What about your parents?"

"My father left when I was little, and my mother was killed shortly after I was raped. I never really had a chance."

"Rachel, that's quite a heavy burden on an eighteen-year-old. It's very possible that even now you're still being affected by those things."

"I'm doing way better. I used to get angry for no reason, kind of explode at times, and that hardly ever happens anymore. And I'm not as compulsive about keeping things so neat."

"Well, that's a control thing, and very common in rape victims. So is the anger. I'm glad to hear that. I volunteer at a rape crisis center, and we have some very good counselors there. I know it's been a long time since it happened, but why don't you come in and talk to someone?"

"I'll think about it. I really just want to put it behind me. I'm married. I've got a whole new life now."

"Still, these things, when left unresolved, can sometimes rear themselves again when we least expect it."

"And what about having sex?"

"It's most likely you're going into spasms, your muscles tightening. It's not uncommon when a woman has been traumatized. Your body tenses up, and penetration can be nearly impossible.

We just need to give you some exercises to relax. Classical conditioning is all it is, really, and once you're able to relax and enjoy a few times, you'll be able to put this behind you."

The doctor opened one of the cabinets above the sink and pulled out a pamphlet. "This should answer any questions you might have, and if you follow these exercises, things should begin to improve. But please come back if they don't. And please consider counseling."

The last thing I wanted was to relive it all and hear others talking about their own horrible stories. Ten minutes later, sitting in the truck, I hid the pamphlet in a zipper compartment inside my purse. Then I pulled out the shard of green glass, turning it over and over. What if my mother hadn't died after I was raped? How different would my life have been? Would I have been able to deal with things years ago, perhaps even have married long ago, with a family of my own now?

It was impossible to guess. Somehow over the years, the guilt over my mother's death and the horror of the rape had become so entwined that I wasn't even certain anymore where one began and the other ended. I knew one thing, though: for years I wouldn't let myself be happy. Didn't feel I deserved love.

Now I had a chance to have everything that had been stolen from me. Everything I'd denied myself. I never thought this would be possible again after all my years alone. I had to do whatever it would take to make it happen. This was something Tillie never had. Because every chance, every hope, had been stolen from her that cold night in April.

* * *

I ASSUMED ADAM WAS IN THE OFFICE, the little seven dwarfs' building by the river, as I saw a car parked there when I came over the bridge. Someone purchasing a plot or making arrangements. I was glad. I wasn't ready to talk about my visit to the doctor just yet. When I walked into the house, I went straight upstairs to my desk in the office and opened my notebook. I took out the shard of green glass and laid it under the desk lamp, where Tillie's picture was propped. I stared into her eyes, as I often did, once again imagining the hard life she must have had, feeling a connection that began from the first moment I stood at her monument. I picked up the shard again, laying it in my hand beside the bandage. Finding this sliver of glass...the cut on my thumb...being in James Titus's house...it was all too much to ignore now. If I'd had any doubt before, it evaporated in Lubber's Run.

I was terrified going into the cabin. I stood in that open door-way knowing that if I got hurt, no one would ever find me. And what if someone was lurking in the woods nearby? Someone could hurt me. No one would hear me scream. My heart was beating so fast, I was almost panting. But I was there. I'd found the cabin against all odds. And I knew I'd gone too far to turn back.

I stepped inside, halting immediately. I looked down, relieved to see a dirt floor. No worries, then, about falling through to a cellar. Dappled sunlight splashed the dark interior where it filtered through the branches and shone through the missing roof. But there were many dark corners. I pulled out the flash-light I always kept in my purse and did a quick scan in case an animal might be nesting somewhere. The log walls were black, splintered with age. The few windows were nothing more than openings to the outside, the glass panes long gone. There was no furniture at all. The big room was empty except for broken glass, cans, and garbage strewn across the dirt floor.

I stood there a moment, trying to imagine their voices in there. Their footsteps across the dirt floor each day. Going about what must have been a hard and meager existence. Tillie and her sisters and brother not even attending school, growing up without knowing how to read or write. At some point Tillie had left home to work for a Dr. Conover, I'd learned from an article, and apparently he had taught her to read finally. The joy and pride she must have felt. And then she'd gone to work at the seminary. Another step up in the world. She'd been trying to make a better life for herself; I had no doubt of that.

I stood in that pitiful log house picturing the beautiful man-sion at Waterloo where her cousins and uncle lived. The fine furnishings, the beautiful clothes. How could she not have longed for it? Wouldn't she have wanted that kind of life instead of this? I walked further inside and began searching.

I spent an hour combing through the interior of the cabin, damp and moldy, probably never quite drying out between rains. I kept checking my watch, a nervous humming inside me, still worrying about Adam waiting for me, still anxious someone might be in the woods outside. I found a crude wooden shelf that had been built into the log wall near the hearth and imagined this must have been the kitchen area. I knelt and scoured through a pile of glass in the dirt, my fingers carefully pushing the pieces apart, looking for anything at all. It was mostly tiny slivers or bigger pieces that told of recent beer parties. At the very bottom, practically embedded in the dirt, my flashlight caught a glimmer of green. I picked it up, expecting another piece of a beer bottle. But it was too thick and a deeper shade. A shard of emerald green glass. I took it to the doorway and held it up to the light, not believing my eyes. There was the raised P.

"Oh my God!" It was the same as the perfume bottle I'd found in the cellar when I tripped the breaker. Salon Palmer. I held it up to my nose, knowing there'd be no scent but imagining this bottle in her hands. Oh, how my heart broke for her, picturing that hopeful look in her eyes that was burned in my brain. How long after she held this bottle, dabbed its perfume on her wrists, her neck, was her life taken from her? Because at some point, she was here. She had this bottle. And she had no idea she was going to die. I was certain of it.

I slipped the shard into my pocket and began making my way back through the woods, praying I wouldn't get lost. A nagging voice of reason began needling me. It probably wasn't so unusual finding the shard. There were only a few perfume makers back then, and there probably wasn't much available in these parts. Still...

Still, I thought, now sitting at the desk and tracing the letter P on the fragment of glass, what were the odds really? That it would be there, that I would even find it? What were the odds for anything that had happened so far?

I thought about the darkened woods when I left the cabin, the drive back to town in the falling dusk, the long grey shadows of the trees seeming ominous. A shiver ran up my back now, but it wasn't the haunting memory of the dark woods. It was James Titus.

Just last night, in a faded and blurred paragraph I'd nearly missed at the end of an article, I discovered the power the janitor lorded over the servants. Which I now knew he held over Tillie.

I picked up my pen and began writing.

CHAPTER 15

January 20, 1886

THE SNOW STOPPED BY THE TIME Tillie reached the village of Waterloo, teeth chattering and feet numb as wood from the cold. She was still more than six miles from town. Even if she'd had any coins left, she was out of luck. The last train of the day had come and gone. A liveryman heading back home offered her a ride as far as Saxton Falls, and she took it, though he was old and smelly and had a lecherous look about him.

She sat to the far end of the bench on the wagon without offering any conversation. It was pitch dark when he stopped the wagon abruptly and turned to her. By the lantern, she could see his horrible grin, the missing teeth. The stench of rum filled the night air. She jumped off the wagon before he had a chance to even touch her. She ran into the woods and hid until she heard the wagon rumble off. She huddled by a tree in total darkness until the lantern disappeared. Venturing out from the trees then, she thanked the Lord for the bit of moon that lit the road. One other wagon came by a while later, and she ran back to the cover of the woods until it passed. She knew only too well what might happen with miners or canal men.

The moon had moved quite a bit when she finally reached the road from Saxton Falls into Star Port, still about three miles from the institute. She wasn't far from the Mosier sisters' place and knew that the odds of someone being there who could give her a ride back to town were good. The thought of being seen there, though, was yet another risk. But she dared not miss the curfew, 'cause that might cost her job. Lifting her skirts, Tillie began running toward their house, praying she'd get back before ten.

Before she even reached the Mosier sisters', she saw a wagon slowly pulling away. She waited in the darkness, then hopped on the back, praying the drunken men didn't notice her. Luckily, they did not.

The ride was slow and bumpy, and she was shivering something fierce now. She turned her thoughts to her visit with her sisters, glad she'd brought them the perfume and not the book she'd first picked. What would have been the purpose? She had to help get them out of Lubber's Run. Nora's daydream of Tillie working her way up, finding a beau, having a home where they could all live a decent life...it was possible. In the meantime, at least Nora had a prospect, and hopefully this time she'd last. Tillie hoped with all her heart she would get the position in spite of her fears. But then there was Catherine. What was to become of her without even Nora left? Like their mother, Catherine was prone to moodiness and nervous fits.

The wagon slowed coming up the hill to Main Street, and she knew this was her chance. She jumped off quietly, not even feeling her feet, and hid behind a bush. Suddenly, she heard the bells of the institute ringing in the distance, and as she hurried, she counted. It was ten o'clock. Oh, she was soon for trouble.

Her feet came back to life as she tried to run, but she was just too worn out. Walking as fast as she was able, she headed up Main Street and three blocks later turned onto Church Street by the post office. Way up the dark street, she saw the institute lit up by the gas lanterns, and now she began to run as fast as she could in her corset and petticoats, grateful for the wooden sidewalks so she didn't have to worry about ice. She flew through the front gates and just then heard the front door lock slide shut. Around the building to the side entrance she ran now, great big breaths of steam coming from her. Slipping suddenly, she fell on her behind so hard that she bit her lip. Breathless, she got to her feet and pulled at the side door, but it was locked as well. Racing to the back of the building, she prayed she wasn't too late, but just as she reached the cellar door, she heard the lock slide.

"Open up, please," she called, though not too loud to wake

anyone. Then she knocked on the door. "Please, I've just gotten here. Please open up." She could hardly speak, she was so winded.

The door opened, and there stood the janitor, Jimmy Titus, a lantern in one hand, a ring of keys in the other. "Well, Tillie Smith, what are you doing out after curfew?" he asked without smiling.

She stepped inside, so tuckered out she about swooned as the heat hit her. But she couldn't go forward. Janitor Titus was but inches from her, blocking her way, his pale skin shiny with sweat and his dark eyes shining hard. He was thin and wiry, and she thought she could possibly just push by him. But she knew better. She'd seen him shoveling coal and hauling the students' trunks up the staircase.

"I went to visit my family and missed the train back," she lied, her words coming in spurts as she tried to slow her breath-ing.

"As I see it, you might be owing me a favor here, seeing as I'm obliged to tell Mrs. Ruckle about you girls coming in late."

She watched the slow smile curl his lips and felt a flash of anger because she was ready to drop and wanted none of this. "Can you let me by, please?"

Then they heard footsteps coming, and her heart about seized up, fearing the worst. She saw a little flicker of worry in his eyes. He'd just let her in after curfew, so perhaps he was afraid she'd get *him* into trouble?

"Sorry I'm late, Jimmy."

The janitor turned quickly, and she saw one of the seminary students coming from the direction of the stairway. She'd thought he was one of the reverends at first, with his black collar and gold-rimmed glasses.

"It's just fine, Mead. I was about to go upstairs and begin locking up. You can turn down the gas lamps as we go."

Titus stepped aside, and she rushed in past him, nearly bumping into Mead, who gave her a sharp look. It was the first she'd seen him since he'd had designs on her up in the dining room. As she hurried along, she heard Mr. Titus close and lock the bolt as he headed down the long hall with Mead, their voices fading. She stopped for a quick bit in the furnace room, hot as the blazes, the boilers thundering loudly. Her bones began to thaw as she sat there catching her breath. She'd be safe as they still had to lock up the rest of the big building.

After a while, she stood up, half asleep, and her purse fell from her lap. When she bent to pick it up, she noticed red spots on the floor, like drops of blood. Fearful, she touched one with her finger. It was dry and sooty, not blood at all, she realized. Quiet as a church mouse, she then tiptoed up the staircase to the maids' quarters, mindful as she slipped past Mrs. Ruckle's room. If she were caught now, that would no doubt be the end of her job.

Once inside her own room, she fell under her covers in all her clothes.

"Whatcha doing coming in after curfew, Tillie? That musta cost you something with the janitor."

"I thought you was asleep, Stella."

"No, too wound up to sleep, Tillie."

"Sakes alive, you best shut your eyes 'cause morning will be here all too soon."

She thought of the janitor again, letting her in after the ten o'clock bells. She didn't want to make an enemy of Jimmy Titus; that was for sure. She hoped he didn't report to the matron tomorrow that she'd come in after curfew.

And then she thought of Peter Mead, looking down his nose at her, still smarting, perhaps, at how she'd talked to him in the dining room that day. No doubt she'd already made an enemy of him. Would he tattle on her to Mrs. Ruckle? But even worry couldn't keep her awake.

As she drifted off, she heard Stella say, "You'll never guess. I have a beau, Tillie."

But Tillie was too tired to even say a word back.

CHAPTER 16

I HEARD A CAR DOOR AND THEN VOICES. I got up from the desk to look out the window. Adam and Helen were coming around her white Cadillac. Their voices were loud enough for me to hear.

"You can't keep doing this," she said. "You can leave anytime you want. Get your life back."

"This is my life."

"And do you think getting married—"

"Stop!"

I'd never heard Adam raise his voice like that.

"Please don't be upset with me," I heard Helen say, her face stricken. "I've never had kids of my own, so you're it for me, Adam."

Adam came closer to her then, put a hand on her shoulder. "I know," he said in a gentler tone.

"It's time to stop punishing yourself. There's life beyond this cemetery. The legacy could end here. You had dreams once."

"I know you love me and you want what's best for me, but you have to respect I'm an adult. This is the life I've chosen. And I still have dreams. I'm happier now than I've been in a long time."

"Oh, Adam, there's something not quite right there. A quickie marriage. No family. I don't want to see you get hurt. You could still do something about this before it's too late."

"You mean before there's a pregnancy? Are you kidding? I want kids, and I know Rachel will, too. The sooner the better."

"Oh, Adam, tell me this isn't about the legacy. Keeping it going."

"Whoa," he said, holding a hand up. "You've been watching too many soaps. Now I'm going inside to my wife."

For some reason she looked up then, and I quickly backed

away from the window. A moment later I heard the car pull away. I waited for Adam to come inside, but he didn't. Then I heard a loud thwacking sound. I went out and found him near the garage, chopping wood, viciously slamming logs until they split with one attack of the ax. It was a few minutes before he noticed me.

He put the ax down and caught his breath.

"Hey," I said, walking closer. "What's going on?"

"Nothing. Just getting some logs split. Supposed to get cold again the next few nights."

"Honey, come on. I couldn't help overhearing you and your aunt."

He looked up at the clouds building in the west, where the weather usually blew in from. Then he looked at me again. "Let's go get some dinner and we'll talk."

"Okay," I said, surprised he gave in so easily.

* * *

WE WENT TO MAMA'S CAFÉ just down Mountain Avenue. Adam asked for a quiet table, and they sat us in a corner. He didn't even touch the bread while we waited for our entrees.

"I feel like something has changed since we got married," I said to him. "We came back here, and...I don't know. You've been different."

He gave me a long look. "I could say the same about you, Rachel."

I opened my mouth, but nothing came out. Instead my eyes filled with tears. "I should have told you the truth in the beginning. I heard you tell your aunt that you want children, and I..."

"Oh shit, I'm sorry, babe." He took both my hands. "I shouldn't be turning this on you."

"Adam, we never really talked about children."

"You talked a lot of about being alone, having no family....I just assumed you wanted them."

"I know, and I do want them. But...what if I can't?"

"Is that what the doctor said? Is there something wrong?"

I shook my head. "She told me I'm perfectly normal, though it does get harder after thirty-five."

"And what about...?"

I took a deep breath. "She said it's not unusual, that I...tense up because...of what happened. But there are...relaxation exercises, maybe...some Xanax the first few times."

"Okay."

"I just need more time, Adam."

"Why would you think I wouldn't give you that?"

"I know it's important to you to carry on your family's legacy. If you don't..." I let the rest go unsaid.

"I didn't marry you to be a baby machine."

I had hurt him, and it was the last thing I'd intended to do. I wanted to comfort him after his talk with Helen. I wanted him to confide in me. Now we were having our first real fight. I was awful at this. I didn't really know how to have a relationship.

Our entrees arrived, and Adam ordered a glass of wine. I ordered one, too. We ate in silence. When Adam was half done, he put his fork down and gave me a long look. I knew what was coming. *This isn't working out. You're a strange woman. Sex hasn't exactly been what I'd thought.* I'd heard it before. How could I be surprised? I'd had one short relationship that was awful. I dated two guys after that until they quickly found someone else. I was doomed to be alone for the rest of my life. It probably wasn't too late for an annulment.

"I'm sorry," Adam said instead. "You didn't deserve that."

"No, I'm sorry, Adam. What I implied was awful. I know that's not who you are."

He sighed. "I've got my flaws, Rachel; don't doubt that. I'm just...I'm trying to be the best person I can. That wasn't always the case. For a lot of years, I didn't care about anyone else. I was just out for myself."

"When you left here?"

He nodded. "I knew my father needed me. And I knew without me here to run interference, my mother wouldn't stay. But...I just wanted a bigger world. A different world."

"You told me you went to college and then did a few years in the military. Are you talking after that?"

"I should have come home sooner," he said with a nod, and I waited for more. "Let's just leave it at that."

I knew there was no pushing him further. This wasn't the right time.

* * *

LATER THAT NIGHT, ADAM WAS SLEEPING and I was still awake when the phone rang. I jumped and grabbed it quickly. It was one of the funeral directors. There weren't a lot of Jewish people in this small town, but one had just died and would need to be buried right away, as was the custom. The deceased had purchased a plot awhile back. I wrote down the name and then woke Adam.

"I'm going to help you," I said as he rolled out of bed, his eyes barely open while pulling on clothes, moving on automatic pilot.

"No, go to sleep. This could take all night."

"Please, Adam, let me help. This way you won't have to call anyone else."

It was one in the morning. I knew how he hated waking up any of the others, always having to call two or three before he finally got one to even answer the phone.

"All right."

A few minutes later we were in the pickup, headlights piercing the blackness as we drove the winding paths across the cemetery to the small cottage that housed the office. I hadn't been inside before. It was one large room with a desk and two chairs facing it for clients. A woodstove sat in a corner, the only means of heat, it seemed. The wall to its right was filled with framed photos and papers or documents, no doubt a history of the cemetery. In front of the window were several tables covered with small file boxes and ledgers. Everything looked ancient, in need of paint and perhaps a good dusting. Adam opened a file box that held hundreds of index cards, searching for the name Cohen. A minute later, he cursed, slamming it shut.

"What's wrong?"

"Nothing."

By the third file box, he was sweating.

"Can I help?"

"No!" Then he turned to me. "I'm sorry. I'm just...tired. It's not well organized. I'll find it."

He pulled a card from the fourth box, and I could hear him sigh with relief. Then he reached for a ledger from a pile on a shelf.

"These are all seriously still done by hand?"

"It's the way it's always been. This works."

I had my doubts. It was cold in there, and I shivered, zipping up my jacket.

"Jesus, I'm sorry about this."

I smiled. "It's okay."

He turned back to the ledger, his finger scanning, finally stopping. "Here he is. Max Cohen. He's in 22A, section 18." Then he walked over to the wall where several old large maps hung, brown with age. "Here it is." After he jotted down the information, we were out the door again, riding in the pickup toward the back of the cemetery. When we reached section 18, Adam parked the truck and left the headlights on pointing toward the headstones. Then he began walking, and I followed as he counted. Halfway across the row, which was mostly empty of graves, he stopped.

"This should be it. Wait here a moment."

He walked back to the truck, pulled out a tape measure, and began walking again. "Yup, this is it. There are four graves between that one and Cohen's."

"Are you serious? That's how it's done?"

He looked at me and smiled. "That's how it's always been done," he said again.

I watched as he measured out and marked the plot.

"Will one of the boys come in the morning with the backhoe?"

"There's no time for that. The vault has to go in early tomorrow, burial either tomorrow night or the next morning, depending on how strict the family is. Jews are usually buried the day after they die. But since he died so late...we'll see. Gotta be ready, though."

We drove over to the equipment shed, and he got the backhoe.

"You can go to bed now. This is going to take a while."

"I don't want you to be alone."

He laughed. "I do this alone a lot. It doesn't bother me."

"Your grandmother told me she used to help your grandfather. And your father. I want to."

He gave me an appreciative smile. "My mother helped my father a lot, too, in their early years. Had to. Once, when he got hurt, she even ran the place for a while. But later on...she just got tired of it."

It was the way he said it. Whatever was going on with him had something to do with his parents. I was glad I hadn't pushed earlier.

"Adam, I could get the office all organized for you. I'm good at that. You said there was confusion over those plots the other day, and now you had a hard time—"

"Stop. It's fine. There's no problem." I nodded slowly as he kept moving, then turned to me again. "Look, we just don't have time for this right now."

I followed in the pickup as he drove the backhoe slowly across the cemetery back to Mr. Cohen's plot. I trained the headlights on the plot and watched as Adam methodically moved back and forth, the jagged teeth of the backhoe's bucket cutting into the earth and removing scoops of dirt, placing them in a pile beside the hole.

Now my eyes began to wander across the silent graves. The eternal flame candles were the only light that broke the darkness since there was no moon. But as my eyes adjusted and time went by, I could make out the fields of headstones in the ambient light. I should have been spooked, but it was actually ethereal and peaceful. There were few cars on the road nearby, and I could hear the river in the distance. Then I heard a low rumble, a sound I now recognized as a car driving over the wooden bridge. Goose bumps ran up my arms. I looked that way, watching, but there were no headlights.

Getting out of the truck, I stretched and caught something in my peripheral vision. A deer, frozen in place a few rows down, stood staring at me. I stood still for a moment watching it until it turned suddenly and ran off, its white tail flashing in the darkness. Smiling, I turned back toward Adam to check his progress, but something far across the cemetery now caught my attention. Two pinpoints of amber light moving in the distance. It looked like a person, or persons, walking through the dark cemetery by candlelight. I waved to Adam, but he was focused on his task. Suddenly uneasy, I got back in the truck.

As I sat there, I thought of all the cemetery keepers in Adam's family who'd been doing this for more than a century and a half. Phineas Miller was the first, Adam had told me, back in the early 1800s. He'd built the house we were living in. I imagined him pulling a horse-drawn wagon and digging graves by hand, lowering wooden coffins with ropes. Loved ones arriving in horse-drawn carriages or by foot. All of those souls still resting right here around me.

I remembered Adam telling me what his grandmother repeated. They were the "keepers of the souls." Though he didn't share much about his father, he spoke often of his grandfather Samuel, who'd taught him to fish and carve things from branches, who told him that one day it would be his time here and that it was a special calling because not everyone could do it.

I watched Adam get off the backhoe and lay a sheath of plywood across the dug grave. Then he drove the backhoe toward the truck.

"Still awake?"

"Adam, there's someone walking over there, toward the river. I thought I heard a car going over the bridge. Then I saw candles moving. I think."

He shook his head. "College kids, probably. Can't seem to keep them away from Tillie."

It was the first we'd mentioned Tillie since he asked me to let her go. I followed him in the truck back to the equipment shed, and he hopped into the passenger side.

"Let's drive up there and make sure they're gone. I don't want any partying going on. You know which way to go?"

"I think so." But in the darkness I got confused and took the wrong path, ending beside the river at a nearly open field where there were few headstones.

"This is the old potter's field, as they called it back then, where the poor were buried."

"Your grandmother told me she used to put flowers on some of the graves several times a year."

"Yeah, most are unmarked, or whatever was there has fallen over or crumbled over the years."

"God, that's so sad."

"Most of their families couldn't even afford a grave much less a marker."

"That's where Tillie was first buried, you know. It's hard to believe the monument she has now. It must have cost a fortune back in those days."

Adam didn't respond. A minute later he said, "Take the next sharp left."

Up we climbed to the highest point in the cemetery. There in the distance I saw the light again. When we finally pulled up to Tillie's monument, the headlights shining on it, I saw two votive candles sitting on its base and a bouquet of fresh flowers set on the grass.

"Why do they come at night?"

"Oh, people expect all sorts of strange things to happen in cemeteries at night. Maybe they're hoping to run into Tillie's ghost."

"Do you believe in that? Ghosts?"

He shook his head. "I believe there's something that goes on, a consciousness, or spirit, or whatever you want to call it. But I've never seen anything to make me believe in ghosts. There's nothing here, believe me."

I felt the same way. And I believed something of Tillie was reaching out to me. "Oh, Adam," I said, my eyes now on the carved letters. "Today is April eighth. It's the anniversary of her death."

"I guess that explains it, then."

I closed my eyes and said a quick prayer.

"Hey, you can't keep your eyes open, and I'm ready to fall down. Let's try to get a few hours' sleep."

We went right up to bed. Adam pulled me into his arms, the tension from our dinner earlier gone. I was glad I'd gone to help him with the plot. Within seconds he was asleep. I kept thinking of Tillie buried in Potter's Field, then her body exhumed and moved to that beautiful plot. Was her spirit at rest? Were there other spirits or forms of consciousness wandering these acres of graves unbeknownst to us? Another world in an entirely different dimension? Was it even possible for a spirit to rest after such a brutal death and the possibility that justice wasn't served?

I shivered, remembering long ago my mother telling me that it meant someone was walking over your grave. Then I snuggled closer to Adam, loving the smell of him, warm and musky, like sunlight and grass and masculinity. I felt safe. And I wondered if Tillie had had any idea as she went about her life each day that she wasn't.

CHAPTER 17

February 1886

TILLIE SAT NEXT TO STELLA ON THE CARRIAGE RIDE to the cemetery with the other female servants. Last week the institute was filled with dread as one of the students, sick with consumption, had to leave suddenly. And now Mr. Alsop, the farmhand who brought her the potatoes most mornings, had died from complications of pneumonia. Everyone was scared, listening to the coughing through the halls, knowing how quickly sickness could spread and how the bitter winter air should be a caution to all.

Riding down the hill from Main Street, Tillie had a sudden yearning to see her ma. Tears popped into her eyes, and she wiped them fast with a handkerchief. The cough she had since going home to Lubber's Run was finally easing some, thank the Lord. She knew it was best to wait for it to be full gone before making the journey out to Independence.

The wooden bridge rattled as the carriage drove over the river, and Tillie looked down at the water rushing by, the edges rimmed with ice. She didn't want to come. Death frightened her, though she'd seen enough to be used to it. And there was something right scary about graveyards. But as the carriage turned left toward the trees in the distance, she thought that this place didn't appear so fearsome at all. The big trees were covered in white, and the river was gurgling so that it was beautiful, even in the harshness of winter. Maybe it was the quiet.

At the institute, it was never really quiet. Even at night with everyone asleep, there were the sounds of snoring, or worse, and always the hiss of the gas jets and the rumblings of the boilers below. And now the hacking and coughing. Here there was no sound at all but the crunching of the wheels over frozen ground. They stopped at the crowd already gathered by the plot, a hole in the ground with but a few flowers surrounding it. Stella grabbed her hand.

"Oh, Tillie, I fear I might faint!"

Stella was nearly hysterical when she learned they were expected to attend. Once, when just a girl, she'd walked across a cemetery and slipped into a freshly dug grave, and the horror had never left her, she told Tillie last night. She'd prattled on and on, keeping Tillie awake, but Tillie felt bad and didn't scold her for once.

"Are you afraid of dying, Tillie?" she'd whispered in the dark just as Tillie was nearly asleep. "Can you imagine being an old woman, knowing your time is coming? Or worse, sick and hearing there's no hope at all?"

"No, I can't see myself as old," she muttered, so sleepy it was hard to talk, "or sick like that."

She thought about it now, standing beside the grave, listening to Mrs. Alsop wail. Five little ones surrounded her, and Tillie wondered how they would survive without his pay. Unless there was family to take her in, the wife would have to find a new husband fast, someone who didn't mind all those mouths to feed. If not, then perhaps a farmer who needed a domestic and had the room for her brood. There were other ways, of course, but she doubted Mrs. Alsop would know about those.

The cemetery keeper and his boy stood off a ways with their shovels beside them. As Dr. Whitney began to pray, she bowed her head, and a shiver ran through her as she looked into that hole in the earth where Mr. Alsop would spend eternity. She peeked then and saw they were all bowed, eyes closed. She looked over the cemetery, the rolling fields and old trees. Across the way was a big white house, and she shuddered to think of the cemetery keeper and his boy, who looked just like him, living here. Turning the other way, her eyes rose to the highest perch and rested on a beautiful mausoleum. She wondered who had the means to afford such a choice spot. Imagine, a small building just for you, to house your body for the rest of time.

When Tillie looked back at the grave, she felt eyes upon her. For a moment there, she thought it was yet another reverend, but it was Peter Mead, standing behind Dr. Whitney, looking himself like a man of the cloth in his black clothes and high collar. He had cold eyes, that one. She could see that even through his gold spectacles. And then she saw that Mrs. Ruckle was eyeing her with a frown, and she quickly looked down again and closed her eyes. The matron had been stern with her since she had missed curfew, but nothing was ever said. She pictured Catherine and Nora and their pitiful cabin with little food. She couldn't take any more chances; that was for certain.

Dr. Whitney led them in "Amazing Grace," and then the institute bells began to ring in the distance as they were climbing the wagons to leave and head back to work. Just past Mr. Alsop's, they saw the paupers' graves, and Stella crossed herself.

"Imagine being dumped there in Potter's Field for all eternity," she said. "What a cruel end that would be."

Tillie couldn't imagine anything sadder. But she knew it was best not to dwell on such things. "It's over and done, Stella. We're young and strong with our whole lives ahead."

"Mr. Alsop wasn't exactly old, Tillie. And he was a might strong."

There was nothing really to say to that.

When they were crossing over the bridge again, Stella asked, "Do you believe in heaven, Tillie? Or the other?"

"I ain't rightly certain, Stella. I want to believe there's a better place, that the good we do here means something." It was too awful to think otherwise.

"But what about when we're not so good?"

"I think how you feel about it is mighty important. If you're sorrowful, then I think God should understand and forgive you."

Stella was quiet for a long time.

"That's what my beau says, too, though he's of a mind to think that most people are bound for the other."

"And are you ever going to tell me who this beau of yours might be?"

Stella looked at the other help sitting beside them in the carriage and got really quiet. Then she shook her head. Tillie knew something wasn't quite right there, not if chatty Stella was keeping a secret. And a bad feeling settled in her belly.

CHAPTER 18

A WEEK LATER, I WAS COMPLETELY UNPACKED, and each room of the house was reorganized and sparkling clean. I had no work, and I was trying to distance myself from Tillie. I was trying to be a good wife. Then my cell phone rang. It was Mr. Finegan. Was I possibly interested in helping him out since his nephew seemed to be MIA? I arrived at the house on Sharp Street within the hour, trying not to look too excited. I knew I was meant to be there. I wondered what I would find.

Mr. Finegan and I sat at the dining room table and made up a game plan. His knees and his back couldn't handle the bending and crouching in an attic or basement, the notoriously dirty and bug-infested spaces. I didn't even flinch. I knew when it came to hiding things, these places were golden.

I began in the attic while downstairs Mr. Finegan was tackling the first floor. Attics were tough, usually chock full of whatever detritus people didn't know what to do with over the years, which was why you had to be so careful. It was easy to overlook something of value in your haste to get the job done. Not me, though.

It took me two hours to sort through the front of the big open area. Next I walked past the chimney, which went right through the middle, pitching to the right a bit and dividing the space in two. The back of the attic was mostly filled with furniture, odds and ends such as old screens and doors. As I inventoried and tagged items, I couldn't help but think of Adam and what I was planning for that evening. I didn't want to wait any longer. I'd been practicing the exercises and had gotten the prescription for Xanax filled. Tonight I was going to be the wife Adam had hoped for. Still, my heart kicked into high gear each time I thought ahead.

Focus, I chastised myself, turning to the back wall of the attic. Then my eyes landed on an old steamer trunk, and I smiled. Lifting the lid, I saw that it was filled to the brim. It took me twenty minutes to sort through lesson plans from Mrs. Freeman's teaching days, artwork by a favorite student, old autograph books, the kind that went out of fashion generations ago. I perused each item carefully, hoping something unexpected might be hidden in there.

Ninety minutes later, everything in the area was itemized on my pad, some of it tagged, the rest to be donated to a thrift shop or shelter. Looking around one last time, I began scrutinizing the floorboards one by one, seeing if any were mismatched or able to be lifted. Once, on a job when I was first apprenticing, I'd found a bag of old coins from the Civil War hidden under an attic floorboard. My boss had been amazed. And I was hooked.

Finally, I went to the eaves of the attic, searching in the darkest corners where beams and wall supports met, scanning with a flashlight and trying to see past thick cobwebs. In the last corner, I spotted something dark and square. I reached in on my hands and knees, finally pulling out a heavy old book. I wiped off years of dust with the hem of my t-shirt and saw it was a Bible.

A thrill of excitement rushed over me as I sat on the floor by the window and opened it. It was the family Bible, and in front was the Titus family tree. It began with James Titus's parents. His father had died before he was grown. Everything I saw I couldn't help referencing to Tillie and the year 1886. Titus married in 1881 and had a daughter in 1882, the older woman in the picture in the dining room. She'd been just four years old when her father murdered Tillie. Titus's wife had died in 1904, I read, though his death in 1952 was not written there. The last thing that was recorded was the birth of Titus's granddaughter Marion, Gran's friend who'd just gone into the nursing home.

It was eerie looking at the actual handwriting, imagining his wife writing the date of their wedding in this book. The birth of their daughter. Happy times. And then learning that her husband had been a predator all along. As I imagined the man who raped me must have been. Charming, kind perhaps, but with a hidden agenda. What must it have done to his wife, his daughter, learning that your husband or father was a monster? And what about the granddaughter, Mrs. Freeman?

I paged through the Bible slowly, searching for loose pages, something slipped into it over the years and forgotten. Instead I found passages underlined in heavy blue ink, from a fountain pen, no doubt. In the Old Testament, I read in Hebrews 8:12, "For I will forgive their wickedness and will remember their sins no more." I paged ahead to the New Testament, and there was another in Luke 23:34: "Jesus said, Father, forgive them, for they do not know what they are doing." And yet another in 1 John 1:9: "If we confess our sins, he is faithful and just and will forgive us our sins and purify us from all unrighteousness."

There were perhaps a dozen underlined passages in all, and each dealt with forgiveness. I looked out the window, wondering. Was Titus's wife trying to forgive him? Or perhaps his granddaughter years later? Or could it be possible these were the scribblings of James Titus himself, asking for forgiveness from God? That seemed the most likely answer. Otherwise, why would it have been hidden away like that?

I shut the Bible and sat there, frustrated. Everything I could find so far was about Titus or his trial. Every article focused on him or the details or the crime. But it was Tillie I wanted. And the truth. Who was she really? Why did he kill her? Why were people still tarnishing her name, as Gran had done? But so far, I couldn't find answers. I could barely find anything at all about her. I sat there in the attic of her convicted murderer, and the sad reality dawned on me. If I wanted to find Tillie, I was no doubt going to have to do it through James Titus. And there was but one obvious place I could ask questions. There was only one person still living who really knew him.

But did I have the nerve?

* * *

FOREST HAVEN WAS ON THE EDGE OF TOWN, on the same road

that led into the state park. It was an idyllic setting for an assisted living facility, with perhaps a dozen little ranch homes and a big main building surrounded by woods and bordered by the Musconetcong. I wasn't sure where Mrs. Freeman would be, so I followed the sign for visitors. The reception area was cheerful, with light classical music, floral arrangements, and colorful prints on the walls. All of it should have calmed me, but it didn't. I knew I was on dangerous ground. I gripped the Bible tighter to my chest.

"I'm here to see Marion Freeman," I told the young woman behind the desk.

She looked at her computer screen and clicked away. "She's in 323. Elevators are through the lounge to your right." She didn't even ask my name, which was a bit of a relief.

"Thank you."

The lounge was lively with card games and people reading or watching a large flat screen TV. I realized she might not even be in her room, which could be a problem. I didn't want to call attention to myself asking around for her. I got off the elevator on the third floor, and my stomach began doing flips. I had an excuse, I kept telling myself. Something that would be precious to her. And it was worth the risk.

I walked down a long corridor and saw that her door was open. I stopped just before it and peeked inside. It was just as I had pictured: a twin bed and dresser, TV and two chairs in another corner, with pictures and personal knick-knacks adorning the room. And there she was, James Titus's granddaughter. The once-young woman who'd stood beside him in the family photo back in the forties. She was tiny, frail looking, dressed in a peach pantsuit and pearls, her grey hair pulled back into a low bun. Rather formal for every day in a nursing home. This was a woman who took pride in her appearance.

She was sitting in a blue wingback chair with a book in her hands, head down, glasses halfway down her nose. I couldn't tell if she was actually reading or if she'd fallen asleep. I knocked gently. She looked up immediately and blinked several times. I could see I must have woken her.

"Mrs. Freeman?" I asked, stepping just inside the room.

"Yes?" she asked in a trembly voice, taking off her reading glasses. "Is it tea time already?"

"Oh, no," I said, coming toward her, so nervous it was almost difficult to speak. She watched me with vivid blue eyes that sharpened as I got closer. "I've actually brought you something."

"Oh, well, why don't you sit down?"

I sank in the smaller chair beside her, turning so I could face her.

"Who are you, dear?"

"Oh, I'm sorry. Forgive me. My name is Rachel, and I'm work-ing with Mr. Finegan, the auctioneer handling your house. I found this in the attic, kind of lost in the eaves, and when I saw what it was, I thought it might be important to you." The Bible was heavy, so I knelt down and set it on her lap.

She stared at it a moment with a little frown. "Why, I've never seen this before." Slowly she opened the cover, then turned a page. She stared at first; then I watched her eyes traveling slowly down the family tree. Finally she looked up at me, and there were tears in her eyes. "I can't believe you found this. It's sad, isn't it? I'm the last entry in here."

"I'm so sorry. I didn't mean to upset you."

But she was shaking her head. "No, dear, it's all right. It's just that you reach my age and there isn't much to do but look back. But I've been fortunate. I had all my students, you know? Many of them come and visit me here. Did I have you? What's your last name?"

"Oh, no, I just moved here. I just married Adam Miller," I said, too uneasy not to be honest with her any longer.

"Oh, I'd heard Adam married suddenly." She looked at me a long moment. "How are you adjusting to living in the cemetery?"

"I don't mind it at all, actually. In fact, I think it's very peace-ful. Which I guess is a bit ironic."

She smiled and reached for a tissue, wiping her eyes. "I didn't mean to get emotional."

"That's okay. I understand. And I think I know why." I took a long breath. This was a gamble. "Mrs. Freeman, ever since I moved into the cemetery, something's been happening to me. Strange coincidences I guess you'd call it, but it started when I saw the monument to Tillie Smith."

Her eyes widened and I began to lose my nerve, but I kept talking quickly. "I've been doing some research, and there's something odd about what I've been finding. I mean, I know your grandfather was convicted, but did you know that originally they thought there was another man involved? And I'm not really sure what it all means...." My words were stalling at the startled look on her face. I was grasping for a way to put this. "What I'm trying to say is that I've heard some doubts about whether James Titus really was to blame for Tillie Smith's murder, and I wanted to see if I could..."

But she wasn't looking at me any longer. She was shaking her head and looking past me. When I turned, I realized why she was all dressed up. She was expecting company: Aunt Helen and Gran, who sat in her wheelchair looking at me in horror.

* * *

I DROVE BACK TO THE CEMETERY sick to my stomach. What had I been thinking? I'd deliberately ignored Helen's request to leave it alone. Then I told Adam I would let Tillie go. And I upset poor Mrs. Freeman, who probably would have been better off without the Bible and reminders of what she had lost. But worst of all, I hurt Gran. Marion was her dear friend, Ronnie's godmother. No matter how much I tried to apologize before leaving Forest Haven, Gran could barely look at me.

I was hoping I'd have time to do some damage control with Adam. But I didn't. When I walked into the house, he was in the kitchen, pacing, obviously waiting for me. Helen had apparently wasted not a moment filling him in on everything.

"Why would you do this?" he asked, his voice full of anguish.

"Adam, please understand, I didn't mean to hurt anyone—"

"But you did," he interrupted. "And you'd been asked more than once, apparently, by my aunt and my grandmother. In fact, I remember last week when you mentioned your interest in Tillie Smith and my aunt's concern, I even agreed you should let it go."

I felt sick at heart. I wished he'd be mad. But he, too, looked hurt. And disappointed.

"I know. But...it's just so hard to explain. Did you ever in your life feel as though you were meant to do something? I know I told you about the coincidences, the weird things happening, but there's more. It's like she's—"

"It doesn't matter, Rachel," he said, enunciating each word slowly. He turned away from me and walked to the window, shaking his head. Then he turned to me again. "There's an old lady sitting in a nursing home who has no one left, and the last thing she needs is to be reminded of what was probably the saddest thing in her life. What the hell were you trying to accomplish?"

"I found a family Bible in the attic, and I thought she'd want it. But I wanted to ask her some things because...Adam, the past is never as simple as everyone thinks. I've seen that time and again with my job, and I'm sure you have, too. There may have been another man involved. Your grandmother seems to think Tillie was some kind of loose woman, but I don't—"

"It doesn't matter!" he shouted. "She's dead. Titus is dead. Mrs. Freeman deserves peace. And my grandmother deserves respect."

I sat down, sick with dread. I'd been running on adrenaline, but I suddenly felt as if every ounce of energy had drained from my body. What I had done was selfish, duplicitous. I knew that. "You're right," I said in barely a whisper. "I...I don't know what came over me."

He lifted my chin so I had to look at him. "You'll stop, then?"

I was in so deep, it would be almost impossible. Tillie had become an obsession, occupying most of my waking thoughts. And there was the belief in my heart I was somehow meant to help her. I looked at my husband, whom I loved. Whom I had hurt and no doubt embarrassed. Who was now looking at me with disappointment in his eyes.

I nodded. "I'll stop."

He went back to work then. I sat there in the kitchen, unable to move, thinking of how excited I'd been about my plans for the evening, to show Adam how much he meant to me, finally becoming his wife in every way.

I'd ruined it all.

CHAPTER 19

IT SEEMED EASTER WAS BARELY OVER when getting the cemetery ready for Memorial Day began. The bare mountains began to soften with green. Pink and white dogwoods burst into bloom. Life was sprouting everywhere, the birds in a frenzy each morning before day even broke. The cemetery became a place of life and beauty, ironically, with squirrels and chipmunks cavorting, and deer wandering through at dawn and dusk. One morning I watched as workers from the nearby state fish hatchery came and stocked the river with trout. Adam had told me once he would teach me to fish. I wondered if that would still happen.

Adam was so busy, I couldn't tell if he was still upset with me or just preoccupied. The cemetery board wanted to build a mausoleum, and he seemed unhappy with that decision. But the morning I left for the auction at the Titus house on Sharp Street, he finally pulled me into his arms.

"I wanted to say good luck today. Though I don't think you'll need it."

"Thanks. Although Mr. Finegan really does the hard part. I'll just be in the background."

"I don't like how things have been," he said, looking down in my eyes.

"I don't, either. It's my fault. I'm sorry."

"Look, I know none of this has been easy for you. Eloping, moving here into the cemetery, suddenly surrounded by my family. And...what happened to you before. I get how you might feel some kind of connection to Tillie because of that, but..." He shook his head.

"But I need to let it go. I know."

"I know that probably seems unfair to you. Maybe after today it'll be easier."

"I understand."

He looked at me a long moment. "You know, sometimes I wake up and just look at you in the morning before you open your eyes, not quite believing you're here. I don't want to ruin this, Rachel."

"Oh, Adam, I've been alone for so long, I wonder sometimes if maybe I'm just not cut out—"

"Don't say that," Adam said, putting a finger on my lips. "I'm in the same boat. I've been here alone for so long, I wonder if it's even fair to expect you to be living in the middle of all these graves."

"It's starting to feel like home."

He smiled. "Good."

I said nothing about the weight of all those souls on my heart.

* * *

THE ANTIQUE DEALERS WERE THE FIRST TO ARRIVE, as usual, before the Titus house was officially open. I was familiar with the drill. They were hoping to score a find, something they could flip with some minor refurbishing, or discover something valuable the auctioneer might have overlooked. There wasn't much chance of anything like that in the old Titus house. They'd lived simply through the generations, and even the furniture being sold that day was modest by the standard of its era, late forties into the fifties. Midcentury modern, now so in vogue, hadn't even hit the scene yet.

Mr. Finegan conducted the proceedings, and I was impressed with his knowledge and showmanship. I knew my field, and no one was better at finding hidden treasures, but I could never quite put the dramatic flourishes into the procedure of auctioneering as he did.

When we opened the door, throngs of people began coming in to view the items. I kept watch inside, going from room to room, making sure items were not manhandled or moved. I was surprised by how many conversations I overheard mentioning Titus and Tillie. Some locals, it seemed, were as captivated by the history here as I was. Ten minutes later, I ambled back into the dining room and saw an old man with a cane looking at the family photos still displayed on the wall. A young woman stood beside him.

"Are you interested in the old photographs?" I asked.

The old man nodded, then turned to me. "You work for the auction house?"

"Yes, I do. We'll be bidding on smaller items later in the morning, after the furnishings."

"Well, I'm Mr. Davidson, and I'd like the lot of these."

"I'm sorry; you'll have to bid on them along with whoever else does."

He looked back at the pictures, staring at the one with James Titus on the porch.

"Did you know him?"

"Not really, but my grandfather did. He was a reporter for the local paper during the trial."

"Oh. Wow."

"He used to talk about how those big city newspapers railroaded Jimmy Titus. He wrote about it back then, and when I was just a kid, he talked about writing a book. It was a big to-do back in those days. But then he kind of lost his gumption for the whole thing."

"What do you mean he thought Titus was railroaded?"

"Just that he didn't do it. He was an easy target."

"But...they must have had reason to charge him. And he was convicted. He served in prison." And there were all those quotes about forgiveness in his family Bible.

"Well, my grandfather said the trial was a farce. That Titus's attorneys were idiots. Botched a case that never shoulda been in the first place."

"Did he ever mention another man? That two men were responsible?"

"Not that I recall. Just that Titus was a decent man."

I opened my mouth, then closed it before speaking. It was

hard for people to believe, I knew, that someone normal, perhaps even charming, could be capable of violence. Maybe for the people in town who knew the family, the good women he was surrounded by, it was even more difficult. Mr. Davidson's mind was set; I could see that.

"So why do you...I mean, what would you do with these photographs?"

He shrugged. "Nothing, really. Just a little piece of history that my grandfather was part of."

"What was your grandfather's name?"

"Denis Sullivan."

"Did your grandfather ever tell you anything about Tillie?"

He turned then, looking at me for a long moment. "There was some talk about her. That's about all."

It was the same way Gran had put it, and I knew what he meant. I could remember my mother using a similar phrase when I got to high school, that I had to be careful about boys because I didn't want there to be "talk" about me.

I wondered if Mr. Davidson might have copies of his grandfather's work. I longed to ask him, but then I noticed Helen coming in. She was a physical reminder of my promise to Adam. I wished Mr. Davidson good luck and left.

Three hours later, when the photos went up for bidding, I was surprised at how many people bid on them. And I was happy to see Mr. Davidson got them. When I drove into the cemetery at the end of the day, I had to resist an urge to drive to Tillie's monument. My thoughts were in turmoil because so much didn't make sense.

But I turned my car toward home. Adam would be back soon. He was no longer upset with me. It was time we were husband and wife in every sense of the word.

* * *

I MADE A QUICK DINNER OF PASTA AND SHRIMP while Adam showered after work. Then I asked him to make a fire. He looked at me with a question in his eyes. I carried in a tray with our food, along with wine and glasses. Then I sat on the floor beside him, raising a glass in a toast.

"This seems like déjà vu," Adam said with a little smile.

"Yes. This is what you did on what was supposed to be our 'wedding night.'"

"So...is this...?"

"Yes. This is going to be...our wedding night. Finally."

He hesitated. "Are you sure?"

I nodded, though my heart was pounding. Was I really ready? I hoped so. But I also knew too much time had gone by already. Our marriage needed this.

He asked me about the auction while we ate. I didn't mention Mr. Davidson. I asked how the plans were going for the mauso-leum. Complicated, he said. Then we were finished. I stood, and he started to gather the dishes.

"Leave them," I said, not wanting to lose the buzz I had from the wine.

I took his hand and led him upstairs to our bedroom. "Make yourself comfortable," I said, pulling back the covers and smil-ing.

"Are you sure?" he asked again.

"I'll be back in a few minutes." I walked across the hall to the bathroom, where I quickly swallowed half a Xanax, afraid to take a whole since I'd had wine. Then I sat on the edge of the tub and did the relaxation exercises, closing my eyes, imagining Adam's hands, his kisses. A tug of wanting bloomed deep within me.

When I went back to the bedroom, I saw that a window was cracked open, and the evening breeze lifted the sheer curtains. Adam sat on the window seat in just his jeans. I walked over to him, and he pulled me down onto his lap, kissing me immedi-ately. I wore my robe with nothing underneath. His mouth roamed from my lips down my neck, softly brushing the hollow at my throat, continuing down and parting my robe before one of his hands began to graze my breasts.

I knew the Xanax had kicked in because I was light-headed. I felt as though I were in a beautiful dream, the room, everything filtered through a soft lens. Slowly he slipped the robe from my shoulders, his lips and hands never stopping, and I thought I might faint from wanting, my heart racing and breath shallow with desire. An ache deep in my abdomen throbbed with a force I'd never known before. He stood me up, the robe dropped, and the cool night air, my sudden nakedness, made me stop for a moment. I'd never felt so exposed. I felt a squeeze of fear in my chest.

"My God, you're beautiful."

The old demons began to claw at me as my hands began to fold across my chest, and I started to pull away. But Adam stood quickly, slipping off his jeans until he was naked, too, pulling me into him. His skin was like fire on mine, and it was the most beautiful feeling. Gently he laid me down on the bed without letting go.

He was on top of me then, his eyes blazing into mine with such love. I wouldn't allow my thoughts to stray, as I always had before. I counted silently for distraction, forcing my muscles to stay relaxed by tightening and letting go, letting myself enjoy the feel of him as he slowly began to enter me. There was some pain, but my heart focused on one thing: This man loves me. This man is my husband.

HOW COULD I POSSIBLY SLEEP? Despite the wine and the bit of Xanax, every nerve in my body hummed with joy. I wanted to open the windows and shout it to the world. I knew now what I'd been missing. I was Adam's wife now, truly.

It wasn't perfect. How could it be? But I believed it would be okay with time. I would have to keep working at it. For a moment, I was afraid to look up at him, remembering what had happened last time, seeing a face that terrified me. But it didn't happen.

I got up to pee, not turning on the light. The room was freezing, and I went to shut the window. For a moment I looked out at the cemetery, lit up by the pearly glow of a full moon. It was beautiful, not scary at all. Even the river shimmered like silver as it curled toward the bridge. My eyes traveled then up to the highest point, and it was as if the marble monument shone from within, a beacon that could be seen from afar.

My breath caught as something crossed in front of it, the light shining right through it. I blinked, widening my eyes to focus better, and it was gone.

Adam would no doubt say it was college kids again, somehow explain it away. But I couldn't tell Adam. And in that moment, sitting on the window seat in the dark, I wouldn't have believed him. It was her. She was reaching out to me.

CHAPTER 20

February 1886

T ILLIE WAS FINALLY FAMILIAR with the maze of rooms in the basement of the Centenary Collegiate Institute. Walking through the halls now, which felt more like dark tunnels, she passed the laundry and drying rooms, where linens were hung each and every day and the smell of dampness and soap lingered. The ladies who worked there fussed all the time about the harsh lye and the constant dampness, but Tillie always took a deep breath when nearby. It was the smell of cleanliness, something she loved.

There was hardly ever anyone up and about in the kitchen at this hour except perhaps Bridget or Daisy, another kitchen maid. Mrs. Ruckle might poke her head in at any time, as if checking to make sure they were about their work. The cook and his assistant were at least a half hour later, waiting for them to get all the preparations ready in the kitchen. Tillie had never met a male cook before and thought there was something odd about a man cooking three meals a day for the entire seminary. But Bridget said it was a plum job and not easy. It paid well to boot, so of course it would be a man's lot.

She walked into the kitchen, and sure enough, there was Bridget.

"Hope you've got all your drawers on 'cause you'll have to fetch your own potatoes today. The fella who took Mr. Alsop's place up and quit."

It wasn't the first time Tillie would have to go to the potato cellar out in the barn, where the potatoes that were harvested in the early fall were stored through winter. It would take too much time now to go up and get her coat, so she grabbed one from the hook in the janitor's room and ran out the building toward the barn. The coat didn't even help. No matter how many petticoats and drawers she donned, it seemed the wind bit right through to her bones.

Opening the barn door, she ventured inside, though it was still dark and she could barely see, despite the gas lamps in the back of the institute. Suddenly she hit something with her foot, and as she began to fall, she heard a groan and then a belch. A moment later, the tramp stumbled to his feet, swaying.

"Begone, you beggar," she shouted. "You've had your night's sleep."

The bum staggered outside, and Tillie filled the potato sack as quickly as she could, praying there weren't others in the dark corners of the barn she couldn't see. The tramps often begged at the back kitchen door or asked for a place to spend the night. Normally they were harmless, but still, she knew what drink could do to a man, especially a desperate one.

Back in the building, she dropped the sack in the kitchen, went to return the coat back to its hook in the janitor's room, and once again halted in her tracks. Jimmy Titus was shoveling coal into the open boilers, shirt off and sweating, his skin red from the heat. He'd been giving her surly looks ever since she'd come in late. Quickly she hung up the coat, and before he turned around, she was gone.

Later on, after the last of the breakfast pots were washed up, she headed upstairs to clean herself up a bit. Passing the staircase that led up to the ladies' quarters, she heard something that caused her to halt. It was music, but this was a different sort than she'd ever heard. She waited a moment and the song ended, but then another started. It wasn't a formal program, the likes of which they had some evenings and all the girls would dress up in their finest to attend. It was too early in the day for that. But it was nothing she'd ever heard at a musical show.

As she crept up the staircase, it grew louder, and before she knew it, she was in the hallway of the ladies' quarters, the music seeming to touch her bones and vibrate within her. A woman sang in the highest-pitched voice she'd ever heard, and though it was a language she couldn't understand, it sounded so beautiful and heartbreaking, it brought tears to Tillie's eyes. There was pain in that voice, and longing. Tillie leaned against the wall and let the music fill her. She felt a sob rise up through her chest, and just at that moment, the music stopped. She opened her eyes.

"What are you doing here?"

"Oh," she gasped in alarm and stood up straight again.

One of the ladies, still in her nightgown and robe, stared at her from the open doorway of a room. Tillie lifted her apron and wiped her eyes quickly.

"I'm sorry, miss. I'll be leaving. I just heard that music, and I didn't know what it was."

"Why, it's opera, of course. Haven't you ever heard it before?"

"No, I haven't."

Just then another girl appeared and looked at Tillie, then at the girl in the doorway. Tillie remembered her. She was the one coming across the parlor the day the perfume drummer was there. To shoo her away, no doubt.

"I'm sorry, miss. I was just telling this lady that it was the music that drew me up here. I'm leaving right now."

"No, don't go. Lila, don't you have your Latin class in a half hour?"

Lila gave the girl a sour look, turned, and shut the door.

"Do you like opera?" the girl then asked Tillie.

"I...I think so. I've never heard it before. Was that you singing it?"

"I'm practicing for my class. Come and hear one more."

"Oh, I dare not. I must get back downstairs before I'm missed."

"I'll sing something short. It helps me to have an audience, as I get nervous singing sometimes in front of people. You can say you were in the water closet if anyone asks. Who will know?" She gave Tillie such a kind smile that she couldn't resist.

"Perhaps just the one song."

"By the way, my name is Faith. Welcome to the halls of Sigma Epsilon Phi. We're a very modern sorority."

Faith remembered her, too, from that day and said she had

not been about to shoo her. She was going to welcome her, as she thought the female help was treated quite poorly. And then she said all women needed to stand up more for themselves, and she had ideas about that.

* * *

FOR THE REST OF THAT DAY, Tillie felt as if she were floating in a new world. The music played in her head, though all was silent save for the usual sounds of the seminary: footsteps overhead, the thundering of the boilers, steam rushing through the pipes, the endless clatter of pots and pans in the kitchen. But above it all, Tillie heard the beautiful voice of Faith singing as that woman in the opera *Florinda*, as if she were haunting her soul.

Loneliness dug into the pit of her belly. She missed her sisters, though she'd just seen them a few weeks ago. Above all, she missed her ma. Her ma worked as a domestic at a farm outside of town, and Tillie saw her every so often. But her ma wasn't really a part of her life anymore, not since she'd left them. No, what Tillie really longed for was a sweetheart, someone to love her, someone to take care of her and share a life.

Sometimes she felt so tired just trying to survive. Even here, where it felt like a dream at first to be living and sleeping in such a nice place, at moments it hit her like a mule kick seeing all these girls, like her cousins, with all their pretty store-bought dresses and music lessons and classes and opportunities in life that she'd never have.

Again her eyes filled with tears, and she wiped them quickly with her apron. Oh, Tillie, you damn fool. She knew what it was. The lady singing the opera, the cramps low in her belly, and the tiredness and moodiness that came with it. It would pass. And tomorrow she'd hopefully be waiting on the servants' tables upstairs.

As she neared the kitchen door to the back of the grounds, she saw the milk wagon pull up. A moment later she opened the door to let Elvin Cutler in with the day's delivery. Imagine her surprise when instead she saw Frank Weeder, the young man who'd given her a ride back to Lubber's Run.

"Why, Tillie Smith!"

His cheeks were pink from the cold, and his green eyes sparkled as he looked at her with a smile. He'd remembered her name.

"Well, hello, Mr. Weeder. What happened to Mr. Cutler?"

"It seems he had a bit of an accident, which makes this my lucky day indeed. What a pleasure it is to be seeing you again so soon."

Tillie felt something lift in her chest. "And it's a pleasure to see you again, too, Mr. Weeder."

CHAPTER 21

ADAM HIRED A FEW HIGH SCHOOL BOYS to help with the Memorial Day preparations. With the auction over, I found myself with too much free time once again. Despite my repeated offers to help with the cemetery office—my fingers were itching to get in there and organize it—Adam was adamant he could handle it. I sat on the big porch with my coffee one warm morning, rocking and thinking about what I might do. I'd dropped my cards at every attorney's and realtor's office in town and still not one call. In the distance I could hear the drone of lawn mowers across the cemetery.

Just then the bells of the college rang, and my thoughts turned to Tillie. It was hard with all this free time not to. There were so many unanswered questions and so many things that didn't add up. Had James Titus really killed her? Was it one or two other men? And why did people insinuate Tillie didn't have a good reputation?

But there was one thing I did not question, one thing I felt deeply in my heart was true. Tillie Smith was trying to make a better life for herself.

Despite my unease at not finding steady work locally, I wondered if this was yet another coincidence. The college bells stopped ringing the hour. It was nine o'clock, and I went inside and got dressed. I was just going to explore, I told myself. That's all.

THIRTY MINUTES LATER I TURNED OFF Main Street onto Church Street, and there in the distance a few blocks up I saw the college.

How many times before that final night had Tillie walked these same blocks? I stopped on Jefferson Street before the front of the campus. I'd only really seen the side of it when we were at Helen's party. The grounds were beautiful. Huge old trees flanked either side of the light brick building that stretched across nearly an entire block, rising up to the gold dome, which shimmered in the morning sunlight. I walked up the front steps of the beautiful portico and through the double mahogany doors. I paused a moment at a front desk, but the woman was busy, so after a few moments I began wandering.

The front parlors were beautiful, spacious and open, one room leading into another, with tasteful formal furnishings that lent a Victorian air to it all. As I meandered through, I noticed the old photographs on the walls of some of the former college presidents and distinguished alumni.

In the last room, which was massive, stretching from the front of the building to the back, I stood there imagining the formal events and recitals that took place in this room. I noticed a glass case against the wall and walked over to it. It was filled with historic mementos: china and silverware from the early 1900s, a dance programme, literary magazines, and lots of photographs from throughout the century. In the midst of it all lay a charred piece of wood. Then I saw the photo of this main building engulfed in flames.

Reading through the captions, I realized that this wasn't the original building where Tillie had worked. That had burned almost to the ground on Halloween night in 1900, and this building was erected on its foundation. An earlier photograph of the original building was much more austere, with a gothic air about it that reminded me of old horror movies.

I wandered downstairs to the basement area, which held offices now, and made my way through winding corridors. Just before the rear entrance, I stopped in front of a little coffee bar, and my mouth dropped open. Above the entrance hung a sign: Tillie's Café. A bolt of anger shot through me. I'd heard the talk several times about Tillie's ghost roaming the college, and of course I saw the evidence of partying college kids at her grave.

But here was yet more evidence that her violent death had become almost a mockery. As I peeked in at the people sipping their drinks, reading or chatting, I wanted to go inside and yell at them. It seemed sacrilegious. What had happened to Tillie had become little more than local legend and entertainment, with hardly a thought to what she had suffered.

I walked out the back of the building, scanning the rear of the campus, the light brick dorms and classroom buildings scattered among grassy quads lined with large old trees. Of course, none of it had been there in Tillie's time, just the original austere building and some outbuildings. But this was the same ground Tillie had walked, where she had fetched potatoes or simply stepped outside to catch a breath of air. It was the very same ground she had walked that night she left on April eighth, having no idea she would never return alive.

Turning in all directions, I looked for anything that might resemble an old barn because that's where they originally thought she was killed, Mrs. Stewart's barn, but there wasn't anything. I saw a sign for the library then and headed that way, but just before I got there, a strange, unsettled feeling crept over me. I stopped beside a huge old oak. Somewhere within feet of where I stood, Tillie's body had been found. I scoured the ground, even closing my eyes and praying to somehow know where. Nothing. I put my hand on the trunk of the tree, pressing into the bark until it almost pierced my palm. The tree most likely had been there that night. I wondered what it had witnessed.

Finally I turned and walked up the library steps. It was quiet inside the library, which was built in the fifties and had large windows looking over the campus. I assumed there were finals going on or the spring semester had ended already.

"May I help you?"

I looked over toward the woman behind the checkout desk. "I was wondering if you might have some information on Tillie Smith."

"We do have some information on Tillie and the trial. She worked here, you know."

"Yes, she was a potato peeler, right?"

"Well, that I didn't know. I'm actually not from around here, and I just started this job a few months ago, so I don't know much, but I have heard about her ghost."

"Really? What have you heard?"

"Oh, that her ghost haunts one of the dorms and follows girls when they go out alone to protect them. And apparently people have heard the piano playing in the little theatre when there's no one in there at all."

"Do you think any of it's true? I mean, I guess you'd have to believe in ghosts."

She shrugged. "Who knows? But apparently even professors have seen and heard things going back many years."

"I'm actually new in town, too. I saw her monument at the cemetery, and then, believe it or not, a few hours later, I found myself in the janitor's house—you know, James Titus, the one convicted of killing her. I've become a bit obsessed with finding out about her."

"Oh my, I can imagine. I'll try to find whatever I can. I'm actually in charge of the archives, but unfortunately they're in disarray because the college needed more office space downstairs, so everything has been boxed up since before I started here. It's going to take me months to get it all organized again, but I'll see what I can do."

"Whatever you can find from the year 1886 would be most helpful."

"I'm Colleen, by the way."

"I'm Rachel. And if you wouldn't mind, I'd like to keep my search quiet."

Colleen laughed. "I don't know anyone I could tell anyway. But of course."

Luckily, Helen or Gran wouldn't find out about this. Or Adam.

"In the meantime, we do have a book in our reference section, *Everyday Life in the 1800s*, that will at least give you the flavor of the period. Let me get it for you."

While Colleen was digging into the archives, I began reading the book she had gotten me. It definitely gave me a picture of what life was like for the years Tillie was alive. In the 1880s, I learned, the Brooklyn Bridge was completed and the Statue of Liberty erected. People actually used words like *pshaw* and *balderdash* and *high-falutin'* and *skedaddle*. Women's suffrage had begun, and even Prohibition, which I'd always thought was an early 1900s thing, was already in full swing and gaining support.

I heard footsteps coming up the stairs then. Colleen was back a moment later with an armful of material.

"Things are such a mess down there. I'm sorry. But I've found some articles reprinted from the time of the murder, though they aren't in any order, and certainly not everything that was printed back then. I also found some of the little booklets written by students each year, and while I don't have 1886, I do have a few from the year before and after, so it'll give you a true feel for campus life back then." She set everything on the table. "Oh, and this might interest you. Here's a map of the campus back then, including a Sanborn map of the layout of the building, which they needed for insurance purposes."

"Thank you."

"Are you writing an article about her?"

"Oh, no. As I said, I saw the monument and have had these strange coincidences happening, and I...I just want to know who she really was, you know? What was she like? What was life even like back then for a girl her age?"

"Pretty tough, I would imagine."

"I think so, yes. Well, thank you for all of this."

"Well, hopefully you'll find what you're looking for in some of that. Happy reading."

As I opened to the first page of material, I thought this would be anything but happy reading.

* * *

HOURS LATER, I LEFT THE LIBRARY after scanning through yearbooks and programs for musical events and socials from the 1800s, as well as stories compiled by the various graduating classes in little booklets. It was a privileged world for the students and seminarians, and I wondered how Tillie felt, surrounded by such advantages that were out of her reach.

I carried a large stack of photocopies, including the maps, which were big and had to be pieced together. My head was spinning, but I couldn't wait to get home to process some of the information.

Walking back inside the rear entrance to the basement of the main building, I stopped, knowing now from the old map that this was where the kitchen had been back then. Coming through the student lounge, a big open area filled with chairs and benches, I paused. It was late afternoon now, and no one was around. Sitting on a bench, I imagined what might have been in this very spot. A big wood cookstove? Wash sinks where they cleaned the day's dishes?

Was Tillie standing right where I now sat, peeling potatoes, dreaming about that better life she was working so hard to find? My head swam with snippets from the articles, and I was also overheated from the walk across campus on this unseasonably warm day. The cool quiet enveloped me, and closing my eyes, I began to doze. But then I felt something crawling across my scalp or touching my hair. Opening my eyes with a start, I looked around. Something was... different. Then I caught my reflection in a glass door. My hair stuck up as if full of static electricity.

"Are you here, Tillie?" I whispered softly.

Just then the eerie quiet was broken by footsteps, and a moment later, two giggling girls came through the lounge. I got up, smoothed my hair, and began walking back to the cemetery.

CHAPTER 22

February 1886

I T WAS LONG PAST THE LAST BELL, and Tillie lay in bed, wondering where Stella might be. She dare not go and ask Mrs. Ruckle if she'd been called home, for if she hadn't been, she'd be in trouble for certain.

The door opened slowly then, and Stella slipped in, quiet as a church mouse.

"Land sakes, Stella, you're throwing caution to the wind."

Stella sat on the side of Tillie's bed. "Oh, Tillie, promise you won't say a word to no one?"

"I promise."

"Caution won't be mattering for me much longer here."

"What are you saying?"

"I'm in love. I told you this fella's been sweet on me and all. We met one night when I was up in the chapel to clean up a bit after the choir practice. And, well, we been meetin' up there regular now, and he's so smart, Tillie."

"You mean he's a student?"

"Yes, and I know what Matron says and all that, but he's just the sweetest thing. Tonight he read a poem to me from Psalms. Told me I was all he could think about and wondered if he might really have a chance with me."

Tillie was sitting up now. "You'd best be careful, Stella. I know that one of these gents could change the world for the likes of us. I've thought about it, too, truly I have, but...it's not about to happen, don't ya see? They're of a different station. Why, even if your fella was of a mind to want to marry you, his folks would never allow it. And if Matron finds out, it'll be your job."

In the weeks since she'd started working at the institute, Tillie saw clearly that the likes of her, a kitchen maid, were never going to be good enough for one of the young men attending there. A dalliance, perhaps, was all she could hope for, and she wasn't going to get caught up in that. She'd heard the stories from Bridget, who'd been there five years now. A girl getting into trouble now and again. A job lost. And a young man graduating with no consequence.

But Stella was shaking her head. "Peter Mead has got a true Christian soul, Tillie, and is goin' to be a reverend. He believes God meant for us to both be here at the same time. He's not one of these fine dandies. He's here because of a scholarship, and he even works some with Janitor Titus. That's how he first noticed me. Besides, haven't you gotten awful friendly with that sorority girl? The one who wants you to attend the women's rights program by the suffragists? We're not so very different from them."

She wanted to say something about this Peter Mead trying to get familiar with her that day in the dining room, that he was not to be trusted. But she knew Stella would just accuse her of being jealous. And Stella knew she'd missed curfew. If she got angry enough...

"Yes, we are different, Stella," she said instead. "Those folks might preach about things changing and rights and all that, but that's all it is, talk. There are lots of fine fellas here in town. Why not come out with me tomorrow evening? I'm going to a revival meeting at the Free Methodist Meeting House up on Main Street. You could meet a fella more suitable."

"I shoulda known better. Peter told me not to be telling anyone 'cause no one would understand. We are meant to be together. And when he's a reverend, we'll move far away from here and have a fine house, and I won't have to be working anymore."

Wouldn't it be grand if such things could really happen? Tillie thought. It was hard not to get excited. Why, just that afternoon in her little bit of off time, she'd gone back up to the sorority girl's hall upstairs. Faith had actually come down to the kitchen while she was working and insisted she must hear about the Ladies Suffragist Movement. But when she started to protest, Faith had said loudly, "Why Tillie, we liberated the Negroes, why not women? Especially women like you." She'd quickly agreed then, only to get her gone before Mrs. Ruckle might show up.

But so much of what Faith had spouted had simply gone over her head. There were words she didn't understand and was too embarrassed to say so. She found herself more caught up in what the girls wore, how they smelled, even their hair. Faith had projects, and Tillie didn't want to be one of them.

THE NEXT EVENING, TILLIE WAS PLEASED as punch to see her old friend Annie Van Syckle waiting outside the Free Methodist Meeting House on Main Street. Didn't Annie look stylish in Mrs. Conover's store-bought hand-me-downs that Tillie gave Annie months ago because they'd been too small for her? Tillie lament-ed her grey muslin dress, the old navy frock coat, and the fraying muff that hardly kept her hands warm. But she had the hat that Faith had offered her, saying it would look much better on Tillie.

"So how are things at the Lamsons'?" she asked Annie as they waited for the doors to open. It was just beginning to snow, but there was little wind.

"Oh, the usual. The missus always complaining that my cooking is never good enough or hot enough, or the wash is too stiff. There's no pleasing that woman. No wonder the mister's got a roving eye."

"Has it been wandering to you?"

"Ha! When doesn't it?" Annie looked away a moment, then back at her. "You know, Tillie, he's not a bad man."

"Land sakes, Annie, you're not..."

Annie blushed. "It's nothing, really. And it passes the time. I get really lonely here away from my family. I'm not so daring to walk home like you. It's too far, so unless there's a wagon com-ing I can hitch, I never ever see them."

"'Course I know that, and how you feel. But you'd best be careful there, Annie. You know—"

"I know, I know. You don't have to remind me." Annie looked around and smiled again. "Ain't that why we're here, after all?"

The doors opened, and they went in and sat on a bench beside two sisters, Mary and Agnes Wright. Mary was a nurse but working as a domestic nearby and wanted to know all about the institute. But the preacher walked out to the pulpit then, and everyone hushed. At first he talked really soft, of God's love and forgiveness, but then Tillie's thoughts took off as he screamed of fire and brimstone and the just lot for those who didn't repent. She knew she wasn't a bad person, but like some here, she had moments she wasn't proud of, moments when she'd had few choices. She closed her eyes and asked for forgiveness from whoever might be listening up there, though she was never quite certain anyone was.

"That preacher was making the windows rattle," Annie laughed as they stepped outside afterward.

"A bit more dramatic than what we see at the seminary, but I guess they're preaching the same message. We'd best turn away from the temptations of this world before we take our last breath."

"But man alive, does he have to scream to the rafters about it?" Mary Wright chimed in, and they all laughed again.

"I bet even God in heaven was holding his ears," they heard a male voice say, and all turned.

And there was Frank Weeder.

"Why, Frank, I didn't see you in there."

"Hello, Tillie Smith. Fancy meeting you here."

Annie's eyebrows lifted, and then she gave Tillie a smile of approval.

"I was wondering if I might walk you back to the institute. That is, if your friends here don't mind."

"We'll be parting down by the post office anyway," Annie chimed in. "So it's no bother to us."

Frank looked at her.

"That would be nice," she said, and he offered her his arm.

The snow had stopped, but as they walked down Main Street toward the post office, Tillie slipped on a patch of it, and Frank held her tight, keeping her from falling.

"Thank you," she said as she caught her balance.

"You're welcome."

A block later, in the dark shadow of a tree on Church Street, Frank suddenly kissed her. He was strong and smelled nice, of bay rum like some of the seminary boys, and she felt warm and safe there in his arms. But when the bells rang the quarter hour, she told him she needed to hurry, and so they ran, he holding onto her arm, until they were through the front gate. Laughing and out of breath, they gazed at each other.

"Will you be my girl, Tillie?"

She didn't say a word at first. She'd never been anyone's girl. For a second she heard Faith saying, *We don't want to be owned by any man.*

"All right, Frank. I'll be your girl."

CHAPTER 23

MEMORIAL DAY DAWNED SOFT AND ROSY, a promise of summer in the morning air as I stepped onto the porch, thinking about the day ahead. In a few hours we'd walk through town and watch the parade, and then go to Aunt Helen's for a family picnic. Part of me wished we could just stay here, cocooned in the graveyard, fragrant with fresh-cut grass and flowering trees, and not have to face the rest of the world. Especially his aunt.

Adam left early to do a last survey of the cemetery, making sure veterans' graves were marked and flowers arranged properly. I had a French toast casserole baking in the oven, complete with blueberries and strawberries to make it look like a flag. I'd seen it on the cover of a women's magazine at the grocery store featuring Memorial Day recipes. When I picked it up and put it in the full cart on top of Adam's favorite foods, I felt my heart swell. I was a wife grocery shopping for her husband. I seemed as normal as anyone else on line. I wondered if anyone else had ever felt such joy checking out of a store. But I wasn't anyone else. I was a woman harboring a secret obsession.

"Smells good," Adam said coming onto the porch.

"I hope you like it."

Adam was quiet while we ate. I knew he was exhausted, working overtime while the plans for the mausoleum were being laid out. And of course getting the cemetery in the best shape possible for today, when hundreds of people would be here. I was the opposite, out of work with so much idle time on my hands. I began tackling the garden around the house, perennial beds his mother had once put in and that had gone to ruin in the years since she left. I didn't know much about plants and flowers, but it was a way to help out. Like my job, it was also the kind of physical work that let the mind relax and wander. And my thoughts and growing theories about Tillie took off.

Tillie, I'd learned, had a boyfriend. In a piece from a New York newspaper that Colleen had given me, Joseph Pulitzer's the *World*, Frank Weeder was described as "the formerly accepted beau of Tillie Smith on the few occasions she went out in the evening." My eyes of course locked on that word *formerly*. I had watched enough crime shows on television to know that the husband or boyfriend was usually the number one suspect. But Weeder had been cleared, it seemed. He'd been drinking with friends at Tineman's Grocery in town. Not only that, he wasn't considered clever enough to have committed such a crime.

I couldn't help imagining Tillie with her beau, walking into town for supper, hoping, perhaps, that something could come of their relationship. What other chances did a poor working girl have back then? A teacher or a wife, and Tillie didn't have the education to be a teacher.

"What are you thinking about?"

I looked up at Adam, a needle of guilt jabbing me. "Just... thinking about today."

"Don't let my aunt get to you, okay?" Obviously he'd miscon-strued my own silence. My guilty look.

"I won't. Promise."

"What do you think about going on a cruise for our honey-moon?"

"Oh...I've never been on one." In truth, I hadn't traveled much at all. "I thought you wanted to go to Europe."

"I did, but I started to think about how maybe it would be nicer to just relax on a ship, get waited on, not have to deal with trains and language issues. We can get off and island-hop and then get back on."

"Actually that sounds kind of nice. And probably a lot less expensive."

"It's not about the money," he said with an edge.

"I'm sorry. I didn't mean anything by that, Adam. When do you want to do it?"

"How does September sound?"

September was the start of hurricane season. It was also pushing the honeymoon back a few months yet again, which made me wonder. "September sounds fine," I said instead.

Of course underneath it all was my insecurity over sex. We'd been intimate more, and I was still struggling at times with what felt like aftershocks from my rape. The act of loving was so similar to the act of violence that nearly destroyed me. Adam was being patient. But maybe underneath he was starting to have second thoughts.

* * *

AT NINE O'CLOCK WE WALKED through the stone arch and turned toward Main Street. Mountain Avenue was closed to traffic in front of the cemetery, and people were beginning to line the road with chairs, waiting for the parade. At Water Street, Adam paused.

"Do you want to show me where you lived back when I saved your bike?" he asked with a little smile. He confessed he barely remembered the incident.

"How about another time?" I suggested, not wanting to cast a shadow on this day. "I don't want to be late."

By the time we got up to Main Street, both sides were filled with chairs, strollers, and clusters of spectators. Flowering baskets of petunias hung from the lanterns that stretched all down Main Street, and flags were draped everywhere. It seemed everyone smiled or waved to Adam, and he introduced me every chance he got. We stopped in front of Stella's Café.

"How's this?" Adam asked.

I stood there beside my husband, surrounded by the people of this small town, and it hit me: I was a part of this life now. "Looks good to me."

We settled in with the crowd. Before I knew it, the local high school marching band came down the street followed by a twirler and the parade was on its way. There were fire trucks and classic cars, cheerleaders, and more bands. The Colonial

Musketeers, a local drum and bugle corps reminiscent of a Revolutionary War army, was amazing. Then there was a float of local dignitaries tossing bags of M&Ms. Of course there were the veterans, in all sorts of uniforms and of all ages.

The parade went on for over an hour, and then Adam took my hand and we began walking down to the cemetery again. By the time we were back at the stone arch, the grassy fields on either side of the bridge were filled with throngs of people. We stood near the river waiting for the last of the parade to arrive before the ceremony would begin. There was a hushed expectation in the crowd, and then it was silent.

A covered platform sat below the bridge, and I watched a few dignitaries and several veterans climb the dais. The mayor welcomed everyone, then turned the microphone over to an old man, an underage veteran of World War II. In a trembling voice and wearing his Marine uniform, he spoke of the friends who had died beside him, the shattered knee that sent him home, and how he would do it all again today for his country. He handed the microphone to a young man who looked to be barely out of high school and who announced he'd just received orders to be deployed to Afghanistan. The crowd cheered their support, and I imagined his mother's mixed pride and terror.

Then the young soldier helped the old man off the dais, and together they carried a small raft covered with red, white, and blue flowers to the river's edge. A lone soldier up on the hill began playing taps, and the men set the raft into the water. As we all watched in silence, they stood there as it floated slowly down the river to the haunting bugle notes until it disappeared. Tears stung my eyes, and I turned to see Adam's eyes brimming. He squeezed my hand.

"My father was in Viet Nam," he whispered. "Gran told me he was never the same afterward."

No one served and came back unscathed, I knew. And here we were paying tribute, feeling such a sense of gratitude, filled with the magnitude of what others suffered for our own freedom. It was one of the most emotional moments I could remember. The crowd began to disperse, many of them walking across the wooden bridge and into the cemetery to visit graves or simply honor the fallen soldiers buried there. Adam stood watching them, and I recalled his telling me the other night over dinner how this day was originally called Decoration Day. It had been established shortly after the Civil War ended so that the nation could decorate the graves of the war dead with flowers. In that moment I understood his pride in how it looked today, and in his calling.

I turned and saw a woman staring at Adam. She was petite, with short blonde hair. Her eyes shifted to me and widened. Quickly, she looked away. I turned to ask Adam who she was, but he was shaking hands with one of the soldiers, who looked about our age. When I turned back again, she was gone.

"I never thought you'd be back, Miller. I heard your band was making some waves in Nashville," the soldier said to Adam in a teasing tone.

"Nah, just playing around after college."

"Well, you're doing a great job here. I think your father and grandfather would be proud."

"Thanks, Ryan."

Adam took my hand, and we began walking home.

"You played in Nashville?" I asked. "You were that good?"

He laughed. "Do you know how many bands go to Nashville? Maybe ten percent make it. That makes ninety percent that don't."

"But that was what you wanted?" I was stunned. "You didn't intend to stay here?"

He stopped and looked at me. "I needed to get away from here for a while. It's a small town. I needed to try something else. And in the end, I grew up. This is where I belong. It's as simple as that."

But I knew that it wasn't.

I HAD A GOOD TIME AT THE PICNIC, thanks in part because Aunt Helen was on the phone most of the afternoon upstairs trying to save a huge deal and the buyer didn't seem to care it was a holiday. It was also a much smaller crowd than our wedding party.

I learned to play quoits, a game that originated in the Slate Belt of nearby Pennsylvania and not all that different from horseshoes. Adam and I even won a few. When we sat at a picnic table in the yard across from each other eating hot dogs and corn on the cob, he reached over at one point and slowly wiped a dab of mustard from my upper lip. It was his way, I knew, of making amends for being cranky.

When Gran got tired, I wheeled her into her room for a rest. As she settled in her recliner, I pulled an afghan over her. "Gran, I want to tell you how sorry I am for upsetting you that day I went to see Mrs. Freeman. Please know I didn't mean to hurt her, or you." I left Helen out of it, but she didn't notice.

"It's all right. I understand curiosity about all that. Believe me, it wasn't as if I didn't wonder about him myself growing up and being friends with Marion. It was so difficult for her. None of our friends were allowed in that house."

"That's pretty awful." I was working up the courage to ask a few questions since she seemed willing to talk a bit. But then her eyes started closing.

I sat there awhile, just enjoying her presence. I'd never had a grandmother or a grandfather. No aunts or uncles, or brothers or sisters. I was lucky to be part of this family now. I wondered about Gran and Aunt Helen, two such different women it was hard to believe they were mother and daughter. But then my own mother and I had been so different. Although maybe that would have changed if she'd lived longer. If we'd had a chance to see what our relationship would have evolved into.

Adam came to get me a short while later to join the party again. An hour later, when it was barely dusk, the children ran around the yard with sparklers, fiery embers of color flying as they waved them in the air, whooping and laughing. It was such a lovely sight, their innocent beauty, their simple delight. I saw Adam across the yard with a beer in his hand, laughing and talking to another guy. He looked happy now, relaxed. I thought about what he had said about leaving his music behind. Then I pictured the blonde-haired woman looking at him with...longing. Was she an old girlfriend? Someone who'd liked him from afar? There was still so much we didn't know about each other.

Someone gave Gran a sparkler then, and she laughed as she twirled it in circles. It was hard to fathom that she had known James Titus. I thought about everything I'd learned so far about life back in Tillie's era and the seminary where she worked, and died, right across the street from where I now stood. As far removed as the murder was, the whole story really wasn't; 1952, when Titus died, wasn't all that long ago. My mother had been born that year.

CHAPTER 24

I COULD TELL ADAM WAS GETTING A LITTLE ANNOYED with my efforts at organizing everything in the house. And then doing it again. We were two people who'd lived alone for a long time, each set in our ways. He continually left doors and drawers open, the top off the toothpaste, and often just threw his clothes on a chair at night instead of ten feet across the room to the hamper. I tried my best not get annoyed.

With nothing else to occupy my time and trying so hard to keep a distance from Tillie, I was probably the only person on the planet looking forward to jury duty. Apparently, when you change your address for your driver's license, you're thrown right at the top of the jury duty pool. Adam drove me early on a Monday morning to the courthouse in Belvidere, twenty minutes west of town.

I was stunned at its quaint beauty. The courthouse was on one side of a town green that was filled with towering trees and benches, as well as a gazebo in its center. Colorful Victorians lined the streets surrounding the square. Even the side streets were lined with vintage homes, complete with porches, cupolas, and picket fences.

"This is like a mini Cape May," I said, looking across at the green. "I've never seen so many beautiful Victorians. They must be stuffed with wonderful treasures."

"You miss working, don't you?"

"I do. There's always that thrill of not knowing what's been hidden away in old boxes and forgotten drawers. You know, once I found a diamond ring in a bucket full of nails under a workbench. Another time I discovered an original Jackson Pollock tucked behind an old screen door in an attic."

"I'm sorry you haven't gotten any real work yet."

"Well, if it doesn't happen soon, I think I'm going to have to start thinking of something else."

"Is there anything else you're interested in?"

"I'm not unhappy, Adam, if that's what you're worried about. I love what I do. Did. But...being with you means a lot more to me than a job."

"We need to get you a car."

"Not until I can pay for it myself."

"We have the wedding money. That belongs to you, too."

"I'll be fine. Don't worry."

He gave me a long look, then leaned over and kissed me softly. "Give me a call when you're done, and I'll come pick you up."

THE COURTHOUSE WAS OLD AND DARK, reminding me of an elementary school I went to decades ago. After going through the security check, I made my way upstairs to a big, brightly lit room with about forty other people. I checked in and was given an ID card. As soon as the rest of the room was settled, the lights dimmed, and we watched a video about the process of being a juror and the importance of the work ahead should we be chosen. Deciding someone's fate, someone's future, was a daunting task. And of course I couldn't help thinking of James Titus.

When the video was over, we were called to the courtroom. It was a big room with light blue walls, wide white woodwork, and wooden benches that were as uncomfortable as the pews in an old church. The ceilings were high, and before us on a raised dais sat the judge at her bench.

"Good morning, ladies and gentleman. I'd like to thank you all for being here and offering your service. This is a historic courtroom, you may be interested to know. Trials have been held here since the middle of the nineteenth century...."

My eyes widened and I nearly gasped, realizing where I was.

This was the very same courtroom where James Titus was tried for the murder of Tillie Smith. Stroking the wooden bench, I looked all around the room. Tillie's mother or Titus's wife could have sat in this very same spot. James Titus himself would have been up there at the defense attorney's desk. Suddenly all boredom disappeared.

As the judge went on, explaining that our service could be expected to last a month or more, I got that otherworldly feeling that sometimes came over me in an old house. There was a sense of history, a feeling of the past. And of course thinking about that theory of time being a river and just behind the last bend is the past, just ahead the future. If I perhaps turned at the right moment, would I see it? Was God once again winking at me?

* * *

I WAS GLAD I HAD BROUGHT A SANDWICH. It had started raining, so I sat in the holding room and ate it with a cup of tea, perusing my copy of *Everyday Life in the 1800s*. In the chapter on "Courtship and Marriage," I was stunned to learn that not only was premarital sex common, but about one in four women were pregnant when they married. Most surprising of all was that abortion wasn't really uncommon, not that women talked about it. It was only in the latter part of the 1800s that states began to one by one enact laws against it. I was stunned because this was the Victorian era, after all.

The author went on to say that unless you were one of the privileged wealthy, life was pretty damn hard. I imagined Tillie peeling potatoes day after day, her poor hands. I pulled out the photograph of her and began to study it once again.

"That's Tillie Smith!"

I looked up to find a woman staring at the picture.

"Yes, it is. Do you know of her?"

"I do, yes. I went to Centenary."

"I'm sort of obsessed with her," I admitted.

"Well, you wouldn't be the first one."

"This portrait is the only picture of her."

"No, it isn't."

"What...what do you mean? Everyone I've talked to has said that. Even at the historical society."

"There's a picture of her taken with our sorority."

"What?"

"Oh, not our sorority now, but back in her era. Ours is the oldest sorority still in existence at the college."

"Are you sure it's the same Tillie? I've seen pictures of one or two girls with the same name at the historical society and got really excited, but one was from around 1900, and the other looked nothing like her."

"Oh no, it's her—same hair and face. She's wearing one of those black maid uniforms, you know with the lace cap and apron."

"So...maybe she was working her way up out of the kitchen?"

"What do you mean?"

"I'm trying to figure out her life. And I keep thinking, who would want to peel potatoes forever? She must have gone there hoping for more. I mean, what were the options for a poor girl back then?"

The woman shrugged.

"I'm sorry," I said, standing then and extending a hand. "I'm Rachel Miller."

"Nice to meet you. I'm Regina Edwards."

"Would you by any chance have a copy of that picture?"

Regina shook her head. "But I'm still friends with the gal who was our historian. I think when they renovated the Reeves building, she took all of our memorabilia. Most of the sororities had their archives in that basement."

"Could you ask and let me know?"

"Sure. I'll call her tonight."

"In case we don't get called back for tomorrow, here's my number. And thank you. I really appreciate this. I know it doesn't seem like a big deal, but it just amazes me that all these years, there's been another picture of Tillie and no one knew about it."

I couldn't wait to see her in it. Would her eyes haunt me, as they did in the photo I had? Would there be a smile? Some hint of how her life was going?

During the long, idle hours of waiting that afternoon as one juror after another was questioned, I couldn't help but wonder what else there might be about Tillie hidden in the folds of time, just waiting to be discovered.

CHAPTER 25

March 1886

TILLIE WAS ALONE IN THE KITCHEN, soaking her battered hands in warm water after the dinner hour, when she heard her name whispered. She turned and saw one of the sorority girls peeking in the door.

"Emmaline," she said in surprise.

"Shhh. Please, Tillie, I need your help. I've got a friend who needs medical attention," she whispered.

Before Tillie could even ask why she didn't go to the nurse on staff, Emmaline's eyes filled.

"Your friend, she's in a bit of trouble?"

Emmaline nodded. "I know you've told us stories about the canal and the mine workers and how things are a bit rough and tumble out there where you're from. I just thought, well, that you might know of where my friend could get some help."

Tillie nodded. "I do. I've heard talk of an old gypsy woman out near Stanhope who might help her."

Then Emmaline's lips began to quiver. "Will she...will it hurt?"

"If it's early enough, it'll just be some herbs and not much worse than a bad monthly. That's what I've heard."

Emmaline gave her a weak smile. "I'm so grateful. You seem to know everything, Tillie."

"I don't, Emmy. I wish I did, for that matter. I just...I heard things from others." And saw a few as well.

"Faith is right about you. She wants to make you an honorary sorority sister."

"Honest, Emmy?"

Emmaline held her hand over her heart. "You've brought a

bit of the real world to our stuffy little group. Maybe one of these days, we'll be able to do something for you."

Emmy took her hands and squeezed, and Tillie let out a little wail.

"Oh, Tillie, your hands are a mess."

She pulled her hands under her apron to hide them.

"I was just soaking them a bit. They get pretty nicked up with all the potatoes I have to peel each day."

"What an awful life," Emmy said. Then her own hand flew to her mouth. "I'm sorry, Tillie. I didn't mean it that way. I just...it's just you've got such a hard life. Compared to the lot of us."

"I'm not complaining," Tillie said stiffly. "I'm getting ahead here."

And didn't she have dreams, just like the rest of them?

Last week, when Mrs. Ruckle was gone for the evening visiting a relative, Tillie had gone upstairs to Faith's room. Over a decanter of wine that someone had "borrowed" from the chapel, they'd all gotten a bit tipsy, then began talking about their hopes for the future. Mostly they were the same: a handsome husband, good-natured children, a nice home with an indoor water closet. When it was Tillie's turn, the flushed cheeks and bright eyes all turned to her, and she'd hesitated. Her dreams were the same, and she could even see it: a little house with Frank, some children, perhaps her ma and sisters even. A good life. Yet it seemed silly to say it aloud. When she did finally, they all began to giggle until they'd forgotten what started it and ended up collapsing in their chairs in hysteria.

"We always have the best time when you're here," Faith had said when she left to go to her room, long past lights out and praying that Mrs. Ruckle, or worse yet Jimmy Titus, wouldn't see her.

She'd collapsed in her bed that night, tipsy as the lot of them, despite swearing she'd never drink, not after seeing what it did to her pa. And if it weren't for the drink, she wouldn't have shared her dreams and watched them laugh at her. She realized she was nothing more than entertainment for them. Why she made the lot of them laugh, or shocked them with stories of Saxton Falls and the canal and mine workers.

But then Faith had given her the kid gloves, and she'd nearly cried. They were hand-me-downs for sure, made for hands smaller than hers. But she managed to get them on, and they were soft as a baby's bottom, the gorgeous leather a lovely shade of cream. Her hands looked lovely in them, and all her bad feelings had slipped away then.

* * *

IT WAS TRUE. TILLIE WAS NOW an honorary sorority sister. And today she'd have her very first picture taken! She was going to put on the parlor maid's uniform she'd borrowed from one of the girls who was off that day. Faith said perhaps she could be in one of the photographs. She was excited, but nervous, too. She'd never had her picture taken in her life, not like her cousins, who had their likenesses at all ages covering the walls of their grand house.

Pulling on the long black skirt and top with the ruffled collar and the white lace apron, Tillie looked in the small mirror above the washstand. Oh, her hair. She pulled it back tight, fastening more than a dozen pins to tame the wild wisps springing out everywhere, and then she donned the little lace cap. There, didn't she look like a proper parlor maid? She smiled, then caught sight of her teeth, not her best feature, and decided to keep her mouth closed.

Just then the door opened.

"Why, look at you, Tillie Smith, all dressed up. And where might you be heading, to a costume ball?"

"No, Stella, I'm just goin' upstairs to help the sorority ladies with the portraits. I didn't want to smell like potatoes or look like a kitchen hand."

"Well, isn't that what you are, then?"

Tillie stared at her. Things hadn't been right between them since she'd warned Stella about Peter Mead.

"I'm sorry I said what I did about that fellow you were going to meet in the chapel, Stella. It wasn't my place."

Stella gave her a hard look. Then she sat on the edge of her bed. "I knew you'd be jealous, and it's all right. I imagine I would be, too, with the advantages about to come to me."

"I wish you the best, Stella." And she did. Hadn't she had grand visions herself when she first arrived? Thinking perhaps she'd meet some nice student? But that was nothin' but a lark.

"And what about your Frank Weeder, then?" Stella said, softening now since Tillie had apologized.

"Well, he ain't quite a gent," she said with a laugh, "as his talk is sometimes a bit colorful. But he's good to me; I can't deny that." She didn't say that he was talking about a future for the two of them.

"I hope so, Tillie, for your sake."

"I'd best be going now. If anyone's looking about for me, would you just say I wasn't feeling quite right? I'll be back down soon as I can." She knew she was taking an awful chance.

"Sure thing, Tillie."

The sorority girls were all dressed in their finest gowns, hair swept up in gorgeous dos and smelling as sweet as a field of wild flowers. Tillie, excited in her starched uniform, stood in the doorway at first.

"Tillie, come here. You're to stand on the end in the back row," Faith called out.

Faith, of course, was in charge of setting up the scene. The photographer fiddled with his camera, a big contraption the likes of which Tillie had never seen before. Faith fiddled with each girl's posture, and when she stood before Tillie, turning her a bit to the side, she whispered, "You look just lovely, Tillie."

When it was time to finally take the picture, the photographer told them to stand as still as statues and try not to breathe. In the hush of those long seconds, Tillie could almost hear her heart beating. She pictured herself as she would appear in the photograph and felt proud. For all her talk about some-how, someway making a better life for herself, wasn't this proof enough that it was possible?

Drifting off to sleep that night, she told herself what she wanted now was a proper photograph of herself. Dressed like a lady, as her cousins had done so many times. She'd have to get herself some better clothes, not her homespun. Perhaps take in some mending on the side to afford it all. Until then, she'd have the picture with the sorority sisters.

But she'd never be one of them. Not really, no matter how much she helped them. In the end there was only one person to help Tillie, and that was herself.

CHAPTER 26

I WAS STUNNED WHEN ADAM BROUGHT ME HOME after the first day of jury duty to see a white van in front of the house. "Who's here?" I asked.

"No one." He glanced at me out of the corner of his eye, but I could see the little smile beginning.

"You...you seriously got me a van today?"

"I've been selfish. I can't expect you to use the truck when it's convenient for me. You need your own vehicle for work."

I wanted to say..."But I have no work." I didn't, though. I didn't want to ruin the look of delight on Adam's face. I knew in that moment he was trying to make up for delaying the honeymoon.

"That was really sweet. Thank you."

He shrugged. "You're worth it. It's not new, but it should last awhile. And you've got plenty of space in the back to haul things. I took the seats out. They're in the garage if you want them back in at any point."

"It must've taken you all day to make this happen."

"Not quite."

While he showered and I started dinner, my cell rang. I recognized Dr. Roberti's number and felt a bolt of alarm in my stomach. She'd already called me a few days after my visit to tell me my pap was fine.

"I wanted to check in and see how you're doing," she said now.

"Things are getting better. A little easier."

"I want to encourage you again to go for counseling, Rachel. I think it would help you. You know, one in four women are sexually assaulted in their lives. But by far the highest statistic is among college freshman. You're not alone."

I hadn't known that.

"And they're often made to feel as if it was their fault—for drinking, going to a party, or simply trusting someone and getting into a vulnerable situation. The shame and the guilt can linger for years."

"I know. I did feel that way for a long time. More stupid than anything, really, but...I'm coming out of it all finally. I have a new life. I don't want to go back there. I'm sorry."

"That's all right. But if you ever change your mind, we're here."

I knew she was right. There were still moments when Adam touched me suddenly that I flinched. Nights when I had to keep my eyes open and make sure it was Adam, my muscles betraying me and trying to tighten up. Despite what I told the doctor, all these years later, I could still see the snickering smiles and hear the whispers as I left my dorm for the last time. *Slut.* He was handsome and popular, and God knows what lies he spread about me.

I'd fought these memories for years. But now they were coming back again with force, the sounds, the smells, the pictures in my mind...and I knew why. It was Tillie. The more I dug into her tragedy, the more my own was floating back to the surface. One more reason I should let her go. But I couldn't. It was almost beyond obsession now. I was like an addict, and I had to find more.

* * *

I DROVE MYSELF BACK TO JURY DUTY the next morning in the white van. As soon as I walked into the holding room, I went right over to Regina at the coffee maker. "Any luck?"

She shook her head. "Sara remembers seeing the photo, too, but doesn't have a copy of it. We're going to have to see if the boxes are still someplace at the college, but she doesn't have a good feeling. During the renovations, they threw lots of old boxes out."

"Oh no."

"It's kind of sickening, isn't it?"

"I'd just like to see her in another setting, in other clothes, and see if I can glean anything else. So much of what I'm thinking about her is pure hunch, you know?" I sat down, feeling defeated. "Everything is about the trial and Titus. Even those articles mention very little about her or her life. Any little thing I could find that would give me a peek into what her life was really like would help."

"Well, I can tell you that I remember there were probably about thirty women in the picture in three or four rows. The sorority was much bigger back then. And Tillie stuck out like a sore thumb. The rest of them were all dressed up, and she was in that typical black maid's uniform with the lace apron and cap. I can't remember if it was written on the back or we just assumed that she was an honorary Sigma sister."

"That just makes me want to see it even more."

"I'll keep asking around, okay? I'd really like to help."

"Thanks so much."

Fifteen minutes later, we were seated back in the jury room, and the individual questioning continued. Cell phones and reading material were not allowed, so I was forced to just sit and listen as one potential juror after another was questioned. My mind kept drifting, imagining the trial for Tillie's murder in this same room, until a sudden commotion brought me back to the present. One of the attorneys was visibly upset about a juror, and the judge called everyone to her bench. As I watched, the stenographer got up and brought her equipment with her to record the conversation.

"Oh my God," I gasped, then covered my mouth quickly, but no one really noticed.

Staring at the stenographer, I couldn't believe it hadn't hit me sooner. The Titus trial was held in this same courtroom back in 1886. Someone must have taken down the testimony. Maybe not with the equipment used now, but perhaps in shorthand.

Was it possible that there was a transcript of Tillie's murder trial?

AN HOUR LATER, I WAS EXCUSED after answering that yes, I'd once been the victim of a crime. I was relieved. I went downstairs to the security desk and asked the cop where the archives were. I was so excited, I could feel my pulse humming.

"Archives?" he repeated, with a puzzled frown. "Why, I don't think there is one."

"I'm looking for the transcript of a trial from back in the 1880s. Where would something like that be kept?"

"Maybe try the prosecutor's office, upstairs to the front of the building. They've got records from way back."

"Thank you."

The administrator in the prosecutor's office was surprised at my request. "A transcript from the 1880s? No, we wouldn't have that. I don't think they had court stenographers back then. Or transcripts."

"What about any records at all pertaining to the case? The grand jury records? The death certificate, perhaps?"

"I don't think so, but let me take a look. I haven't been here all that long."

Five minutes later she returned from another room with an older gentleman in a suit. "This is attorney Pat Richmond. He's been here for years."

"I'm sorry, miss, but our grand jury records just go back to the 1940s."

"The coroner's inquest, maybe?"

He shook his head. "I think you're going to find this a dead end. The courthouse was renovated in the 1950s, and all that stuff was thrown out."

"You...can't be serious?"

"Listen, this is a small courthouse. It's not like anyone's going to be appealing a case from a century ago. It's not like today with computers and you can store things digitally. Back then they needed the room."

It was unbelievable. I felt sick with disappointment. I turned to leave and already had the door open when the administrator asked me to wait.

"There's someone who might be able to help you. Michael

Cassidy. He's an attorney here in town. So was his father. He's also a local history buff. Maybe he could point you in the right direction." The woman told me where to find his office.

Luckily, the attorney was in, but he had a morning filled with appointments. I waited for ninety minutes until his lunch break, when his secretary told me I could have just a few minutes because he had to be in court that afternoon.

Michael Cassidy ushered me into his office, where I sat and quickly spilled my request. Middle-aged and nice looking, he began to smile as soon as I mentioned Tillie.

"I know I'm not the first person to look into this, but it's important to me. For personal reasons."

"I can tell," he said with a nod. "I don't know if a transcript exists, though I disagree with the information you got at the courthouse. There were court stenographers and transcripts back then. But where would a copy of it be now?"

"That seems to be the big question."

"I can take a look here when I'm finished with court. I'll only be an hour or so."

"What do you mean? You might actually have a copy?"

He looked puzzled. "Isn't that why you came here? Because of my office?"

"I don't know what you mean."

"This was the office of J. G. Shipman and Son. They were the defendant's counsel."

"What? This was the actual office of James Titus's attorney?"

He laughed. "Yes, it was. And there are boxes and boxes of old case records downstairs."

"Oh, I'd be happy to—"

But he put his hand up. "It's dirty and disorganized, and you'd have no idea what to look for. I'd be happy to give it a shot."

"I can't thank you enough."

"Actually, I should thank you. No one's ever asked me this before. And honestly, I can't believe I didn't think of it. I love his-tory, and I imagine that would be a fascinating transcript."

"Can I come back later and check in?"

"Sure. Don't get too excited, though. I can't promise anything.

In the meantime, if you're still going to be in town, why don't you see if they have anything at the county law library pertaining to the case?"

The county library on the outskirts of town had nothing on the transcript, of course. But they had lots of old copies of the *Belvidere Apollo*, which had apparently covered the case. I hadn't seen this newspaper before. I knew I didn't have enough time to read it all, so I simply photocopied everything I could find for later. By now I was starving and went to a little café around the corner of the courthouse, Thisildous, and ordered a burger, though I found I couldn't eat it.

I felt I was getting so close to something that my entire body was vibrating. Two bites of the burger and I pushed it aside. Instead I began racing through the copies I'd made. Much of it was the same basic information that had been covered in the *Hackettstown Gazette* and even the *New York Times*...until I found an article from 1887, long after Titus had been found guilty and sentenced to hang "until you are dead, dead, dead." I had read that quote before, and the big mystery was, of course, that there he was sitting in a rocker in the family photo at nearly ninety years old, obviously escaping the hangman's noose.

Now I learned that after Titus was found guilty and sentenced, his attorneys took the case all the way to the state appeals court. So maybe he'd been exonerated after all? But then I read further that the appeal was denied. It still didn't make sense. Why didn't he hang? What happened to get him off?

I asked for the check, anxious to get back, hoping against hope that almost 130 years later, that transcript was still sitting in the basement of James Titus's attorney's office.

* * *

WHEN I RETURNED TO MICHAEL CASSIDY'S OFFICE, his secretary sent me down into the basement. He was right; the stairs were steep and wobbly, and it was dark and low ceilinged.

"I'm just finishing up, but so far nothing," he said as he uncovered a cardboard box. "This is the last one."

I sat on the bottom step, so disappointed I thought I might cry. "Oh, I was so hoping, but I guess what were the odds?"

"I'm sure there was a transcript at one time."

"I've read so many articles, anything I could get my hands on, but I find it all confusing. First she was supposedly killed in a barn by two men, but the papers then say it looks like the murder would go unsolved. Suddenly Titus is then arrested, and the theory is that he killed her alone in the basement of the seminary. Yet some locals think he may have been railroaded."

"It was supposedly a very confusing case from what I recall."

I sat there shaking my head. "But it's more than that. Tillie seems to have been forgotten in all of this, you know? I just want to see if there's anything else about her and her life in there that didn't make the papers. I imagine her family and friends would have testified at the trial."

"I'm a history buff. I totally understand."

"Maybe the papers were right and it really was Titus, because apparently there was an appeal and he lost that too."

His eyes widened. "What did you say?"

"There was an appeal."

"Ha!" He began to chuckle. "Well, that could explain it."

"Explain what?"

"Where the transcript is. If they appealed the case, the transcript would have gone to the state Court of Appeals in Trenton."

I stood up. "So it might be there? Still?"

He looked at his watch. "I guess there's only one way to find out."

I followed Mr. Cassidy up the stairs and listened as he got on his phone. He went through person after person and finally hung up.

"It's late, but this young guy apparently loves a good mystery and doesn't mind a little overtime without pay. He's looking and said he'll call us back within a half hour."

A half hour came and went. Mr. Cassidy was killing time reading through depositions for the following day. I knew Adam was probably wondering where I was, no doubt thinking I had been picked as a juror. I just stood up to leave when the phone finally rang.

"Yes," Mr. Cassidy said after a few moments. "Okay, then, thank you for your time."

My heart sank at his words. "So no transcript?"

"Apparently there are some pages missing, but yes, there is a transcript! It's been filed away in the archives at the state library for decades, it seems."

"Oh my God," I whispered.

"Now all you have to do is go to Trenton and see it, although it could take you days to read through. And hopefully there should be some evidence filed away with it."

"I can't thank you enough, Mr. Cassidy. I would have never found this on my own."

He came around his desk and shook my hand. "Oh, I have a feeling you would have. Good luck."

"Thank you. And if you don't mind, I'd like to keep this private. I live in Hackettstown, and there are people there who still get upset because of Titus's granddaughter, Mrs. Freeman, and how this whole thing has affected their family."

"No problem at all, as long as you come back at some point and let me know what you've found."

"It's a deal."

It was after six when I finally got in my van and began driving home. I was on autopilot, my mind racing, every cell in my body twitching. This was it. The thing I'd been waiting and hoping for. The pages of the transcript would take me back to Tillie's world—the words, the language, the real story of the people who were part of her life. I so wanted to find out more about her family. My heart broke at the sorry state of their lives. I could only imagine her sisters' despair when she was killed.

I was back in town, with no recollection of the drive at all. Finally I would be able to discover who Tillie really was and hopefully be able to understand the strange coincidences that had begun the moment I saw her monument. There was a reason; I was certain of it. Maybe by reading the transcript, I could also figure out what really happened to her on that last night of her life. I couldn't wait. I wanted to go as soon as possible. Tomorrow, perhaps. But...it wasn't that simple.

What would I tell Adam? I'd given him my word that I would let go of Tillie, that I'd forget about Titus. I was going against everything I had promised him and his family. Not only that, if he knew, then he would also know I'd been lying all along. Driving through the stone arch, across the rumbling wooden bridge, I couldn't shut my thoughts down. I knew I wouldn't be able to stop myself. I knew what I was risking. And then I saw him and stopped the truck suddenly.

Adam sat on a flat boulder at the river's edge near the cottage. He wasn't fishing. He was just sitting there, looking forlorn, staring at the water tumbling over the rocks, not even hearing the van or looking up. A hot wave of dread rose up in my chest. Somehow he already knew. He was upset, angry. Things were going to begin falling apart now, as they always did. And of course I had only myself to blame.

CHAPTER 27

March 1886

TILLIE COULDN'T SLEEP. All night she kept seeing Nora's face and couldn't stop worrying about what was to happen to the lot of them.

When Matron came to the kitchen yesterday to tell her she had a visitor in the parlors, and then she saw her sister white as a sheet and shivering, her heart about stopped. Someone musta died. But no, Nora had come to say goodbye. She was in her faded Sunday dress and leaving for Newark on the noon train.

"Have you been to tell Ma?" she'd asked.

"Oh, Tillie, I barely had time to come see you. Catherine's in a state, and I didn't want to leave her. You must go tell Ma for me. Promise?"

"Of course. I've been trying to see her awhile myself. And you did right. You must go. This position is your chance."

That was when Nora began to cry. "We're all scatterin' like seeds in the wind, Tillie. I miss you all the time, and I already miss Catherine, no matter what her moods. She's so much like Ma."

"Catherine will be fine. I'll see to it. And maybe..." She'd sat there, her own insides aquiver by then. "Nora, I've got me a beau. And he's a hard worker. We talk about saving all our money and getting a little place of our own and...I'm hoping that one day soon, perhaps we can all be together again."

"Oh, Tillie. Are you going to marry him, then?"

"Well, it's a bit soon for that, but he's got prospects, and he cares for me."

"And you care for him, too?"

She giggled. "He's got some lovely green eyes that just about melt me at times."

The seminary bells rang the half hour then, and Nora jumped up. "I must go, sister."

"I'll write you, Nora. I'll..." She stopped then. Of course she wouldn't. Nora couldn't read.

"Maybe once I get settled, I'll ask someone to write a letter for me so's I can send to you, and you can let everyone know I'm doin' fine."

She hugged Nora, who was trembling even harder, like a baby bird.

"I don't know when I'll see you again, Tillie."

"Just work hard and save your money, Nora. Perhaps in the spring I'll take the train and come see you in Newark if I can get a few days off. And remember, the future is lookin' up for us."

She was lying now in her warm bed. Tears slid down her cheeks onto the pillow as she thought about how she'd watched Nora through the parlor windows walking through the front gates and across Jefferson Street, hurrying to the train. And the promises she made. Bridget said once that luck was a matter of birth. And she was right. But Tillie was going to change that luck. And with Frank beside her, maybe it would happen even sooner.

* * *

IT SEEMED BUT MINUTES LATER she was down in the kitchen, only to find hardly enough potatoes for the students, much less the workers. There'd been yet another big snow during the night, and nothing was as it should have been that morning

"The new hand for Mr. Alsop's position quit again," Bridget told her.

"Another one? You can't be serious?" Tillie wanted to cry. "I've got to trudge through this snow to get potatoes? Why, no doubt there'll be no path cleared yet."

"Yes, Mr. Titus is out there shoveling now, with some of the students helping him out."

"But I've not the proper boots for that. It's still blowing like mad out there." Besides, she didn't want to be anywhere near the dark barn with Mr. Titus, who was in the habit now of staring at her bosom when she was waiting on the men's help table.

Bridget didn't reply. Instead she began to set pots and pans on the big stove.

"What are ya doing?" Tillie asked.

"Well, it seems the snow has brought you a bit of bad luck and me a bit of good luck. The cook's assistant is not able to make it in, and so I was asked to be Mr. Finger's helper this morning. I told him I'd be happy to show him how to make real Irish oatmeal, the likes of which he's never tasted."

"Lucky you is right."

"Now, you'd best be getting those potatoes, Tillie, because I'm also going to make some real Irish breakfast potatoes."

The wind nearly knocked her down just a few steps from the building, and she regretted not running upstairs for her coat. But there was no time. When she got to the barn, she stopped, catching her breath.

"Please, miss, would you have some food you could spare?"

She turned with a start. Coming into the doorway from the dark inside, where the snow's reflection cast some light, was a young man, skinny as a scarecrow, with no shoes and an old coat that hung on him.

"Land sakes! You near scared me to death."

"I'm mighty sorry, miss. I just got caught in the storm, and..."

She watched him begin to sway, then steady himself on the barn door.

"When was the last time you ate?"

"Don't rightly know, miss. I fell on hard times a while back."

"Have you got enough strength left to fill a potato sack?"

He nodded, and she handed him a sack and led him to the potato cellar. Each of them filled one up. Just as the sky was brightening, they walked back to the building, huddled together, her hands nearly frozen. She could only imagine his poor feet.

Tillie took him into the kitchen and led him behind the big cookstove. "Set yourself there where you can't be seen, and warm up. We'll have a meal for you shortly."

Bridget looked at her with raised eyes. "Ye best not be bringin' tramps inside here, ya know. Matron will boot you out the door for good if yer caught."

"He's not a tramp. He's a poor boy down on his luck. Have a heart, Bridget."

"And you don't be a fool, Tillie. Don't ya ever read the papers? That kind's always drinkin' the whiskey and gettin' into trouble, even killin' folks at times."

"Hush up, Bridget. He's just a boy." And something about him reminded her of James, when her brother was a skinny lad working long hours on the farms. Her ma couldn't fill him up, never having enough food for that to happen.

Tillie turned to the potatoes, her hands still not thawed, which made it fairly impossible to peel as her fingers could hardly bend. Bridget, on the other side of the kitchen preparing her oatmeal, began singing some cheery Irish ballad, pleased as punch at the turn of events and her chance at cooking.

A little while later, Tillie brought a bowl of the oatmeal to the boy sitting on the floor behind the cookstove. While he gobbled it down, she stared at him, seeing James again, and her sisters, the four of them waiting on their mother for a meager meal. She knew hunger, that fierce gnawing at your belly. And she knew helplessness, when you thought there was nothing that could change your lot in life. But now she had better, and she would not be like Bridget and turn her back on someone who needed help. No matter what.

When Bridget went to the water closet, she checked to make sure Jimmy Titus was still busy outside. Then she slipped into the furnace room and grabbed a pair of the work boots the janitors always wore when shoveling the coal into the furnaces. Hopefully the young lad would be long gone before Titus noticed the boots were as well. And hopefully he'd have no idea how they'd disappeared.

LATER THAT EVENING AS THEY WERE FINISHING cleaning up the dinner dishes, they heard voices singing outside. Bridget was upstairs as she didn't have to wash up. Stella, who'd come in to chat after her supper, went to the window and wiped a clearing in the steamed glass.

"They're off ice skating on the canal. Imagine that."

Tillie joined her, watching the girls in their pretty sweaters and crocheted hats and mittens, the boys in heavy wool cardigans and earmuffs, all of them with skates tossed carelessly across their shoulders, heading toward the Morris Canal, frozen over now where it curved below Buck Hill.

"Have you ever been ice skating?" she asked Stella.

"Not once. You, Tillie?"

She remembered trying it just the once when she was a girl, visiting her uncle John's grand house that one Christmas. Her cousins had gotten new skates, and one of them let her try them. But her ankles bobbled and she kept falling, and her mother near had a fit she'd crack her head open.

"No, never tried it," she told Stella.

They watched as the merry group walked behind the building, and Tillie about gasped 'cause one of the ice skaters looked an awful lot like that Peter Mead, his gold spectacles flashing with the light of a gas lamp as he passed by holding hands with one of the sorority girls. But Tillie didn't have to say a word because when she turned, she saw the look on Stella's face. Just days ago, she'd seen Stella comin' outta the red barn across the way with that cad, her face all flushed.

"I'm sorry, Stella. You deserve better than that."

But Stella had already turned away, crying. And Tillie wished she could just run right out there and smack him. Just then, Janitor Titus came into the kitchen, wondering if anyone had seen a pair of boots that seemed to have disappeared from the furnace room.

CHAPTER 28

I PARKED THE TRUCK ON THE SIDE OF A LANE and walked over to Adam. I was nearly beside him when he finally looked up.

"Hey," I said, sitting.

"Hey," he said with a weak smile.

My heart was pounding now, waiting for him to speak because I couldn't. He took my hand then and squeezed it. "I have to tell you something. Something I should have told you from the beginning. It's about my father."

"Your father?"

He nodded. "I should have been honest with you, but I thought I'd gotten it under control, or I wouldn't have...I wouldn't have married you."

I was nearly breathless, so taken aback by what he was saying, expecting something so different.

"You would've loved my father. He was kind of an odd guy, but he was funny, and really smart. A loner. He must have read every issue of *National Geographic* since he was ten years old, and he could tell you anything about anyplace in the world. But except for his time in the army, he never really left this place. It was almost like he was...afraid or something. Maybe that was from the war. He told me once he saw a lot of horror over in Viet Nam and thought he'd probably had PTSD, though he never went for help. He didn't really believe in doctors, said they just pumped you full of pills for whatever they thought ailed you. Ironically, I think he just used alcohol to self-medicate."

"I think a lot of vets have issues with alcohol."

"My parents didn't have such a good marriage, and...I felt like I was all he really had. When I went off to college, I felt guilty because my mom finally left for good. I came home in the summers and on breaks to work here, but I could see he was going downhill. Then after college I did a few years in the army, came back, and joined a band. We went on the road trying to build an audience, and I wanted to keep going with that. I kept coming back when I could to help out here, but...I could never do anything right in my father's eyes. He wasn't one of those jolly drinkers. He'd go someplace dark, get belligerent. But he was so proud of our legacy here. It's a sacred job. I believe that, though I doubt anyone on the outside would get it. He resented my not taking over back then. When he was dying, I left the band and came back to take care of him and run the cemetery until I figured things out. That's when I began to realize he'd messed up pretty badly here. Not on purpose. He just forgot things, like writing down who bought which plot. Or keeping his accounting ledgers up to date."

"Oh, Adam, I had a feeling you were doing some kind of damage control for your father."

"I don't want him to go down as the one who fucked up the legacy and tarnish generations of men."

"No one could blame you for any of this. I'm certain Gran and Helen would understand, and—"

"No, I don't want them to know. I don't want them to remember him like that. It's the one thing I can do for him, because I feel like..." He stopped, blinked several times, and I could see he was fighting tears. "I feel like I failed him."

"You mean you weren't planning to stay?"

He sighed, shaking his head. "I know you're probably shocked. I was supposed to be the seventh generation here, the next in line, and...I remember reciting the names to you of all the cemetery keepers, just like my grandfather taught me. But...I don't know; when I got older, I just didn't want it."

"And you've stayed on all this time to try to fix this?"

"I guess sometimes life just goes in the direction it's supposed to; you know what I mean? My band got tired of waiting, found a guitarist to fill in while I was gone, and...next thing you know, they got really big. And I started to think maybe this was meant to be. Maybe I wasn't supposed to do something else. I have a legacy to follow, a family who expected things of me. And I disappointed my father in that. The least I can do is try to make things right for him. For his memory here. He worked long and hard for more than forty years here. He deserves that."

Of course I knew of the drinking from what Adam had told me, and then Gran, who also mentioned how hard his father was on him. But I didn't realize what a long shadow his father had cast on his life.

"How can I help? Maybe if I organize the files in the office and—"

"I need the wedding money to pay for a few plots I can't find records for. The deeds were issued, but there's no accounting for them."

"That's fine. Just do it."

"It's not fair to you, though. None of this is fair. I should have told you from the beginning, I just thought it was getting better, and since we got married, there have been four different discrepancies."

"Adam, if this is what you need to do to, it's okay. I don't care. My God, you bought me a van."

He looked at me then, shaking his head. "But I care."

I could almost feel him withdrawing. Adam, I knew, was a fixer. Gran had also told me how he'd tried to keep peace in his own family, something we had in common. And how in the end he couldn't. Something else we shared.

"Why are you telling me this now? Did something happen?"

"Because of the mausoleum and the declining revenue due to cremations, the board's decided it's time to do an audit."

"When was the last time they did one?"

"Never."

"Adam, maybe you should just tell them. I mean, you didn't do anything wrong, and it sounds like an almost impossible situation to fix." I thought of that little office with the index cards and ledgers. Where would you even start? But I could see his face hardening.

"No. I will not disgrace my father. I just need to make up the shortfall."

I wondered how much money he'd put in already. And when would it stop?

"Look," he said, getting up. "This is not your worry, okay? I'll make it right. No one ever has to know."

He held out a hand, and I stood up. He didn't ask me about jury duty or why I was so late. I could see his mind was racing, and I was worried, despite what he said. Because I wasn't sure there really was a way to fix this.

It wasn't until later that night when Adam was sleeping that I realized what we hadn't really talked about. If he was here out of a sense of duty, because he felt he had no choice, what did that say about his decision to marry me? If living here and leaving his music behind was settling, was I part of that, too?

* * *

LONG PAST MIDNIGHT, I GOT UP and went downstairs, unable to sleep. My witching hour. Doubts about Adam's feelings, and even our marriage, were taunting me. What if he'd simply married me because he couldn't leave the cemetery? What if he just wanted to have a child to take over one day, as I'd overheard Helen insinuate? My old insecurities roared in my head, which I had to stop. They would only make things worse.

I went into the spare room, sat at the desk, and turned on the light. I needed distraction, always my rescue when I wanted to escape my thoughts and fears. I took out all the articles I'd copied that afternoon from the *Belvidere Apollo*, and in a matter of minutes my mind was drawn back into Tillie's life. Because in a very short piece in the paper, there was a mention of the inquest that was held right after her body was found.

The mother of the dead girl was seen, but her story is omitted as it can have no bearing upon the case, at least so far as the public are concerned, and only told a sad story of domestic affairs.

I was praying the entire inquest would be in Trenton because obviously her family would have attended and been questioned.

It might give me so much more information than the trial would about her life. They must have been devastated.

I pictured the cabin, Tillie and her sisters without a mother, the father no doubt a drunk. Then I pulled out her photograph, staring into her eyes again. She just broke my heart.

CHAPTER 29

February 1886

"**Y**A CAN'T BE SERIOUSLY VENTURING OUT INTO THAT?" Tillie heard Bridget call to her as she opened the basement door to leave. "Not even for a proper meal with that handsome beau of yours. Why, there must be another foot or so out there since yesterday."

She poked her head into the kitchen. "I'm going to tell Frank I've got to see my ma, Bridget. If I don't today, God knows when I'll have another chance. I need to tell her about Nora."

"I swear, I don't think I'll ever be used to these harsh American winters. Even in winter, the fields in Ireland are still as green as an emerald."

"Oh, I don't know that we ever get used to it, either. We just bear it. Now I'm off."

Tillie opened the door again and stepped outside. The one thing she did love about a big snow was the quiet, as though the world were asleep in the daylight and everything so pure and glistening. The farm lane was partly packed down from those who'd gone to the barn earlier, and Tillie picked her way slowly in that direction, though it was longer. When she reached Moore Street, she saw that sled tracks from carts and wagons that had gone through had carved grooves into the middle, as she'd hoped, and that was where she walked, heading into town. By the time she reached Main Street, her boots were soaked through, and her toes hurt from the freezing wetness.

Main Street was a sight, the sled tracks and horse hooves already worn through the snow to the dirt so that it was all brown and slushy. The wooden sidewalks had been cleared in most places, but from time to time she had to venture out into the street to avoid an icy patch. If she fell, there'd be no help for her as she'd be soaked and filthy, and too far from the seminary to make it back without catching her death.

She saw Frank waiting for her in front of the stagecoach office, talking to some fellas. Then he turned and smiled, and her heart fluttered. He was so handsome.

"Hello, pet. You're lookin' lovely as always. What do you say to a bite over at the American House?"

"Oh, I'm so sorry, Frank, but I'm needing to get out to Independence to see my mother. She works as a domestic there for a farmer's family."

"You can't be walking all the way out there? Not in this?"

"I thought I might see if anyone was heading out that way, perhaps."

Frank looked down at the wet hem of her skirt and shook his head, smiling. Then he turned to one of the fellas. "George, the lady here is needin' a way out to Independence. I think we gents can help her out, don't you?"

The fellas turned and ran down Main Street. Frank lit a cigarette and kept smiling at her. Before she knew it, a horse was stopping in the street before her, pulling a handsome buckboard sled. Frank's friend hopped off, and then Frank took her arm.

"But I..." she didn't know what to say.

"I'll drive you there, Tillie, my girl, but we can't be too long."

It was like she'd wished on a bottle, and here was her way to see her Ma.

He helped her up to the seat, then climbed up beside her, took the reins, and with not another word, they were off, flying up Main Street. She started laughing because it felt like they were birds swooping through town, especially as they rode over the railroad tracks and seemed to float in the air before coming down onto the snow again.

Tillie began to shiver. Frank reached behind, pulled out a blanket, and spread it across both their laps. She tucked her hands underneath. Frank put his arm about her and slid her closer. She could feel his warmth and didn't protest a lick. She was going to see her ma, and in style! She couldn't wait to tell Stella and Bridget about this.

The houses grew sparse and the woods thickened as the road wound up past Buck Hill and out of town. Tillie knew this way, having worked a few miles farther out for Dr. Conover last year. She'd seen more of her ma then because they weren't working too far from each other.

"You're going to turn to the right soon, before the big hill that'll take you down into Vienna," she told him. "Do you know where they found that mastodon skeleton everyone was talkin' about a while back? My ma is just near to that."

"Sure do. Why, that put Hackettstown on the map for a bit, didn't it?"

He pulled on the reins, slowing the horse, and they turned, the buckboard slipping suddenly till they were almost off the road. Tillie and Frank nearly slid off the seat, and as he righted the sled, he turned to her, his cheeks all pink, the breath coming from him in little puffs of steam. He kissed her then before she even knew what was happening. When he pulled away, she leaned and kissed him back. They both laughed out loud, and she couldn't remember ever feeling so happy.

The road here was steep and narrow, and a few times the rudders seemed to get stuck. But Frank kept at it, working the reins, and before Tillie knew it, she saw the white farmhouse with the porch up ahead.

"I'd ask you in, but—"

"No, I'll wait right here, case someone needs to get by."

"I won't be long, promise."

He hopped off and helped her to climb down, then held her arm as she made her way to the porch, as it wasn't shoveled well. Then he went back to the buckboard, and she knocked on the front door.

When it opened, her ma stood there with wide eyes. "Why, Tillie, what on earth are ya doin' out here in this?"

"I wanted to see ya, Ma. It's been a long time."

Her mother looked back over her shoulder a moment, but then she said, "Come warm up a few minutes. But I can't take too long. This snow has set us all back, and the missus is havin' a bad day with her rheumatism."

Tillie followed her mother into the kitchen, where a wood stove was blazing, pots boiling away on top so that the one window was all steamed up. On a wooden table there were bottles and towels.

"She wants a bath, says she can't warm up."

"Oh, Ma, like you don't have enough to do around here." Her mother's face was thinner, with more lines than the last time, and her hair was nearly all grey. Her hands shook all the time now as she went about dumping pots into a metal tub in a corner of the room.

"Here, let me help ya. Sit down, Ma."

Her mother didn't even set about to argue, just sat in a kitchen chair. That wasn't like her. Normally she'd argue she was just fine.

"How are the girls?" her mother asked.

"Well, that's one reason I'm here, to tell ya the news. Nora has gone to Newark to work for a fine lady."

"Well, that's a relief. Nora's pretty enough. Maybe she'll find her a good husband there. But Catherine, she's a right old maid by now, don't ya think? Not that she'll ever be leavin' him, I imagine."

"I don't know, Ma." Tillie picked up the bucket of water from the floor and filled another pot on the stove, set it to boil. She knew better than to argue and get her mother's nerves up. Her ma had always been crazy jealous of Catherine.

"And your pa, the wasteful drunkard? Still spending all his coins over at Elsie's?"

"I don't know, Ma. I've only been home once in months, and...everything was much the same." She sat across from her mother now, catching her breath.

"Well, I'm glad you got out of there. You're like me, a survivor." Her mother surprised her then by squeezing her hand. Tillie's eyes began to water, and she blinked hard.

"You been taking care of yourself, Ma? Taking those pills the doc said would help the nerves?"

Her mother just nodded, staring at her now. "Ya know I woulda stayed if I could. You know that, don't ya?"

"I know, Ma. I know." She remembered the day her mother left after a horrible fight with her pa, the both of them swinging at each other and screaming things she didn't want to remember.

"You were just a wee girl, and Nora not much bigger. Catherine shoulda been more help, but she was always her pa's pet. She shoulda—"

"Ma, it's all right. We're all doing all right. No need to fret yourself. And did ya hear about our James gettin' work on a ship? He's always dreamed of sailing."

Now her mother's eyes filled. "It's likely we'll never see him again. You realize that, don't ya? Maybe Nora, too."

"Nora's not so far, really, and our James'll be back. You'll see."

"Things shoulda been different for all you kids. Your pa—"

They were interrupted by pounding on the ceiling overhead. Her mother stood with a sigh. "That'll be the missus wantin' her bath. I best be gettin' up there to help her down the stairs. The mister is out tendin' to the animals."

Tillie hugged her mother, so thin she could feel her rib bones. "Things are gonna change for ya, Ma. I'm comin' up in the world. They've got me waitin' tables, and I'm doin' a good job. The matron likes me, and even the sorority girls have me upstairs now and then. I'm even doing some mending for them. And I've got me a fine beau. He's a hard worker, and..." But she could see her mother's mind had wandered already.

WHEN TILLIE WENT BACK OUTSIDE, Frank hopped off the buckboard and helped her up. As he climbed beside her, she turned to him, then caught the whiskey on his breath. It was still morning.

"Somethin' to warm ya up, Tillie?" He held a flask out to her then.

She shook her head, unable to speak, feeling like she had swallowed a stone that was working its way to her middle. Finally she took his arm. "Frank, tell me straight; are ya one for the drink?"

"Why, Tillie, how could you ask such a thing? This is just to keep the chills away on such a cold ride."

God in heaven, she hoped that was the truth. She had only to look at her pa to know where this could go. As much as she cared for Frank and was starting to see a future with him, she couldn't bear the likes of that.

"I'm glad to hear that, Frank."

He shook the reins, and the horse was off. It was impossible to turn around, so the ride back was even longer, as they had to wind through Petersburg. When they came toward town, just past Buck Hill, she saw two police on horses riding at them. One held up a hand.

"Sorry, Tillie," Frank whispered. "I hoped to get ya back to the institute, but I think our ride might be about over."

"What...?"

"I think maybe my pals mighta borrowed the wrong sled for our ride."

It took a moment for her to realize the truth of the situation. Frank's pals had stolen the sled. But how could Frank put her in such a position? If Mrs. Ruckle were to find out about this, she'd have her job for sure. He couldn't have known, she kept telling herself.

On the long walk back to the seminary, Tillie fretted about what the police might to do Frank. As for herself, she'd best be careful. She couldn't lose this job. It was her only hope to try to make things right for her family.

Frank had such a big heart. She'd have to caution him about whom he chose for his friends.

CHAPTER 30

A DAM BEGAN WORKING LIKE A DEMON, gone from morning to night. The footings for the mausoleum were in already. I assumed he was hoping to get it finished ahead of schedule. And a new section for cremains was being cleared. Whenever I brought up the problem or asked if I could help, he kept telling me not to worry; he'd handle it. I wasn't sure how he'd do that short of continuing to pump money into the cemetery account whenever a discrepancy showed up. I wondered how much he'd put in before the wedding money, which was several thousand dollars.

When I got upset at his distance, I couldn't help picturing that little boy who'd come to my door with my bike all those years ago. Living here and hearing all of his life that this was his future. Eventually growing up and trying to make a break from it all. Only to be paying now in his own mind for that longing to make his own way, as any young adult might do.

As for me, I gave Adam his space. But Tillie continued to haunt me. I dreamed of her at night now, snippets and scenes without words, as if I were watching her go about her day-to-day life at the seminary in a silent movie with no idea that her life was about to end violently. The transcript was there in Trenton, just waiting for me to find whatever I was meant to discover. But I was determined to be a good wife. I cooked. I tended his mother's garden. A few times I cut flowers and brought them to Tillie's grave, or Adam's father's or grandfather's. I brought fliers to surrounding towns, hoping to drum up some work. In the hours I couldn't fill when Adam was gone, I kept going over all of the information I'd gathered about Tillie, trying to be patient.

There were so many discrepancies, so many questions I wanted to find answers to.

EARLY THAT NEXT MORNING I was awakened by the sound of sirens. Reaching with my hand, I realized Adam wasn't beside me. In my grogginess, I reasoned that there must have been an early call I didn't hear.

The sirens were getting closer. I got out of bed and looked out the window. My heart froze when I saw the flashing lights wind - ing through the gravel lanes toward the equipment shed. I pulled on shorts and a t-shirt and ran out the door. The truck was gone, parked near the shed I saw now, so I kept running across the cemetery, arriving at the shed in time to see Adam being carried on a stretcher into the back of the ambulance.

"Oh God! What happened?"

His face was swelling, his eyes barely visible, and angry red welts covered his arms and his neck. He seemed to be gasping for breath. One of the paramedics came over and took my arm, leading me into the ambulance. They slid an oxygen mask over Adam's face and stuck an IV into his hand.

"Looks like multiple stings," said the paramedic, whom I recognized from the softball team. "One of the young guys cut- ting the grass said they hit a yellow jacket nest in the ground. Adam was standing there and took the brunt of it."

I laid my hand on his cheek. It was hot to the touch. "Is he going to be okay?"

"We gave him a shot of adrenaline and Benadryl. He's getting IV fluids. Anaphylaxis can be tricky."

"I didn't know he was allergic."

"I don't think he was. I remember once he got stung during football practice in high school, and he was fine. But this was quite a few stings, so..."

This man who was a stranger to me knew more about Adam than I did. I held my husband's hand, praying he would be all right. If I lost him...I couldn't think that way. That I would always lose those I loved. That I would always be alone.

* * *

THE EDEMA WORSENED BEFORE IT BEGAN TO RESPOND to the drugs. His eyes swelled shut, and it was difficult to tell if he was awake. So I stayed quiet, waiting for any kind of response. Nurses came in and out checking his vitals, each one assuring me he was going to be fine. Still, seeing him hooked up to machines and looking so awful, it was hard to believe.

Helen came and went over the course of the day, her face a mask of worry. I tried to give her space, going to the cafeteria for coffee and coming back to find her standing next to his bed, holding his hand. I assured her I'd be staying the night, and she said she'd come back in the morning so I could get some rest.

Old friends popped in every few hours to offer their help, to make sure he was going to be okay. The cemetery would be taken care of, I was assured. Later in the afternoon, I was surprised to see Doris, Aunt Helen's friend whom I'd met at the picnic, peek in.

"It's okay, you can come in," I said, getting up from the chair beside Adam.

I was surprised when the door opened fully and Doris entered with a basket of cookies and a younger woman with short blonde hair and a shy smile. The woman from Memorial Day. My stomach lurched.

"This is my niece, Sandra."

I blinked. Gran had called me Sandra the first time we met.

"We'll just stay a minute. I'm sure they want things quiet in here," Sandra said softly.

I opened my mouth, but words failed to come. Sandra was staring at Adam, and now there was no mistaking her look.

I forced myself to eat a cookie, the dry crumbs sticking in my throat as Doris whispered on and on what a nice boy Adam was and how he was always there to lend a hand when anyone needed him, as if she were eulogizing him.

"He was never allergic before," Doris piped in during a stretch of silence. "Isn't that right, Sandra?"

Sandra shrugged, clearly embarrassed.

"Did you go to school with Adam?" I asked Sandra then.

Doris began to giggle. "Why, didn't you know? Adam and Sandra used to be sweethearts. We all thought they'd get married."

The dagger in my gut twisted again.

Sandra turned maroon. "It was a long time ago."

Just then a nurse came in with a new IV bag.

"Well, we'd better be going," Sandra said, pulling on her aunt's arm. "We just wanted to say hello and see if you needed anything."

"No, I'm fine."

But I wasn't. Adam had once loved this woman. And as much as we shared our past relationships, he'd never once mentioned a sweetheart or someone he thought he might marry. And yet here she was popping in out of the blue at the first sign of a problem. I looked at him, unconscious and swollen, hooked up to machines.

I knew I was holding things back, and I knew why. Guilt. And shame. Clearly there was way more to what Adam was holding back than I'd first thought. This went beyond the cemetery and his guitar. I was certain now that Sandra was part of it.

* * *

IT WAS LATER THAT EVENING when the doctor on staff came in to check on Adam and told me he would be fine after a few days. I was so relieved. I curled up in the chair, wrapped the blanket around me, and fell asleep. But I kept waking up, uncomfortable, twisting and turning to get in a better position. Sometime in the middle of the night, I heard my name whispered. I opened my eyes to see Adam holding one of his eyes open with his fingers. I went to his side.

"How long have I been here?"

"Since this morning."

"My eyes feel really weird."

"They're getting better, but they were swollen shut."

"Can we go home now?"

I smiled, relieved. "The doctor will be back in the morning, so we'll see. You gave us all quite a scare. You're going to have to carry an EpiPen from now on."

"I need to get out of here tomorrow."

I knew where this was going, what was worrying him. "Adam, I'll stay on top of things; don't worry. I'll go right home in the morning, and I'll answer any calls that come in."

"Thanks. But I still want to get out of here tomorrow. Why don't you go home and get some sleep?"

"I'm not leaving."

"You can't sleep in a chair all night."

"Watch me."

He fell asleep then, and I curled back into the chair, knowing I'd be an aching mess by morning but not caring at all. The time for questioning Adam about Sandra and his past wasn't now. He would come home, and I would take care of him. He was going to be fine; that was all that mattered. And somehow I had to help him fix this nightmare situation with the cemetery. In the long hours I couldn't sleep, my thoughts kept going round and round. How could we solve this problem in the cemetery once and for all? There had to be a way.

CHAPTER 31

H ELEN CAME BACK EARLY IN THE MORNING. Adam was still sleeping. In the long hours of a restless night, I had figured out a way to start doing some damage control at the cemetery. But I was going to need her help.

"Can I speak to you in the hall?" I whispered when she walked into the room.

Helen followed me back out, and I led her to the lounge. I knew I was taking chances. I was betraying Adam's trust. I was assuming Helen would come on board. And I was hoping we'd get it all done before Adam was ready to go back to work. But they were chances I had to take. I told Helen everything her brother had done: the messed-up records, missing plots, money that never made it into accounts. And how Adam had been trying to fix it for years. I could see her anger grow while at the same time her eyes filled.

"I knew there was something. I...I just couldn't figure it out. How stupid I was. And poor Adam."

"He might never forgive me for telling you, but I just can't stand not doing anything, especially now. He's so afraid that while he's here, something will go wrong again."

"And Ronnie will be blamed."

"But what if they blamed Adam, too? Accused him of theft? I mean, who's to know, really?"

Helen sighed and didn't answer right away. "Adam has a heart of gold, sometimes to his own detriment. He's a fixer, can't stand to see anyone hurting. That was especially true with his parents. When his mother left for good and Ronnie started to get out of control, Adam came back and tried to help. He felt guilty for not coming back sooner, and ...here he still is. I know he was torn. When he left for college all those years ago, he told me this wasn't the future he wanted."

"Was Sandra part of that future?"

Her eyes widened for a moment. "I think it's best if you ask Adam about that."

"But she's part of this whole thing, Adam leaving..."

"Yes, but it's not my place to tell you."

For once Helen wasn't smug about the things I didn't know about Adam's life.

"Now," she said, putting an end to our previous conversation, "why don't you tell me how you think you can fix this if he hasn't been able to?"

"Well, I started thinking last night that if all of the plot and money issues were during the time after Adam's mother left until...his father was too sick to work anymore, then those are the years we should focus on. We need to get all of those little file boxes and ledgers and everything organized into a database."

"That should have been done years ago. But Ronnie was a stubborn man. And obviously his judgment got worse and worse."

"I know."

"All right, so we get it into a database and focus on that time period, but how do we know what's missing?"

"I'm hoping we can use a process of elimination. Also maybe even call around to area funeral homes, see who has preplanned theirs, and cross-reference. I know it's a lot of work and there's not much time. Once they let him out of here..."

"We can't seriously get all of this done in a couple of days."

"I was thinking, what if we got some kids from the college, maybe technology or business students? Kind of like a mini-internship."

"I know people at the college."

I'd been counting on that. "Would you mind making a few calls? I'm going to go home and shower and then see what I can do to get started in the office."

"He'll kill us."

"I know. I'm nervous doing this. I feel like I've betrayed him in a way."

"We don't have a choice," she said. "Go home. I'm going to make some calls. And then I'll find out how long we can make them keep him here."

We went back to Adam's room. He was still sleeping, and I got my things. As I was walking out the door, I heard Helen whisper my name and turned.

"Thank you," she said.

* * *

THE OFFICE, THE LITTLE SEVEN DWARFS' COTTAGE, as I always thought of it, was dark and probably hadn't been cleaned in months. I brought some extra lamps as well as my laptop, pads and pens, and bottles of water. It was nearly noon when a car pulled up and several young people got out, all carrying computer bags.

"I'm Jared. We're here to help," the tallest one told me.

An hour later, there were ten of them in total, and the room became too crowded. I went back to the house and got a few folding tables to set them up under one of the big trees just outside the office. Hours went by. I felt guilty not going back to the hospital to check on Adam, but I knew this was more important.

I went for a quick visit in the late afternoon. Adam's eyes were still swollen, and I was secretly glad. They wouldn't let him out until he could see. I went back to the cemetery. The cottage windows and doors were open, the soft night air coming in on a summer breeze, a new batch of students working.

"I'm going to go pick up some coffee at Dunkin' Donuts up the road to keep these guys going," Helen said.

"Do you really think they can get this done in a couple of days?"

"I hope so. I've got another group of students lined up for tomorrow."

"I'm dreading when I have to tell Adam."

"Once it's done, there's nothing he can do about it."

"I know, but..."

"He'll get over it. And at some point he'll realize this had to be done. If my brother were alive, I'd smack him silly."

"Adam really loved his father."

"He did. He would have done anything for the man, and the sad thing is...it enabled Ronnie. Because he knew Adam would always be there for him."

* * *

WHEN ADAM FOUND OUT WHAT WAS GOING ON two days later, he was furious with me. He was home, looking out the bedroom window and watching people going in and out of the office.

"How could you betray me like this? And my father?" he asked in a cold voice.

"Adam, this wasn't going to go away by itself, and...I could see it was eating away at you."

"This wasn't your call. You had no right. And I was managing."

"I've been scared for you. And worried sick. You've obviously been putting your own money into the cemetery account to cover up for a long time. I mean, how long can you keep doing that?"

"Oh, right, and because I borrowed some of the honeymoon money—"

"No, that's not it. Please don't say that. I don't care about money. I care about you. I was only trying to help."

"This was the opposite of helping me." He turned his back to me.

I went downstairs and called Helen, desperate. Fifteen minutes later she arrived, going right upstairs, and within a minute I could hear them shouting from the hall, though I couldn't make out the words. After a while she came down with a tear-stained face.

I slept on the couch that night, sick with dread. What if he never forgave me?

* * *

I BROUGHT ADAM BREAKFAST THE NEXT MORNING, but he was still silent. The swelling had gone down considerably, but his face and eyes were still puffy, and I could see he was tired. I knew the best thing I could do was give him space. One thing I knew about Adam; he'd come around when he was ready and not a moment sooner. I just prayed he would. I knew I broke what he considered a sacred trust. There was nothing I could do but wait.

Later in the morning I walked across the cemetery to the office to check on the progress. They were nearly finished cataloguing everything, and several of the college students were on their cell phones, calling all the funeral homes within a thirty-mile radius. It wasn't a perfect plan, I knew, but it was a start. Helen had bought a computer, and Jared was setting it up on the old desk. Before they left, all of the data would be downloaded and easily accessible for Adam. The cemetery, after nearly two centuries, was entering the modern era finally.

I took a good look around the office and thought it really wouldn't take much to give it an update. The old maps on the walls were yellowed and tattered and could be salvaged if put in some nice frames. The walls themselves were a horrid shade of beige that bordered on brown and probably hadn't been painted in decades. A soft yellow would brighten it and give it a more cheerful ambiance. I envisioned how cozy it could look. But I knew I needed to wait on all of that. I'd done enough for now.

Walking outside, I went and sat under a tree by the river. I needed a break. I had barely slept in three days. The rush and flow of the river was like music that calmed my heart. Everything felt heavy. I closed my eyes.

SLOWLY I CAME AWAKE UNDER THE TREE, my eyes still closed, just listening to the sounds of the cemetery. I wondered if it were possible to hear the souls of those who hadn't found rest. Could their now-silent voices, their unmet yearnings, somehow find their way into the calling of birds? The rush of the wind? The soothing ripple of the water over rocks? I could almost feel it somehow. I knew that anyone you asked would say the cemetery was a place of death. But to me...there was more.

I stood and stretched, still groggy, an otherworldly feeling consuming me despite the afternoon sunlight. I began walking home to check on Adam. I would need to be patient with him, put up with his silences, his disappointed looks. Though I meant well and had his best interest at heart, he felt betrayed.

I took the long way back, walking up the gravel lane to Tillie's monument. I stood there a long time, listening to the bells of Centenary ringing across town. The gold dome of the college was no longer visible across the valley, hidden by the trees in full summer leaf. How many times over the past days had I thought about the transcript, still waiting for me in Trenton? Tempting me. Torturing me. Knowing that to go back there, to have Adam know I'd betrayed him not once but twice, would no doubt be the end of us. Yet staring at her name, I felt as though I was letting Tillie down.

My cell phone rang just then, breaking the silence all around me. I jumped, then dug it out of my pocket.

"Hello?"

"Hi, Rachel, this is Colleen from the archives at Centenary?"

"Oh, yes, Colleen. Hello."

"You called me last week and asked if the sorority archives might be here in the library with the other things, and I told you no. I thought everything was gone, all thrown out, and I'd pretty much given up. But I found out some of the sorority collections are in the basement of Lotte Hall." I could hear the excitement in her voice. "I'm going to check it out tomorrow. Want to come and see?"

I turned from the monument to our home, where Adam was resting, where I would go now and cook him a good meal.

"I'd like to, Colleen, but I really can't."

I kept walking, wondering if she'd find that photo of Tillie, and perhaps even something else linking Tillie with the sorority. It would be like a treasure hunt, digging through boxes and unearthing what I'd been hoping for. But I wouldn't go. How could I leave Adam alone?

But five minutes later, when I walked in the door, Adam was gone.

CHAPTER 32

March 1886

AFTER SEEING HER MA, Tillie worked the next two weeks with barely a moment off, hoping to show how hard a worker she was. She took hours from those out sick or who couldn't make it in 'cause of another snow. Whatever she could. She feared for her job, especially after Maggie Donovan was fired and left sobbing. Mrs. Ruckle stood there watching her go down the servant's hall with her little suitcase, giving the rest of them a sharp look. Maggie had missed curfew three times, according to Janitor Titus. Tillie knew she could be next if the matron knew half of what she'd been up to.

Tillie lay in bed that night, Stella long asleep and snoring softly. She was so tired, she could barely stop her muscles from twitching or her mind from fretting, picturing her ma shaking with exhaustion, the wife talking to her like dirt as Tillie was closing the door to leave. What if her ma were to lose her job? She looked so old and worn out. Where would her ma go? When she left, she swore she'd never go back to Lubber's Run. And that was most likely for the best.

And there was Catherine, with nerves and fits that seemed to come from nowhere, withering away in that cabin barely fit for farm animals. Tillie saw that now. It broke her heart, as Catherine was pretty and sweet and funny when she was in a good spell. At least Nora had gotten a position, but what if it didn't work out for her? Her belly churned with worry, and she turned over, trying to stop the onslaught of fear. Even James was no hope, gone to sail the world. He was a hard worker, but he'd had just that one dream, to leave. And her pa...well, that was never going to change.

When he wasn't working the fields or drinking at Elsie's tavern, her pa whittled ax handles for pay. As the wood took shape, he'd drink and whistle a war tune, carving ever more slowly until he'd slump to sleep in his chair. Her ma, ever busy cooking or sewing or whatnot, would notice then and bang the wooden table until he jumped in the air. Then the real trouble would start. When he was sober, her pa was quiet and gentle. But when he drank, the temper got hold of him, especially toward her ma. How different their lives mighta been if her pa had been of a different cloth. She only had to look at her cousins in Waterloo.

Tillie knew she was her family's only hope. But even with all the extra hours and mending at night, she knew it would never amount to enough. A sob of frustration caught in her throat. Would they simply all scatter and go their own ways? Perhaps never to see each other again? She couldn't bear the thought.

Closing her eyes again, she thought back to that day they were all so sick, and these same hopeless feelings were about to swallow her whole, so scared her sisters might die that she went to Susie Mosier's to make some money for the doctor. Even now it was as if she could smell the sweat and stink on the miner who'd been the first that night, grunting and pushing on top of her till she felt like she was being split by a hot poker. She'd bit clear through her lip so that when he got up, he asked why there was blood coming down her chin. It was the only way she could stop herself from screaming. Or crying. When he left the room, she threw up in the chamber pot, barely able to stand up. Then she cleaned herself up, as Susie told her to do, and waited for the next one.

When she got home late that night, she burned Nora's dress in the fire and swore to God above, *Never again*. The doctor came the next morning. It took nearly a week before she could stop her body from shaking. Nora thought she was coming down with the sickness. But Tillie never said a word.

Her pa took longest to get better but seemed changed after that, quiet and hardworking for a few days, whittling away and whistling. Tillie thought if it took what she'd had to do to bring about this hope, it was worth it. But it lasted not a week. As soon as he made a few coins, he was gone, up the road to Elsie's Tavern, leaving barely enough to buy flour and coffee.

How could she ever go back to Susie Mosier's? She rolled onto her back again, staring at the ceiling in the dark. She couldn't. Just the thought twisted her insides into a knot. Didn't she attend regular revival meetings to wash the stains off her soul? Hadn't she made a good name for herself here, and with Dr. and Mrs. Conover? There had to be a better way to make a decent future for someone like her, and she knew what it was.

A husband.

If she kept working here and perhaps advancing, and if she married a hardworking fella, it was possible to make enough to buy a little place of their own. And they could even add on to it and bring her sisters and her ma in one day. She imagined them all laughing and cooking in the kitchen, and it was Frank she saw, sitting at the table and smiling at her with those green eyes. Frank was generous and a hard worker, though there was the problem of the drink.

But she hadn't heard from Frank since the day his friends stole the sled.

CHAPTER 33

ADAM WAS BACK TO WORK despite being not being fully recuperated. The day I walked home and found him gone, I knew exactly where he was. At the little office, sending everyone away. Taking over the project himself. Nothing Helen or I said could dissuade him. I brought meals over and lots of homemade iced tea and lemonade to keep him hydrated. My guilt was starting to fade, and annoyance was starting to take over. Yes, I had betrayed a confidence, but I'd had good intentions. He was being unreasonable. A chilly distance continued, and I didn't know how to make it better. Late at night, I would look at him sleeping and think, *I'm losing him.* He wouldn't let me in, and I felt sick. I would go back to a sad little furnished rental, try to pick up the pieces of my pathetic old life. I would miss Gran. I would miss the cemetery. My heart would never get over Adam. It was just a matter of his saying the words aloud. Words I'd heard before. *This isn't working out. I don't know how to be with you.*

What did it matter now if I called Colleen back?

* * *

LOTTE HALL WAS AN ADDITION onto the main building of Centenary College that was rebuilt after the fire of 1899. Light brick and four stories high, it curved to the left, with a twin dorm curving to the right on the other side of the Seay Building. It was now over a hundred years old, and as I followed Colleen down to the basement, which was massive and dark, she chatted away, flipping on lights as we made our way deeper into its cool recesses filled with row after row of boxes stacked floor to ceiling, old furnishings, storm doors and windows, as well as screens, and even props from the Little Theatre upstairs.

"I finally found a janitor who'd been here back in the nineties and remembered putting these things down here, because I was drawing a complete blank," she explained as we walked slowly. "Everyone working here today just told me this stuff was long gone. But...obviously it's not."

"Thank goodness."

"He also told me some interesting stories...possibly about Tillie. Apparently when painting the dorm above us in the summer one year, they heard strange noises, and he said he got a very odd feeling. Then all of a sudden there would be this strong scent of lilacs. And another one of the maintenance crew shared with him that whenever he was in the Little Theatre at night, he would see dark shadows coming toward him, though he never saw a full apparition." She stopped before a little alcove near the back of the basement.

"Colleen, I actually found a piece of glass from an old perfume bottle in Tillie's cabin that I discovered in Lubber's Run. It was falling down, but there it was, buried in dirt, and I matched it to a perfume maker, Salon Palmer, from the 1800s. The green bottles were for their Spring Lilac scent."

"Oh my God."

We stood there staring at each other, shaking our heads.

"I'm praying we find something here," I said.

The alcove was full of boxes that appeared to have been tossed with little care onto the floor.

"I started going through them after work the day after I called you," Colleen said as she began pulling them out into the main part of the room. "It's a mess, I'm sorry to say, though I'm sure at one time it was all organized. From what that janitor told me, the boxes were rotting from age and damp, so they just kind of dumped everything in new ones without really going through anything."

"Well, thank God they didn't throw them out after all."

"I know. Now these," she said, grabbing a stack near the wall, "I think you're going to find exciting. They're from the late 1800s, it seems. I haven't really looked yet. I just peeked at the top and saw the ledger with the minutes from 1889 to 1890. I thought we should do this together."

"That's really so kind of you." The thought of finding anything about Tillie here was simply incredible, something I was afraid to even hope for.

"I get the feeling this means a lot to you, Rachel."

"It does. Thank you."

"Well, I'm glad to be included. This is kind of fun. Like a scavenger hunt across time."

We knelt beside the boxes on the dusty concrete floor. I was glad Colleen had suggested wearing old clothes. We each took a box and sifted through stacks of papers, minutes, newsletters, etc. The overhead lighting wasn't the best, so Colleen went and scrounged up a few floor lamps from the theatre props. It took us almost two hours to get through six boxes.

Slowly we lifted everything item by item out of each box. I paged through the first ledger, from 1890, excited to see the minutes of Delta Sigma Epsilon from that year, wondering if even that far from 1886 something might be mentioned about Tillie, but there was nothing. In the meantime, Colleen kept digging, putting aside awards, programs, souvenirs, class photos, and more. At the bottom we found another year's minutes, 1888–89, but again, there was nothing about Tillie. The next box yielded much of the same, and we were halfway through it when Colleen lifted yet another ledger out. 1885–86.

"Oh my God." I took it from her.

Together we read it page by page. It began in September of 1885 with the nomination of that year's officers. Faith Seiler was president and Emmeline Henry vice-president. The minutes were mundane and much as expected, discussing social events, programs, and ideas for fund raising. Their pet project, it seemed, was women's rights, and one of the goals was to bring in a major speaker of the time, Victoria Woodhull, who I'd never heard of but had apparently run for president.

It wasn't until months later, February of 1886, that there was mention of something that caught my attention. Faith wanted to include one of the servants in the sorority, but there was resistance. No name was mentioned. The next meeting, in March, the minutes recorded that the annual sorority photograph was taken and that Tillie Smith, a kitchen worker who'd become an honorary member of their society, had been included.

"Oh, Colleen!" I sat back on my heels, staring at the words, tears coming into my eyes. This was real. This was proof of everything I'd been only guessing at. "Tillie became involved with the sorority girls. It's just as I've imagined. Her life before coming here was so damn hard. Her family destitute. And she was trying so hard to improve herself, better her life."

"That must have been unusual, for a servant to be included in something like that."

"Oh, yes."

Nothing further was mentioned about Tillie in the minutes until the next month, April, which Colleen read aloud.

At the suggestion of our president, Faith Seiler, we held a memorial vigil for our honorary sister, Matilda Smith.

Colleen looked up at me, both of us looking stricken. Weeks after that photograph, she was dead. My throat ached with grief, with tears I tried to hold back. It was as if it was all happening in real time as we read it. Those sorority girls horrified and screaming, Tillie lying dead somewhere behind the building we now knelt in.

Colleen began reading again: *On the morning of April 9th, Tillie's body was found in the back field of the campus. At the sound of servants screaming, several of us ran outside, and we nearly collapsed when we saw our Tillie lying there as though she'd fallen asleep on her back. But her neck was covered with purple bruises.*

Dr. Whitney tried to push us back until Faith protested that one of our own had been murdered, and it was nonsense to worry about our sensibilities. And now, two weeks later, we know that Tillie had also been ravished.

It is said our Tillie had gone to sleep in a nearby barn because she could not be admitted back into the institute past ten o'clock. We protest the treatment of the servants here, especially the

*women. That she should have been locked out to fend for herself on
a cold, dark night is barbaric.*

*We hereby petition Dr. Whitney to change the working condi-
tions for women. We do this in our friend Tillie's honor.*

Colleen held the pages up for me to see the signatures of
more than thirty young women.

"Oh, Rachel. This is just unbelievable."

I couldn't speak.

"I feel sick," Colleen went on, her eyes filling. "This isn't a
scavenger hunt. This just made it all so real. That poor girl."

It was as if I were seeing that morning unfold in my mind,
the chaos, the screaming, and Tillie just lying on the cold
ground, gone.

"She was real," I said finally. "Not a legend or a mascot or...
anything like that. After all this time, she's become nothing
more than a footnote in her own life. It's not right. And I've had
this feeling for such a long time now that I'm meant to do something about that."

I told Colleen about jury duty and my wild goose chase, then
finding out about the transcript from the trial. I also confessed
about Adam's family connection with Titus's granddaughter and
their order to leave it all alone.

"Oh my God," Colleen whispered, shaking her head. "But how
do you just let it go?"

"I've been trying. I don't want to get them any more upset.
Especially Adam."

"Still...I don't know if I could just let it go. I mean, from
everything you've told me, there does seem to be some kind of
hand of fate at play here."

"I know."

We were silent for a long moment. Then Colleen said, "Look,
why don't we finish up for now? It's getting late."

We finished looking through the box together. There was
nothing else as the school year ended in May. When the minutes
began again in the fall, Faith was no longer president, and the
minutes took on an entirely different tone. Someone less pro-

gressive and more devout had taken over. The minutes were full of prayers and social news about the various members.

We came to the very last box.

"Oh my God," Colleen said, "it's all photographs. Hundreds of them, I think."

We lifted out a batch, portraits of members. We also saw with excitement the yearly sorority group photos. They were in no particular order, and Colleen and I began to sift through them, hoping against hope, my heart beating faster and faster. Some were brown with age, brittle, and some even stuck together from dampness. Others in the later years were in color.

"Rachel."

I looked up. Colleen was looking at me, another photograph in her hand. She nodded, then handed it to me. "I can't believe this."

I took the photograph. There they all were, the young ladies of Delta Sigma Epsilon 1885–1886, all lined up in three rows, in lovely silk dresses, upswept hairdos, and pearls. In the back row on the end stood a servant girl in a classic black maid's uniform with white lace apron and cap. There was the barest hint of a smile. It was Tillie.

I stared at her face. At her eyes.

"I can't," I said to Colleen. "I just can't let her go."

CHAPTER 34

March 1886

THE SNOWS FINALLY BEGAN TO MELT by the third week of March, though the change also brought the seasonal fatigues and maladies to many at the institute. When Tillie was little and her ma still at home, her ma used to spoon out black-strap molasses every fall and spring, and sometimes even the dreaded cod liver oil. But spring this early was a false gift. Tillie had seen too many snows in April and more than her share of frosts in May, listening to her pa cursing about crops gone bad before they barely sprouted. He seemed to have a better hand at crafting handles for tools than farming.

It was still dark when she made her way down to the kitchen, Stella and the rest still asleep. She was hoping to get the potatoes for breakfast and supper done this morning so she'd have time to finish some of the other work she'd taken on in the afternoon. She was just past the laundry when she stopped suddenly.

"What do you make of the potato peeler, that Tillie?"

She knew the voice. It was that Mead, who'd tried to get fresh with her in the dining room, the one Stella had been sweet on.

"She's a plump little morsel," she heard Mr. Titus say. "Good enough to take a nibble out of."

"Pshaw, Jimmy, you would not dare."

"Why, I've had my hand on her leg, mind you, and a fine leg she has."

Her face flamed, and she nearly charged into the furnace room. Why, the nerve of those two, talking so familiar about her.

"And how about that Daisy? Whatcha think about her, Jimmy?"

"A bit too skinny for my own taste. I like 'em with some flesh on their bones. Now, that Irish gal, Bridget..."

Tillie shook her head and kept going, wishing she could dump some of Bridget's hot Irish oatmeal into their laps. Mr. Titus was bad enough, always with the lecherous looks at her bosom or the sly remarks under his breath, knowing she wasn't about to say anything to the matron, especially after Maggie Donovan had been fired. 'Cause who'd believe her over him? She'd wager her best petticoat he was all talk about ladies. But Mead was a bit scary, that one. Walking around so pompous with his nose in the air and all. Dressed like a reverend, then talking and acting like he was from the gutter. He was the kind who could do real damage to someone if he had the mindset.

Bridget was not long behind her in the kitchen.

"Why, Tillie, look at the mountain of potatoes already peeled."

"I aim to take a few hours to myself after the noon meal, if Matron will allow it. I've got me some mending to do for some of the girls that I need to finish up. They've got a fancy do this weekend."

"Anyone with eyes could see you been workin' yourself to the bone. I don't know how you're still standin', lass. Ye must be savin' for something special. That store-bought dress you been dreamin' about?" Bridget asked with a teasing smile.

Tillie didn't answer at first. "No, I got bigger dreams than that."

"Then why such a long face?" When she didn't answer, Bridget said, "Would it have somethin' to do with that handsome beau of yours?"

Tillie sighed. "It's been fifteen days and not a word."

"And you're fretting perhaps he's found another gal?"

"I...I don't think so. He really seemed to care for me, but...I don't know."

"You care for him, then."

"I do. It's so nice to think that there's someone thinkin' about ya, you know? Just you. And that you could rely on someone if need be."

"Oh, I do know, truly. It's a hard world we've got for us. Doin' it alone makes it even harder."

"What about you, Bridget? Hasn't there been someone claiming your heart?"

Bridget's eyes filled with tears, and Tillie regretted her question.

"There was, back in Ireland. As handsome as they go with eyes so blue, I swore they were real sapphires. And a tongue full of the blarney."

"What do you mean?"

"When I left Ireland, he promised to be right behind me. He'd been workin' to save for passage. And...well, he never did come. Or if he did, he didn't come to find me."

"I'm sorry, Bridget."

"Oh, I'm long past it."

But Tillie could see she wasn't. Just then Matron popped in on her rounds, and all talk stopped as they went back to their tasks. Cook arrived a short while after that, and by the time the breakfast was over and cleaned up, Tillie felt as though she were melting, the kitchen was so hot. Grabbing her shawl and stepping outside for a breath of fresh air, she was stunned to find Frank sitting on one of the cellar steps. His cheeks were red as apples and his green eyes bright with the cold. He musta been waiting for her a long time.

* * *

BY THE TIME TILLIE SAT IN HER ROOM finishing up the hemming and stitching that afternoon, the fretful mood that had taken hold of her for days was gone. All thoughts of Titus and Mead and their horrid bawdy talk had disappeared, too. She was fairly bubbling with excitement, her foot tapping as she worked her needle and thread. This must be what real love felt like. She knew now all the fuss in songs and plays and books. She felt as though she was born anew inside. Not like what they talked about at the revival meetings. This was something more akin to joy.

When she first saw Frank, though, her mood was sour. "I

was afraid you might be in jail over taking that sled," she'd said, wrapping her shawl tighter against the cold and watching his smile fade. "The police didn't look too pleased."

"Well, when I explained the situation, that my girl needed to go see her ma, and my pals wanted to oblige..." He shrugged, as if nothing more need be said.

"So you truly weren't in trouble over it?" she said in disbelief.

"Well, Tillie, sometimes you gotta know how to deal with situations," he said, patting his pocket and smiling again. "Everyone has their price. And it was worth it to get my girl where she needed to be, snow be damned."

She stood there, stunned. No one had ever taken such a chance on her. Or cared so about what she wanted or needed.

"So where've ya been for these past weeks, then?"

"Actually, my pet, I went out to Danville to help rebuild a farmhouse that caught fire. Had to stay there, too, 'cause we were in a hurry, which I didn't mind 'cause that paid extra, and I been saving up for something special."

"And what would that be?" she asked, feeling her heart lift like a wish on the wind.

"Well," he said, coming closer and giving her a wink, "I think you'll just have to be patient and find out on Saturday."

She laughed suddenly and kissed him right on the mouth. Realizing her folly, she took his hand and hurried him to the old red barn on the other side of the grounds, where she knew some of the gals went with their beaus. Inside the dark barn, he pulled her to him tight, kissing her right back, and she felt all the worries that had been gnawing at her fly up to the rafters. She really was his girl.

CHAPTER 35

"I'M SORRY," I SAID TO ADAM YET AGAIN one morning as he was leaving for work. It was early, barely after six. His face had finally returned to normal, but he still looked pale and exhausted. He hadn't touched me since he came home from the hospital.

"You don't have to keep saying that," he said as he walked into the foyer.

"Who's Sandra?"

That got his attention. He turned and gave me a long look.

"She came to the hospital when you were still unconscious. Her aunt said you two were high school sweethearts and were planning to marry."

"I never had any plans to marry her," he said, closing the door behind him.

I decided to go to Trenton. I doubted Adam would miss me. Or even care.

The old insecurities had come back, unwanted visitors I knew well from my lonely years since the rape. The ones that told me I wasn't good enough, pretty enough, interesting enough. Who would really want me? Maybe Adam didn't after all. And didn't know how to get out of this. And of course, I kept picturing Sandra, petite and adorable.

I told myself not to feel this way. I wanted to trust Adam while giving him the space he needed. But along with the old insecurities, I felt my defenses rising, the cranky, argumentative behavior that managed to ruin the few other relationships I'd tried to have. I knew what it was all about even as I'd acted out. I would pick the relationship apart before he even had a chance. I would control the demise and salvage my pride. I was a fool.

I LEFT A LITTLE AFTER SEVEN-THIRTY, taking Route 29, which paralleled the Delaware River, with Pennsylvania on the other side. It was a scenic drive, the road lined with orange tiger lilies and other colorful wildflowers, the wide river glistening in the early morning sun. My mind, though, was far from tranquil. Eleven hundred pages awaited me, and I knew I wouldn't be able to go through it all in just a day. My first goal was to find anything to do with Tillie's family. But my real hope was to hear Tillie's own words through someone else. This was no doubt going to be the closest I would come to her.

My dreams of Tillie were becoming more vivid. The new photo-graph was the impetus, no doubt. After all these years and the long-standing belief that her portrait was the only known photo-graph, Colleen and I had found something remarkable. We made copies of it, and she let me take the original. I had both photo-graphs with me.

As I approached Trenton in the heart of rush hour, traffic thickened. I'd had nothing but toast and coffee before leaving, and now even that began to churn in my stomach as my excite-ment and nervousness grew. I turned onto State Street and recognized the library just ahead from the photos online, the plaza and fountain fronting the road. My knees actually trembled as I walked into the big building. I waited as a group of seniors were directed to a conference room for a government talk on health care, and then it was my turn.

"Hi. I'm here to see Colin Frinzi. He's expecting me. My name is Rachel Miller."

"Just take the elevator to the fourth floor. I'll let him know you're here."

Mr. Frinzi was waiting for me as I stepped off the elevator. He'd already pulled the volume and escorted me to a big oak table near a window.

"This is it?" I asked, looking at him.

"Yes, this is it," he said with a smile. "Be careful; it's brittle."

"I will. You don't have to worry."

After he left, I stood there looking down at the immense book, the brown leather cover worn with age. Then I placed a palm on it, closed my eyes, and prayed.

I sat and carefully opened to the first yellowed page: *The State vs. James J. Titus: Warren County, September 29, 1886.* The trial had begun nearly six months after the murder. I quickly inventoried the book and saw that the first half was the prosecution's case. Then there were the pages of the defense. And finally, the closing arguments, which weren't much because those seemed to be most of the missing pages.

The opening pages were typical courtroom business, but it was fascinating, and I realized I'd have to skim fast or I'd never get to what I really wanted: anything that could give me a clue into Tillie's real life. Perhaps I could also find things that had been missed about the murder.

As I began reading, the sounds of the library faded, as did everything else, and it was as if I were sitting once again on one of those hard wooden benches in that same courtroom in Belvidere, but now it was 1886, and here was the entire cast of characters, except for the one person I wanted, Tillie. The language was quaint and the pages often difficult to read because the handwriting was tiny and slanted. Then it changed, as obviously the person transcribing the stenographer's notes changed. I raced past witnesses and was more than four hundred pages into it when I found a name that halted me. *Nathan Smith*, Tillie's father!

The prosecution went first and asked Nathan Smith only four questions: *Where do you live? Waterloo. Was Matilda Smith your daughter? Yes, sir. Can you tell me when she was born? She was born in 1867. What day and what month? 20th of June.*

I paused. Was it possible her father didn't know her real birthday? Tillie's date of birth was listed in the census as well as in the newspapers as January 20, 1867. Or was it an error on the stenographer's part? Either way it was sad. To have pieces of your life so quickly forgotten.

The defense took over then, and Mr. Shipman, Titus's attorney, was hostile from the start. *You don't live at Waterloo, do you? In the neighborhood of Waterloo, I use the Waterloo post office. How far do you live from there? About a mile or more. Which of your children lives with you?*

The prosecution then objected: what did this cross-examination have to do with the questions asked by them, which were simply to prove Matilda's age? Titus's attorney explained that he *simply wanted to show the surroundings of the parties.* The judge allowed it. A little drumming began in my gut. I had a bad feeling about this.

Is your wife living? I believe so. Where is she? Living in Warren County somewhere, with John Grey, I think. She don't live with you? No sir. How long has she been living separate? About eight years, I think. Keeps house for John Grey? I believe so. How long has she kept house for him? I can't tell you exactly.

Then the questioning took a very disturbing turn.

You live with your daughter, you say? Catherine. She keeps house for me. And you and Catherine live in the same room at night? We are in the same room; that is, she sleeps at one end of the room. Don't you and she sometimes sleep together? No sir.

I stared at the pages, stunned. Abruptly, the questioning changed then.

How long has Tillie been away from home? Well, she has been away from home, as near as I can remember, about two years now, somewhere near that. Did you have any difficulty with Tillie at your own house about her going about? I think not.

I took a deep breath, trying to calm myself. I saw now where this was going, and I wanted to scream. They were going to attack Tillie's home life and character. The prosecution objected again, but the judge overruled: *It seems to me to touch the character of the deceased. In a charge of rape, the character of the woman alleged to be ravished is open for inquiry. It is relevant undoubtedly.*

My fist hit the table. Then I looked up. Luckily, there was no one else nearby. This was a horror. They were going to insinuate that Tillie's character or her chastity was to blame somehow?

She'd been brutally raped and murdered, and now it was as if she herself was on trial.

It went on for pages. *Didn't she run around a great deal? Didn't she go out a great deal at night with boys?* Nathan Smith answered no to all of it, admitting only that he advised her to *stay in and keep away from bad company.*

Were there not some houses that were rather disreputable about there, and didn't you find fault with her for going there? Didn't she stay a while in that house and live there as a servant and work there? Not to my knowledge.

Oh, Tillie...I felt sick at heart. The defense was implying incest in her home. That she'd been to a brothel. I couldn't help but picture the little cabin at Lubber's Run. Her home life must have been awful. And the fact that such testimony was allowed, that the victim could be deemed at fault for the "*character of her chastity.*" My God, what woman would ever bring a man up on charges back then?

If Titus's attorney was stooping to such awful lengths, weren't they desperate? Maybe he was guilty despite those doubts by some locals I'd heard, and their only recourse was to attack the victim. Paint her as a whore, to prove it wasn't rape. I felt nauseas. Closing my eyes, I laid my head down for a moment, hearing nothing but the hum of a machine in the dis-tance. Until suddenly a whisper broke the quiet.

Slut.

And then a chorus of snickers. I felt like someone was squeezing my brain. I stood up, turned all around, searching the room. No one...was there. I hurried to the stairwell, down four flights, out into the parking lot. I stood there in the blazing heat, disoriented, trying to make sense of what just happened. And then I heard a man laughing. A laugh I'd heard once before.

I started walking to my van, certain I was going to throw up. He was still laughing. Goose bumps ran up and down my arms despite the heat. I stopped walking, turned in a circle looking... and there he was. Talking and laughing on his cell phone. I stood there blinking, dazed. He was heading right toward me. I knew that laugh. The red hair...

He was in front of me now, and my heart stopped. I stared at him. His eyes met mine. He kept walking past, barely noticing me, still talking on his phone. I started shaking as I watched him get into a white Mercedes. Somehow I got in my car. I turned it on, blasting the air, my brain feeling as if it might explode.

It was all coming back. Images flashing across the windshield. The sound of his cackle. Everything I had fought so hard to forget for the past eighteen years. And there was nothing I could do to stop it.

CHAPTER 36

I T WAS ONE OF THOSE SPECTACULAR AUTUMN DAYS. The sun so golden, leaves bursting with color all over campus, the world full of promise. I had a date! I'd never really dated in high school, so I was excited. And really nervous. He was a junior and a football player. He was also tall and broad with bright red hair. He looked like a Viking, and everyone called him Thor. We lived in the same coed dorm, and when he was hanging out in the lounge on my floor, I could hear that laugh from my room.

I was fairly floating as I went to my dorm room after class to change. I picked out my outfit carefully: a black jean skirt, emerald green sweater, black suede boots. My mother thought green highlighted my auburn hair, and when we went shopping before I left for my freshman year, she told me I looked beautiful in the sweater. She had tears in her eyes. I knew my going far was difficult for her, but for once she was trying not to show it. As for me, I needed space. I wanted to live, finally, far from her fears and phobias.

My mother nearly went insane, though, when she first found out I was assigned a coed dorm. She'd even called the college requesting a reassignment, but there were no other options. There were separate bathrooms, I assured her, and a dorm counselor on each floor. She bought me pepper spray and insisted I have it on me at all times, even just going to the bathroom. For a while I did. And then I didn't.

One day when I was walking through the lounge, I saw him there reading. There was no one else around. As I walked by, I felt a tug on my hair, and I turned to see him smiling. I blushed.

"You have beautiful hair."

My heart slammed in my chest. He was so handsome. "Thank you," I managed.

"Where are you from?"

And so it began, a conversation that lasted more than thirty minutes about our classes, our majors, where we saw ourselves in five years. He listened to me so intently, frowning as I spoke, his eyes searching my face. When I had to leave for my next class, he asked me to have pizza with him the next day. I couldn't believe it. I was a nobody, and he was one of the most popular guys in school.

I met him at Campus Pizza just across the main street that ran through the college. He ordered a large pie with pepperoni, and as he ate four slices, he told me he was excited because some scouts were coming to watch him play that weekend. He was hoping to make it to the pros. I just sat there, dazzled, barely able to eat one piece, listening to it all. I just kept thinking, *He's so nice, not stuck up at all like you'd expect.*

We walked back to my dorm afterwards, and then he walked me right to my door. There was an awkward moment when I wondered if he'd kiss me, but he didn't. It seemed the most natural thing to invite him in. I was going to make tea in my hot pot. I had homemade cookies my mother had sent. And we were deep into a conversation about music. I didn't want the date to end.

I was standing near the window, and he was sitting by my desk. We were talking about how much we liked the music of our parents' generation: the Beatles; the Stones; Crosby, Stills, Nash & Young. He kept looking at my mouth.

"Do you like the Moody Blues?" he asked, standing and coming toward me, his voice getting softer. "'Nights in White Satin'?"

I could only nod because I knew he was about to kiss me. He did, his lips so soft on mine. I hesitated, then kissed him back, a rush of wanting flooding through me. He started kissing harder, pushing his tongue in my mouth, a strange yet thrilling sensation. Then he began pressing himself into me. I wasn't sure what to do, and after a moment I tried to pull away, to get back to talking. But he pushed me back so I was sitting on the bed, and he sat with me, his arms wrapped around me tightly and not let-ting go. I was getting nervous, but he just kept kissing me harder and faster, his breath coming in gasps now. I tried with more force to pull away again, to say something, but then he grabbed my hair and pulled me backward onto the bed. My heart was racing, and I was having a hard time breathing. Then suddenly he was on top of me, his hand up my skirt. I tried to scream, but his mouth was on mine, the weight of him on my chest. I couldn't breathe. Terror ripped through me. I was being crushed as his fingers pulled at my underwear. I tried to get my hand between us, to grab his and stop him, but I couldn't, and his belt buckle tore my thumb as he was undoing his pants. Suddenly he was shoving himself into me, grunting and pushing, and a moment later it was as if my insides were splitting in half, my flesh tearing and burning. Over and over he kept ramming him-self into me. I wasn't even crying. I was suffocating. My lungs were collapsing. I was going to die.

And then it was over. He lay on top of me panting. Finally, he rolled off me, and I gasped for air. He got up, zipped his pants, and grabbed his jacket from the chair. I lay there, unable to speak, my body paralyzed.

"Thanks. That was nice," he said.

And then he was gone.

I sat in my van now, sobbing. Remembering all that had happened in the days and weeks that followed, I began to wail. How stupid I was. How utterly fucking stupid.

I OPENED MY EYES AND SAT UP WITH A START, gripping the steering wheel, completely disoriented. I looked at the dashboard clock. I'd been asleep for almost an hour. Grabbing a water bottle on the passenger seat, I downed it quickly. I felt as if I'd run a marathon, my body spent, my muscles quivering. How had this happened?

I sat back, turned the air conditioning off, and rolled down the windows. I thought about every coincidence, every single moment since I'd first seen the monument to Tillie Smith that caused me to be at this library today. That brought me face to face with the man who ruined my life. And relive the horror of that day that changed everything for me. I lifted my hand and looked at the tiny scar across my thumb from the fishing wire around her monument. Then I looked at the scar beside it from eighteen years ago.

What were the odds?

I sat there for a long time, not sure what to do. Then I got out of the car and walked back into the library.

CHAPTER 37

March 1886

I T WAS THE QUIET HOUR AFTER THE DINNER'S CLEANUP and before the ten o'clock curfew. Student programs were over, studying finished up, and even the servants' quarters absent the usual rushing about to jobs and chores. Besides the ever-banging steam pipes and the hiss of the gas lamps, the only other sound was the clatter of freezing rain hitting the windows.

Stella was having a hot bath, hogging the water closet for nearly an hour now, something Tillie longed for herself. But Tillie was too exhausted from her long days of late. Tonight there was a revival meeting, and though she wanted to go see Annie and tell her all that was happening, she dared not. Even if the weather were less fierce, she couldn't manage the time off.

Yet there were things in her heart she needed to clear. Worries that gnawed at her, though she was more hopeful than she'd ever been. Perhaps that was the problem. Hope was a risky thing. Didn't she know that well? Having your expectations soar only to be crushed by disappointment again and again.

Instead of changing into her nightclothes, Tillie opened her door and peeked out into the servants' hall. No one was about, not even Mrs. Ruckle, who she heard was having a meeting with Cook about a special luncheon tomorrow for some visiting clergy. Quietly she closed her door and walked down the hall, the gas sconces not yet lowered by the janitor. Slowly she climbed the two flights up, staying to the sides of the wooden steps, where creaking was less likely. When she got to the chapel doors, she said a quick prayer, then opened them cautiously, looking about. No one was there.

Stepping inside, she paused a moment and took a deep

breath. The chapel was so quiet, the only sound the hissing of the gas lamps. She'd been up here only a few times, and once again she was awed by the beauty of the colorful stained glass windows, the grand altar, the gleaming pews and woodwork. Stella did a fine job here, she'd give her that. And thanks to Stella's endless stories about when she was meeting Peter Mead up here, Tillie knew this was the best time to sneak up to the chapel.

She knelt on a cushioned pew, staring at the large wooden cross on the altar, wondering where to start. She prayed all the time. Nothing formal, mostly quick prayers when she needed something during the day, like she'd just done before opening the doors. Or before going into the barn, afraid of murderous tramps lurking. Even for good weather before attempting a trek home. But this was different. This prayer was for...everything.

Folding her hands, she bowed her head and closed her eyes.

"Dear Lord," she whispered, for she believed your voice had to be spoken for prayers to truly be heard, as her mother had taught them. "I don't come here often, as you know. And you must think I'm lacking sometimes in piety and devotion, but I have tried mightily to follow your path. I try to be kind to others and not judge my neighbor. In all my life, I have never stolen or taken your name in vain. The sins I committed in the past were not for wanting but for necessity. I know that doesn't excuse those sinful deeds, but I'm hoping...I am praying...if Jesus could forgive Mary Magdalene, perhaps he could forgive me. I'm here now not just for myself, Lord. I'm here for my family. I know to some we're a sorry sight, but I believe we have a chance for a better life.

I thank you for this position here at the institute, Lord. For the strength of my hands to keep peeling potatoes each day, and I will stay with this job until the end of my days if I must. Thank you for bringing into my life a man who is good and kind. I'm praying that Frank loves me enough to ask me to be his wife. I'm praying for steady employment for him so we can make a home. And I'm praying to bring my sisters and my ma to come live with us, Lord. Nothing fancy, just enough to get us by so we can be together. And Lord, if possible, I'm praying that my pa could stop drinking. Thank you for listening, Lord. I am your most humble servant, Tillie."

She stood and walked to the back of the chapel, then turned to look at the altar once more. She had to have faith. *With faith, all things are possible.* How many times had she heard that quote from the Bible?

Just then the bells began to ring, near deafening as the bell tower was just about this floor. Turning quickly, she made her way to the stairs, pausing suddenly. *Where did that noise come from?* she wondered, turning to look back at the chapel doors, her heart in her throat. She looked all around, but no one was in sight. Slipping downstairs and back into her room, she was relieved to find Stella asleep already. She undressed quickly, turned down the light, and got into bed.

A shiver ran down her arms despite the thick covers. Someone had been up there, she was certain of it.

CHAPTER 38

I T WAS DARK WHEN I GOT BACK TO TOWN. I turned my van into the cemetery and stopped when I was over the bridge. Except for the eternal flame candles and the occasional solar decoration, the cemetery was dark, the graves silent. What was I going to say to Adam? Would I even tell him? I knew I should, but I was terrified of saying it out loud, reliving each moment. Making it real again. Going back to that dark place that once owned me. Wouldn't it be better to bury it again?

I was physically drained, yet my insides pulsed with nervous energy. I needed Xanax, or a few glasses of wine. I pulled up to the house and got out of the van.

"You've been gone all day."

I jumped, startled. From the light of the living room window, I saw Adam sitting on the porch in the dark.

"I..." My voice was rusty, and I cleared my throat. "I'm sur-prised you noticed."

"I deserve that."

I waited, trembling.

"I came back this morning to talk to you," he said, "but you were gone. I've been waiting all day."

"You could've called me."

"I did. It went straight to voice mail each time."

Stupid me. I realized then I had never turned my phone back on once I'd left the library.

"Where were you?"

"I was just driving around."

He stood then, coming toward me. Without realizing, I took a step back. He stopped.

"Look, I want to apologize. I've been a real ass. What you did...I know you didn't mean to deceive me."

I started to cry. I wasn't even sure why. Loud sobs, the kind that take your breath away.

"Oh, baby, I am so sorry," he said, reaching for me.

I jumped back.

"Whoa, honey..."

"I..." But I had no words. I felt like I was falling apart.

He was saying something else, but I didn't hear it because I was running to the house now, up the stairs to the guest bedroom. I locked the door.

* * *

WHEN I FINALLY WENT DOWN THE NEXT MORNING I found a note on the kitchen counter.

Rachel, I know I overreacted. You meant well, and I know I punished you for far too long. I'm fixing it, so don't worry. I pushed the board audit back due to my illness. I think in a few weeks the worst will be over. I understand if you need some space. But please don't take too long. I miss my wife. Love, Adam.

He missed his wife. I sat in a kitchen chair, holding the letter in a trembling hand. Could I really be a wife to him again? Everything I'd fought for years to wipe out of my memory bank was back. The horror of what that bastard did to me that day, and then what I did, causing my own mother's death a few days later...it had broken me for a long time. I was so alone.

Mrs. Bejarano, a nice lady next door who'd befriended my mother, began coming over with meals, trying to get me to talk, to even just step outside. Otherwise there was no one. The day I didn't answer the door, she broke the window in the sidelight, reached her hand in, and unlocked it. She found me at the kitchen table with a pile of my mother's pills in front of me and called 911.

I was hospitalized in a psych ward because I was considered

a danger to myself. Finally, I told the therapist everything. I told her I wanted to block it out, make believe it had never happened. That might work for a while, she'd cautioned, but at some point it would come back. Eventually I'd have to face it. But I told myself she was wrong. And for a long time, I thought she was. I'd managed to make a life for myself, building a career that was a perfect escape and keeping to myself. A lonely existence, per-haps, but one I felt safe in.

That afternoon I sat in front of my computer, my fingers poised above the keys for a long time before I finally began typ-ing, searching for websites dealing with rape. I could hear my therapist all those years ago encouraging me to continue coun-seling, to face what I only wanted to forget. And here I was, eighteen years later, with Dr. Roberti saying the same things

The first website I pulled was takebackthenight.org. At the very top in big bold letters were statistics: one in three women worldwide are victims of sexual violence. I sat back, wondering. This meant the odds were that someone in my life was probably also a victim. The average rapist, it went on, would assault twelve to seventeen women before going to prison. My blood stilled. Were there others before me? After me? I couldn't help picturing him, so confident and cocky on his cell phone, laugh-ing and getting into his expensive Mercedes. How many other girls and women had he destroyed?

Why didn't I walk up to him and smack him? Scream that I knew what he was? Why did I fall apart again, a pathetic bundle of shame and guilt?

I kept reading. There were survivor stories, with names and photographs. Women who, unlike me, were courageous enough to face the world and tell about their rapes. An overweight black woman who admitted she'd been committing slow suicide through food and cigarettes since her rape. A mother in her thirties who confessed that even having her kids hug her would sometimes bring on panic. A middle-aged woman who'd once been a pariah at her college because she'd had the gall to report her rape by a popular soccer player. They shared obvious traits:

the need for control often morphing into OCD, panic attacks, out-bursts of anger. Traits I recognized in myself.

They had all been raped while freshmen in college. Like me. Even now, twenty or thirty years later, despite finding some kind of closure, they all admitted they were still affected by what had been labeled "date rape." In each case they were made to feel that somehow it was their fault.

And while there were rarely any physical scars, the damage to their souls was brutal. I wasn't alone. I wasn't even an oddity, I began to see. The difference was that they'd had the guts to step forward and tell their stories.

* * *

TWO DAYS LATER THE TRANSCRIPT WAS EMAILED TO ME. When I'd gone back into the library, Colin Frinzi told me it wouldn't be cheap to have it scanned and digitized, but after the run-in with my rapist, I felt reckless and didn't care. I paid with a credit card still in my name only.

It was easy to hide on my computer. I read the transcript all day. Adam came in after work simply assuming I was looking for some kind of job. Now I was the distant one, living in fear, waiting for myself to fall apart again. Buried in the trial of Tillie's murder. I could not tear myself away. I was living in another time, totally absorbed in the testimony.

I was still troubled by the allegations that Tillie had been working at a brothel. I knew nothing about her life before the institute, really, until I came upon another name I recognized: Dr. William Conover. He testified that Tillie had come to work for him the previous year and had been with them until just prior to working at the seminary. I remembered that he was the one who'd taught her to read.

The prosecutor asked, *What was her general reputation for chastity in the community?*

I knew now what they were doing. There were two charges against Titus, one for rape and one for murder. They were trying to prove it was not rape by insinuating Tillie was a loose woman.

Dr. Conover: I knew her general reputation in the community as long as she lived with me.

Prosecutor: What is it?

Dr. Conover: It was very good indeed.

Dr. Conover was then admonished by the judge: *The question is not what you thought....The question is, what was her general reputation in the community, not the family?*

Dr. Conover: I can answer that very quickly. It was good, sir, extremely.

I closed my eyes a moment, thanking God for that. The defense then went on the attack.

Shipman: Did you ever hear anybody speak about her reputation for chastity?

Dr. Conover: No sir.

Shipman: Then you don't know, as far as your general knowledge extends, anything about it from what you heard people say about it?

Dr. Conover: I can state that—

Shipman: It is not what people said about it.

Dr. Conover: All the employees on my farm.

Shipman: Never mind the employees on your farm. Did you ever hear anybody in the neighborhood speak of the general reputation of Tillie Smith for chastity?

Dr. Conover: I heard of Mrs. Bailey. She lived down the road a short distance from my place.

But the defense objected because they didn't want anything said about Tillie after the murder. I assumed they would figure sentiment ran high for Tillie after she had been killed. They were looking for evidence of her reputation before the murder. So the testimony was struck and ended with Dr. Conover stating he knew nothing at all of it prior to her death, and the defense won that volley, casting doubt on Tillie's name prior to that.

Samuel T. Casey, a farmer from Mount Olive Township who had employed Tillie in 1882, was up next for the prosecution. At just fifteen years old, Rachel calculated, Tillie took care of Samuel Casey's house for six months.

Prosecutor: Were you acquainted with her reputation for chastity in that neighborhood?

Samuel Casey: Well, yes. It was good as far as I know. I heard nothing against her at all. All the time that she was there.

He was followed by William P. Osborne, who testified that Tillie worked for him on his farm about a mile away in Stanhope until the end of June 1883. No one had a bad word to say about Tillie. So Tillie had left home at fifteen and begun working for various farmers, eventually taking a position with Dr. Conover, her last before Centenary, which took her farther from home but closer to her mother...and perhaps away from the mines and the canal?

Still, there was the gap in employment in the last six months of 1883, when she'd been seen at the brothel. I picked up the photograph, staring into Tillie's eyes. "I won't let them get away with this," I whispered.

"Won't let who get away with what?"

I turned with a start. Adam stood in the doorway.

"Did you forget Gran's party?"

I'd lost track of time. Again. "Give me five minutes."

"Where's the present?"

I'd forgotten that, too. It was the one thing he'd asked me to do that day.

CHAPTER 39

ON THE RIDE OVER TO GRAN'S PARTY, Adam didn't speak.
"Let's stop at the florist. I'll run in and get flowers," I said.

He shrugged, eyes on the road. Then he turned to me. "I'm worried about you. Something's different. You're so...distracted. You won't even let me near you."

I didn't say anything.

"Look, I know I hurt you by being mad for so long. I...I tried to let it go."

"You needed space. Now it's my turn."

"Okay. Fair enough."

Five minutes later we pulled up to Helen's Victorian. The street was lined with cars.

"Well, if it isn't the honeymooners," Aunt Helen said as we walked into the house, already full of guests.

A banner across the dining room read, "HAPPY 90TH BIRTH-DAY, CORA." Aunt Helen gave Adam a kiss on the cheek, then turned to me, hesitating.

"It's okay. You don't have to," I said.

It came out before I even realized it. Aunt Helen's eyes widened. I'd just killed our brief armistice. Adam took my hand, leading me away.

"I'm sorry. She just puts me on edge."

"Maybe she could say the same about you."

Then we were in the big living room. Gran was sitting there in her wheelchair with a glass of something bubbly in her hand.

"There's my handsome grandson!"

Everyone turned, and I prayed the strain between us wasn't

obvious. Adam handed Gran the flowers. Then Gran looked at me a moment and broke into a smile.

"Rachel!"

I hugged Gran, who kept hold of my hand, and then I noticed who was sitting right beside her. I felt my face turn red. "Hello, Mrs. Freeman," I said.

"Hello, dear," she said, giving me a tiny smile.

I stood beside Gran as Adam began talking to people through-out the room. A little while later, Justine, Gran's aide, came into the room with a tray of appetizers.

"Oh, don't those look delicious," Gran said, letting go and tak-ing a small plate and a few appetizers.

I made my way across the room to a punch bowl, wondering if Mrs. Freeman remembered me.

"Hey, Rachel," Justine said, now on this side of the room, holding up her tray for me to choose from.

"Oh, hi, Justine. No thanks."

"Did you see that amazing cake Sandra made?"

"What?!" I had no idea I had said it so loud until I realized people were looking at me.

I followed Justine to the kitchen, stopping in the doorway. She began refilling her tray, but my eyes were riveted to Sandra, standing beside a large cake and, next to her, Adam. They were in deep conversation and didn't even look up.

"What a pretty cake," I said.

They both turned. Sandra's eyes widened, and Adam actually blushed.

"Helen asked me to make the cake," Sandra said.

Of course she did, I thought.

"Sandy's starting a business," Adam said.

"Well, it's just perfect, isn't it, Adam?" I said, turning and walking out of the room.

I went back into the living room after getting another glass of champagne punch from the bowl on the dining room table. Adam came back in and sat on the other side of Gran. The room was silent as they were all focused on the television. He glanced up but didn't smile. The punch went sour in my stomach.

"What are you all watching?" I asked Justine, who stopped with yet another tray of appetizers.

"Oh, one of Gran's neighbors, Betsy Rider—she's the one in the yellow blouse—was on *Jeopardy!* a few weeks ago, and it's airing tonight," she whispered.

"Oh."

Just then the show cut to commercial, and everyone started talking. I looked over at Adam. He was smiling and talking with Gran, who seemed so happy, her cheeks flushed, giggling like a girl. Betsy Rider was also chatting up a storm with them. I stood by myself, feeling like an outsider, and turned to leave the room, but suddenly my eye caught a face on the silent TV screen, and I stopped.

It was him again. Looking straight at me and smiling, saying something I couldn't hear because the television was muted. Somewhere close by, a glass shattered. I couldn't seem to take a breath. Adam was beside me then, taking my arm, but my eyes were glued to the TV.

"Rachel, what is it?"

"I...I think I'm getting a migraine," I said, turning to him quickly. "I can't drink champagne. It just gives me a headache."

I saw then that everyone was looking at us and realized it was my glass in shards on the floor. "I'm sorry. Clumsy me," I said aloud, pulling away from Adam. "I'll go get something to clean it up. Please, go back to Gran and apologize for me breaking her glass."

The show was back, and the sound came on suddenly. Everyone turned back to the TV. Adam stared at me a long moment, then let go of my arm and turned to Gran. I escaped to the kitchen, my heart pounding, only to find Sandra putting candles on the big cake, which was now on a cart to be wheeled into the other room. She looked up at me. Tiny, blonde, adorable. The creator of this amazing cake.

I went out the kitchen door, knowing I wouldn't be coming back. And that my husband, already annoyed, would be even more disappointed in me. What could I expect, really? He'd lasted far longer than the others.

* * *

BY THE TIME I WALKED INTO THE HOUSE, I was out of breath. I'd practically run across town. From the moment I saw his face on the television screen, shaking hands, smiling, saying words I couldn't hear, my heart felt as though it might explode in my chest. And then Sandra in the kitchen, it was simply the icing on the cake. I couldn't help laughing out loud at my pun, until I realized I sounded hysterical.

I walked upstairs, then stood a moment looking at my computer where the transcript waited for me. The desk was covered with pages I'd printed, notepads filled with scribbling. I didn't want to think about the man with the red hair. I knew now why he'd been at the state library. He was talking about health care. I didn't want to think about the horror of what I'd done tonight at Gran's party.

I sat down and turned the computer on, my hands shaking. *Focus*, I ordered myself. Here were the pages detailing Tillie's final weeks alive. I opened the drawer, pulled out her two photos, and looked into her eyes. I tried to imagine it. Spring was coming, and she had a beau whom I still knew nothing about, really. She must have been excited. Hopeful. I could remember such feelings myself, having no idea how badly it all would turn out.

CHAPTER 40

April 1, 1886

B EFORE THE DINNER HOUR ON FRIDAY, Tillie brought the mending up to the sorority hall. She was proud of the work she'd done. She had Mrs. Conover to thank for helping to improve her stitches, though it was a slow labor as she had to be so careful not to bleed on the fine garments from the nicks on her hands. She was not halfway up the staircase when she could hear the ruckus of the ladies' voices.

"Oh, Tillie," one of them yelled coming down their hall, "our Annabelle has gotten engaged."

Annabelle, who had the fairest blonde hair Tillie had ever seen and light blue eyes, was what Tillie imagined an angel would look like. She was sitting on the bed in her room, surrounded by the others, and held out her hand as Tillie entered the room.

"It's just lovely." The ring was gold with a large pearl.

"Her intended has a big farm out near Chester and is quite well to do," one of the others chimed in.

Tillie nearly told them she expected she might soon be engaged as well, but they were chattering like magpies and didn't seem to really notice her.

"He's got a domestic and a cook."

"Well, she's still got a year left to her education," Faith said loudly from the doorway.

"What for?" several others laughed. "She'll be settled for life."

"Oh, Tillie, I'm so glad you're here," Annabelle said then. "Walter is taking me to meet his family in a few weeks. I have a blue dress that has a tear on the hem. Would you be able to mend it for me?"

Annabelle hopped off the bed, opened the wardrobe, and pulled out a dress of some silky material Tillie had never worked with before. It would be slippery and difficult, but perhaps she could charge a bit more.

"Why, sure, I can manage it."

She then returned the dress and petticoats in her arms to the girls they belonged to and collected her coins. On her way back to the staircase, Faith called out to her.

"They're fools," she said, shaking her head. "Selling themselves for life and abandoning their educations to be a slave to a man."

Tillie looked at her. "Why, Faith, don't ya believe in love? And don't ya hope to get married one day?"

Faith shook her head. "Sure, it might start out that way, but little by little he will own her, and whatever bit of life she's wanted for herself will disappear. She's not even going to finish her education."

Tillie knew what Faith was getting at, had seen it in her own house and then the ones she'd worked for, marriages gone sour. But then there was Doctor and Mrs. Conover. They had been different. He'd been so kind and caring to her. And she was always calling him "sweetheart."

"It sounds like she'll have a comfortable life."

"I do wish you would come to one of our suffragist meetings, Tillie. We have another one Saturday, and we have a famous speaker coming, Victoria Woodhull. Do you remember she ran for president back in 1872 for the Equal Rights Party?"

"A woman ran for president? But we cannot even vote."

"She was sabotaged by the press, but trust me, Tillie, she is a champion for us women, and in particular the working class. Do promise you'll come?"

She stood there thinking about Frank. Her ma slaving away over at the farm in Independence. Susie Mosier and her sister and the god-awful things they did to survive. And of course Catherine and Nora.

"I'm sorry. I won't be able to make it, Faith. I'm meeting my

beau. I know you might be disappointed, but I think he may propose."

"Oh, Tillie." Faith looked as though she might cry. She sat on
her bed, unable to speak for a moment.

"I wish you'd be happy for me. He's truly good to me, and
with both of us working, I'm hoping we can get a little place of
our own."

Now Faith's eyes did fill with tears. "I'm sorry, Tillie. What
right do I have to expect you to follow my beliefs? Why...I can't
even imagine how difficult your life must be."

Now she felt ashamed, not wanting Faith's pity. "I manage
just fine. Don't be worrying about me."

"Yes, of course, I know you do. But you work so damn hard! If
you can't come to the meeting, Tillie, would you promise you'll
let me interview you for an essay I'm writing for the next suffragist pamphlet? It's about the conditions of working girls and
women. How they're paid less to do the same jobs as men. And
how they have little opportunity to even have certain positions or
even advance."

She hesitated.

"Please, Tillie? I won't use your name, of course. I know I'm
blessed. Privileged. I just want to use my station to make a difference."

"Well, all right." She liked Faith; she truly did. She'd been
good to her, introducing her to so many new things she'd never
have known.

Faith hugged her. "Now, come with me for a minute. I have
something for you for your big day Saturday."

She was so happy as she went down the staircase a short
while later and turned toward the servants' hall that she nearly
bumped into Peter Mead.

"And what have you got there?" he asked.

"A bonnet from one of the sorority girls."

"Something you liked and helped yourself to?"

Oh, how she wanted to smack him. "'Twas a gift. I'd say
you're the one who's been helping yourself to things you've got
no right to."

His face burned red, and she kept going, hoping she didn't regret her tongue later on.

CHAPTER 41

"YOU'RE UNBELIEVABLE, YOU KNOW THAT?"

I stood up and turned to find Adam in the doorway, hands on his hips. I opened my mouth, but words failed me. A stack of transcript pages slipped out of my trembling hands onto the floor.

"What the hell happened? You walk into Gran's party and first insult my aunt, then act like you've seen a ghost. You break a glass and don't even make an attempt to pick it up. Then you lie about getting tea and...you completely disappear."

I couldn't seem to speak.

"Not to mention making me look like a fool. There I was, looking all over the house for you, and you were gone."

"I'm sorry. I—"

"I don't want to hear it. What I want for once is the truth. Something's been going on with you."

"I'm sorry, Adam. This was a mistake."

"What?" And then he noticed the suitcase on the side of the desk. "What are you doing?"

"We shouldn't have gotten married. We really didn't know each other."

"I can't believe this." He stared at me, shaking his head. "Rachel, I had no idea Sandra would be there tonight. And I should have told you about her before. It's just...I don't like to think—"

"I shouldn't have married you, Adam. It wasn't fair. We can probably get an annulment."

He didn't respond. Then he looked at the pages that had fallen to the floor. "What's all that?"

I hesitated, my heart galloping. "It's the transcript for James

Titus's trial. For the murder of Tillie Smith." I knew there was no turning back now.

"Where on earth did you get that?"

"At the state library in Trenton. When I was on jury duty—"

"I thought you stopped all that," he interrupted.

"I...I never stopped."

He stared at me for a long moment. "What do you mean you never stopped?"

"I tried to, but then things kept happening without my even trying. All those coincidences I told you about in the beginning, how we both had the same odd cut on our thumbs from our attacks...and...there were even more. I found out there was a transcript of the trial when I was in Belvidere, and then I discovered there was another photo of her. Adam, it felt like...I was somehow meant to uncover some truth about her, some—"

"So...you lied?"

I hesitated. He stood there waiting, and I could see the hurt in his eyes. "I couldn't help it. I'm sorry."

He shook his head in disbelief. "Did it ever occur to you, Rachel, that this...obsession to find out about Tillie might be because you never had closure of your own?"

"Adam, that isn't about me. It's about doing right by her. Honestly."

"I think maybe in your subconscious it is. This guy got away with something horrible. I know you think maybe Tillie didn't have justice, but what about yours?"

I took a deep breath. "Even if you're right, I'm not going to put myself through all that agony for nothing. Because that's what it would be. And nothing would come of it. He's a politician, a lawyer. It will be my word against his. Who will believe me?"

"I think you'd have closure."

"Or is this more about you having closure? Wanting to...do something to him?"

"What happened at Gran's tonight?"

"I saw him."

"What?! He was there?" I saw his fists clench.

"No, no. On the television, on a commercial. Apparently he's running for attorney general in New Jersey."

"And that's the first time you've seen him since then?"

Slowly I shook my head. "I saw him in Trenton last week."

"That was the day you were gone? When you came back and wouldn't let me near you?"

"You were so wrapped up in trying to fix things here, and you were so angry with me, I didn't think you'd even care."

"And he was there?"

"It was totally by accident. It must have been a political thing he was there for, and I saw him in the parking lot. I couldn't even say a word. I nearly fainted."

"Fuck." He turned suddenly, punching the wall. Plaster dust fell to the floor like snow.

"You can't fix this, Adam."

"Do I even know you? Why have you held so much back from me all this time?"

"You're not blameless, either. We each came into this not being completely honest with each other."

"Look, I apologized for the problems my father caused here and for using our money."

"I'm talking about Sandra. It's a small town. How could you think I wouldn't find out that once upon a time everyone thought you two were going to get married?"

"It didn't even cross my mind. It was over years ago. I didn't think it mattered."

"It matters to me because I think there's still something between you. I see how she looks at you. And then we walk into the party, and there she is, with this beautiful cake, you beside her blushing. Your aunt seems to prefer her, doesn't she?"

"Do not turn this around on me, Rachel."

I began picking the pages up off the floor.

"Are you done with Tillie now? Will you stop?"

"No. I can't," I said, not even looking at him.

A moment later I heard the front door close and the truck start up and drive away. I stood there, unable to believe what had just happened. Though why should I have been surprised? I'd managed to sabotage every relationship since the rape. But...I'd never actually loved anyone before. Adam was no doubt going back to the party to save face. Where they probably all thought I was crazy. And Sandra would be waiting patiently with her ador-able smile.

I clutched the transcript pages containing the final days of Tillie's life to my chest. Because something was swirling in my head, something I couldn't quite put my finger on yet. I was get-ting close. And I couldn't help but wonder now about God wink-ing at me. What if the quirk of fate that brought me back here wasn't because of Adam? What if it was because of Tillie Smith?

CHAPTER 42

April 3, 1886

A SOFT WIND GREETED TILLIE when she left out the servants' entrance Saturday afternoon. The farm fields round the college were being cut and readied for planting in a few weeks' time, and the air was rich with the smell of plowed earth. She loved this time of year, the softening of the mountains, the daffodils beginning to show their smiling faces. But her mood was anything but gay.

It had started before she'd even left to meet him, dressing with such care in her room. And then Stella coming in with that little smile of hers, holding a newspaper. Like the cat that swallowed the canary.

"Ain't this your Frank Weeder?"

She looked at the headline: *Rowdies Arrested Outside Tineman's Grocery.* She felt like a big hand was squeezing her heart right inside her chest. She could barely draw breath as she read the article. What a fool she was for not listening to her conscience when she began having doubts about him. The grocery was where you went for spirits. It seemed Frank was a regular there, and it wasn't his first time getting into trouble with the police. And now she knew he hadn't been working out in Great Meadows.

When she got to Main Street, she turned left and looked for Liberty Street. A young girl no more than ten was on the corner peddling spring flowers. She was filthy, her clothes hanging, obviously hand-me-downs from someone older.

"Lovely daffodils for just two bits, miss."

Tillie stopped and looked at the bouquets of daffodils and tulips. The girl eyed her with hope. She couldn't spare two bits.

"Here ya go. That's for you," Tillie said, tossing a dime into the girl's cup.

"Thank ye much, miss."

A few blocks up, she turned onto Liberty Street and looked for the right number. Now her heart was hammering away.

"Tillie, where ya headin', girl?"

She turned, and there was Frank, standing on a porch with another fella. He said something, then came her way.

"Was ya comin' to see me, pet? This is a surprise. I thought we were to meet at three."

"I need to talk to you, Frank."

He led her up a few doors to where he boarded, and they went onto the porch. He reached over to her, but she pulled away, smelling alcohol on his breath.

"What's botherin' my girl, eh? It couldn't wait till later?"

"I can't see ya no more, Frank."

"What's taken hold a you, Tillie? Don't I have a say in this?"

"I don't want to keep steppin' out with ya. I saw your name in the newspaper. I been hearing too many things."

He narrowed his eyes at her. "And you're gonna be believin' gossip and snivel that—?"

"It don't matter what I believe. It's what I feel. I don't want to be with someone who has such a taste for the whiskey."

He smiled then. "Oh, Tillie, don't ya understand? It's gin I use, for some rheumatism I got after breaking my arm. Why don't ya read the advertisements? Gin can cure just about anything."

"I don't care. I feel we are not suited for each other. I need to protect my name."

He slipped a hand in his pocket, then took her hand and set a pair of earrings in her palm.

"I was planning to give ya these today. We've been talking about a future, you and me. Don't ya care about me anymore?"

The truth of it was she did. She'd never had a beau before, and Frank made her feel special. And looking into those light green eyes, sometimes she felt her heart melting. But she couldn't give in to that.

"Did ya steal these, Frank?"

"I won them, fair and square, in a card game. They're a gift, and if ya believe nothin' else about me, believe that I'm a generous man. And I'd be good to ya, Tillie."

"My mind's made."

His gumption faded, and he shook his head, looking sad. "I care for ya, pet. You and I's of the same cloth. Workin' class just tryin' for a better way. Sometimes we gotta make that way happen. That's all I been doin', 'cause ya know things ain't ever fair for the likes of us."

"I'm sorry. I want to find a better way than that."

He gave her a sly smile, folding her fingers and holding them tight so the earrings nearly cut into her skin. "Ya think I ain't heard the talk about you and those gals up to Saxton Falls? You know how to get by, girl, just like me."

"I'm not your girl." She held out the earrings again.

"Keep 'em. They're yours."

She dug into her purse and pulled out a two-dollar bill. Quickly she stuck it in his pocket, then turned and walked away, trembling like a leaf.

The sun was setting over Buck Hill, and as Tillie turned onto Main Street, the lamplighter was tending to the gas lamps. The little girl with the flowers was gone, and the wagons tied up at the hitching posts were starting to head home one by one. When she came to the Flock Building, she stood in front of the big windows looking at the lovely clothes. No homespun. No hand-me-downs. Dresses and skirts like the sorority girls wore. Then she looked at her own likeness in the glass, tears shimmering in her eyes.

"Why, Tillie, is that you?"

She turned to find Faith walking toward her, wrapped in a gorgeous emerald green cloak. Quickly she wiped her eyes. "Well, hello there, Faith."

"Tillie, are you crying?"

"Oh, it's just the cold makes my eyes water. I was just standing here admiring the dresses."

"Did you have your date? Did your sweetheart propose?"

Tillie hesitated. "I decided Frank wasn't the fella for me after all."

Faith stared at her, waiting for more. Then she put her arm through Tillie's.

"I'll tell you what. I'm on my way to Niper's Photography Shop to have a portrait done for the suffragist pamphlet. Come along with me. Have you ever had your own portrait done, Tillie?"

"No, Faith."

As Faith led her along chatting away, she wondered how long it would take for her heart to stop hurting. Her dream of someone to love her, a little house, her family together...it had all flown away like a wish on the wind.

CHAPTER 43

I HAD NO REAL PLAN THE NIGHT I LEFT, so I went to the Emerson House, a B&B on the other side of town. I felt like a top spinning out of control. I'd lied so much to Adam, betrayed him twice, hurt his family, though they didn't know the half of it. Hatred for my rapist gnawed at my insides, eating away at me bit by bit. I had to leave Adam. I wasn't fit to be with anyone.

I should have gone far from Hackettstown, but I couldn't just yet. Not until I finished everything that had been set in motion from the first hours I'd come here. Finding the truth about Tillie's life. And her death. Without roadblocks, I figured it wouldn't take me long.

I spent hours reading in the beautifully appointed room at the Emerson House, all lace, floral wallpaper, and Victorian furniture. It wasn't hard to imagine I had traveled back in time to 1886. Tillie's life was happening in real time as I read. And as the days passed, as one person after another in her life testified, I grew more frantic. And more confused.

I'd been printing pages here and there, but now I went to an office supply store and finally had the entire transcript printed. I worked mostly on the bed, where I had more room, surrounded by legal pads and various colored markers, making notes as I read. To an outsider it would have looked crazy. Obsessive. I'd just left the life I'd always wanted, the man I loved. Now I was alone again—my worst fear—tracking the final days of a woman who'd died nearly 130 years ago, someone who I believed in my heart had somehow reached out to me across time. All these months I'd kept wondering why. Was it to bring me face to face with the man who'd raped me and all that I'd managed to push to a far recess of my mind? Or was it because there was something I needed to set right for her? I wasn't sure.

Besides reading, I did a lot of walking, mostly before dawn or after dusk, not wanting to risk running into any of Adam's family or friends. I wondered what he had told them. I imagined Aunt Helen was smirking with satisfaction. She'd been right all along.

In my witching hour each night, there was simply no turning away from what I wanted to forget yet again. That bastard. What he did to me. How I reacted. The fallout that lasted for years. And then there was Adam's face, an emotional brew of hurt, anger, and confusion.

* * *

I WOKE LATE ONE NIGHT TO A PHONE RINGING INCESSANTLY. I'd fallen asleep in my clothes with all the lights on. I sat up suddenly, and a stack of pages on my chest fell to the floor. The phone kept ringing. Why wasn't anyone answering it? I got up and walked to the door, intending to see what was going on. The ringing just got louder and louder, and then my heart slammed in my chest. I grabbed the dresser. Suddenly I was back in my dorm room eighteen years ago, listening to my own phone ringing and ringing. My mother called each night to make sure I was in safe. But this night...I just couldn't answer. I couldn't tell her. And this was the second night I hadn't answered. The ringing wouldn't stop.

One of the other students pounded on my door then. "Answer your goddamn phone."

I picked it up.

"Rachel?" I could hear the hysteria in my mother's voice.

"I..." My voice cracked, and then I was sobbing.

"Rachel, what's wrong? What happened?"

I couldn't talk.

"Did someone hurt you?"

I looked at my thumb, still bleeding through the paper towels I kept wrapping around it, probably needing stitches. My insides felt as if they'd been scraped open with razor blades. I'd been hid-ing in my room, too ashamed to go to the infirmary.

"Honey, did someone do something bad to you?"

"Yes," I whispered.

"I'm coming there, honey. Don't worry. I'll bring you home. Don't say anything to anyone, okay? Just wait for me to get there."

She never came. I waited all night, not knowing a drunk driver had flown through a red light, broadsiding and killing her on impact. If I'd just kept my mouth shut. If I'd just gone home myself....My mother shouldn't have been driving all those hours. She'd always been fragile. She wasn't a good driver. It was my fault.

HOURS LATER, I STILL LAY AWAKE IN THE B&B with the lights on, unable to stop reliving that time. It wasn't until I found my mother's diary when I helped the auctioneer get our house ready to sell that I learned the truth about her own life. Why she'd always been overprotective to the point of embarrassing me. She'd been molested in a few foster homes, once by a teenage boy when she was just twelve. Another time by the father in the house when she was fifteen. She did nothing about it. Because she was finally in a school she liked with friends she liked. She didn't want to change that. But she was so ashamed. She never told anyone, even blaming herself for wearing certain clothes. She found ways to protect herself. Barricading her bedroom door at night. Making sure she was never alone with him. Even now, remembering, sitting on the floor and reading those pages, it simply broke my heart. What happened to her when she was young colored the rest of her life. I finally understood my mother, but it was too late.

I turned out the light now, desperate for sleep, but my thoughts wouldn't stop. One decision, one quick moment in time. How my life would have been different if I'd not said yes to that date. If I'd gone right home afterwards and not ignored my mother's calls. If I'd not taken that job in Kearny at Adam's aunt Eleanor's. If I hadn't stopped at Tillie's monument the day I came back to the cemetery. Or tucked those flowers into the fishing wire.

So much of life seemed to be just a trick of destiny. Was life really preordained? How much did we actually control? Was I supposed to meet Adam again? And now, after all that had happened, was I meant to be alone again for the rest of my life? I couldn't bear that thought. I wouldn't allow myself to dwell on it.

I turned the light back on, got up, and gathered the pages I'd been reading again. It was easier for me to think about Tillie than myself. I would finish this. I needed to finish this. And then I would figure out my own life.

As I read more testimony about Tillie's family circumstances, my thoughts kept drifting back to my mother's diary and my years of being ashamed of her. I wondered if Tillie had felt that way about her father.

CHAPTER 44

April 5, 1886

TILLIE WALKED INTO THE KITCHEN Monday morning wishing she could go back to her warm bed upstairs. She'd not been sleeping well and couldn't blame it on Stella's snoring or the banging of the steam pipes. No, it was still her own foolishness over trusting Frank. And why would her heart not stop aching? Scrubbing the first bushel of potatoes, she wondered if this was it, her lot for the rest of her life. By herself, it would take years to earn enough to make a real change for her or her sisters.

She turned at a sound in the doorway, expecting Bridget. Instead there stood Janitor Titus, looking peaked and holding onto the wall.

"I was wonderin' if I might be able to get a cup of tea."

She was just about to remind him that he could have all the tea he wanted at breakfast in a bit, but then he held his stomach, and his face went white.

"Why don't ya sit yourself down and I'll fetch it? Water's hot already."

"I'm just gonna have a lie down in the furnace room. I'll be back in a few minutes."

When he didn't return, Tillie brought the cup over to the furnace room, where the janitor was sitting on the edge of a bench, his head hanging between his knees.

"Ya want me to fetch the doctor?"

He looked up and shook his head. "I've been. He gave me stomach bitters."

It was hot as blazes in the room, but Titus was shivering. Tillie thought it must be the diarrhea, remembering how it had spread through her own house like wildfire sometimes.

"Don't look like it's working much. My ma always used cod liver oil. Said a good cleanout was the best medicine."

"Your ma don't know more than a doctor."

She held her tongue, then set the tea on the bench, not so close as to catch something. She was about to leave when she turned back to him. "Mr. Titus, I'm going to be going out to a show on Thursday. I can't be certain I'll be back by curfew. I was wondering if you might be able to help me out with that."

He picked up the tea and looked at her. Then, surprisingly, he nodded.

"Thank you kindly. I'll be sure to remind you when the day comes." She went back to the kitchen, hating that she had to grovel to that lecherous man.

Bridget was there, getting her big pots on the stove.

"Where's me potatoes? Whatcha' been doin' down here all mornin'?"

"Land sakes, Bridget, what's got your petticoats all bunched in a twist?" Tillie said, getting back to the first bushel.

Bridget gave a long sigh. "Oh, I just miss me ma and da is all. Me sister Colleen writes to tell me all the goin's-on to cheer me, but...well, it just makes me homesick."

"Well, can you not go back to Ireland if you're so unhappy here?"

"Ha, ye must be daft. Go back to starvation and no opportunities and too many mouths to feed? No, I send back most of what I make here, and even that's not enough. But still, aren't we warm and fed and have a bit of a future here? That's more than there'd be for me back in Ireland."

"I'm sorry for you, Bridget. It must be hard."

"No harder than you missin' the ones you love, Tillie."

"At least I sometimes see them, though Nora's gone all the way to work in Newark, and I've been wonderin' how she's doing. And my brother could be anywhere; I have no idea."

"Well, I've got me letters saved, and when I cannot stand it, I'll sit up at night and read the lot of them and weep me eyes out and wake all cleared up."

She'd never thought to write a letter to her family since none of them could read. But perhaps Nora was learning. If not, someone at the house could read it to her. That would be exciting and maybe cheer her a bit. It would be even more wonderful if someone could help Nora to send a letter back to her.

Just then Mrs. Ruckle came in. "Matilda, there's a man here to see you."

Tillie's heart skipped a beat. Matron hadn't called her Matilda since that first day, and her tone was stern. And then she felt her face flame, wondering if it could be Frank.

"He says he's your father. I asked him to come around to the cellar door."

Of course the matron wouldn't want her pa in the front parlors.

"Yes, ma'am. I'll be quick about it."

She put her peeler down, praying her pa wasn't drunk. And knowing that this must be something bad.

CHAPTER 45

April 5, 1886

TILLIE'S PA LOOKED LIKE A VERY OLD MAN, hunched over in the cold, in a threadbare coat, his beard and hair unkempt. One would think he was shaking from the cold, but she knew better. He was needing a drink, and it wasn't nine in the morning yet. He turned at the sound of the cellar door closing.

"There's my Tillie. And a sight for sore eyes, you are."

Tears sprang to her eyes. He hadn't called her "my Tillie" since she was but a wee girl, when he could still make her laugh with his silly songs. But it had been a long time since he'd done anything but disappoint her. Or fuel her anger.

"What's wrong, Pa? Why are ya here?"

He just looked at her as if he couldn't muster up the words, and her heart beat faster.

"Is it Catherine?"

Slowly he nodded.

"She's passed?" she cried, having trouble standing now, as though her knees had turned to water.

"No, no, she's still with us, but she needs some tending to. I spoke with a doctor who knows all about nervous ailments, and he feels he can help her. It's just...I don't have..."

She stared at him a long moment. "You're needing money."

He nodded, unable to look at her now.

"And how does he think he might help her?"

"He's from New York City, and ailments of the nerves and the mind are his specialty. He says the rest cure we been trying ain't gonna work. She needs tonics, and when her nerves get worked up, laudanum."

"And where did you find this city doctor? At Elsie's?"

"Now, don't ya be sassin' me, girl. I mean to be getting help for your sister. She's been in a right bad way lately. I fear leavin' her alone, and there's no one left but me to tend to her."

Words she knew would be of no use caught in her throat. How he'd driven them all away one by one. How she had to take care of herself and hopefully her sisters 'cause he couldn't. But more than angry, she was frightened. She knew how Catherine could get in her lowest moods when drawing breath seemed more effort than she could muster.

"How much does this doctor fetch for his medicines?"

"Five dollars would be enough for all she'd need. It'd carry her for three months, he says, and hopefully it'd turn her around."

She had seven dollars. Her entire savings. If it would help Catherine, she'd give it in a minute. But what if her pa was simply wheedling his way to more drink? He'd done it before.

But Catherine was his pet. She'd always been. And there was no hope now of a little house of their own away from Lubber's Run, so what good would her dollars do anyway? It would take years to make that happen. Catherine needed her help now.

"I'll give it to you, but I can't get it now."

"The doctor is coming back through this way on the Friday train."

She stood there thinking, knowing she'd best get back to the kitchen before Mrs. Ruckle came looking for her.

"I'll be going into town on Thursday evening. Meet me on Main Street in front of the post office. I'll be there between seven and quarter past, and if you aren't...then I'll know what's truth and what isn't."

She didn't want him back at the institute. And giving it to him now...there'd only be the temptation to spend it on drink waiting for the doctor. If he was being truthful, if he really feared for Catherine, he would be there.

She turned to go back inside, then froze. Peter Mead was standing in front of the cellar door with a coal bucket. She wondered how much he had heard.

CHAPTER 46

WALKING INTO TOWN FOR LUNCH, I was startled to notice mums and other fall flowers dotting the sidewalks. There was a chill in the air as well. Days had passed, the seasons were beginning to change, and I was caught in a world between past and present. I went for hours without even speaking to anyone. I needed to take more breaks.

I missed the cemetery. I loved hearing the birds come awake just before five, chirping and calling as they flew about searching for food. I loved the peaceful feeling of looking out the window across the fields of graves toward the river curling around the cemetery, as if holding us back from the real world. Most of all I missed Adam. How I would look up to find him gazing at me with tenderness across the table while we ate. How he would wrap his arms around me as I fell asleep, making me feel so safe. I couldn't bear the thought of him looking at Sandra that way.

I imagined he was hard at work cleaning the summer flowers from the graves. I wondered how the mausoleum was coming along. We would have been leaving soon for our honeymoon. He hadn't been honest with me about Sandra or his father. He had held his anger for far too long after I'd meddled in the cemetery business. But what I'd done...it was far worse.

I walked to Stella's Café for lunch later that day. It was such a cheerful place, and I was glad to be enveloped in the comforting sounds of people talking, dishes clanking. Laughter. I ordered soup and tea, then grabbed a copy of the *Hackettstown Gazette* from a stack of papers on the end of the counter.

"Say, aren't you the gal who works with Mr. Finegan?"

I turned to the old man beside me, recognizing him at once. "Yes. And you bought the family photos at the auction, if I recall correctly."

"That I did. Harry Davidson," he said, extending a hand.

"Rachel...Dempsey," I said, shaking it. No sense bringing up the Miller name at this point, I figured.

"Nice seeing you again."

"You, too," I said, hesitating, then continuing. "I was glad you were able to get those photos you wanted at the auction. Of the Titus family."

He laughed. "A silly thing, probably. They're still sitting in a closet."

"Well, I know you mentioned your great-grandfather, Denis Sullivan, was a reporter for the *Hackettstown Gazette*," I said, holding up a copy of that day's paper. "And he had hoped to write a book?"

"That's right. You have quite a good memory."

"Well, I'm actually very interested in what he may have written."

"He was quite a prominent journalist in these parts in his day."

"You know, I've been doing some research of my own, Mr. Davidson. I've heard some say that Titus wasn't really guilty, just as you mentioned your grandfather had told you. But I've been reading the trial transcript, and...there's quite a lot of circumstantial evidence that makes him look...far from innocent. Would you be willing to let me look at your great-grandfather's articles? I would even pay you for the—"

But he held up a hand. "No need for that. I'd be happy to let you look at them. But I'll need to find them. They should be up in the attic, I guess. I'll have to get one of the grandkids up there. Why don't you give me your number, and I'll give you a call when I get my hands on it? Though it'll be a bit. The wife and I are leaving on vacation to see our son in California tomorrow."

"I really appreciate it, Mr. Davidson. I have so many unan-swered questions. Most of all about Tillie."

I gave him my business card, disappointed it would take so long.

I OPENED THE *HACKETTSTOWN GAZETTE* and read while eating my soup. Centenary College's new performing arts center was all over the front page with their coming fall and winter lineup. A sidebar was headlined "Lantern Tours," and I began reading about guided strolls up Main Street to Church Street and then up to the college on Halloween night. They were also known as "Tillie Walks," as they followed Tillie Smith's footsteps the last night of her life. It was uncanny. I was actually reading about her final days, learning so many details already about the night in question. It made me sick that her last steps alive were being mimicked for entertainment.

The last line read, *On Halloween night, 1899, the original building burned to the ground. Many think Tillie's ghost was responsible.* I sat there staring at the words, pushing my soup away. I left cash on the counter and walked out.

As I went down Main Street, I could just picture what those tours would be like. Someone tracing Tillie's last moments on earth, perhaps dressed in Victorian garb. People giggling as they got spooked imagining her popping out of the shadows. Suddenly I stopped.

I was in front of the antique shop I'd gone into earlier in the summer. There in the window was the mannequin I had seen, still outfitted in the kind of clothing I imagined Tillie would have worn to see her show. The long muslin dress with the bustle back cinched tightly at her waist, with a corset underneath, of course. An ivory lace collar tied around her neck to dress it up. Fitted gloves to hide the scars from peeling potatoes each day.

I turned and went inside.

CHAPTER 47

April 8, 1886

W HEN BREAKFAST WAS ALL CLEANED UP and she had a few moments, Tillie slipped upstairs, hoping Faith was in her room. Luckily she was. She told Faith about her sister's nervous spells, her despondent moods, and the possibility of a new tonic and laudanum.

"Oh, Tillie, women have been putting up with these 'rest cures' for nervous exhaustion for years now. And there's no proof it helps with this so-called neurasthenia. Why, there's a wonderful piece about it in one of our newsletters. Oftentimes it simply adds to the malaise."

"So do you think it would be a good thing to try this new treatment?"

For once, Faith didn't seem to have an opinion or an answer. "I honestly don't know, Tillie. But as for your father, I think you'll have to use your own best judgment."

Tillie had spent days turning it over and over in her mind. Feeling herself slipping into a despondent state herself since breaking with Frank, worrying about her future and her family, and now the added worry of Catherine. A memory of her sister crying for days, unable to leave her bed, came to her then. The dark rings under her eyes, her face all hollowed out, as if she had already passed.

She would give her father the money. What choice did she have, really? She couldn't live with herself if something were to happen to her sister. She turned to go, thanking Faith anyway.

"Wait, Tillie. Don't you want to see your portrait? I picked them up just this morning."

She turned to see Faith picking it up from her desk and hold-ing it for Tillie to see.

"Oh..." was all she could manage.

BY THE TIME THE DINNER HOUR WAS OVER and she was hurrying upstairs to ready for the evening, she felt a spring returning to her step. She'd give her pa the money. And then she would go to the show. She deserved a bit of fun. More than that, she needed it. And what would two bits matter now? She'd be starting her savings all over again.

The bells rang six-fifteen as she layered on three petticoats, then pulled on the dress she'd worn for her picture. She laid out her sacque coat and the kid gloves Faith had given her, then tied on the delicate lace collar that had been Mrs. Conover's. She pinned up her hair, thankful she'd picked up more hairpins. She hesitated a moment, then clipped the earrings on, figuring she'd paid for them after all. She knew they were just glass, but they sparkled so in the gaslight, and she felt another twinge of regret about Frank. But it was best she had ended it before her heart was fully his. She only had to look at her pa to know where her life would have ended up.

Finally she went over to the bureau for her red purse. But it was her portrait lying there beside the purse that she picked up.

When she'd seen her likeness in Faith's room that morning, Tillie couldn't even speak. It was hard to believe it was herself, looking for all the world like a real lady, wearing the same fine lace collar and ribbons round her neck. Looking at it now, she knew she wasn't beautiful, had only ever been called handsome. But there she was for all the world to see. The only one in her family to have a proper portrait.

She couldn't help but smile. Why, she looked as fine as one of her cousins. And wasn't it all her own doing? They might have their luck of birth and all the advantages of a wealthy father, but she had the gumption. Faith had made her see that now. She couldn't wait to take the portrait to her ma. Wouldn't she be stunned to see her Tillie looking so much like a lady? If only she had another for Nora. But there on the night table as well was the letter she had written to Nora. It had taken her hours these past few days since Bridget had given her the idea, and more crumpled sheets of paper than she should have. But she needed to be careful of her words, knowing that someone would have to read it to her sister. Still, she thought, picking up the envelope now and slipping it into her purse, in less than a week Nora would hear these very words. And hopefully someone would write back for Nora.

The door opened, and Stella came in and whistled. "Well, don't you look a fine sight, Tillie."

"I'm off to a show at Shield's Hall."

"And where would that be, New York City?" Stella teased.

"Don't be daft," she said, laughing. "It's in town somewhere. I was hopin' you might know."

"Sorry, I don't. But I guess you'll be impressin' all the fellas, that's for sure."

"You never know who might be there," Tillie said, repeating her friend Mary Wright's words.

She opened the wardrobe, biting off a piece of blue thread from Annabelle's hem. "I need to stop and get a spool of this color, so I'll just ask the shopkeeper where the hall is."

If she hadn't spent so much time on the letter, she'd have returned the frock already. There was nothing for it now but to get up extra early in the morning to sew the hem before starting her duties.

"What time will you be back?"

"I don't know for certain, but I might not make curfew."

Stella made a face. "Have you asked Matron?"

She shook her head. "I asked Mr. Titus a few days ago, and he agreed."

"That might cost ya somethin', if you know what I'm getting at."

"Oh, I do, Stella. But I think I'm safe there."

She opened her drawer then and began counting her money.

"Land sakes, you've got quite a heap there, Tillie. You'd best be careful carrying all that."

"I won't have it long. I'm meeting my pa. My sister needs some doctoring."

"Oh, so that accounts for all the mending and late nights you've been up to. I thought you still had your eye on that store-bought dress in town at the Flock Building."

"I've never had a store-bought dress in my life. I guess I can wait a bit longer."

"Oh, I've had a hand-me-down one or two."

Tillie put the money in her red purse, then pulled on her sacque and tied her bonnet.

"Well, you look right smart already," Stella said.

"I'm feelin' smart at that," Tillie said, opening the door. She then turned back to Stella with a smile. "And I aim to have a swell time tonight."

* * *

SHE WAS SO BUNDLED UP FOR THE COLD WALK BACK later that by the time Tillie reached the basement hallway, she was starting to sweat. As she neared the furnace room, she heard voices, and then Mead came into the hallway carrying a chair, the caned seat all fixed up. He gave her a hard look.

"And where might you be going at this hour all gussied up?"

She stood a moment, stunned. "That would be none of your business, mister. Oh wait, I mean REVEREND."

She hated him for what he'd done to Stella, so holier than thou, getting the poor girl's hopes up for nothing. He whispered something, but Tillie couldn't hear it. She wondered now if he knew she'd prodded Stella to end it. He went by her then, deliberately banging into her with the chair.

"Arse," she said under her breath and walked on.

Titus was in the furnace room in his overalls, as if about to shovel coal into the boilers. He looked a bit better than the other day.

"Mr. Titus?"

He looked up at her.

"I just wanted to remind you that I'm goin' to meet my girl-friends for a show in town, and it might be a bit past ten by the time I make it back. When I brought you tea the other day when you weren't feeling well, you said you would let me in if I was to miss the curfew."

"That would be breaking the rules, wouldn't it?"

She hesitated. "It's been done before, from what I hear."

"I been hearin' things myself. About you." He smiled then, that slow smile that gave her shivers.

"I could say the same, Mr. Titus, but good Christians as we are here don't put much stock in gossip. Ain't that what Dr. Whitney preaches?"

His eyes narrowed, and she could see he knew what she was getting at. If Dr. Whitney, the president of the seminary, got wind of Titus's questionable actions, it would not bode well for him, that was for sure. Not that she'd ever go that far, 'cause mightn't that cause some trouble for herself as well?

"You'd best be askin' the matron."

"You know Mrs. Ruckle doesn't approve of missing curfew. I'm askin' you a favor, Mr. Titus. You were agreeable the other day."

With his eyes still on her, he picked up the shovel leaning against the wall. "I lock the laundry door last."

"Well, would you be able to lock that door after I come in if it's past ten?"

He didn't reply but turned then and opened the boiler. A blast of heat came at her from across the room. He began shoveling coal into the boiler, ignoring her.

Tillie turned and left, stopping for a dab of vanilla in the kitchen. When she opened the door to the outside, the cold air turned her sweat to ice. She shivered despite all her petticoats. Walking around the big building, she headed out to Jefferson Street. It was nearly dark and bitter as winter. But the smell of the plowed fields nearby reminded her that warm days were soon coming. It also reminded her of home, and a lump of sadness grew in her throat. She would go and see Catherine on her next Sunday off. Somehow she would get her sister away from Lubber's Run.

CHAPTER 48

S TELLA SLIKER, BRIDGET GROGAN, FAITH SEILER, Mrs. Ruckle. None of these women who had seen Tillie before she left for her big evening out had any idea she might be in danger. And then there were those who might have known more than they were telling: Peter Mead and James Titus, two men who seemed rather unsavory from what I'd read of them. And then there was Tillie's ex-beau, Frank Weeder. I imagined them all.

Closing my eyes, I pictured those people who were in my own life all those years ago. Did anyone ever suspect that bastard? He must have targeted other girls. The quiet, the meek. I was shy, far from home, in a big college with thousands of kids, with little experience because I was overly protected by a neurotic mother. It seemed the other girls were always more confident in themselves, in what they said, what they wore. They formed friendships and cliques quickly. On weekends I'd hear them leaving for frat parties or dates as I sat in my room alone, reading or writing poetry for a creative writing class, wondering when my real life there would start. Or if my mother had been right and I'd made a mistake coming there. Then he asked me out. And I said yes.

Hope, I knew now, was such a dangerous thing. It fueled expectation, even spurred confidence. Bolstered you with moments of joyful anticipation. And often clouded reality. I should have known better than to believe that guy would be interested in me. I should have known he would be after something. But I still had learned nothing after all that. Because I should have realized it was folly to marry someone after knowing him just twelve weeks. That the past I'd always been fighting to escape would no doubt come back. That intimacy would still be an issue. But I'd been floating on a cloud of hope. I was so happy. I saw it all, my future with Adam, a family perhaps. A life where I belonged. I was so tired of being alone. And once again hope had led me to heartache.

I looked at the final pile of pages I was about to start, knowing I wasn't alone in this mistake. Tillie'd had hope, I was certain of it. Stella, Bridget, the Wright sisters, and even Annie Van Syckle testified how excited she'd been to go to that show. It was painful and so sad tracing her steps that night after she left the institute. I picked up the transcript and began reading once more.

IT SEEMED AFTER TILLIE WALKED OUT of the building, no one saw her again until she was noticed coming from Church Street to the corner of Main, where the old post office was, directly across from the Methodist church. A liveryman had seen her drop a letter into the mailbox somewhere between seven and seven-thirty. According to Bridget Grogan, Tillie was writing to her sister Nora.

She was seen next at Beatty & Karr's Dry Goods a few blocks up Main at the corner of Grand Avenue. The shopkeeper there testified that he had showed her an assortment of threads until she found just the right blue to match one she'd brought with her for a mending job.

What broke my heart was that when she went to pay, Tillie struggled with the buttons on her kid gloves. She told the shop-keeper the gloves had been given to her weeks ago by one of the sorority girls. I knew it had to have been Faith. Tillie went on to say she'd hoped they'd stretch but guessed she hadn't worn them enough. She was in a hurry, though, so she opened her red purse and let him count out the right amount. He was surprised to see she had about seven dollars, a significant amount back then. When he finished, he put the rest of the money back into her purse

The shopkeeper then testified that she asked him where Shield's Hall was because she couldn't seem to find it and was to meet a friend to see Fitzgerald's Merrymakers. Ironically it was on the third floor of his building. He led her outside and showed her which door would take her up to the show. She thanked him and hurried off. By then it was close to eight.

I imagined Tillie climbing those stairs, anticipating the show about to start. Happy to be seeing her friends. Hopeful. I put the pages down, got up, and paced the room. Tillie was just hours away from being murdered.

CHAPTER 49

April 8, 1886

T ILLIE HURRIED UP THE THREE FLIGHTS OF STAIRS, wishing she hadn't laced her corset quite so tight. She knew she must be late as there was no one else about, and she hoped there'd still be a seat left. On the last flight, the sound of voices came to her, and she could tell the show had not started yet. At the ticket booth she purchased a bench seat, the cheapest one offered, and went inside, looking for Mary.

"Tillie, over here."

There she was on a bench to the right of the hall with her sister, Agnes.

"Why, Tillie, don't you look smart with your fancy bonnet and red purse," Agnes said with a bit of sass to her.

Tillie sat then, turning to Mary, who was rolling her eyes.

"Don't mind her, Tillie. She's just a bit green."

Then she noticed her other friend, Annie Van Syckle, up near the front beside a nice-looking gentleman. Before she could say a word to Mary about it, a man came out on the stage, and the crowd hushed up as he announced the performances about to begin. She hadn't been to but a few shows in her life and soon found herself caught up in the excitement.

There was one act after the other, starting with a magician who pulled flowers out of a hat, a bird out of one man's ear, and then somehow made himself disappear into a box. Then followed the musicals, with some of her favorite songs like "Oh! Susannah" and "My Darling Clementine," followed by show tunes. She especially liked the one called "Sailing, Sailing," from a new Broadway musical, *The Pirates of Penzance*, as it made her think of her brother, James. How was it possible that it had been more than a year since she'd seen him?

When that song ended, a woman in a bright orange gown and lots of flashy diamonds walked onto the stage and began singing. It was the very same song that she'd heard Faith sing from the opera *Florinda*. Even without understanding the language, Tillie recognized the heartache in the woman's voice as it rose above them. The music seemed to swell in her own chest, the sadness rising into her throat until she felt consumed with longing and had to fight back tears. All the hope that she'd held in her heart these past few months was gone. She had nothing. Frank, whom she was starting to love and picture a life with, had been just another disappointment. Her pa hadn't even shown up tonight, though she'd waited near an hour for him. He was either drunk or lying. Her ma was struggling, working herself into an early grave on that farm. And there was Catherine, hopeless back in Lubber's Run. Could she possibly help her, or was she just fooling herself?

The applause brought her back to the hall as the song ended. She'd never heard anything so beautiful. Faith had told her the grandest operas were in New York City. Perhaps one day she'd be able to see one.

All too soon the show was over, and as she and the sisters made their way down the stairs, Agnes suggested they walk over to the American House. It was bitter cold outside, and she envied those who got into carriages. As they crossed Main Street, she heard her name called and saw Annie Van Syckle waiting on the wooden sidewalk.

"Why, Tillie, I thought that was you," Annie said.

"I saw you in the hall, Annie, but I was too far to catch your eye."

Tillie looked at the two gentlemen beside Annie.

"This is Mr. Hunter," Annie said, introducing the man who had sat beside her at the show.

"Good evening, ladies," he said to them all, lifting his hat. "May I introduce my good friend, Mr. Schofield?"

They were fine looking and well dressed, Mr. Hunter taller

and nicer looking than his friend. Annie gave Tillie a quick smile and raised her eyebrows. They all talked about the show for a bit, and then Tillie heard the institute bells ring but couldn't make out if it was the half or quarter hour before ten. As they all began walking up Main Street, Mr. Hunter explained that they were drummers in town on business, having arrived on the train just that afternoon. Tillie thought they seemed like fine gents of a different class from Frank, and she remembered Mary's words just the other day: you never knew who might be at the show.

As they kept walking, Mr. Schofield paired off with Annie far in front. Then the other gent, Mr. Hunter, stepped beside Mary. Tillie found herself beside Agnes in the back of the group.

"Ain't we the popular ones now," Agnes complained.

"Well, being a sourpuss won't help," Tillie said.

Soon they were in front of Trinity Methodist Church, and the group stopped, except for Annie and Mr. Schofield, who were chatting up a storm and kept walking up Main.

"I'd best be getting' back to the seminary," Tillie said.

Just then they all heard someone call out to Mary. As she stepped away, Tillie turned to speak with Mr. Hunter and froze. Just beyond him, near the church doorway, stood three fellows. One of them was Frank, and he was looking straight at her. Then he said something to Mary and turned away with his friends. Mary came back over. Tillie wondered what Frank had said to her but didn't want to ask in front of the drummers.

"Now, Mr. Hunter, I must say goodbye," Mary said. "I must be off to meet another friend. Come, Agnes. Goodbye, Tillie."

"Well, good night, Miss Wright. And Miss Wright." He smiled at his own humor and tipped his hat to the sisters. Then he turned to Tillie. "Might I walk you home, then?"

"Why...sure, that would be nice. Especially as Church Street up to the seminary is quite dark," she said, pleased at the turn, though not happy at seeing Frank.

Mr. Hunter offered her his arm, and he and Tillie crossed Main Street, passing the post office on the corner. He smelled nice, of bay rum like so many of the students wore, and up close she could see his suit was finely made. He had a nice smile and looked right into her eyes when he spoke. She asked what he was here in town selling. Before he could answer, they both turned at a low whistle that came from the doorway of the post office. In the shadows she could make out two men.

"This town seems to have its share of unsavories," Mr. Hunter remarked.

Then one of the fellas stepped a bit forward, his eyes aimed right at her, and Tillie felt her heart go still.

CHAPTER 50

S O FRANK WEEDER WAS THERE ON MAIN STREET the night Tillie died, warning Mary Wright to be careful of the drummers. How did he feel seeing Tillie there with another man? He couldn't have been happy.

Stella testified that Tillie had asked Titus to let her in after curfew, but Titus wasn't testifying. She must have spoken to him again before leaving. Mead wished her a good evening as he saw her leaving the building, but somehow I didn't think it was that simple. I already had an eerie feeling about him.

Then there was Charles Munnich, the drummer, whose testimony I was now reading. Reminding me so much of Thor, luring her in with his surprising attention and fine appearance. But a bastard if there ever was one. Even lying about his name, telling her it was Charles Hunter.

And who were the fellows in the shadows at the post office? What must have been going through Tillie's mind, I could only imagine.

I wished I could have screamed to her across time. Stopped what was already set in motion, an evening of fun, a walk back to the institute seemingly full of promise. Oh, Tillie.

I needed a break. I hadn't eaten all day, and it was already dusk. Life had taken on a surreal rhythm, and I realized I was now living more in the past than the present. I could hear the geese flying overhead as they made their way back to the fish hatchery on the other side of town for the night, another sure sign of fall. I'd been at the B&B for several weeks now. Adam had called twice. I hadn't called back.

I walked over to the dresser. Next to my piles of notes was

the newspaper from a few days ago. I stared at the front page and the photo of one of the candidates running for state attorney general, Thor, whose real name was Barry Marshall. The bastard who raped me was looking back at me with that killer smile. I turned the paper face down.

I grabbed a muffin I'd saved from the morning's breakfast. Then I went and sat on the bed and continued reading.

CHAPTER 51

April 8, 1886

TILLIE STOOD THERE, UNABLE TO MOVE for the moment, looking over to the post office entrance where the two men lurked in the shadows.

"Oh, give me just a minute, if you please," she said, trying to sound natural. "I think I might know one of those fellas."

She was gone but a few minutes and tried to hush her voice to keep Mr. Hunter from hearing. When she walked back to him, she took his arm again.

"Come, it's getting late. The seminary is just a few blocks up this way."

"Who was that fellow?"

"Oh, never mind that."

"Fancy you, does he?"

"I guess you might say that." She laughed to make light of it, then changed the way things were going. "So what is it that you're on the road selling, Mr. Hunter?"

"Please, call me Charles. And may I call you Tillie? I heard your friends address you so."

"Certainly." *Certainly* was a word Faith used often, and it sounded more refined than saying, *Why, sure*, which is what she would have said.

"I sell shoes, very high quality shoes. And I tell you, I do very well at it."

"Do you sell to the fancy shops in New York City?"

"Of course."

"I've never been to New York, though my sister Nora lives in Newark now."

"Oh, there are some fine shops there as well."

As they stepped off the wooden sidewalk to cross Washington Street, Tillie slipped on a bit of frost, and Charles held her arm tight, pulling her closer and steadying her.

"Thank you, Charles." She liked saying his name; it sounded dignified. She liked how this all felt, walking with a gentleman after a lovely show, someone with fine manners who was treating her like she was a lady. "This is a new street, you know, and the walks aren't the best, though I hear they'll be improving them come summer. They made the street not long ago so the seminary students could walk right up to the Methodist church there."

"Oh, so that's why they call it Church Street," he said with a laugh.

"Yes, that's right," she said, laughing too, feeling more light of heart than she had in weeks. "And it's a might easier coming this way to Main Street at times. There ain't many houses yet, so it can be quite dark, but I imagine that's about to change as well, what with people coming to work at the institute more and more."

"Tell me, what you do there, Tillie?"

"Why, I..." She hesitated, not wanting to say the truth, that she peeled potatoes till her fingers bled, and sometimes waited on the help at meals. "I help the matron with various things throughout the place."

"Oh, kind of like her assistant?"

"Yes."

"It's an impressive sight," he said as they crossed over Monroe Street. The building sat a block before them, lit by the gas lanterns, rising up five stories to the clock tower in the center.

"That it is."

"I bet lots of those divinity students must have their eye on a pretty thing like you."

"Oh, I don't pay them any mind. They're just boys. I'm interested in someone a bit more grown up and worldly than that."

He didn't say anything, and she wondered if she wasn't being too forward. Still, there weren't many chances like this.

"You strike me as a resourceful gal."

"I'm quick on my feet."

They crossed Jefferson Street then and walked through the front gates onto the grounds. A moment later he stopped and turned to her, then smiled. He had straight white teeth and a thin mustache. "I'll tell you what, Tillie. I'm staying over at the American House. Have you ever been?"

"Why, no. Just outside, like tonight." Though wasn't she to have gone there with Frank the day she broke it off? The day he was going to propose? But here she was now, with a fine gentleman who seemed to like her.

"I'd make it worth it to you if you'd come back with me."

She stared at him, but he kept smiling that sweet smile. "It's a bit late for a meal."

Just then they heard the lock on the front door of the building slide shut.

"Oh, do you have the time?" she asked.

He pulled out his pocket watch and held it up for her to see. It was ten past ten.

"I wasn't talking about a meal. You're a pretty girl, and I'd like us to get to know each other better."

"I..." Words failed as she stood there, her spirits sinking, realizing what he was proposing. "Why, I don't know what you mean."

"I'd pay you well for the favor, Tillie."

And then it was all too clear. He had no intention of anything further than a dalliance. He'd simply been sweet-talking her to get what he intended all along.

"I'm sorry, but you've made a mistake here, Mr. Hunter," she said then, looking him square in the eye. "I'm not the kind for such things. And I mistook you for a gentleman."

"Well, since you're now locked out and all..."

"Why, they've promised to let me in," she said, backing away, not wanting him to get any more ideas.

"Well, goodbye then, Tillie."

She turned and began walking to the side of the building, her footsteps echoing on the wooden walkway. She could hear Charles Hunter's steps fading as he crossed back over Jefferson

Street. For a moment, she stopped, the shock of what he'd just proposed filling her with sadness. Why would he think such a thing of her? She pushed back tears and pressed on, hearing yet another lock slide shut. She started to run then, but when she tried the laundry door, it was locked. She ran faster, out of breath now. It was a quiet night but bitterly cold, and she shivered as she hurried round the building to try the cellar door. But when she walked down the steps and turned the knob, the door wouldn't open. She was locked out.

She'd taken her time walking home with the drummer, thinking he was a fine gentleman, knowing she risked coming back late but thinking it was worth the chance. And now she had no way to get in. She was shaking with the cold and angry with herself for being taken in by the drummer. A flicker of fear began to beat in her chest. What was she to do? She knocked softly several times.

If Mr. Titus had locked up the entire building and turned down all the gas lamps, by now he might just be nearby in the basement or soon would be coming back down to the furnace room. If she waited a bit, perhaps he might hear her. But it was god-awful bitter, and she was suddenly so worn out. She turned, looking around at the outbuildings and the barns, wondering what to do. Wishing she'd never met Charles Hunter at all.

CHAPTER 52

"OH, TILLIE," I PLEADED IN MY QUIET BEDROOM, "where did you go? What happened to you?"

It was hard to even breathe. She was about to die, and it felt like it was happening now, in real time. How could this be it, the end of the testimony for April 8, and I still didn't know what had really happened? It was unbearable.

I sat on the bed, reading and rereading the testimony of a student, Arturo Rivera, who was smoking out the window of his bedroom on the third floor. He was the last known person to see Tillie alive after she said goodbye to the drummer. He verified the drummer's testimony that he left the grounds, heading back up Church Street to the American House. At the same time, Tillie Smith rounded the side of the building toward the servants' entrance. The last time she was seen alive.

I got up and began pacing laps around the bed, back and forth. What must have been going through her mind? It was a bitterly cold night. She had to have been freezing. Did she have any idea she was in danger? Was someone lying in wait for her?

I thought about Titus, Mead, and Weeder. All three of them saw her that night at various times. One of them, I felt certain, was responsible. Only Titus had been accused. Or convicted. Yet even after reading over a thousand pages of testimony, I wasn't sure he was guilty. And obviously there was still doubt by old-timers in town.

The prosecution had laid out their case in their opening arguments, how Titus had lain in wait for her, knowing she'd be late and miss curfew. This was according to Peter Mead. He was the only one who could have let her in, giving him an opportunity, Mrs. Ruckle had testified. The prosecution went on to say that Titus tried to take advantage of her because she was at his mercy. She could lose her job, and when she resisted, he strangled and raped her. Then he carried her outside, far from the building, to avoid suspicion.

It was plausible, but...aside from the testimony of Peter Mead, it was all speculation.

I couldn't help think of what I'd read in the first articles in the week or two after Tillie was found. That there were no real suspects, and they thought the crime would go unsolved. Until James Creelman, the reporter for Joseph Pulitzer's New York newspaper, the *World*, began building a case against Titus. Back then, jurors were allowed to read the newspapers. Creelman became a celebrity as he fueled a tide of outrage that this poor girl had been murdered and dumped in a pauper's grave. He even began the monument fund.

And then, within weeks, Mead stepped forward and solidified the case with nearly a dozen verbatim conversations with Titus that were incriminating. Particularly his last, the night of the murder, when Titus supposedly told him to come back down after his studies because Tillie was coming in late, and *we will have a chance to pump her.*

Bridget Grogan, whose room was right above the furnace room, never heard screaming. No one else in the building heard a thing.

What if it was Mead who'd really killed her? Then plotted a case against Titus to save his own skin?

And how could I overlook Frank Weeder, her ex-beau? He had also seen Tillie that night in front of the church on Main Street, just hours before she was murdered. Today, I knew, the husband or boyfriend was always the prime suspect. How did Weeder feel, seeing Tillie walk away with the drummer after he'd just warned her friend Mary Wright about them? I knew nothing, really, about him. Except for Mary Wright's testimony about seeing him that night, he was never mentioned at all in the transcript.

I looked at the final pages sitting on the dresser. The autopsy. How I dreaded reading it. I didn't want to know the horrid details of her suffering. Tillie Smith had been a living, breathing girl. Not a mascot or a legend. And on that night of April 8th, she had endured a nightmare of horror. Along with her life, every hope and dream she had was brutally taken from her.

I heard the college bells ringing then, just blocks away. Each time I heard them now, every hour of the day, I felt like it was a plea from her. And I was failing.

Oh, Tillie, I prayed, *I wish you could somehow let me know what happened. Who really did this to you? If only you'd lived, if only you could have made him suffer, too. Brought him to justice.*

But would she have? Would she really have reported her attacker? I only had to think of myself to know the answer. For me, the stakes were not so high. The only thing holding me back was my own fear. My shame. For Tillie, it would have been nearly impossible.

I walked back to the dresser to pick up the autopsy pages but suddenly picked up my laptop instead. I didn't type *Tillie* or *Titus* or *Weeder* as I normally did. I typed a name I had not spoken aloud in eighteen years. Before I even clicked on "search," my heart began to pound. I could hear the blood roaring through my head.

There were pages of hits, as there would be for anyone running for political office. What I hadn't expected were the photographs. A row of them like a little album popped right up, and there he was. But what I also hadn't expected was the pretty wife. The adorable children, two girls and a boy. The oldest girl looked about twelve or thirteen and had his red hair. The wife looked sweet. And he...there was that disarming smile, the crooked tooth. He looked...like a nice guy, someone you could vote for and feel good about.

He'd raped me. He'd ruined my life, and he'd gone on to have everything. And at that moment it almost seemed, looking at this man with his perfect family, that it all must have been a bad dream. Something that had happened in another lifetime, to other people, and he couldn't possibly have anything to do with it.

But he did.

I WENT TO STEPHENS STATE PARK, needing the woods and nature to help calm my racing thoughts. I missed the Musconetcong River, which cut through the trees here and around several tiny islands with picnic tables and benches. As I got out of my car, yellow leaves fluttered slowly to the ground on this windless day. The afternoon sun was angled now, a halo of gold lower on the horizon. Most mornings, a glaze of silver frost covered the grass. Everything was changing, had been changing. Porches were decorated with pumpkins and mums. I'd come back to this town in early spring as a bride. Now it was nearly Halloween, and I was...separated.

I sat on a bench and looked down at the water, clear and glistening with rocks and leaves scattered across the bottom. I felt like everything I needed to know, to do, was there in my mind, like those rocks and leaves just below the surface, if only I could reach it.

What if Tillie had lived? Would she have spent her life blaming herself for being attacked? Would she have told her sisters? Would the shame of it have paralyzed her for years? I didn't think so. Closing my eyes, I pictured Tillie's own. How many times had I stared into them, searching? Tillie wouldn't have given up, that I knew. She'd been a survivor, fighting for her family, for a better life. Bridget and Faith and so many others had testified to that. And her sisters, her mother...they would never have blamed her for what happened.

I opened my purse and took out my mother's prayer card from her memorial service. I stared into her wide brown eyes. Valerie Dempsey, forty-three years old. She looked so young, frozen in time eighteen years ago, just eight years older than I was now. He didn't just rape me. He was responsible for my mother's death. For years I blamed myself, hated myself, carried the burden of guilt. A young girl in shock, traumatized and frozen with shame. And what I was coming to see, and feel in my heart, was that I didn't need my mother's forgiveness. I'd had it all along. I just needed to forgive myself. I wasn't to blame; he was. The guilt was his.

CHAPTER 53

WHEN I GOT BACK TO THE BED & BREAKFAST, I was stunned to see Adam waiting for me in the formal living room.

"I need to talk to you," he said as soon as I walked in the front door.

He looked as though he hadn't slept in days, a shadow of a beard beginning, dark circles under his eyes. My heart was hammering in my chest.

I could hear Alyson in the dining room, setting up for the morning meal. Another guest was looking through brochures in the foyer. "Come upstairs," I said, and he followed me.

The room was a wreck, papers everywhere. A moment later, Adam stood in the open doorway.

"I've been trying to reach you," he said.

"I know. And I know you think I've been unfair, but it wasn't just about you."

"Please, let me talk. There are some things I need to tell you."

"Okay. Sit down."

He sat on the wing chair, and I sat on the edge of the bed a few feet from him. I could see his hands shaking.

"There's so much I want to say to you. About what I've done wrong and how I...should have been more honest. But I really came to ask you if you'd come and see my grandmother. She's been asking for you."

"Oh." I was surprised, but really, why should I have been? I felt a bond with her from the very first, and then...I basically disappeared.

"My aunt had a stroke, and Gran's—"

"What? Your aunt Helen?"

"Yes. I've been running back and forth between Gran and the hospital. My aunt's going to be okay hopefully. It was on the mild side, they're saying, though she could have some lasting effects. But Gran is pretty overwhelmed."

"Oh, I'm so sorry. You should have..." *Called me*, right. He had, and I hadn't answered.

"I didn't want to leave a message about that. It didn't seem right."

"Who's with your grandmother now?"

"Justine, but she's leaving, so I don't have a lot of time."

"Where does your grandmother think I've been?"

"I told her you left. I basically...told her everything—about Tillie, what happened to you—"

"You told her I was raped?"

He nodded slowly. "Listen, don't think I wasn't careful about this. I've been talking to a psychologist, Dr. Monday, who I know from town, because I don't think I fully understood what you were going through, and...I didn't want to make any more mistakes. Are you angry I did that?"

He must've seen how stunned I was. "You told your grandmother and someone who is a stranger to me... about something so personal."

"He's a psychologist. Everything is in confidence, and he thinks I was wrong, that I shouldn't have stood in your way when you were searching for the truth about Tillie Smith."

"He did? Did you tell him about your family, and Mrs. Freeman, and how I betrayed all of you?"

"I did, yes. But he said it was more important that you followed your feelings and your gut because maybe, hopefully, it could help you get some closure with your own assault."

"I...I don't even know what to say."

His phone beeped. He looked at it, then stood. "Look, there's a lot more I want to explain to you. But there isn't time right now. Justine has to leave, so I need to get back. Do you think you can please come and see Gran?"

Slowly I nodded.

* * *

I ARRIVED AS JUSTINE WAS LEAVING. The front door was already open, and she and Adam were talking.

"Oh, hey, Rachel. Gran will be glad to see you. She's been asking for you." Then she turned back to Adam. "I'm sorry. I couldn't change my vacation, but I'll be back next week. She's all settled in her recliner, but she's been asking for Ronnie."

Justine left. Adam sighed, then turned to me. "She thinks I'm my dad more and more."

"I'm sorry. I'm sure it's the stress of this whole thing."

He grabbed his jacket. "If you could give me an hour, I'd appreciate it. I'm going to run up to the hospital. My aunt's been giving them a hard time."

"Gee, why isn't that a surprise?"

He smiled, and so did I.

I found Gran in her recliner in the parlor, the television turned to *Jeopardy!* It struck me as I stood in the doorway that this was exactly the scene the last time I'd been in this room, the night of her party. I'd seen my rapist on TV and nearly fainted. Then I ran home, packed, and left Adam. Two weeks had gone by.

I walked into the room, and Gran looked up. "Oh, Rachel, I'm so happy to see you." Then she started to cry.

I pulled a chair close to her, sat, and took both of her hands. "I'm sure Helen is going to be fine. She's a strong woman. Don't worry."

"It's just...she's my child. I couldn't bear if..."

"Don't even think that way."

"You know I'm so dependent on her. And now poor Ronnie is trying to work and be here with me and run to the hospital. I'm not being fair to anyone."

"You mean Adam, don't you, Gran? Adam's been here with you. And yes, he does look so much like his dad, Ronnie."

"Oh, yes, yes. I'm sorry. I haven't been sleeping well, dear, and...sometimes the past doesn't seem all that far away, don't you think?"

Hadn't I been living in the past for a while now? "Yes, I believe you're right about that."

"It must be my age. Sometimes I imagine when I wake up that I'm still living in the cemetery and Sam is already out working. My heart lights up thinking he'll be back for lunch. And then I open my eyes, and everything looks so strange until I realize where I am and that part of my life is all over."

"Oh, Gran." She was breaking my heart. I gave her a hug, squeezing her for a long moment. "I'm sorry I haven't come sooner."

"You're here now."

"I'll stay with you. We'll have a pajama party. How does that sound?"

She smiled then. "That sounds wonderful. And Ron...Adam... can go home and catch up on some rest."

"That's a great idea. I'll stay as long as you need me."

"Adam needs you, too, you know," she said, taking hold of my hand again. "You need to give him a chance, Rachel."

"He said he told you about...everything."

She squeezed my hand. "You've been alone for a long time, dear. It's time you let someone love you. Be there for you. You know I saw that with my friend, Marion, all those years ago. So ashamed of her grandfather, she almost didn't even get married."

I was stunned by her bringing up Marion Freeman.

"I know. You're probably wondering about this old memory of mine, but it's long ago that's clear, not so much the now."

"Oh, Gran, I understand."

"I was the one who pushed her to marry, you know. I told her if he truly loved her, nothing else would matter. That's how it was for my Sam and me. And I think for you and Adam. Not everyone is that lucky. Look at Helen. But Rachel, please give him a chance."

"I will, Gran. I promise."

"Good," she said.

"So did Marion tell her fiancé everything? And he's the one who married her, then?"

"Yes. He really loved her. It didn't matter to him at all, even after she told him about the confession."

"What...confession?" My heart began to hammer away. "Did James Titus confess? I thought he denied it all along. There was even an appeal."

"Oh, I don't know the details, dear, just that Marion told me she knew that at some point, her grandfather had confessed, though she didn't say to who."

"So...he really did murder Tillie Smith? Even though many locals still don't think so and...the case against him seemed weak?"

"That seemed to be, yes. Of course, none of us girls were allowed near her house," she told me, repeating what she'd said once before. "I felt bad for her because of that."

I sat there with Gran still holding my hand, my thoughts colliding. Who on earth had Titus confessed to? And how had I not seen anything about it? Maybe it was to his wife or his daughter. Perhaps years later? It still didn't make sense because although he was sentenced to hang and now I knew at some point had confessed to someone, there he was on that porch more than half a century later.

"Rachel? Dear?"

"Oh, I'm sorry," I said, realizing Gran had been talking and I hadn't heard a word.

"I was wondering if you'd help me get ready for bed. I'm so tired now."

"Of course." I stood up and helped her into her wheelchair.

"You'll give Adam another chance, then?" she asked yet again, looking up at me. "I can't bear to see him so unhappy."

"Oh, Gran, I betrayed him. I lied to all of you. I didn't just leave because of what he did. I didn't feel like I...deserved all of you."

"You love each other. That's all that matters. You'll get through it."

I gave her a kiss on the cheek.

"It's tough to get old," she whispered into my ear.

* * *

WHEN ADAM RETURNED, I hurried over to the Emerson house and quickly packed up my things and came back. He was in the kitchen, about to wash dishes.

"Leave them. I'll do them later or in the morning. You go home and catch up on sleep."

"Are you sure about this?"

"Yes. I feel awful I haven't been here to help."

"It's not your responsibility."

"Not everything is yours to fix, Adam. I love her, and she's going through hell. Hopefully when the stress of this is over and she gets enough rest, she'll bounce back." Though I wasn't as cer-tain as I sounded.

"Hopefully my aunt's tests go well tomorrow."

"You'll be there at the hospital?"

"Of course."

"I'll be here with Gran. For as long as you need."

We walked into the hall, and Adam saw my things, including the box with all the papers.

"Have you found what you were looking for with Tillie?"

"Actually, I think I do know now who she was, as much as I could with so little to go on. As for what happened to her that night she died...I think I'm more confused than ever."

"What do you mean?"

"I read almost the entire transcript, and I was honestly hav-ing doubts about whether James Titus really did it. But your grandmother, out of the blue, just told me he confessed."

"Really? Are you sure she's remembering correctly?"

"Yes, I think she is. But there are no details."

"So you're not finished?"

I hesitated. "No, I'm not."

He looked at me for a long moment. "Good. Let me help you then."

"What?"

"Let's do this together. I want to. You shouldn't have to do it alone. It can't be easy."

I nodded. "It's not. She's real to me. But Adam, you've got your hands pretty full already."

"I'll be off for two weeks starting tomorrow."

And then I realized...he'd taken time for the honeymoon. The honeymoon we'd never finished planning.

"Thank you," I said.

I SAT IN GRAN'S ROOM AS SHE LAY IN BED, our conversation dwindling until I heard her soft breathing. My mind was whirling at everything that had happened today. The last page of Tillie being alive. Seeing my rapist and his family online. Feeling the burden of guilt over my mother's death begin to soften. And then Adam coming to me, confessing about talking to a psychologist and asking if he could help me with Tillie. Wanting to help *me*.

I was overwhelmed by my hope that something could be salvaged with Adam, while at the same time feeling as though I were drowning in sadness over Tillie's final moments on earth with no closure.

In my heart, I knew who she was now. At nineteen, Tillie was trying so desperately to make a better life for herself and her family in a difficult world that was even more difficult for women. I only had to listen to Bridget Grogan and Faith Seiler in their testimony to know that. Tillie admitted to Faith about the working conditions and the challenges in surviving there. How a seminary student tried to get fresh with her and one of the janitors continually giving her lecherous looks. Mead and Titus, of course. Bridget talked of Tillie's dreams and the sadness often present in her eyes.

I needed to know who took those dreams from her. Who made her suffer. I couldn't leave it to chance that justice had already been served. Or to Gran's distant memory. There was a reason I had been put on this path.

I got up and left Gran's room, leaving the door cracked so I would hear if she woke. I knew I wouldn't sleep. And I knew what I had to do.

* * *

HOW TILLIE WAS FOUND THE NEXT MORNING was not in dispute by the coroner or any of the other witnesses. She was lying on her back with her bonnet still tied but fallen behind her head onto the ground. Oddly, there was a wooden board lying in the grass beside her, which seemed to be from a nearby fence. Those who first saw her said she looked as though she might have been sleeping, except for the purple bruises encircling her neck and a trickle of blood on her thumb. I closed my eyes as a crushing sadness filled my chest.

I imagined her battered hands hidden inside those kid gloves so no one could see them. So tight she couldn't even remove them to pay for a spool of thread. Her red purse was missing. More mysterious, there wasn't one pin left in her hair, and there were none to be found anywhere. One earring was still in her ear. The other was found later during the autopsy, lost in her thick hair.

The autopsy testimony by several doctors left no doubt as to how she must have suffered. How she'd been brutalized. No won-der I started having nightmares.

The testimony of the doctor who first examined Tillie and then the coroner was brutally graphic, beginning with the appearance of her body when first examined. Tillie was about five feet four inches and about 145 pounds. She had *a very heavy head of hair...disheveled, disturbed, and disarranged. A bruise on the side of the head. The neck had such marks as might have been made by grasping the throat severely and by making a severe pressure over the windpipe...such as would be likely to produce complete closure of the windpipe. The only bruise we could find upon the body was upon the left arm between the elbow and the shoulder...as if it had been grasped firmly by the hand. A cut in the bend of the thumb had the appearance of an old cut that had been torn open.*

They opened and removed the scalp, examined the skull and brain, and found *an effusion of dark blood between the scalp and the skull, such an appearance as would be presented by a powerful* blow to the head. *The scalp itself presented no external appearance of injury.* Next they opened her chest, and *the right lung was entirely collapsed....The left lung was not so much so.* I felt as though my own lungs were squeezing closed. It was too awful to imagine. Someone had crushed her.

Tillie's abdomen was cut open then, and they *removed the womb, the uterus, and the ovaries; we found them healthy, but we found them virginal in size.* When asked what that meant, the doctor stated, *That the person had never been impregnated.* The doctor went on to state that *there was no appearance of external injury whatever, no bruise or laceration, no blood. We found the vagina in a perfectly relaxed condition with no blood, with a large deposit of what appeared to be semen.* When asked about the hymen by Titus's attorney, the doctor stated that *there was no hymen; there could not be with this perfectly relaxed state.*

His conclusion was that she'd died of strangulation, and that *in all probability was crying or screaming at the time the pressure was commenced,* and that she would have died within two or three minutes. I closed my eyes, unable to go on. It was unbearable to imagine. And to think that now...she'd become entertainment. There would be Lantern Tours reenacting her last moment on earth, walking to her brutal death.

Minutes later, I forced myself to continue. As for the condition of the vagina, *it would show that the person died very suddenly, and there was a complete relaxation of all voluntary and involuntary muscles, the same as it is in hanging.*

The prosecutor asked, *What opinion did you come to as to the time she had been ravished relative to the time of her death?* The doctor answered that *the act was accomplished about the time she died or was in a dying condition.*

I stood up then and had to bend over to breathe. How she had suffered. Poor Tillie. It brought back the terror of that day, his body crushing my own, my gasping for air, thinking I was going to die of suffocation. Silent tears streamed down my cheeks.

I went downstairs, checked on Gran, then walked laps around the house for a while, through the living room, the dining room, the hall and the kitchen, over and over, trying to fight the images burned in my brain. Tillie's body in the field. Then on the table at the furniture maker's, where the autopsy was performed as they built the casket. Cutting her open. It felt as if it were all in real time.

When that feeling of panic began to subside and I felt more in control, I made tea, peeked in on Gran again, then went back upstairs.

The coroner then stated that he believed from the condition of the body in the field when he first saw her that she'd been dead about six or seven hours at least. I counted back, noting that meant she'd been killed within an hour or two of leaving the drummer.

The defense then began its cross-examination and once again went to attack Tillie, insinuating the "relaxed" state of her genitals could indicate she'd had frequent intercourse. I wanted to go back in time and smack them all.

They began a volley of questions about the lack of any kind of bruising or blood on the genital area as indicating her participation. This was followed by getting the doctor to admit that the amount of semen indicated more than one man. I stood up again, wanting to punch the walls. The defense was trying to paint her as a whore who'd had sex with more than one man, then happened to be strangled to death. Now I knew where the theory about two men had come from. And of course there was the prior testimony about the brothel.

"Oh, Tillie..."

I wished I could leave, go back to the cemetery, walk through the fields of headstones and past the river to the highest point. I imagined myself looking up at her monument. *She died in defence of her honor.*

So despite Titus's attorney's efforts to disparage Tillie's reputation and get the rape charge eliminated, there were still those who believed in her back then. The New York newspapers, and James Creelman at the *World* in particular, had fanned the flames of outrage that this poor kitchen helper had been ravished and murdered on the campus of a seminary. But I knew they weren't doing it for Tillie. No, it was a story that they used to sell newspapers. The monument fund and Tillie's death had become a *cause célèbre.* James Creelman became famous.

I picked up Tillie's portrait and looked into her eyes. "I will not fail you," I whispered. "I don't care if they're all dead. Somehow I will find out the truth." Because from everything I'd read, and despite Titus having confessed to someone, it didn't add up. Someone else had gotten away with murdering Tillie, I was convinced of it.

When I put her photo down, I caught my own reflection in the mirror. The irony of what I was doing taunted me. Before he left, Adam had told me that he admired my courage in trying to find whatever I could to right what had happened to Tillie, despite what I'd risked. And yet, I thought now, looking into my own eyes...I didn't have the courage to do the same for myself.

CHAPTER 54

"WHAT ARE YOU READING?"

Adam stood in the kitchen doorway. I was sitting at the table, surrounded by pages from a legal pad with my notes. My theories. It was after nine, and Gran was still sleeping.

"I went over the autopsy last night. I'm trying to focus on the three men in Tillie's life: Titus, a seminary student named Peter Mead, and her former beau, Frank Weeder."

"That had to be pretty rough, reading the autopsy."

"It was gruesome. What they did to her..." I didn't tell him about the nightmares I was now having.

"Hey," he said, coming over and sitting across from me at the table. "You could have waited. I would have read it with you. It might have been a little easier."

I nodded, and then out of the blue, my eyes filled with tears.

"I need to explain to you about Sandra," he said. "I want you to trust me again."

"Okay."

"I had no idea Sandra would be there at the party, Rachel. You have to believe that."

"What hold does she have on you?"

He gave a pained sigh. "It was so awkward seeing her there. I didn't know what to do, and the next thing...you're standing there looking at us. I should have told you about her in the begin-ning. I just...I don't like to think about it. It was so long ago, it seems like another lifetime."

"Adam, I saw the way she looked at you. She had tears in her eyes, and you looked pretty emotional."

"It's not what you think. We were seniors in high school.

We'd been together for a while, though I hadn't been thinking any further than that. Then she got pregnant."

"You have a child?" It felt like a bullet pierced my heart.

"Please, let me finish. I didn't want to marry her. I'm not proud of that, believe me, but we were way too young."

"But you loved her," I interrupted.

He nodded. "I thought I did. Anyway, a few months later she miscarried. Sandra was always a bit fragile. When I said that perhaps now we could move on with our lives separately, she didn't take it too well. I was...relieved. I felt so damn guilty, but I was eighteen and scared to death."

I could well imagine. Eighteen and suddenly everything changes in a devastating way. "So what happened then?"

"Well, she tried to kill herself."

"Oh my God."

He nodded. "Believe it or not, it was Aunt Helen who helped me through it."

Of course, I thought.

"My father wanted me to 'be a man' and stay with her," he went on. "But my aunt convinced me that in the long run, that would be a disaster. That Sandy would get over it. And eventually I think she did."

"Oh, Adam. I think she still loves you."

He shrugged. "It's funny. When you're eighteen, you feel so grown up, so ready to be an adult and take on the world. And something big happens...but you already know that, don't you?" He looked at me with a small smile. "I didn't push you about sex because I knew firsthand that it's not something to be taken lightly, though too many people do. I learned that the hard way."

I nodded.

"I should have told you before. I should have trusted you to understand. I was just ashamed. I felt responsible for her suicide attempt. When I finally left for college, I felt so free. Not just of that but of the problems with my parents over my father's drinking. I knew he was so disappointed in me that I didn't man up."

"You were still a kid, Adam."

"I didn't come back much for years. And then when I did, it

was kind of too late. He was so far gone, and the cemetery...well, you know all that."

"And that's when you stopped your music."

He nodded. "In some way, it was like, how could I let myself enjoy what I believed was partly responsible for my not doing what I should have done? Come home sooner. Help him. And then...as I said before, the band moved on without me."

"You can't fix people, Adam."

"You sound like Aunt Helen."

"Well, that's a first. But you don't feel guilty about Sandra, do you?"

He shrugged. "In theory, I don't. But there's still the guilt that jabs me from time to time. Like when I see her. Or over my dad when something goes wrong at the cemetery."

We sat there in silence for a long moment.

"I know you think we made a mistake, Rachel, but I don't. Despite everything, I think we found each other for a reason. Maybe we jumped into things a little fast, but I don't have any regrets. I hope you can forgive me."

I looked at him a long moment, remembering that little boy with the birthmark across his throat all those years ago. The scars of his childhood still beating inside the man before me. Just as my own still lingered in me.

"I can, Adam. But can you forgive me?"

"I already have."

There was a softness in his eyes again when he looked at me. But I could see he still felt hesitant.

I got up and walked into his arms.

* * *

GRAN SEEMED TO AGE A DECADE over the next few days worrying about Helen, who she said needed to stop being a workaholic. And who she lamented had no one to take care of her but Adam.

"He'll make sure she gets the best care possible; don't worry," I told her. "And I'll be here with you for as long as necessary."

Gran smiled, her eyes filling. "You're a good girl, Rachel."

It pleased me so much to hear those words.

Adam had been staying at the cemetery nights but during the day was in and out between his hospital visits. It was early after-noon now when he returned with news that Helen would soon be transferred to a rehab facility.

"She'll probably be there for a few weeks; then she'll be able to come home. Her left side is pretty weak and her speech is still affected, but with therapy, they think she'll be able to go back to a pretty normal life."

"Your grandmother will be so relieved."

He nodded to the papers all over the dining room table. "Want to tell me what you've found so far?"

"You don't have to go back to the hospital soon?"

"No. They're doing a few more tests before she leaves tomor-row, and she pretty much ordered me to get a life again."

I hesitated. "And...you really want to do this?"

He smiled. "I told you I do. Honestly."

"Thank you. Maybe talking it out will help me see things I've been missing."

He sat down. "Let's get started."

"Those are my bullet points on that yellow legal pad. How about I make us some coffee?"

I went into the kitchen and filled the pot. When I opened the garbage drawer under the sink to dump the coffee grinds, I felt my blood go still. There sat the day's *Star Ledger*, which Adam usually recycled for Gran. The headline read, *Attorney General Race in Dead Heat*. But where there was obviously a photograph of the two candidates, one was missing. It had been carefully cut out. He must have thrown it out last night before he left.

"Oh, Adam," I whispered to myself. "Don't do this."

I went back in the dining room. Adam was sitting at the table, head down, reading intently. He looked up at me with that smile. I hesitated, knowing I didn't really want to do this now. I smiled back at him, then sat down.

I began laying out the facts as I knew them so far. "The drummer, which is what they called a salesman back then, Charles Munnich, walked Tillie back to the institute on April eighth, and they heard the bolt on the front door slide shut. It was after curfew, and Tillie was locked out. He was the last one to see her alive."

"And he wasn't a suspect?"

"He was briefly. First he lied about his real name to her, saying it was Charles Hunter. Then he went back to the American House and bragged that he'd had his way with Tillie. Later on when he was being questioned, he admitted propositioning her but said she had turned him down. A student, Arturo Rivera, testified he saw Munnich walk back up Church Street and Tillie hurry toward the rear of the building."

"What a bastard."

"I know. My heart broke for her—out for a night of fun, possibly even excited to be with a nice gentleman, then having it go so badly."

"So she obviously didn't get in, right?"

"Titus was the only one who could have let her in. He did not testify. Almost the entire case against Titus was based on Peter Mead's testimony, a divinity student on work-study." According to Peter Mead, I went on, Titus said to him earlier that evening that Tillie was getting in late, and he should come back down because "*then we will have a chance to pump her.*"

"Wow, that's pretty vulgar."

"Adam, I looked up the slang in my book on 1880s culture, and it wasn't there. Honestly, I think he made it up. Not only that, Mead had recalled nearly a dozen conversations almost verbatim regarding Titus's comments about Tillie. The defense tried to portray him as a Judas and to rattle him in their cross-examination, and he finally admitted to writing down his conversations with Titus. When accused of simply seeking the reward, he insisted he was only trying to do the right thing. To me, though, it seemed almost plotted."

I handed Adam the reward letter. "Wow, there's his actual handwriting."

"I know. It's fascinating, isn't it? I mean, they all lived; this isn't some legend. These people were all here in this town, living out their lives. One of them murdered her and possibly got away with it."

"So do you think perhaps Peter Mead was guilty? That he did it?"

"Well, I did, actually, but his roommate testified that after he came back from helping Titus in the furnace room, when Titus made that vulgar remark, he began studying for an exam and never left the room again."

"And you believe that?"

I shrugged. "I don't know. I really sense the guy was a worm, and I wonder if he was the divinity student who'd tried to get fresh with Tillie. But he's got an alibi."

"Okay, keep going."

"So during the autopsy, they found Tillie's hair and skirt were full of dust and wood fibers that you'd find in the furnace room. There were red spots on her petticoat from some kind of red lead that was on the furnace room floor. That's it for physical evidence. The prosecution alleged that after he raped and strangled her, Titus threw the hairpins and red purse into the furnace. Then he carried her body outside, laying her in the field so that no one would know she was killed inside the building."

Apparently the day after the body was found, Dr. Whitney told Titus not to sweep up the furnace room. But he did it anyway, according to Mrs. Ruckle. The prosecution insisted he was making sure there was no evidence left, not a hairpin.

"Add that all up, and it doesn't look good, Rachel."

"I know. Titus acted guilty. He asked Bridget Grogan the day after Tillie was found, while standing outside and looking despondent, if she thought God could forgive the murderer. She wasn't the only one to testify about his manner. His health began to deteriorate further, as if his guilt was eating away at him. He tried to escape. They even suspected him of trying to commit suicide when a rope was discovered in his cell. The trial actually had to be delayed until he was strong enough to continue."

"Geez, Rachel, I know most of this is circumstantial, but again when you add it all up..."

"I know. Do you remember the Bible I found in the attic at his house? It was full of underlined passages about forgiveness."

"So I guess while it certainly looks bad, none of it was solid proof."

"Right. I've watched enough TV to know that. And there's something in my gut despite the confession. None of the missing items were ever found, not the hairpins or the red purse. But the thing I keep going back to was that Titus weighed 135 pounds and Tillie weighed 145 pounds. He had stomach and intestinal problems before the murder and was supposedly weak from them. The defense in cross-exam made the point that he couldn't possibly have carried her from the basement of the building to where she was found in the field."

"But when there's a crisis, adrenaline has enabled people to pick up cars."

"I know. But perhaps the most telling point in Titus's favor was that nothing shifted inside of Tillie. This is kind of graphic," and I was embarrassed a bit by having to explain, "but there was '*a large deposit of semen*' high up inside of her. Neither doctor disputed that, and it was originally why it was thought two men were involved."

"But only Titus was convicted."

"Correct. But Adam, think about this. If Titus carried her alone to that field, the semen would have shifted due to gravity. It would have dripped down inside her. There's no way it would have still been high up inside her."

"Unless two men carried her horizontally."

"Do you know, in the very beginning, before the press began pointing the finger at Titus, the police originally thought she was carried and laid in the field on that board found beside her. If she had been flat on the board and carefully placed on the ground, nothing might have shifted. And that would have taken two men."

"Why didn't Titus's attorney hammer that home more forcefully? And why didn't the jury pick up on this?"

"His attorney, honestly, was terrible. They failed him in so many ways. But it had become a circus, with the New York press camped out and building their own case against Titus. It had become a witch hunt thanks to James Creelman and the *World*.

And get this: jurors had free access to reading the newspapers, not like today. And Creelman had vilified Titus. Do you know he's considered the father of yellow journalism?"

"Rachel, my head is spinning. How have you managed to keep this all straight?"

"It hasn't been easy. I just keep reminding myself...this is for Tillie. The truth has to come out."

I went on to explain that when they cut Tillie's beautiful hair off and it fell to the ground at the cabinetmaker's, there was no care taken to keep the hair uncontaminated. Titus's attorney was good at getting the various witnesses to admit that it was possible the wood shavings and dust found on her could have come from the floor right there and not the furnace room. But where I believe his attorney really failed was in not bringing in the original conclusions of the police and the coroner's jury in that early article, which I handed Adam now: that Tillie was killed in a nearby barn. Not one person heard anything in the building that night, any kind of screaming. Bridget Grogan's room was directly above the furnace room, and she heard nothing.

"When it came down to it, the most incriminating evidence is the red lead on the back of her petticoat. You would find it only on the furnace room floor, where supposedly Titus had raped and killed her."

"But was that really enough?"

As much as I hated James Titus, convinced he was a lecherous man, I had to admit it wasn't a strong case. But there was the pressure of the city papers and the town being shamed into giving a reward of $1,000. Creelman even had people sending in sketches for the monument while pleading for funds. It was a groundswell. Even the seminary wanted it over because it was bad for business.

I picked up Tillie's photo, then handed it to Adam. He stared at it for a long moment. "Knowing everything I do now...her eyes are kind of haunting."

"So you understand now? Ever since this whole thing began," I said, lifting my thumb and pointing to the scar, "I feel as if there's something I'm meant to do. I have to figure this out,

Adam. And what if I've missed something? I keep looking at all of this, and sometimes I feel like it's one of those drawings, you know, where you look at a bunch of blotches, and if you focus a certain way, suddenly you see what it really is."

"I do understand, Rachel." He took my hand. "I promise we'll figure it out."

I took a deep breath, trying to calm myself. "Thank you."

"So...if Titus didn't rape and murder Tillie, then who do you think did? What really happened in those final hours?"

"Mead and Weeder both saw her that night."

"So your other two suspects are Mead and Weeder? And Mead seems to have an alibi."

"So does Weeder. I read long ago in a snippet from an article about the inquest that he was in town drinking with friends. And get this: the police didn't believe he was smart enough to have pulled this off."

"So where does that leave us?"

"I've exhausted all of the information I could find. That's why I'm so frustrated. And worried. How do I reach back through time and find the truth?"

Just then my cell phone rang, as if in answer. Adam's eyebrows shot up. Eerie timing. I looked at the name on the caller ID, and my jaw dropped.

"Oh, Adam, you're not going to believe this."

* * *

MR. DAVIDSON'S FARMHOUSE WAS AT the base of Buck Hill, with fruit orchards rising up in the fields behind it. A sign out front read, "Best Peaches in NJ." They also had fields of Christmas trees, where Adam told me he and his parents had come when he was little to cut their trees. He stayed behind with Gran, knowing I didn't want to wait for someone else to come and sit with her.

I sat at Mr. Davidson's kitchen table while he talked about cider and how they used nearly eighteen different kinds of apples in their signature blend. I could barely keep myself from grabbing the cardboard box that was sitting on the counter.

When he finally paused for breath, I jumped right in, asking if he'd found all of his grandfather's articles and writings.

"Oh, it wasn't easy. My grandson came and dug through the attic. I couldn't remember the last time I actually saw it. But it's all in there," he said, getting up and going for the box.

"Here, let me help you," I said, taking the box and bringing it to the table.

I lifted the cardboard flaps, no longer caring about courtesy. The box was filled nearly to the top with onionskin papers covered in blue ink from a fountain pen. I couldn't believe it. I lifted a chunk of pages. There were also old articles, yellowed and brittle with age. I pulled one out.

"It looks like this is an editorial by your grandfather. 'The Power of the Press,' by Denis Sullivan, April 23, 1886. That's two weeks after Tillie was murdered." I began reading it aloud.

It is no secret that our small town has become home these past weeks to not just reporters from the New York newspapers, but also a noted Pinkerton detective. The murder of Tillie Smith seems to have captured the attention of our vast nation, and this reporter wonders if such notoriety is not turning the heads of those in charge. Even our local police and detectives have been seen hobnobbing with the big city press, and the worry should be this: what sway does such attention bring to the truth?

While the coroner has determined that Matilda Smith's murderer is still unknown, and that may never be rectified, Mr. Joseph Pulitzer's reporter, James Creelman, reporting for the WORLD *out of New York City, is building his own case against a certain seminary employee he has not yet named. Yet all here in town know of whom he speaks.* I looked up at Mr. Davidson. "This is incredible. And here your grandfather refutes Creelman: *If we are to use common sense, then the only logical step for the local police would be to go back to the origins of their investigation and further interrogate those let go.*"

"I do remember my grandfather talking about that reporter. How once he set the law's sights on Titus, they didn't bother pursuing anyone else. I can still hear his voice shaking. That reporter stuck in my grandfather's craw, that's for sure."

"It's continued on another page, but..." I lifted another chunk of pages, and one of them fell apart, fluttering to the table. "Oh, I'm sorry. I promise I'll be careful. I can even laminate the pages and try to put this all in order."

"Well, I'm sorry it's not very organized."

"I'm so grateful you're willing to share it with me. I was just wondering if you could remember anything else at all about what your grandfather may have said about Titus or the trial. If they ever talked afterward about what happened?"

"They were in school together as boys; I do remember him saying that. Of course this was a tiny town back then. Titus died in 1952, I believe, and my grandfather in 1950. They both lived good long lives. I do remember him telling me that Titus never spoke of the murder or the trial after he got released, not even to him. Kept to himself and got a job keeping books, which he learned at the prison in Trenton."

"Did your grandfather ever mention Tillie's beau, Frank Weeder? He was obviously one of those who was questioned and let go."

He stood a moment thinking, then shook his head. "I'm sorry; I just don't recall."

"Did he ever say anything about Titus confessing?"

Mr. Davidson frowned for a long moment, thinking way back. "Seems there was something about that, but..."

I stood there waiting, but then he shrugged and shook his head.

"I understand," I said, trying not to sound disappointed. "I'm just thrilled with what you've been able to share with me...and for allowing me to take the articles."

As I drove back through town, I kept looking over at the box on the seat beside me. Denis Sullivan had been there throughout the months of Tillie's murder and Titus's trial. These were his own words, his thoughts, his theories during that time. Though he knew Titus, they weren't good friends, and he seemed to have no bias, not like Creelman. In fact, it seemed from the little bit I'd read so far, he had no respect for Creelman. Yet Creelman went on to have a storied newspaper career, and Denis Sullivan quietly left journalism to tend the family farm.

I pulled into Helen's driveway and carried the box into the house, praying that somewhere in Denis Sullivan's work lay the key to everything I'd been trying to find.

CHAPTER 55

H ELEN SPENT A FEW EXTRA DAYS IN THE HOSPITAL after a complication, having her carotid artery unblocked. We spent what should have been our honeymoon taking care of Gran and reading Denis Sullivan's work. Adam and I were touching again, even kissing. But he was still sleeping at the cemetery while I spent my nights with Gran. I knew he was hesitant to become intimate again. Reading and rereading so many graphic, brutal details of Tillie's rape, I was also nervous about taking that step. I was having nightmares every night now, dreaming of Tillie's final hours alive.

By the third day after getting the box from Mr. Davidson, we were just about finished reading through it all. I think we both had eyestrain from the slanted script, faded over time. We'd each taken copious notes. There weren't just articles; there were also notes, random scribblings of ideas and thoughts. And each piece was fascinating, from an interview with Faith Seiler, president of the sorority, who began a protest against the treatment of women servants; to an article two months after the murder describing how Tillie's body had just been exhumed from Potter's Field and moved to the choicest plot after the town had been shamed in the city press.

"Adam, he mentions one of your ancestors!" I cried as he came into the dining room with refills on tea. "Samuel Miller."

He nodded. "He's the second portrait coming down the stairs. My grandfather was named after him."

"He said he never had to do anything so awful and thought it was perhaps sacrilegious, but...oh my God, listen to this. They pulled out her petticoat when they exhumed her to check those red spots, and..." I looked up at him. "It was blood, not red lead."

"Wow. That must have been in one of the missing chunks of the transcript."

"And that eliminates a huge piece of evidence against Titus, though it didn't seem to matter. It's unbelievable."

"Well, I've got some background on Weeder."

"Oh, that's great. It's like there's nothing anywhere about him."

Frank Weeder was born in 1859, he read. In the 1880 census, he lived on Main Street with his mother, Emma, and her second husband, John Coldbeck.

"So in 1886, when they were 'stepping out,' as it was called back then, Tillie was nineteen, and he was twenty-six," I calculated. "That's a big age difference, though maybe back then not so much."

"And get this: his occupation was listed as 'peanut vendor' in the 1880 census."

"I wonder if that's what he was doing when he met Tillie."

Adam shook his head. "Look at this. It's a directory of some sort from 1886 for Hackettstown. Frank Weeder was listed as a 'laborer' and was living on Liberty Street. And...that's about it."

"Nothing on where he went afterwards?"

"I went on Ancestry.com and filled in some blanks, but I could not find a death record, marriage record, anything related to arrests, nothing. I checked everywhere with the obvious name misspellings. It's like he disappeared."

"Or changed his name?"

"That's what I was thinking."

Why would he want to disappear? His family was here. His job. "Do you think that house on Liberty Street is still standing?"

Adam grimaced. "You can't be serious."

"I am."

"The lumberyard covers a lot of that block now, so it's possible it was knocked down a long time ago."

"But what if it's still there?"

WHEN ONE OF THE LADIES FROM CHURCH came to visit Gran later that afternoon, we flew out the door. Minutes later we pulled onto Liberty Street just off Main, and there it was, still standing. I got out of the truck and stood in front an old Colonial, perhaps from the early 1800s, with a sagging porch, boarded-up windows, and peeling yellow paint. It was directly next to the lumberyard.

I stood staring at it. "Adam, this is unbelievable; do you realize that? I mean, this is where her beau lived. Someone she may have loved. Who could have been her hope for a better future."

"And who it seems disappeared after her murder."

"How can we find out more about this house? Who owns it? How can we get inside?"

"You can't go inside. It looks like it's ready to fall down."

"Can you call your aunt's office? They're Realtors; they should have access to the tax records."

Adam got back in the truck to use his cell. I stepped onto the porch, grateful for the streetlight. The boards sagged under me, and I quickly stepped back onto the sidewalk.

"The lumberyard owns the house now," Adam said as he got out of the truck. "They're expanding, so it's going to be knocked down soon."

"I have to get inside."

"Rachel, I know what you're thinking, but what could possibly be in that house from Weeder living there 130 years ago? Think how many people have lived here since then. It was a boarding house."

I knew the odds were slim to none. But this was all I had, the only tangible link to Frank Weeder.

"Please, Adam. We can come back in the morning. I always find something."

I heard him sigh.

* * *

THE FOLLOWING MORNING WE CALLED, but the lumberyard would not give us permission to go into the house. It was condemned and would be knocked down in a few weeks. I wanted to scream. What if we signed a hold harmless? Maybe we could just quietly break in? But there was no way around it.

"I want you to promise me you won't do anything foolish," Adam said.

"I will, but..." I hesitated, then went on. "You have to make the same promise."

"What are you talking about?"

"I saw the newspaper in the garbage. Where you cut out his picture. I'm afraid you've been thinking about doing something stupid."

He looked at me, saying nothing.

"Don't scare me, Adam. The last thing I need is for you to get in trouble because of that bastard."

Still he said nothing.

"If you try to hurt him, you'll end up hurting me. Think about that."

We stood there in silence. I started the dishes, but when I turned to finish clearing the table, Adam was standing there.

"I promise."

I smiled. "Okay. Me, too."

I SPENT HOURS UPSTAIRS ON OUR BED with the remainder of Denis Sullivan's papers scattered around me, scanning for Weeder's name. Page after page of nothing, until...

"Oh my God!"

It was Titus's confession! It was an original article, yellowed and brittle looking, but someone at some point had laminated it. And paper-clipped to it was a similar page with his statement just prior to his sentencing, again vehemently denying guilt. This was pure gold. I wished I could read it to Adam, but he'd gone to be with his aunt, who was getting moved to rehab today.

I couldn't even sit. I pulled the pages apart and began reading the confession as I paced the room. It was from the *Warren Republic*, the county paper back then, dated April 1, 1887, long after Titus was found guilty and sentenced to hang. No wonder I never saw it.

The confession of James Titus is in the form of an affidavit,
sworn and subscribed by him, and was made solely for the use of
the Court of Pardons. It sets forth that Tillie Smith was not the
chaste girl she was supposed to be. In fact, Titus acknowledges he
had been unduly intimate with her from the time she first entered
the institute as a domestic.

I reread the last sentence, shaking, telling myself I was not
wrong about Tillie.

He states that on the night of the murder, Tillie Smith notified
him that she was going to the show, which she attended, and that
she would not be in until late, and she wanted him to let her in
when she returned. He told her to go to the matron and get per-
mission, but she refused to do so, saying it was against the rules.
After persuasion, he consented to wait for her and let her in. She
then went with him to the furnace room, sat on a settee, and
began taking off her outer wraps and gloves. Titus banked up the
fires and then left her for a few moments to make his usual
rounds, as sworn before a coroner's jury.

He returned about 10:30 and found Tillie waiting for him, who
consented to every proposition made her and offered no resistance
whatever. Titus claims this meeting was a prearranged one and
with a full knowledge on her part of its import, the occurrence
transpiring in the same room on a robe spread on the floor. She
afterward communicated to him her fears that she was in trouble,
from which he endeavored to dissuade her, not successfully, how-
ever, and she finally told him that if such should prove to be the
case, she would expose him as the author of her ruin.

"How is this possible?" I moaned out loud.

Titus protested against that course, and she insisted on it 'til,
he says, he in anger grasped her by the throat and held her for a
moment. He heard a gurgling sound and, thinking that some-
thing serious had happened, went for a light, and when he
returned found that she was dead and had fallen from the sitting
posture she was in to the stone floor, causing those bruises on the
head so puzzling to the physicians.

"I don't believe this!" I had to take deep breaths to slow my
racing heart. This couldn't be true.

It is also said that this confession was laid before the Court of Pardons in the shape of an affidavit as the last card to be played by the adept counsel for the defendant. Suffice it to say to our readers that if this confession be authentic, Titus, outside of the mere acknowledgment of the accidental killing, attempts to shield himself by besmirching the character of Tillie Smith.

Anyone who has read or heard the evidence will readily observe that there is absolutely nothing to uphold any statement that Titus (especially under the circumstances) might make against the chastity of the poor and uneducated girl. As to the details of the confession, he evidently has not hesitated to lie again, at a time when the attempt to relieve himself by blacking his victim's character might be one factor in saving his cowardly neck from the halter.

I knew now what it meant to feel as if your blood was boiling. He had confessed to save his neck. And of course his family, I'd learned, was politically connected.

But this...this became the last word on Tillie. This was her legacy, that she'd had an affair with a married man and was pregnant. My head was reeling.

* * *

THAT NIGHT BEFORE HE LEFT, Adam took me in his arms. He, too, had read the confession.

"Thank you for giving up all of these days to help me with this," I said.

"Well, I could say the same to you, helping with my grandmother."

"I love her."

"And she loves you. So do I." He kissed me then, long and deep. When he finished, he looked at me and said what he'd said that day long ago in the car after undoing my braid. "I've wanted to do that for a long time now."

"And I've wanted you to."

"Justine will be back in a few days. I'd like you to come back home then."

Home. Something swelled in my chest. "I'd like that, too."

He gathered his things. Gran was already asleep. I sat back down at the dining room table, papers scattered everywhere.

"Rachel," Adam said from the doorway, "what if there's some truth to Titus's confession?"

"You can't be serious."

"I know you don't want to believe it, but…"

"Adam, Tillie wasn't just raped and murdered. Her name, who she truly was, has been destroyed for eternity, and not just by the allegations during the trial. Whether anyone believed it or not, Titus's were the last words in history for Tillie Smith. Now I understand."

"What do you mean?"

"Now I understand the coincidences. The need to find her. My…obsession. She was the victim here, and Titus, whether he killed her or not, did to her what rapists do to their victims— make it seem it like it was her fault, that she was the guilty party."

"Rachel," Adam said, and I could tell by the sound of his voice he was about to say something I might not like, "what if there's some truth to his story? What if they had been carrying on? She could have been pregnant. It's possible."

"I can't believe you're even saying this. No one ever saw them together. There's been absolutely nothing to indicate it was even possible, not even in the autopsy."

"It probably would have been too early to tell back then. Look, I don't mean to upset you. I just think at this point, we shouldn't discount anything."

"I am discounting it. There's still the question of how she was carried, the probability she'd been raped by two men. Don't get me wrong—innocent or not, Titus was a coward. His confession became her legacy, the last word on her life. And I just can't let that stand."

CHAPTER 56

TILLIE STOOD IN THE DARK NEAR THE BIG BUILDING, shivering. Grey shadows lurked beneath the giant oak tree by the library. She was looking all about, and I knew she was trying to decide where to go. I needed to warn her. She turned toward the tree and whoever was lying in wait there. She began walking.

"No!" I screamed, though nothing came out but a guttural groan. It was as if my lips were paralyzed, and I couldn't seem to stop her. She was walking to her death!

Tillie turned suddenly, her eyes burning into me. Tears streamed down her cheeks. She knew...

I bolted upright in bed. I reached for the bottle of water on the table and swallowed, my hands shaking and spilling some on me. The nightmares were getting worse. I was no longer just watching it happen. Now it was as though she were pleading with me.

I lay back again, trembling, a sick feeling of dread squeezing my stomach. Wind and rain rattled the windows in the dark. Each night, it was as if it were happening over and over again. Tillie walking to her death.

I got up and went downstairs. I turned on all of the kitchen and dining room lights. I wouldn't sleep, I knew, so I got back to work. And as the sky began to brighten and the rain finally subside, I found something that made me pause. I got my legal pad and began a timeline. There was something confusing, an inconsistency that it seemed everyone, including the Pinkerton detective, had missed. I was getting closer.

* * *

THAT AFTERNOON, HELEN WAS TRANSFERRED to the rehab facility
to begin speech therapy and to hopefully strengthen her left side.
Adam stopped by on his way to accompany her; then Gran
insisted she was fine and wanted me to take her to see Helen
later on. I could barely hold back tears as I wheeled Gran into the
room and there sat Helen in sweats on a hospital bed, trying to
smile, her face still drooping. Gran burst into tears. Afterward
Adam took Gran down the hall to the gift shop, and Helen tried
to speak to me, her words stilted and guttural.

"Taaank ya."

After a moment I realized what she was saying. "Oh, you're
welcome."

Helen took a pad and wrote laboriously. *For taking care of
her.* Then to my astonishment, tears slipped down Helen's face,
and she reached over and took my hand.

"I am sor-ree."

"It's all right. Please don't worry about it."

Helen kept talking, slowly, with great effort, and it was painful to watch. I tried to assure her it wasn't necessary. But there
were things she needed to say, most of which I already knew,
which made me wonder if her memory had been involved. She
loved Adam like a son. But Adam often put his own needs, his
own happiness, on the back burner for others. He was the glue
that held his parents together, and though he had other dreams,
she always felt he stayed on at the cemetery out of obligation to
continue the legacy. Then she apologized again, saying she felt
responsible for my leaving Adam, which had devastated him.

I shook my head. "I know you've had doubts, but that wasn't
why I left. It was complicated."

Slowly she nodded. So he'd told her everything, too.

"I love him, Helen. I know I haven't exactly been the best
wife, but if he gives me the chance, I'll do everything in my
power to make him happy."

She gave me a crooked smile. I went and gave her a long hug.
Then Adam returned with Gran, who gave her daughter a lovely
chenille bed jacket.

"Let's give them some time alone," I whispered to him, and

we slipped out and walked over to the lounge. "What does the doctor say?"

"She'll be here for a week or so; then they'll have a home health aide and occupational therapist come to the house."

"Do they really think her speech will improve? I can't imagine her actually working again."

"Not a hundred percent, but yes, they do say it's remarkable what can be accomplished."

"They can't stay there by themselves, Adam."

"Actually, Justine is coming back tomorrow, and she's going to live in for a while. And I'll go and check on them every day."

"I can, too. Gran's doing fine today, but there were moments the past few days when she was just so tired and confused."

"Thanks. You've been amazing. But listen, I want you to pack up and go home later and get a good night's sleep. You've been with her day and night, and I know it's been exhausting. Besides, I don't mind that hard bed."

I laughed. "I think the floor is softer."

"Seriously."

"Okay. My back could use a break, and if you're sure you don't mind staying alone."

"Don't be silly." He put his arms around me. "And I'm sorry I haven't been able to help with the research the past few days."

"Please, Adam, they needed us. Besides," I said as casually as I could, "I've done a little more reading. And I have a few ideas."

"Oh?"

"Not now. Wait until things settle down."

He kissed my forehead. "Fair enough."

But I knew that for me there would be no waiting. During the night, I'd been able to reread more of Denis Sullivan's papers, going back to those inconsistencies I found in some of the newspaper articles, wondering again at how these things had been missed, knowing I was just about there.

My head was swimming with visions of Tillie, Titus, Mead, and Weeder and her last night alive. It was like a movie trailer playing over and over in my brain, and I had no idea how it would end.

Tonight was Halloween, and it was time for me to find out.

CHAPTER 57

I T WAS ALREADY DUSK WHEN I TURNED MY VAN through the high stone arch into the cemetery. Heavy grey clouds raced above the trees, and the wind buffeted the car. I prayed it wouldn't rain again. Crossing over the old wooden bridge, I turned left toward the house, stopping then for a long moment as I gazed over the rolling fields of graves, headstones surrounding me. Home.

For most people, driving into a cemetery on Halloween night might have been eerie, but not for me. I'd missed this place so much. The peacefulness and beauty of the towering trees, the river rushing behind me, the wildlife. Mostly, though, it was the presence of something greater than myself. A connection with life through death, and the history of all of these souls that had come and gone.

I continued on, pausing for a minute at the battered stone of that mother who'd lost so many children. Time didn't erase heartbreak. It only served to soften it with distance. Time, the healer of all wounds, it's said. I turned toward the hill and the white marble monument barely visible in the falling darkness. But not always.

I pulled up to the house and left almost everything in the van except the heavy grocery bag I'd just picked up and the shopping bag from weeks ago. Inside, I took off my coat, then turned on the downstairs lights and went straight to the kitchen, emptied the ten pounds of potatoes in the sink, and turned on the water. I scrubbed them clean, my hands pink by the time I finished. Then I began peeling.

I was terrible at this. I wasn't even halfway through, and my hands were already red and raw, nicked in half a dozen places. I couldn't imagine doing this all day every day. But while I peeled, my mind kept going over what I'd discovered again and again, and it all began to fall into place.

AT SEVEN-THIRTY I LAID EVERYTHING OUT and began to dress. First I pulled on woolen stockings, then a pair of muslin drawers, a white petticoat, and a corset.

"You're lucky I still have all of these items," the woman in the antique store had told me when I got them that day I'd read about the Tillie Walk in the newspaper. "These are usually snapped up way before Halloween. Guess you're meant to have them."

That's exactly what I'd thought, especially since she had so many items similar to what Tillie wore that night. Not that I was sure at the time what I was going to do with them.

Tying the corset, I wondered how women endured them, feeling as if my ribs were being crushed. I pulled the coarse brown dress over my head; then I watched myself in the mirror as I pushed the tiny buttons through the holes, feeling some- thing I could only describe as surreal. There was a humming inside of me, as if every cell in my body were vibrating.

I arranged the lace collar around my neck and fastened it with a pin. Then I put my hair up with more than a dozen pins. Finally I put the straw hat on, its rim covered in faded flowers. Everything had that smell of "old," but it was all clean. What was strangest was that it all fit as if it were meant to be. And in my heart, I believed it was.

Finally I sat in the chair by the window, holding the red purse. Inside it were seven dollars and a fragment of blue thread. Closing my eyes, I pictured Tillie leaving the institute and walk- ing into town. I'd thought of starting at that moment, but there would be too much time to wait in town during the hours Tillie was at the show. And I knew what had happened there.

When the idea first came to me, it seemed that I should do it on April 8, the anniversary of Tillie's last night alive. But I couldn't imagine waiting months until then. Then I thought of Halloween and realized it was perfect for two reasons: it was the night the institute had burned to the ground, supposedly caused by Tillie's ghost, and walking through town in costume wouldn't arouse anyone's curiosity.

When I heard the college bells strike nine across the valley, I looked in the mirror one last time, touched Tillie's photograph, and walked out the door.

IT WAS A FRIGID NIGHT, LIKE THE ONE TILLIE WALKED, but also like that night, it was clear and there was a partial moon. The porch lights were all out as I headed into town, trick-or-treaters long gone except for an occasional group of teenagers rushing to make it home. The town had instituted a curfew for this night, and I thought how ironic that was since I was reliving Tillie's curfew.

A short while later, I crossed over Church Street, pausing to glance left toward the college, its gold dome lit up, the front gate visible even from there. I turned right toward Main and stopped on the corner across from the church, where the post office once sat. It was long gone, but I pulled an envelope out of my purse, a letter to Nora Smith, and slipped it into the mailbox on the side-walk.

I turned left onto Main then, and two blocks later turned left onto Grand Avenue, stopping before the building just past the corner. This was where Shield's Hall had stood, a big four-story building with the little store tacked on the side like a shed. I stood there looking up at an old building that now housed a chil-dren's consignment shop on the side and a cell phone store fronting Main, with apartments above. The original structure had also burned in a fire. Here was where it all really began that night.

Closing my eyes, I stood there picturing Tillie and her friends, Mary and Agnes Wright, coming down three flights and spilling onto the wooden sidewalk with the throng of people, all of them milling about on the corner, laughing and talking about the show. There were musical acts, a comedy troupe, and even a bit of opera. Perhaps they'd remarked on the cold weather, talked about warming up at the American House, because they soon crossed the corner there to the other side of Main Street.

I followed their route now, crossing to the corner of High Street where the American House once stood. An auto garage and a uniform store now occupied the corner. But again I closed my eyes, imagining it was 1886 and there were horses and buckboards tied up on hitching posts, the street dirt and the sidewalks simply wooden planks. Gas lamps cast their golden glow every block or so. Tillie heard her name called right at this spot and turned to see her old friend Annie Van Syckle.

I saw the scene unfold as if it were happening. Annie was with a finely dressed gentleman. They chatted a moment, it being somewhere between 9:30 and 9:45, though no one knew exactly. Then they all headed east up Main, stopping in front of the Methodist church. They were now across the street from the opening of Church Street. Tillie was then just four blocks from the seminary.

Someone called to Mary, and she left the group a moment and walked over to Frank Weeder, who was with his buddy George Search, standing nearby. Annie, deep in conversation with the other salesman, kept strolling up Main with him, not noticing. Tillie must have watched with unease, wondering what Frank might be saying to Mary, imagining it had to do with the drummers they were with. Mary liked his friend, George Search, and Tillie wasn't surprised when she returned and explained that she had to leave to meet someone later on.

When they said their goodbyes, the drummer, Charles Munnich, asked if he might walk Tillie home. I imagined Tillie was quite pleased at this turn of events. As Mary and her sister, Agnes, continued up Main, Tillie and the drummer crossed to the entrance to Church Street alone, heading to the seminary. They were lost in conversation, but suddenly at the post office on the corner, someone whistled at them. Tillie turned and to her horror saw that it was Frank again, with one of his buddies in the shadows.

She had to be nervous, I thought as I stood in the exact spot, that same old building now a Vietnamese restaurant closed for the night. And most likely she'd been embarrassed, being with a fine gentleman and having a run-in with Frank. Excusing herself to the gentleman, she went over to Frank, and it was as though I could hear their words on the cold night air.

Frank, what are you doin' following me?

Why, you're my girl, Tillie. I'm worried about you with a strange man.

I am not your girl anymore, Frank. Leave me be.

Then who's to watch out for you?

I don't need watching. I can take proper care of myself.

These dapper gents come into town and leave on the morning train, and there can't be any good in it for you, my pet.

I am not yours any longer. Besides, he treats me like a lady.

Ha. You must be joking. You reckon he's thinking you're a lady? He's just looking for some sport out of the likes of you.

Leave me be. You're nothing but a drunk and a rowdy, and you have a bad name all over town. I don't want anything to do with you and regret I ever did.

She turned and left, and her heart must have been pounding. Tillie took the drummer's arm, leading him up Church Street while Frank watched. He must have been seething, watching her walk away with another man after she shamed him.

I began to walk up Church Street, and it was so dark now, it wasn't hard to picture the new street back then, the light of the gas lamps fading from Main Street, very few houses, the wooden sidewalks slick with frost. What happened on these blocks to the seminary gate was lost in some of the missing pages of the transcript of the drummer's testimony. The only thing I knew with certainty was that they'd walked slowly. How I lamented those missing pages as he was the only one who could have given any inkling of what they'd talked about, something I desperately wanted to hear, for these would have been some of Tillie's last words.

But it wasn't hard to imagine. *What do you do for employment, Miss Smith?* What girl of her position wouldn't claim to be something more than she was? *And what is it you do, Mr. Hunter?* Tillie had never known his real name, Munnich. He'd testified he bragged about the fine shoes he sold and his travels across the state. With each step, I felt the weight of something slowing me down as I drew closer and closer to the truth.

Half a block from the front entrance of the college, I realized it didn't matter that it wasn't the same building. I looked up and saw the original institute, that imposing Gothic structure rising up five stories to a square clock tower, surrounded by young trees, with an iron fence stretching all around the perimeter of the campus.

Crossing Jefferson Street, I stood before the front gate, and my skin began to tingle. At this moment, Tillie must have been so thrilled with her evening, seeing her friends, going to a show, wearing her Sunday best, and meeting a fine gentleman, with the hope of perhaps something further. Having no idea as she took these final steps how wrong this night would turn. I could see her standing there and felt a scream rising in my throat. *Oh, Tillie, turn around! Don't step any farther.* But it was a sob that broke the quiet night instead.

I walked through the front gate, about ten feet into the grounds, where the transcript commenced again. They turned to each other. Tillie waited, hoping Charles might ask to see her again when he came through on the next train, but he was still going on about his travels. I knew what was coming next.

Do you have the time? Tillie asked.

He took out his pocket watch and held it up. *It's ten past ten.*

Just then they heard the lock on the front door slide.

Oh, I'll have to go around to the laundry now to get in.

Or you might consider coming back with me to the American House. I have a fine room, and I'd give you a dollar for your time.

Did Tillie stand there in shock? Her heart broken at this turn of events? Did she want to smack him? And was she regretting treating Frank so poorly when this gentleman turned out to be the cad?

I think you've mistaken me, Mr. Hunter. I must go now if I want to get inside.

Well then, good night, Miss Smith.

She walked as quickly as she could around the right side of the building, but the wooden walkway was slippery, and she nearly fell. She knew Titus was making his rounds, closing up the locks one by one and turning down the gas jets, but he knew she was most likely coming in late so would tend to the laundry door last. And hadn't she asked him to wait to lock it? She began to run, but when she got there and turned the knob, it was locked up tight.

I stood on the side of the building, my heart pounding in my chest. What would she do? Tillie kept on, running to the back of the building until she got to the cellar entrance in back, where she'd bring in the potatoes sometimes and the milkman and others brought their deliveries for the kitchen. She pulled on the door with all her might. It was locked, too.

Damn that Jimmy Titus, she whispered. She dare not bang on the door and wake the matron. She turned, her eyes roaming the back of the grounds. She would not go to the potato barn for fear of tramps. She waited for long, cold minutes, realizing with dread that Titus had betrayed her. When her teeth began to chatter and she could not stop her shivering, she began walking over toward the barn she knew. The red one where she'd once kissed Frank. When she still dreamed of a future with him.

I crossed the grass in the dark, my breath now coming in spurts, imagining the old barn beside the huge old oak, the door opening and Tillie going in. I stopped then, and by the light of the stars it was as though I could see Tillie through the doorway taking off her hat. Then one by one removing the pins from her hair and putting them into her purse. Shaking her hair out and rubbing her head. It must have felt so good. Then Tillie disappeared into the darkness of the barn.

I crept closer, imagining peeking in the doorway. In the ambient light, it unfolded as though I were watching a dream as Tillie took off her outer layer, the sacque coat, and spread it on the ground because it would be cold and the dirt and dust would soil her good dress. She lay down on it then, drawing the sacque about her and closing her eyes. I stood there, terrified there might be tramps inside, drunk and asleep, wakened by Tillie's movements. But nothing happened.

Then I heard a noise from behind. I turned toward the big oak and saw two figures emerge and begin walking toward me. Frightened, I stepped back where I couldn't be seen. They were drinking, passing a bottle back and forth, and as they drew closer, I wanted to step out and scream at them, scare them away. Protect Tillie.

But I didn't. I was too afraid.

As I watched, they came past me, and I could smell the whiskey on their breath, hear their soft laughter. Then they were inside, in the darkness, and I couldn't move. My body was stone, and then it was crumbling into pieces. I was falling to the ground, sobbing, and in the darkness I heard one word. *Frank.*

CHAPTER 58

I BECAME AWARE OF THINGS. The sound of a car or truck. The grass, cold and soft under my cheek. Shivering, my body curling into itself for warmth. An ache in my hip from the ground beneath me. And a whimpering I could not stop.

Then a door opening. A shout. Hands grabbing me, and I began to scream.

"Rachel, stop! It's me!"

He pulled me into him, burying my face and silencing me, and it was the smell of him, sunlight, and earth, that brought me back. "Adam," I cried.

Somehow I must have walked or run back to the cemetery in the dark, not even quite remembering except that I'd been crying. He held me for a long time on top of Tillie's grave. Then he picked me up and carried me to the truck as I looked at the monument over his shoulder. *She died in defence of her honor.*

Adam drove me to the house, then carried me upstairs and sat me on the closed toilet while he ran hot water in the claw-foot tub. Then he removed the bonnet, the sacque, the dress, the petticoat, bustle, drawers, and stockings, not even asking about the clothes. When I was naked, he helped me into the tub. My teeth chattered as I sank into the blessed warmth.

Kneeling beside me, he touched my cheek. "When I saw you lying on top of Tillie's grave, I thought you were dead."

"I'm sorry."

When my teeth stopped chattering, I told him what I had done. When I finished, he closed his eyes, shaking his head. "Jesus."

"I know. It was horrible and frightening. At first, I was

simply following her steps that night. Then at times, it was like I was seeing it all unfold. But at the end, it was like...I was inside this dream, and I was her."

"Do you know what really happened, then?"

I turned away from him, looking out the window at the dark night. Tears filled my eyes. "I think so. But please, I can't talk about it yet. I feel as though I just watched her die."

"It's okay," he whispered.

He helped me out of the tub, dried me tenderly, and put me to bed in my robe. He stripped and got in, curling around me.

"Wait, what about Gran?"

"Justine got back early. Don't worry. She's fine."

"I'm too hot."

He lifted the covers, and I took off the robe. Then he was covering me with himself, skin to skin, and I melted into sleep, wondering if I'd ever felt so loved. So safe.

* * *

I SLIPPED OUT OF BED AND PULLED MY ROBE ON, then tiptoed downstairs and made coffee. Standing at the kitchen window, I gazed out at the sea of gravestones, like waves rolling across the fields of grass and up hills. Across the cemetery, at the top of the highest knoll, I could see Tillie's monument, where I must have fainted.

In the light of day, last night seemed surreal. I was still exhausted, my body drained of energy. Yet there was this quivering of emotion deep in my chest. I felt heartsick. I knew now what that term really meant: each breath, each beat of your heart aching with sorrow. I had to make this right somehow. I threw a coat on over my robe, ran out to the van, and grabbed the box with Denis Sullivan's work and parts of the transcript.

When I got back inside, I began laying it all out on the dining room table. Sometime later I heard a noise and turned.

"What are you doing?" Adam stood there in jeans and a t-shirt, looking sleepy.

"I'm just sorting things. Go back to bed. You still look tired."

He shook his head. "I can't sleep anymore. I need to know what happened."

I took a long breath. "Okay. Why don't you get a cup of coffee? I have a lot to tell you."

He pulled a chair beside me when he returned, then took my hand and kissed it.

"I'm sorry I scared you," I said.

"I couldn't bear it if anything happened to you."

"How did you know where to find me?"

"I called a few times, and there was no answer. Then I decided to drive over and make sure everything was okay—you know, kids partying or getting into mischief on Halloween. I didn't want you dealing with that. But you weren't here, and then I found your clothes in the spare bedroom. I got really nervous, so I started driving around town. I finally came back to the cemetery, and then it hit me."

"I'm sorry. I should have told you, but you had so much on your mind already what with Aunt Helen and Gran and all."

"It's okay. You're fine. Now, tell me everything."

I took a deep breath and put my cup down. "First, I think James Titus, the janitor, was guilty."

"What?" he nearly shouted.

"Yes, but not in the way you think. You know all the circum-stantial evidence afterward: how he looked ill, wouldn't talk about it, kept asking if God could forgive the sinner? The scrib-blings in the Bible? Well, I think he was consumed with guilt. Because he did lust after her. And he'd locked her out."

"He never actually said he left the door open, though, did he?"

"I found the rest of the inquest in Denis Sullivan's papers. Remember in the very beginning, they were simply trying to trace Tillie's movements before Titus was even a suspect. Back then he testified he'd left the door open and assumed she'd gone upstairs to her room. But I didn't believe it. I think he lied because he was scared. And he was already plagued by guilt because she was locked out. And if he hadn't locked her out, she would have been up in her room safe. She wouldn't have died that night."

"That makes sense."

"Adam, that one decision by Titus changed everything for Til-lie. Where could she possibly go in the dark and freezing night? She went to Mrs. Stewart's red barn, where they initially found signs of a struggle on the dirt floor. A few streaks of blood on the door. Evidence they quickly dismissed as old or from tramps when they zeroed in on Titus. The red barn, according to Faith Seiler, the sorority girl, was where the girls sometimes went with their sweethearts. It wasn't a barn known for tramps. But once Titus was arrested, no one was listening to this anymore."

"But how do you really know for sure she didn't get in?"

"It was her hairpins."

"I...I don't understand."

I smiled. "What finally helped me put all the pieces together were the hairpins. As I continued imagining her last movements, I kept coming back to them. What man would be able to get each and every one out of all that thick hair? Women themselves have a hard time digging through their own hair to get them all, and Tillie had a lot of hair. Yet not a pin was found anywhere, not even on her head. Why? Because she must have taken them out herself. When she got to the barn, before lying down, she care-fully removed each one, no doubt counting to be sure, and put them in her red purse for safekeeping. She had so little, even hairpins were precious."

I told him the rest then, how I felt Tillie had gone into the barn to sleep, not knowing she'd been followed by Weeder and his friend, George Search. "She probably had no idea what was going to happen at first because he'd cared for her and for the most part was nice to her."

"She trusted him."

"Yes, just like I trusted the guy who was nice to me, who... hurt me."

"But it's not your fault."

"No, it's not. And it wasn't hers. But I think a row ensued. He was drunk, his girl was with another man, he had been mocked and shamed, and his friend had seen it all. Tillie tried to calm him down, but it got out of hand. He decided she was going to be his, and she began to fight him. But he was going to show her, and he needed to save face in front of his friend. He beat her, but she kept fighting him, so he choked her, threw her down, and knelt on her chest, and then...and then he raped her."

"Oh, Rachel."

"Then...his friend raped her."

"Jesus. Two men."

I nodded. "And she was dying while they did this to her. Taking her last breaths."

Neither of us spoke for a while. I stood up and walked to the window, looking toward the river.

"Afterward, they carried her out toward the institute to make it look like she'd been killed there, like a random killing, perhaps by tramps. He didn't want her found in that barn. Perhaps they'd gone there before together, just as Faith had described."

"How do you know all this for sure?"

"I did more reading, and I began to find what might seem trivial inconsistencies in Weeder's statements. But when you put them all together..." I went over to the table and found the papers I'd clipped together. I began to explain to Adam.

I now knew from Weeder's statement at the inquest, which was in one of Sullivan's articles, that Weeder admitted to being on Main Street with his friend, George Search, stopping Mary Wright in front of the church when she was walking with Tillie and the salesman, and then leaving. And Mary Wright testified at the trial the same thing, that he was warning her about strangers.

But in an article weeks later, after Titus was arrested and in jail, Weeder told Creelman for an article that appeared in the *World* that as Tillie and the stranger walked by the *post office*, he whistled to her and warned *her* about the stranger, too. He must have rushed right over there without anyone's notice, knowing she'd have to walk that way to get back to the seminary."

"So he was following her."

"Correct. Sullivan covered most of the inquest, and in that

box were some articles that must have been lost over time. At the inquest, Weeder had stated that after stopping Mary Wright and warning her about the strangers, he went to Tinsman's grocery with a few of his friends and drank hard cider until 12:30, which I'd read somewhere before. That was his original alibi and why he was let go. That was during the time Tillie was killed. But in the article by Creelman weeks after the inquest, he claimed he went to Tinsman's *after* stopping Tillie and the drummer at the *post office.* So which one was it? He couldn't have been two places at the same time."

"One of them was a lie."

"I got a sense of Weeder through all of this and began to real-ize he was getting sloppy in his cockiness. Titus was in jail, a trial was coming...and he'd been let go with little questioning by the police because Sullivan had written in notes for a book he never did write that Weeder *was not considered smart enough to have accomplished such a complicated crime.*"

"Sullivan was the only one paying attention."

I nodded. "Finally, another member of Weeder's gang from that night also testified about going to Tinsman's to drink. He named all who were with him but never identified Weeder. Yet Weeder told the reporter for the *World* that he *was* one of them. So he wasn't drinking hard cider directly after the post office. He couldn't be in two places at one time. And there was another lie."

"It's unbelievable that no one caught this."

"What erased any doubts I may have had came from Mary Wright, and I thought it was big," I went on telling Adam. "When Tillie started walking back to the seminary with the drummer, Charles Munnich, Mary Wright and her sister kept walking up Main Street. Mary told them she had to go meet 'a friend.' His name was George Search."

"The friend who was with Weeder."

"Right. Only she never did find him. He never showed. So Weeder never goes to Tinsman's, Search never meets up with his girlfriend..."

"He was the other guy in the shadows at the post office."

"Right. What boggles my mind was that no one figured this out back then."

"So Weeder is telling all sorts of stories to cover for himself that night, and George Search is MIA. Two men."

"Tillie's ex-beau and his fellow gang member. I'm certain he was the accomplice. And Weeder wasn't even worried anymore about his stories because they already had Titus locked up."

Adam sat there shaking his head. "Do you realize what this means, Rachel? This murder happened in 1886, and I think you finally discovered who the real killer was."

"I just finished what Denis Sullivan started a century ago. He was absolutely right about the power of the New York press. Joseph Pulitzer's reporter James Creelman built the case against Titus. And it seemed there was no turning back."

Sullivan was starting to put all of the pieces together, then suddenly stopped. I imagined that was when he'd quit writing to go back to farming. What a shame. Things could have turned out differently for James Titus. And Marion Freeman. She probably would have had a family. The scandal probably would have dis-sipated. History would have been written differently for that family.

"What are you going to do with this?"

I shrugged. "What can I do with it? We have the discrepan-cies in Weeder's statements and my gut."

"But you did what you hoped for. You found out the truth about Tillie's life and her death."

"To a point. But it's not solid proof. And I doubt it's enough to clear Titus's name. His granddaughter is still alive. I'm sure she'd be grateful after living with this stigma her entire life. But I don't think this is enough. Who's going to believe me?"

"What are you getting at?"

"We need more, something concrete. I want to go back to the house on Liberty Street. The last place we know Frank Weeder lived in 1886."

"Rachel," he cautioned.

"Adam, I'm getting in that house with or without you."

CHAPTER 59

I TRIED TO KEEP BUSY while Adam went to check on his aunt at the rehab, but I was climbing the walls. I started cleaning the kitchen, then found myself staring out the window across the cemetery. When I tried to get back to work, I couldn't even remember where I'd left off. My brain was racing.

I pulled on my coat and went outside, the first day of November, sunny and cold. I walked the gravel lane toward the river. The trees were nearly bare, dead leaves blowing across the grass and piling up around the headstones. More work for Adam. Soon the landscape would be stark and barren here, yet I still saw its beauty, still felt the pull of all these souls.

What if I couldn't ever set history right for Tillie? Or bring justice for Marion Freeman's remaining time on earth? Would it really matter to anyone else other than the two of us? I couldn't believe that. The truth should be told no matter how much time had gone by, no matter what the risks. If we didn't hold fast to truth, what else would matter, really?

I came to the river, the cold water rushing over the rocks, flowing beneath the old wooden bridge. The water was like liquid crystal, and I stared at it for a long time, thinking. If time was truly like a river, then here I stood again, the past behind that curve in the riverbank just to my right, where everything had already happened in my life, in Tillie's life, and in the lives of all the souls that surrounded me. Slowly I turned to the left, and it was as if I could see the future just ahead on the other side of the bridge. But for now I stood in that fleeting moment of the present, knowing that that future depended on whatever I chose to do next.

I went back to the house and called Michael Cassidy's law office in Belvidere. He was in and took my call. Of course his first question was about the transcript. I told him I'd gotten it and read it, as well as the nearly complete works of Denis Sullivan.

"I'd like to bring you a copy of the transcript if you'd be inter-ested."

"Absolutely."

"I'd like to get your opinion, but I think I've figured out what really happened."

"But you don't want to tell me?"

"Not until you finish reading it."

"That's a deal."

"Thank you again for your help."

"Are you kidding? This is close to home for me. Titus's attor-ney sat in the same room that I do day in and day out. I love stuff like this. So thank you."

"Oh, I almost forgot," I said. "What's the statute of limitations on rape?"

"Well...it wouldn't really matter in Tillie's case. Obviously everyone is long gone."

"I...don't mean for Tillie. I mean now. In the present."

There was a moment of silence. "In New Jersey, there's no statute of limitations for sexual assault."

"What about...Pennsylvania?"

Again a pause. "I think it's twelve years. At most fifteen. But if you give me a minute, I can find out for certain."

"No, no, it's all right. I was just curious. Thank you."

I said goodbye before he could ask anything further.

* * *

IT WAS AUNT HELEN WHO PULLED SOME STRINGS and got us permission to go into the house later that day. The catch was that someone from the lumberyard had to accompany us to ensure our safety. As we got out of the truck, a guy about Adam's age was coming up the street.

"Hey, Adam," he said.

"Hi, Pete. Thanks for doing this. This is my wife, Rachel." Of course they knew each other. Adam knew everyone in town.

"We'll be going in the back. The front porch is too dangerous," Pete said.

We went around the house, walking across a small dirt yard filled with debris that backed to the lumberyard parking lot. Pete unlocked a padlock on the door, and Adam held my arm and went in first. We stood in what must have been the kitchen because there were pipes sticking out of the wall, but there were no cabinets or appliances, not even a sink. The house was completely empty and smelled of damp wood. Most of it had been paneled years ago, so it was dark, and there was no electricity on, so it was hard to see.

Adam and I went room by room with a flashlight. Pete stayed behind, talking to his girlfriend on his cell phone. Adam was by my side, holding the light while I went inch by inch, scrutinizing ceiling tiles, floorboards, closets, and even gaps in the wall paneling. Any square inch of the house that might hide something, anything, that could possibly be a link to Frank Weeder.

There was no real attic, just a flat roof and a bit of a crawl space, which was easy to scour in a short amount of time. When we finished that, I told Adam it was time for the basement, which I'd saved for last, knowing it might be moldy and wet. As we descended the cellar steps, I could feel the cool dampness on my skin.

"This reminds me of the basement in our house," Adam said.

"Yeah, it's probably the same era."

The floor was dirt, the foundation stone and mortar, and it was wet all around the edges where the old windows no longer did their job. I instructed Adam to follow me around the foundation walls as I scrutinized them, feeling with my fingers stone by stone. Once in a while I could hear Adam sigh. It was tedious, and we had been at it for more than an hour when he tapped my shoulder.

"Rachel, I think we've done enough. There's nothing here."

"There's always—"

"Honey, I know there's always something, but we're done."

I turned to him, wanting to cry yet knowing he was right. I'd been so certain. There was always something hidden in a house. But really, what were the odds that Frank Weeder had left some-thing behind from 130 years ago? From a murder for which another man was punished?

"All right. Let's go."

We were halfway to the stairs, the flashlight still on, when I shouted, "Wait!"

I spotted something shiny, just a tiny reflection from the flashlight underneath the cellar steps. I crawled under them, kneeling on the dirt floor, pointing to where I wanted the light to hit. I dug with my fingers.

"Oh...it's just a piece of mica in the rock."

"I'm sorry."

We backed out on our knees. Adam stood first, and as the light hit higher up, I stopped suddenly, staring. "Adam, wait. There's something else shining. Between the stones."

There was a tiny glint of something wedged between two fieldstones. He trained the light on it as I stood and for long minutes began carefully working the stones back and forth, try-ing to pry one loose. Bits of dirt spilled to the floor, and the edge of one stone started to crumble. And then I could feel the stone give way. Carefully I stuck my fingers in the crevice and pulled at the shiny object, and with it came something soft and brown that fell to the dirt floor.

I bent down and carefully scooped it up, and as I did, the damp and mildewed lump of something fell apart in my hands. But there was no mistaking the dull glint of the metal clasp.

"Oh my God, it's her red purse."

As I held it out to show Adam, metal hairpins fell to the floor.

CHAPTER 60

L IFE SEEMED TO FALL BACK INTO A RHYTHM over the next days, with Adam working tirelessly to finish the prewinter cemetery cleanup, and early morning frosts now a normal occurrence. The audit was finally finished, and he had a board meeting later that day. I felt guilty. In the past weeks I had been so consumed by Tillie that I'd forgotten all about it and how he'd worried so much. When I apologized, he waved a hand as if it were nothing. But I knew that wasn't the case. I promised myself I was going to be a better wife.

I had actually gotten an inquiry a few days before from someone needing an auctioneer, and I began to think again about growing my business, perhaps going partners with Mr. Finegan. But through it all, Tillie was never far from my thoughts. And now that I knew the truth, I began laying the groundwork for what I needed to do.

That afternoon, when it seemed the last of the leaves were blowing from the trees and the cemetery took on its stark sepia winter palette, I went to see Mrs. Freeman. I didn't call ahead, afraid she would refuse me, so now I stood in the open doorway and peeked into her room. She was in the same wing chair, head bowed over a book, and once again I couldn't tell if she was sleeping or reading. She could have been any other old woman in this nursing home. But she wasn't. This was a woman whose life had been ruined by chance.

How many hours, how many days in her nearly ninety years had she wished for different genes? A different family? A history untarnished by shame and guilt? It was ironic that though I loathed James Titus for his lechery and his small act that resulted in Tillie's death, he was the one whose history I could now change.

I stepped inside the room. "Mrs. Freeman?"

She looked up with those bright blue eyes. She'd not been asleep.

"Yes, dear, come in."

I wasn't sure she knew who I was. Hopefully she wouldn't ask me to leave.

"Mrs. Freeman, I'm Rachel Miller, Adam's wife. The last time I was here, I upset you, and I am very sorry about that. But I'm here with some news I think you will want to know."

She stared at me a long moment, her head trembling, and I wondered if she had Parkinson's or if she was nervous.

"Why don't you sit down?" she said then.

I sat, and I told her everything from the very first moment I saw Tillie's monument and my thumb was pierced to finding the decomposing red purse in Frank Weeder's boarding house. When I finished, her head was shaking harder, and even her chin trembled. Her hand slid back and forth across her lap. Parkinson's, then.

"Are you saying that my grandfather had nothing at all to do with Tillie Smith's death?"

"That's what I'm saying, yes." She didn't need to know he was a lech, or perhaps she already did. As far as locking Tillie out...it wasn't necessary to point that out. "Your grandfather did not kill Tillie Smith. Or assault her."

"But he confessed..."

"Yes, he did confess, but it was after all other options had failed. By confessing, he went to prison but saved his life."

She turned from me and looked out the window, her eyes filling with tears. I could only imagine what was going through her mind. The children she never had. Friends who wouldn't come to her house. The whispers, the looks. Most of all the shame. And here she was, alone at the end of her life. All because of a miscarriage of justice.

I realized that what I'd hoped for would never come. A look of joy, relief, some satisfaction that finally the truth was out. She simply turned back to me and nodded.

"Thank you, dear."

I couldn't help it. I got up and hugged her. "I'm so sorry," I said, fighting tears. I wished I could have done more. But it was too late. Her life was nearly lived out, and everyone she loved whom it would have mattered to was gone.

* * *

WHEN I GOT HOME, I HEARD MUSIC as soon as I walked in the front door. I followed the sounds upstairs to the bedroom. Adam sat on the window seat, strumming a guitar. There was such a look of serenity on his face as he played, unaware I was watching. It was a haunting ballad.

"Did you write that?"

He looked up in surprise. "I did, a long time ago."

"It's just beautiful."

I went and sat on the bed. "I take it the audit and board meeting went well."

He shook his head, and for a moment I thought it was bad news.

"I've been such an ass."

"Oh, Adam, are you in trouble?"

"No, everything finally is out in the open. And I feel like this is the first time I can really breathe in years." He was smiling, as if he couldn't quite believe his own words.

"You told them about your father?"

He nodded.

"Everything?"

"You know, I never wanted to tarnish my father's legacy here, but I just couldn't live with the pressure anymore. Plus, it didn't feel right. Turns out, they weren't surprised. Don't forget this is a small town, even smaller back then. You couldn't really hide a drinking problem."

"And they just let him go on?"

"They were all buddies, the old-timers. Enough of them are still on the board. Anyway, I 'fessed up that I'd been putting my own money in when I had to and that the digitization was really about trying to catch any more problems. They actually thanked me for the damage control I'd been doing since my father died. I realized there would never be an end to this. No matter how organized we were, there might be another surprise around the corner."

"But the likelihood is a lot less now."

"Right. Anyway, the fact that it's now all digitized and they didn't pay for that, along with the money I've been putting in to... hide the errors...it's all out in the open."

"Adam, that is so wonderful."

"I feel so free."

"I can imagine."

"They all loved my dad, in spite of his drinking. You should have heard them talking about him. One of them was in 'Nam with him. I never knew that."

"So...do you still want to stay on and live here? Now that you don't have to worry about your father's mistakes?"

"I've been thinking about that for a long time. If I had a choice, you know, what would I do?" He sighed. "I'm not really ready to make any big changes. You're here; that's all that really matters to me right now. Let's go someplace warm for our honeymoon. We've got all the time in the world to figure out the rest."

I smiled. "Would you play one more of your songs before we leave?"

"Sure." His fingers began lightly strumming again, and then he looked up at me.

I listened to him for a long time, the music allowing my mind to drift back to my visit with Marion Freeman, and then Tillie's sisters, and all of the people affected by that one horrible act of violence. And then my thoughts went to Tillie, picturing those hopeful eyes that had haunted me from the beginning. It was all just as I'd first imagined months ago. She was who I'd imagined. Tillie was trying to make something of her life and to help her family. She learned to read. She was befriended by the sorority girls. She'd gone to revival meetings. What would her life have become if she'd been given the chance? I would never know. But through all of my searching for Tillie, I'd begun to understand myself better, who I'd become because of my own rape.

"Adam?"

He looked up.

"Can I show you something?"

I led him across the hall to the guest room I'd been using as an office. I opened the closet and reached deep inside for the bin with my mother's things. Sitting on the floor, I opened it and began to explain each item and what they meant in the story of my family's life: my father's trophies and his archaeology books he'd left behind; my mother's stuffed giraffe and Beanie Babies, a jewelry box with nothing of real value; the robe she always wore that I couldn't part with; and a few trinkets from a childhood she couldn't remember. And then there was the diary.

"I found this when I was selling the house and everything in it. It's funny; it was my first 'find,' as I call it, a thing hidden from the world. A secret you think you can keep till the grave. Only this was my mother's. After I read it back then...."

I explained how she'd been molested in foster care, which no doubt fueled her obsessive need to protect me. And how she stayed on in those houses, finding ways to protect herself because the next place might be worse. And she had friends, finally.

"Jesus, sometimes I'm embarrassed to be a man."

"You are nothing like that. Do not feel that way. I don't know any other man who could have helped me to finally start healing from what happened to me. No one else had that kind of sensitivity."

"Thanks."

"Anyway, her need to protect me...well, in the end it backfired. That night after I was raped, she called and I couldn't answer. I couldn't call her back after what he did to me," I told Adam now. "I was so ashamed, so traumatized, I couldn't even leave my room. When I did finally pick up...I started crying so hard, I could barely speak. She asked me if someone hurt me, and I said yes. She...knew somehow what it was. Then she said she was coming to get me and that I shouldn't say anything to anyone....If I had answered the phone at first...if I'd kept my mouth shut...if I'd just gone home...it would have all been different."

"Rachel," Adam said, taking my hand and pulling me onto his lap, "you cannot blame yourself."

"I know, but...I did for years. I don't know what was worse, the shame over what he did to me or the guilt over thinking I killed my mother."

"Your mother had a lot of hang-ups, and you were a kid. Please tell me that you no longer blame yourself."

"I...I'm trying. I so didn't want to be like my mother. I wanted to trust guys. I didn't want to think the worst of people, but then..." I shrugged. "So you see, I had trust issues before the rape, and that only made it worse. I'm sorry I didn't trust you to tell you the truth about everything from the beginning, Adam. I should have. I've only had a few relationships in the past twenty years, and they've all ended badly. I know I have some anger issues, too. Control issues. And honesty issues. I think I've been hiding from myself more than anyone. I've learned a lot from reading online about rape victims."

"I'm glad you're doing that."

"It's making me see how it's affected others, and...I'm going to call your Dr. Monday. I think I'm ready, finally, to start talking about all of this."

"I'll go with you if you want."

"Maybe later on. But I need to go myself the first time."

"Okay. Just let me know. But are you sure you still want to do this tomorrow?"

At that my heart began to race. "Yes. It's about time."

* * *

WE WERE DRIVING OVER THE WOODEN BRIDGE, and neither one of us had spoken since we'd gotten in the truck. Adam seemed nervous, his fingers tapping the wheel, his mouth set tight. I felt surprisingly calm.

There was a press conference in Newark in ninety minutes. I'd met with Michael Cassidy and gone over my case, and he contacted a reporter, who began leaking the story that there was a scandal about to erupt for the state attorney general candidate. When the press conference ended, I promised the woman an exclusive interview.

Before we turned onto Mountain Avenue, Adam slid the truck back into park and turned to me with a look of concern. "I don't want you to do this because I told you that you should out him. I don't want you doing this for me."

"I'm not, Adam; I promise. I've thought about it long and hard. I'm a little nervous, but I'm no longer scared."

He sighed, and I imagined this wouldn't be easy for him, standing beside me when I faced the press and accused a promising political candidate of rape. Would anyone take me seriously?

"I know you'd like to hurt him, but this is the right way. I've spent a lot of time these past months thinking about the problems in my life since it happened. Yes, it would have been labeled date rape. As if that term lessens the impact on a young girl's life. But I look back now and see how for years I was half alive. I was raped, lost my mother, spiraled downhill, and hated life. But I was alive. I think Tillie really brought that home for me. She never had that chance to go on afterward and try to make a new life. She had so few chances. And her killer and rapist got off, died unpunished. But the guy who did it to me is still alive. Still unpunished. And I can finally do something about that."

"I know no one can fully imagine the horror you went through, and it can't be easy to relive it."

"He ruined my life for too long. I lived behind this veil of shame, as if it were somehow my fault. But I'm finally beyond it and know that the shame should be his. Today, after I give my statement and then tell the reporter my story, that's it. I'm never looking back again. We have a good life, Adam. I am so blessed that you walked into that house in Kearny that day. Most of all, I am so blessed to have your love."

He lifted my hand and kissed it. "No, Rachel, I'm the lucky one."

* * *

IT WAS JUST AS I HAD IMAGINED, like scenes I'd watched in TV movies—a podium in front of a large room, several dozen reporters, including camera crews. My nerves kicked in as soon as I entered, trembling knees, butterflies swooping through my stomach. Now I stood before the microphone with my heart slamming against my ribs. I turned to Adam beside me, and he gave me a nod.

"My name is Rachel Miller. Nearly twenty years ago, Barry Marshall raped me. I was a freshman in college. I was also...a virgin. Why, you might ask, am I coming forward now? Am I politically motivated? Am I seeking fame or notoriety?" I paused, my nerves waning, my voice growing stronger.

"I'm here now because of something that happened to me earlier this year. Something that made me realize that it is never too late to seek justice. I stumbled upon the case of a young woman named Tillie Smith, who was raped nearly 130 years ago. Unfortunately, she was also murdered by her assailant, so unlike me, she wasn't able to seek justice for herself. In the process of trying to find out who she was and what really happened to her all those years ago, I also discovered who I believe with certainty raped and killed her. His name was Frank Weeder, and he is now long dead. It was through those months of finding Tillie Smith, and researching her life, and the trial of the man unjustly con-victed and punished that it began to dawn on me that justice has no expiration date. And that the truth, when possible, should never go to the grave."

I paused again and turned quickly to Adam. His face was filled with surprise. I hadn't intended to speak of Tillie. It wasn't part of my scripted statement. But once I began to talk, I realized the truth. That if it weren't for Tillie, I wouldn't be standing there at all.

"For a long time, what Barry Marshall did to me nearly ruined my life. I lived with the shame that keeps so many rape victims silent. That shame doesn't belong to me any longer. That shame belongs to Barry Marshall for the crime of raping an innocent young woman. The statute of limitations is long over, but I still believe it's possible to seek justice in the court of public opinion. Barry Marshall should not be our next state attorney general. He should never be allowed to do to another woman what he did to me. Thank you." The barrage of questions began immediately, but I answered none, as was my agreement with the reporter Michael Cassidy had contacted. I turned from the podium.

"You were incredible," Adam said, taking my hand.

Together we walked out of the room.

EPILOGUE

April 8, 2016

I PLACED THE BOUQUET OF YELLOW ROSES at the base of the monument. There were other flowers, lined up as if a procession had come during the night. Votive candles sat on the ledge above Tillie's name, burned out hours ago. I'd seen the lights of cars at various times the previous evening. Adam told me they would come at all hours of the night, many hoping to catch sight of Tillie's ghost.

If there was a ghost, I never saw her myself. But I'd felt something, her energy, her consciousness or spirit, whatever the thing was that went on afterward. From the first moment I'd seen this monument, read its words, which I now knew by heart, I had been touched by something unsettling, uneasy, that propelled me to find the truth. Now I looked up at the shaft of white stone in the early spring sunlight, and that feeling was gone.

Tomorrow, along with the articles that appeared each year in the local papers on the anniversary of Tillie's murder, my own story would be printed. The reporter who interviewed me and wrote the piece thought it might even get picked up by some of the bigger papers toward the city. After all, discovering the real murderer after almost 130 years and clearing the name of a man wrongly convicted didn't happen every day. I didn't want accolades or notoriety, though. I simply wanted the truth told.

In setting Tillie's spirit free to move on, I set myself free. The man who raped me would not go to prison, but my accusations cast a stain on his character he would never be able to fully erase, and not surprisingly, others came forward after me. He would never hold political office.

The college bells across town chimed eight o'clock, and I turned, walked down the hill and toward the back of the cemetery until I came to another grave, that of James Titus. His entire family was buried there, and I read the headstones, one by one, saying a little prayer for each, knowing there would be no others. The line ended with Marion's, where I placed another bouquet. She had died a few weeks after the press conference.

I then walked on to another section and a grave where the grass was just coming in, the pink granite clean and new. *Cora Jacobs Miller*. Ninety was a good long life, but it was hard not to grieve for someone you'd come to love. Aunt Helen's stroke and recovery took a toll on Gran, and then she caught pneumonia over the winter, and slowly, like a clock winding down, she let go of this life. I placed the last bouquet there, then looked at the others: Adam's grandfather, Samuel; then Samuel's parents and others going back generations to Phineas Miller, with whom the legacy began.

I turned to Adam's father's headstone, Ronald Miller, marked with an American flag and a plaque to honor his service. In the grassy space beside Ronnie's plot and the gravel path, I knew that one day Adam and I would take our places, and perhaps a lineage that would follow. An unbroken chain of our lives laid out here, as so many already were.

Strangely, there was comfort in that, being one link in that chain of humanity, a mystery that perhaps would never be solved. But here I was, alive, just as all of these souls once were, breathing, loving, hopeful. And now silent. A mystery I was no longer afraid to face.

I saw my own gravestone as if it were already there. *Rachel Miller, Beloved Wife*, and I smiled. Then I turned and walked across the cemetery to home, where my husband was waiting for me.

Acknowledgements

This is the most challenging book I've written so far. Writing it took place during one of the most difficult times of my life. There were days it seemed futile, and moments when I wanted to give up. But deep inside was an almost visceral need to tell Tillie's story. Besides, those who know and love me...they wouldn't let me give up. And for that I am most grateful.

I saw the monument to Tillie Smith decades ago as an eleven-year-old. I didn't really know what the words meant, but I was intrigued. Throughout my life there have been coincidences, much like Rachel's, with Tillie's story. Perhaps the most astounding was during my earlier real estate days when I walked into a house on Sharp Street only to find out it belong to James Titus's family. How I describe it is how I saw it that day.

Tillie Smith is famous in my hometown, and has become a bit of a legend regionally. For more than a century it's been said her ghost prowls Centenary's halls. But no one really knew who she was, what her life was like. She truly became a footnote in the sensational story of her death. My hope with this novel is that I have portrayed her as accurately as possible. That my interpretation of her life would have pleased her. Some scenes I began with a gut feeling, only to get a bit of verification with a surprising bit of research. Or a coincidence, once again. Tillie and the sorority girls was one of those hunches.

There are so many people I must thank, but no one more than Denis Sullivan, author of *In Defence of Her Honor*, a non-fiction book detailing the trial of James Titus. His own research helped immensely, as well as his sleuthing. He was kind enough to give me a copy of the missing transcript, which he discovered. My character Denis Sullivan is, of course, named for him.

At Centenary University, I must thank Catherine Rust, Annamaria Lalevee, Dr. Boris Gavrilovic and Dr. Sharon Decker. Also Colleen Bain, who helped with my research in the archives. Regina Evans, a Centenary Alumnus, happened to see me holding Tillie's photo at jury duty, and told me of the other photo, which astounded me.

The Hackettstown Historical Society and genealogist Gwen Char were wonderful in their assistance, as well as the Hackettstown Public Library and the Belvidere Public Library.

The late Bob Smith, as well as Mary Smith Ritzer, descendants of Tillie's prominent relatives, helped me to understand the dynamics of her family. In researching cemetery life, I turned to Roger Hines, our former cemetery keeper, and his son, Kevin Hines, who now runs Union Cemetery. Also, many thanks to Joyce Ort Berninger, who was a former cemetery keeper's wife, and shared many of her adventures there. Joyce's nephew, Charlie Ort, happened to share some old bottles he collected with me, and the beautiful green one for Salon Palmer inspired that storyline.

Though there isn't a house in Union Cemetery, I discovered that there once was one for the cemetery keeper across the river on Mountain Avenue.

Many thanks to Dr. Lee Monday, psychologist, and Dr. Robert Taylor, gynecologist and oncologist, for insight into sexual assault and it's repercussions. There are many sites online which also helped with my research, especially takebackthenight.org.

My writing buddies helped me through moments of panic and doubt. A huge shout out to Judy Walters, Jenny Milchman, Dottie Frank, Kate Brandes and Kathryn Craft. To Mary Alice Monroe and Adriana Trigiani, incredible authors who were so kind to read my novel and share their wonderful words. To my wonderful writing partner, the talented novelist Julie Maloney, I hope you know how much your support means to me.

To my family of friends who got me through the last few years: Debora Messina, Vicki Malanga, Lynn Vergano and Michael Cassidy, thanks for always being there. Joe Englert, for providing thousands of printed pages, and Frank Kasper for keeping my garden and writing view beautiful. Robin Hoffman Abourizk and Joni Cassidy, I'm so grateful not just for your wonderful friendship and support, but for reading many, many drafts. I'm heartbroken my third reader, my mother, didn't live to see this book in print.

Alan Donaghey, thank you for my exquisite book cover. You are brilliant! I can never thank my sister Jacky Abromitis enough for all of her hard work on anything technical! What would I do without her! And to her wife, Kathy Ulisse, who has also read and commented on pages.

Many thanks to my agent, Ruth Pomerance, at Folio Agency, as well as Michael Harriot. Your continued support and passion for this book has meant the world to me.

And finally, to my children, Patrick and Marisa, amazing writers themselves. And my children-in-law, Mike and Karen. They have never stopped believing in me and my writing. And to my darling grandchildren: Alice, Lily, Julia, Phoebe and Jackson, writers of the future!

I burned through 3 laptops writing this book and many e-mail files were lost. So for anyone I've forgotten to thank, please forgive me.

To see photos, read about my research, and see some deleted material, please visit my website: maryannmcfadden.com

I love meeting Book Clubs, either in person or via skype. For a Reading Group Guide or to contact me, please go to maryann mcfadden.com

CPSIA information can be obtained
at www.ICGtesting.com
Printed in the USA
LVHW070010160623
749893LV00003B/423